PRIEST OF BONES

PETER McLEAN

PRIEST OF BONES

Jo Fletcher
BOOKS

ı Great Britain in 2018 by

Jo Fletcher Books
an imprint of
Quercus Editions Ltd
Carmelite House
50 Victoria Embankment
London EC4Y 0DZ

An Hachette UK company

A CIP catalogue record for this book is available from the British Library.

HB ISBN 978-1-78747-348-5
TPB ISBN 978-1-78747-347-8
EBOOK ISBN 978-1-78747-350-8

10 9 8 7 6 5 4 3 2 1

Typeset by CC Book Production
Printed and bound in Great Britain by Clays Ltd, Elcograf S.p.A.

For Diane.
Always.

'If you must break the law, do it to seize power.'

—Julius Caesar

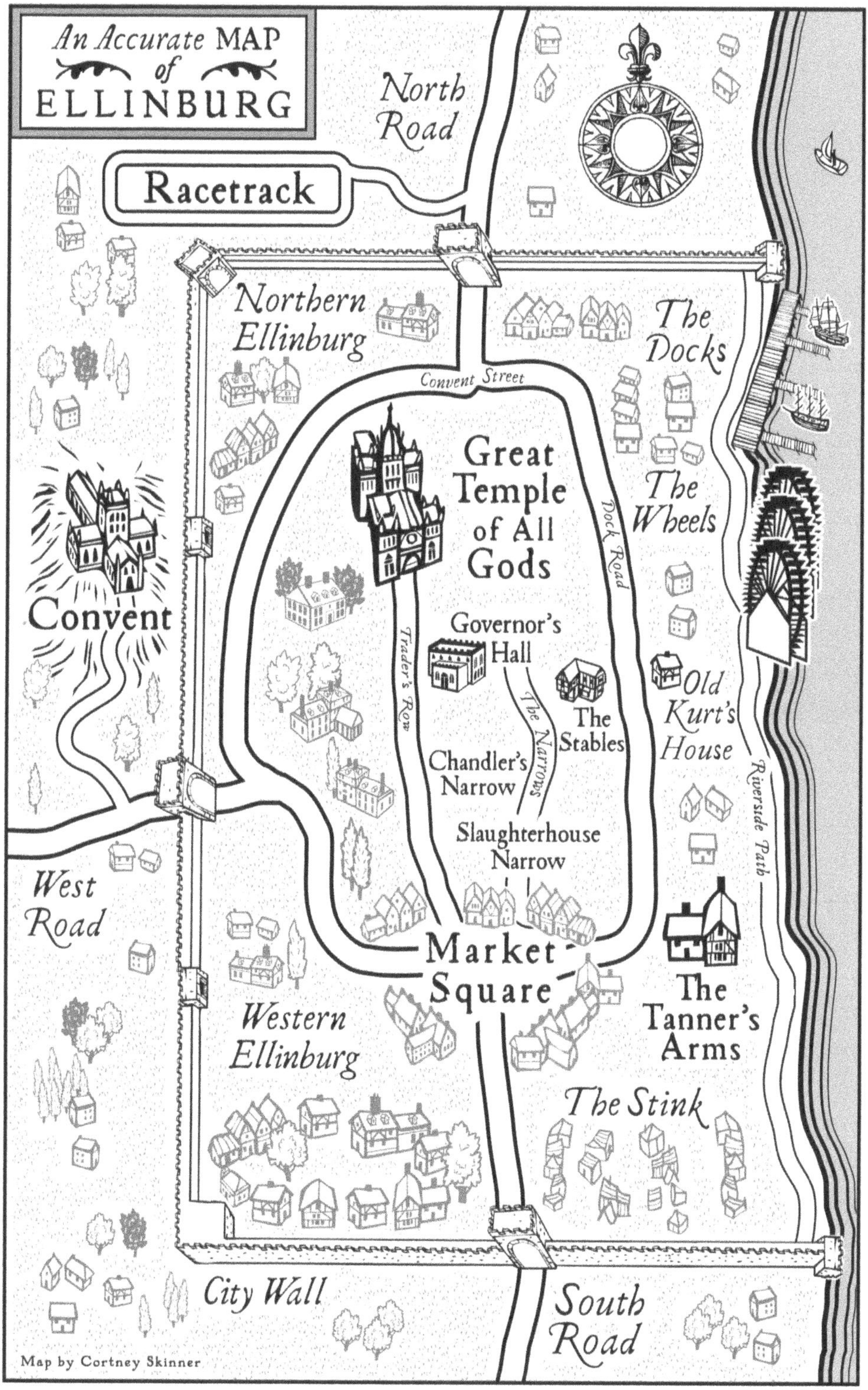
An Accurate MAP of ELLINBURG
North Road
Racetrack
Northern Ellinburg
The Docks
Convent Street
Great Temple of All Gods
The Wheels
Dock Road
Convent
Trader's Row
Governor's Hall
Old Kurt's House
The Stables
The Narrows
Chandler's Narrow
Riverside Path
Slaughterhouse Narrow
West Road
Market Square
The Tanner's Arms
Western Ellinburg
The Stink
City Wall
South Road
Map by Cortney Skinner

Dramatis Personae

The Piety Family

Tomas Piety: An army priest, a veteran, and a businessman. Leader of the Pious Men. Your narrator.

Jochan Piety: His younger brother, a very disturbed man.

Enaid Piety: Their loving aunt, sister to their da. A spinster of some sixty years. She had been a soldier in the last war, and she took no shit from anyone.

Tomas' Crew

Bloody Anne: A sergeant, a good soldier, and a loyal friend. Anne always had preferred the close work; that was how she got her name in the first place.

Sir Eland: A false knight with the eyes of a weasel. Not a man you'd trust.

Kant: A corporal and a psychopath. Kant the Cunt, the crew called him, but never to his face.

Brak: Kant's second, a young thug of some twenty years. He was only tough when he had the big man in front of him.

Cookpot: A cook, a forager, and a thief. Cookpot had grown up in Ellinburg, but he didn't know how business was done any more than Simple Sam did.

Fat Luka: Another Ellinburg man. If he had managed to stay fat on army rations then it was just his natural shape and he'd be fat for life.

Simple Sam: A slow lad but a faithful one, and he certainly had a good size to him.

Black Billy: Black Billy was proud of his arms, and rightly so. Good with his fists too.

Billy the Boy: An orphan of twelve years, touched by the goddess. A very strange young man.

Grieg: A conscript with some unpleasant habits.

Nik the Knife: Not such a bad fellow, despite his name. Nik was well liked in the crew.

Stefan: A soldier. There was little more to be said about Stefan.

Borys: A thoughtful, older man who said little. He could move quiet when he wanted to, for a big man.

Erik: He was good at the close work, was Erik.

Three other ruffians whose names are not recorded here.

Jochan's Crew

Will the Woman: We called him that because every time Will kills a man he weeps afterward, but he's killed so many men it ain't funny no more.

Hari: Not a natural soldier, but a man of hidden talents.

Mika: He could think for himself, could Mika, which is more than some of the lads could.

Cutter: A professional murderer with a mysterious past.

Ganna: A shithead.

Their Friends, Acquaintances, and Enemies in Ellinburg

Governor Hauer: The city governor of Ellinburg. A frugal man, or so he let it be thought. Overly fond of wine.

Captain Rogan: Captain of the City Guard. A hard man and a ruthless bully, but he was greedy and he had his vices.

Ailsa: An Alarian barmaid. Among other things.

Rosie: A whore with a heart of secrets.

Doc Cordin: A barber-surgeon. He had always been a better surgeon than he was a barber.

The Mother Superior: Head of the convent of the Mother of Blessed Redemption. Can't take a joke.

Sister Jessica: A nun at the convent. Good with a halberd.

Old Kurt: People called Old Kurt a cunning man, and that had two meanings.

Ernst: A barber.

Pawl: A tailor.

Georg: A baker.

Desh: An Alarian lad from Hull Patcher's Row. As far back as he could remember, he always wanted to be a Pious Man.

Captain Larn: A career army officer and a pain in the arse.

Ma Aditi: A gangster and an enemy, the head of the Gutcutters down in the Wheels.

Gregor: A gangster who sits at Ma Aditi's left hand.

Bloodhands: A very, very scary man.

Part One

Chapter 1

After the war we came home.

Sixty-five thousand battle-shocked, trained killers came home to no jobs, no food, and the plague. What the fuck did Her Majesty *think* was going to happen?

'Drink up, lads,' I said. 'It's on the house, now.'

'That it is,' Bloody Anne said as she threw the innkeeper out of the door and locked it behind him.

He had wanted silver, for food and beer barely worth half a clipped copper. That was no way to welcome the returning heroes, to my mind, and it seemed Anne had agreed with me about that. She'd given him a good kicking for his trouble.

'That's done then,' she said.

Bloody Anne was my sergeant. Her hair was shorter than mine and she had a long, puckered scar that ran from the corner of her left eye down almost to the tip of her jaw, twisting the edge of her mouth into a permanent sneer. Nobody messed with Bloody Anne, not if they knew what was good for them.

'You drinking?' I asked, offering her a tankard.

'What do you think?'

She had a gravelly voice that had been roughened by the smoke of blasting powder and too many years of shouting orders. No amount of beer would soften that voice, but that didn't stop her trying every chance she got. We sat at a table together and she took the cup from me and drained half of it in a single swallow.

A couple of the lads were dragging the innkeeper's daughter up some splintery wooden stairs while the others tapped a fresh cask. Kant grinned at me from those stairs, his hand already thrust down the front of the girl's kirtle. I shook my head to tell him no. I don't hold with rape and I wasn't allowing it, not in my crew.

I'm a priest, after all.

Over Anne's shoulder, I watched Kant ignore me and drag the girl up onto the landing and out of sight. Those were the times we lived in.

All the same, there were limits.

I got to my feet and shoved the table away from me, spilling our tankards of warm beer across the sawdust-covered floor.

'Oi,' Anne complained.

'Kant!' I shouted.

Kant stuck his head back around the rough plaster arch at the top of the stairs. 'What?'

'Let the girl go,' I said.

'Good one, boss.' He grinned, showing me his shit-coloured teeth.

Bloody Anne turned in her seat and saw what was going on. 'Enough, Corporal,' she growled, but he ignored her.

It made me angry, that he thought he could ignore Anne like that. She was a sergeant and he was only a corporal, although that sort of thing didn't matter much any more. Kant was a head taller than me and maybe thirty pounds heavier, but I didn't care. I knew that didn't matter either and, more to the point, Kant knew it too. There was a devil in me, and all my crew knew it.

'No,' I said, letting my voice fall into the flat tone that warned of harsh justice to come.

'You're joking,' Kant said, but he sounded uncertain now.

'Come here, Kant,' I said. 'You too, Brak.'

Spring rain blew against the closed shutters, loud in a room that had otherwise plunged into nervous silence. A smoky fire crackled in the grate. Kant and his fellow would-be rapist came back down the stairs, leaving the girl crying in a heap on the top step. She had maybe sixteen or seventeen years to her, no more than that, putting her at barely half my age.

I could feel Anne and the rest of my crew looking at me. Men set down their tankards and bottles to watch. Even Fat Luka put his cup down, and it took a lot to stop him drinking. The crew knew something had been ill done, and when something was ill done in my eyes there was *always* harsh justice.

Bloody Anne was giving me a wary look now. Sir Eland the false knight just stood there sneering at everyone like he always did, but he was watching too. Billy the Boy was halfway to drunk already, but then he was only twelve so I supposed I had to let him off not being able to hold his beer. Grieg and Cookpot and Black Billy and the others just watched.

I met Kant's eyes and pointed at a spot on the boards in front of me.

'Come here,' I said. 'Right now.'

A log popped in the grate, making Simple Sam jump. Kant glared at me but he came, and Brak followed in his wake like a little boat trailing behind a war galleon.

'Would you like someone to fuck, Kant?' I asked him.

Kant was bigger than me, huge and ugly. Kant the Cunt, the crew called him, but never to his face. His chain-mail byrnie strained across his massive barrel chest over a jerkin of boiled leather. The scars on his face stood out livid and red as he started to get angry right back at me. I remembered how he had earned those scars at Abingon, forcing his way through the breach in the west wall when the citadel fell. Kant had led his squad over a mound of corpses, and never mind the archers waiting for them. He had taken an arrow through the cheek for his trouble. He had kept fighting, had Kant, spitting blood and teeth as he swung his mace into this head, that shoulder, those balls, crushing and bludgeoning and forcing his way forward. Bludgeon and force, that was how Kant the Cunt made his way in the world.

Kant was a war hero.

But then so was I.

'Course I want someone to fuck,' Kant said. 'Who don't?'

'You want to fuck, Kant?' I asked him again, and this time my voice went soft and quiet.

All the crew had been with me long enough to know what *that* tone meant. That tone meant the devil was awake and there was harsh justice coming for sure, and soon. Kant was drunk, though – not booze drunk but rape drunk, power drunk – and I knew he wasn't going to take a telling. Not this time.

'Yeah, I fucking do,' he said.

I didn't like Kant. I never had liked Kant, truth be told, but Kant was a good soldier. In Abingon I had needed good soldiers. Now I needed good men, and the Lady only knows the two ain't necessarily the same thing.

'Come here,' I said again. 'If you want to fuck, come here and fuck me.'

I held Kant's gaze. I wouldn't have put it past him, under different circumstances. If I had been some other man, some peasant lad, I doubted Kant would have been picky. A hole was a hole as far as he was concerned, and if he could stick his cock in it then it made him happy.

'Tomas . . .' Anne started to say, but it was too late for that and I think she knew it.

The Weeping Women hung heavy on my hips. They were a matched pair of beautifully crafted shortswords that I had looted from a dead colonel after the last battle of Abingon. I had named them Remorse and Mercy.

My crew knew all too well what the Weeping Women could do in my hands.

'You didn't ought to force yourself on lasses. It's not right,' Black Billy said. He nudged the man beside him with his elbow. 'Ain't that so, Grieg?'

Grieg grunted but said nothing. He was a man of few words, was Grieg.

'Lady's sake,' Brak muttered, scuffing his foot at the beery sawdust underfoot while Kant tried to stare me out. 'We was only having a bit of fun, like.'

'Does she look like she's having fun?' I asked.

Kant saw me point to the girl, he saw my eyes and hand move away from him, and he took his moment. I had thought he might, for all that I hoped he had more sense. He was quick, was Kant, and he was brutal, but he wasn't any kind of clever.

He lunged at me, his hand going to his belt and coming up with a long knife. I dipped and turned, and swept Remorse out of her scabbard and across his throat in a vicious backhand cut. Kant dropped in a great spray of red foam, bubbling and cursing as he fell.

I could feel Billy the Boy watching me.

'Good fucking deal,' he said, his voice not yet broken, and he drained his tankard.

'Fuck,' Brak said.

'That's what you wanted, Brak,' I said. 'The offer's still open. My arse, if you can come and take it.'

He looked at me, and at Kant bleeding out on the floor and at the length of dripping steel in my hand. He shook his head, and that was as I had expected. Brak was Kant's second, but he had barely twenty years to him and he was only tough when he had the big man in front of him.

'Nah,' he said at last. 'I ain't in the mood no more.'

'Didn't think so,' I said.

I wondered where this left Brak now in the pecking order of my crew. Truth be told, I didn't care. That was Brak's problem, not mine. Staying boss was my problem – how they sorted out their own hierarchy was up to them.

Matters of rank and the chain of command had gone to the whores after Abingon, but I had been the company priest. That put me in charge of the crew by default after the captain died of his wounds on the way home. That and I was used to leading men, and no one else was.

Simple Sam stood looking down at Kant for a long moment, then gave him a hefty kick as though checking to make sure he was dead.

He was.

'What's the colonel going to say about this, Mr Piety?' Sam asked.

'We ain't got a colonel any more, Sam lad,' I told him. 'We've been disbanded, remember?'

'What's disbanded?'

'Means they've stopped paying us,' Anne grumbled.

She was right. Our regiment had gone from being three thousand paid, organised murderers to three thousand unpaid, disorganised murderers.

That had gone about as well as might be expected.

'Bollocks,' Sam muttered, and kicked Kant again to show us what he thought of that.

The Lady only knew what had happened to our colonel, but the rest of us had stayed together in a loose mass of independent crews as a matter of habit more than anything else. There were nearly three thousand men camped in and around this town, but no one was really in charge any more. No, I wouldn't be getting court-martialled for killing Kant. Not these days.

I looked down for a moment and gave thanks to Our Lady of Eternal Sorrows for my victory. She hadn't guided my hand, I knew that much. Our Lady doesn't help. Not ever. She doesn't answer prayers or grant boons or give a man anything at all, however hard he might pray for it. The best you can hope for from Her is that She doesn't take your life today. Maybe tomorrow, aye, but not today. That's as good as it gets, and the rest is up to you.

She was a goddess for soldiers and no mistake.

'Well done,' Sir Eland the false knight said in my ear. 'You've kept the men this time, at least.'

He was a sneaky bastard, was Sir Eland. I hadn't known he was there until I felt his hot breath on the back of my neck. I turned and looked at him, carefully keeping a bland expression on my face. Sir Eland had been the captain's champion, this man who called himself a knight. He was nothing of the sort, I knew. He was just a thug who had stolen himself a warhorse and enough ill-fitting armour to carry off the lie. He was about as noble as my morning shit. All the same, he was dangerous and he needed watching.

'Sir Eland,' I said, and forced myself to smile at him. 'How gratifying to have your support.'

I turned away before he could say anything else. I could feel his eyes on my back, boring through my hooded black priest's robe and my chain-mail byrnie and boiled leather jerkin and linen shirt all the way to my heart. Oh, yes, Sir Eland the false knight would stab me in the back the first chance he got. It was my job to not give him that chance. That was what it was, to be a leader of men like these.

At least Anne hated him as much as I did, that was something. I knew she had my back; she always did. I made my way to where Billy the Boy was sitting. Kant was still lying on the floorboards in a spreading pool of his own blood, but no one seemed to be in any sort of hurry to move him. I sat down at the scarred trestle table across from Billy and nodded to him.

The lad looked up, light catching the smooth planes of a face that had never seen a razor. A slow smile crept across his moist, young lips.

'Speak, in the name of Our Lady,' he said.

'I killed Kant,' I confessed to him, keeping my voice low.

'It was his time to cross the river,' Billy said. 'The Lady knows Kant needed killing and She forgives you. In Our Lady's name.'

He'd needed killing, all right. No one would miss Kant, I knew that much.

Billy was only twelve years old, but he wore mail and a shortsword like a man. I might be a priest, but Billy was my confessor, strange as that may seem. I bowed my head before the child.

'In Our Lady's name,' I repeated.

Billy the Boy reached out and brushed the cowl back from my face to put a hand on my forehead. It looked ridiculous, I knew, me giving confession to this child-man. I was the priest there, not him, but Billy was special. Billy was touched by Our Lady, all there knew that. That was the only reason the crew left a young lad like him alone. I remembered when Billy first joined us, an orphan refugee from the sack of Messia. The regiment had been recruiting by then, replacing its losses, and had accepted Billy, even young as he was.

Sir Eland had taken a shine to him at once. He liked lads, did Sir Eland. He tried to get into Billy's bedroll one night, to have his way with him. To this day, I don't know exactly what happened, and to be sure Sir Eland was never likely to raise the matter in conversation. All I remembered was a campfire by the roadside. I'd had the watch that hour, and the rest of the crew were curled up asleep in their blankets as close to the fire as they could get. I remembered a sudden shrill scream in the darkness.

It hadn't been Billy who'd screamed, but Sir Eland. Whatever he had tried to do to Billy – and I suppose that was his business really – his attention hadn't been wanted. Billy had done . . . something, and that was the end of it. That was how the pecking order got worked out, and no one ever mentioned it again. The crew adapted and moved on, and after that Billy the Boy was one of us.

The one touched by the goddess.

'Thank you, Billy,' I said.

He shrugged, indifferent. So simply was atonement given. There was no expression at all in his flat brown eyes, and Lady only knew what went on in his head.

I got up and looked around the room, my gaze taking in the rest of the crew. They were drinking and laughing and cursing once more, throwing dice and stuffing their faces with whatever Cookpot had found in the kitchen. At some point the girl had run away, and I thought that was wise of her. Simple Sam was being noisily sick in a corner. I went to join Bloody Anne at her table. All was well.

Right up until several armed men kicked the door in, anyway.

'Fuck!' Brak shouted.

It was his favourite word, I had to give him that.

I sat quiet and stared at the newcomers as my crew drew steel. I knew the one who led them, but I hadn't thought to see *him* again. I kept my hands on the table in front of me, well away from the hilts of the Weeping Women.

Six men shouldered their way inside with the rain blowing in behind them. Their leader shoved the hood of his sodden cloak back from his face and showed me a savage grin.

'Fuck a nun, Tomas Piety!' he said.

I stood up.

'Brother,' I said.

Chapter 2

My brother Jochan looked around him and roared with laughter. He was four years younger than me but taller and thinner, with wild hair and a three-day growth of beard on his prominent, pointed chin.

'Fucking priest?' he said, staring at my robes. 'How are you a fucking priest? If I'm any judge, half your crew are puking shitfaced and you've fucking killed one of them yourself.'

Thanks to the mercy of Our Lady, Jochan wasn't a judge. Still, I had to admit he had the right of it this time. I showed him a smile that I didn't feel.

'Those are the times we live in,' I said.

'Fucking right,' Jochan agreed, and turned to his crew. 'Lads, this is my big brother Tomas. I ain't seen him since the war started but he's a fucking priest now, apparently. Still he's all right, despite that. His boys won't mind sharing, will they?'

That last was pointed at me, of course. I shrugged.

'Be our guests,' I said. 'Ain't like we paid for it.'

If my crew could feel the tension between my brother and me they had the sense not to show it.

Jochan's lads started helping themselves to beer and food, while he came and joined me and Bloody Anne at our table. I didn't know any of his crew. Jochan and I had ended up in different regiments, and if he was here now I could only assume he had led his handful of men cross country from wherever they were supposed to be to join us.

'Oi!' he shouted. 'Woman! Bring us beer.'

Anne's head snapped around in anger, but he didn't mean her.

One of Jochan's men came over with tankards for us, then went to rejoin the others. He was as rough-looking as the rest of them and there was nothing remotely womanly about the fellow, to my mind. I raised an eyebrow at Jochan.

'Woman?' I asked.

'Aye, that's Will the Woman,' Jochan said. 'We call him that because every time Will kills a man he weeps afterward. Mind you, he's killed so many fucking men it ain't funny no more, but you know how a name sticks.'

I did.

'He must have wept a lot, at Abingon,' Anne said.

'Aye,' Jochan said, and fell silent.

We had the war in common, us brothers, if little enough else. The war and the memories of it, of home before it and of childhood things long past and best forgotten. We were nothing alike, me and Jochan. We never had been. We had worked together before the war, but I wouldn't have called us friends. My aunt always told me that I didn't feel enough, but to my mind Jochan always felt far too much. Perhaps between us we made a whole man. I wouldn't know. That was a philosophical question, I supposed, and this was no time for philosophy.

I looked across the table into my brother's eyes, and in that moment I realised what the war had done to him. Jochan had always been wild, but there was a feral quality to his stare now that I hadn't seen before. I could almost see the flare of the cannon in his pupils, the clouds of dust from falling walls rolling across the whites of his eyes into corners that were as red as the rivers of blood we had waded through. Whatever little sanity Jochan possessed before the war, he had left it in the dust of Abingon.

'Brother,' I said, and reached out a hand to him across the rough tabletop.

Jochan lurched to his feet and drained his tankard in a long, shuddering swallow, spilling a good deal of it down the front of his rusty mail. He turned and hurled the empty vessel into the fire.

'What now?' he bellowed. 'What now for the glorious Piety boys, reunited at the outskirts of Hell?'

He leaped up onto the table and kicked my tankard aside, spraying beer carelessly across Kant's cooling body. He'd have looked drunk to anyone who didn't know him, but Jochan wasn't drunk. Not yet, anyway. Jochan was Jochan and this was just his way. He'd never been quite right in the head.

'What now?' he roared, arms outstretched as he turned in a circle before the assembled men.

His own crew were obviously used to this sort of thing, whereas my lads watched him with a mixture of suspicion and barely concealed amusement. Best they keep it concealed, I thought. One thing you didn't do was laugh at Jochan.

Simple Sam obviously didn't get that note, not that he could read anyway. He sniggered. I remembered this sort of thing from the schoolrooms of our shared, lost youth. I remembered how some of the other boys had laughed at Jochan, once.

Only once.

No one laughed at Jochan a second time. Not ever.

He launched himself off the table without a word, without a warning, and ploughed into Simple Sam. Sam was a big lad, but he was slow in body as well as mind, and Jochan caught him full in the chest with his elbow and slammed him back into the wall beside the fireplace. He had Sam on the floor a second later, and then the beating started. His fist rose and fell in a merciless rhythm.

I couldn't let that pass, brother or not. Bloody Anne began to rise, to make something of it. I put a hand on her arm to tell her to be still. Sergeant she might be, but Jochan was my brother and that made him my problem, not hers.

'No,' I said, in that special voice even Jochan recognised.

He knew what harsh justice looked like, and he'd felt it once or twice himself when we were young.

He let Sam go and turned to face me, blood dripping from his knuckles as he stood up. '*No*, is it, war hero?' he sneered. 'You think you can order me about? What's your big fucking plan then, Tomas?'

He was testing me, I knew that. Testing the limits of that harsh justice, with his men around him and mine with me. I'd like to say no one wanted a bloodbath, but I wasn't sure that was true. Even though we outnumbered them better than two to one, I didn't think Jochan realised that, or that he would care even if he did. I knew *I* didn't want blood, though, not now. That wouldn't help anyone.

'We go home,' I said. 'We go home with my crew, and yours, and any of the rest of the regiment who'll follow us. We go home and pick up where we left off.'

'Pick up *what*?' Jochan demanded. 'The county is on its fucking knees, Tomas. There's plague. There's famine. There's no fucking work. And we *won* this fucking war?'

'Aye, we won it,' I said. 'We won, and Aunt Enaid has been keeping the family business for us while we've been away.'

'Away?' he roared at me. 'We've been in *Hell*! We come home as devils, tainted by what we've seen.'

I looked at him, at the tears in his mad eyes.

Jochan had always felt too much, and I not enough. If the war had changed me I had noticed it little enough. Running the business back home, running a crew in Abingon, it was all the same to me save that the food was better back home and there was more drink to be had. I spread my hands in a gesture of conciliation.

'You have a place at my side, Jochan,' I told him. 'You're my brother; you'll always have a place. Come home with me.'

He spat on the floor in empty defiance, then sniffed and looked down at his boots.

'Aye,' he said, after a moment. 'Aye, Tomas.'

He had always been like this, after his rages left him. Quiet, contrite. Sometimes tearful, like now. I could see he was fighting to hold that back in front of his men, and that was wise of him. Will the Woman might get away with weeping among that lot, but I didn't think Jochan would. Not if he wanted to stay the boss of them, anyway.

I looked at Simple Sam, sitting half unconscious in front of the fireplace with blood streaming from his broken nose and one eye already swollen shut. Anne got up and handed him a rag for his nose, but held her peace about what had happened. Sam had been lucky, all things considered. He wouldn't have been the first man Jochan had beaten to death with his fists.

So there we were, the Piety boys.

I had been intending to return home anyway, with my crew and any others I could raise from what was left of the regiment, return home and reclaim what was mine. Jochan's lads would follow him, I was sure, and in time they would become *my* lads.

I might well need them. Aunt Enaid was keeping the family business for us, I had told Jochan. I hoped that was true, but I wasn't prepared to bet on it. I wouldn't have bet a clipped copper on it, truth be told, not with the state of what I had seen so far since we returned. That was only in the countryside, mind. The Lady only knew what the city looked like by now.

'Good,' I said. 'That's good, Jochan. Have another beer, why don't you? There's plenty.'

There *was* plenty, and that was good too. There was famine, as I have written, and the land south of here had been foraged to within an inch of its life. This inn, though, this nothing little country inn in the middle of this nothing little market town, this place still had barrels in the cellar and stringy meat and a few root vegetables in the kitchen. That meant we were ahead of the main march of the army, and for that I gave thanks to Our Lady.

I sat back in my chair, thinking on it while the boys drank themselves silly all around me. After a while Bloody Anne joined me again, a fresh tankard in each hand. She put them down on the table and gave me a look. Anne wasn't as drunk as the others, perhaps wasn't drunk at all. It was hard to tell, with her.

She was my second, in my eyes anyway, for all that Sir Eland assumed that role was his. I didn't know how much I could trust Anne, not really, but I couldn't trust Sir Eland at all. Oh, I would trust Anne with my life on the battlefield, make no mistake. I had done in fact, many times, and had been pleased to call her my friend. But now we were almost home and business was calling, that might be a different matter.

'Have a drink, boss,' she said.

She pushed one of the tankards toward me. I nodded and took a swallow to say thank you even though I didn't really want it.

'Did you notice what this town was called, Anne?' I asked her.

She shrugged. 'Someone's ford,' she said. 'Harrow's Ford? Herron's Ford? Something like that.'

'Anything strike you as queer about it?'

Again, she shrugged. 'Market town,' she said. 'All the same.'

She was right; they *were* all the same. Burned out or starved out or everyone dead from the plague, every single one we had come across on our long, slow march back home. Until this one.

'This one isn't,' I said. 'This one's not dead.'

'Soon will be,' she said. 'There's three thousand hungry men here.'

She had a point there, I had to allow.

Those were the times we lived in.

We might as well make the most of it while the inn was still there.

Chapter 3

I woke up the next morning, my face pillowed on my arms on the table, stiff and sore and with an aching head. I sat up and swallowed spit that tasted of stale beer. Most of the crew were still lying where they had passed out, all but Bloody Anne. She was sitting by the door, picking at her nails with the point of her dagger and obviously keeping watch. She was a good soldier, was Anne.

Someone had to be.

'Morning, boss,' she said.

I nodded to her and got up, heading out the back for a piss. The kitchen had been ransacked; all the cupboards opened and anything fit to eat already taken. Cookpot knew how to give a place a thorough foraging, I had to give him that.

I stood in the muddy yard behind the inn, pissing into a thin morning rain. It was cold, and everything seemed to have taken on the colour of fresh shit. This town might not have been dead yet, but I could see now that it wasn't far off, and the arrival of our regiment would surely be helping it along its way. I looked up at the overcast sky and guessed it was an hour past dawn.

I laced my britches back up and leaned against the door for a moment, thinking. We were three, maybe four days' march from Ellinburg. The regiment would break up here, I knew. This was farming country and most of them were farm boys, with land and wives and pigs and sheep to get back to. If they were lucky, those things might even still be there waiting for them.

Jochan and I, we were city boys, the same as Fat Luka and Cookpot. We had grown up together, the four of us, been in school together. Those two knew what my business was, and before the war Luka had even helped out now and again. He was a good man, handy in a pinch. He might be fat but he was strong with it and he could fight. Lady, but could he fight. Cookpot couldn't, not worth a spit, but he could steal and he could cook, and those things made him useful too. In a regiment where almost everyone could fight and hardly anyone could cook, it had made him very useful indeed. I had been glad to have him in our company then, and I was glad to have him in my crew now.

I wondered what the rest of them would make of the city, Sir Eland and Brak and Stefan, Bloody Anne and Borys and Nik the Knife and the others. Sir Eland said he'd been to Dannsburg, to court even, although that part was about as believable as him being a knight at all. Court was where the queen lived, this queen we had gone through Hell for, and they didn't welcome the likes of Sir Eland there.

I didn't even know what the queen looked like.

All the same, Sir Eland had spun a yarn you could almost half believe if you were drunk and stupid, so I supposed he must at least have seen a city somewhere along the line.

Not Ellinburg, though. He wouldn't have been there. His accent spoke of the south and the west, and we had been going north for weeks now. North was home, far away from the border. Away from the war. Our regiment had been founded there, among those cold, wet hills, and there it would break apart again. I didn't know what would happen to them. Those lads who thought they were going back to their old lives were in for a hard surprise, so far as I could see. They'd find their wives starved or dead of the plague or run off with anyone who had food to give them, most like. They'd find their sheep fucked and their pigs eaten and their lands burned.

Those were the times we lived in.

We had won the war, but at what cost? The queen had beggared the country to do it, and trade had died out and then the weather turned and the crops failed and the plague came. A superstitious man might say those things were related, but I wouldn't know. I was a priest, not a mystic, and Our Lady gave no answers.

I pushed the cowl back from my head and ran my hands through my hair, letting the rain dampen it. It felt good just to stand there, to breathe the fresh morning air, to feel the rain on my face and listen to it pattering into the puddles. I remembered days of choking dust and tearing thirst, the bellow of the cannon and the acrid fumes of blasting powder.

The rain felt good on my skin, clean and fresh. There had been nothing clean or fresh at Abingon, nothing but fire and dust and shit and death, men dying of wounds and burns and the bloody flux. What we would have given for a cool rain, there.

What we would have given . . .

I felt a touch on my shoulder and whipped around. Remorse flashed from her scabbard and I laid steel against flesh. I had the blade against the side of Jochan's neck before I knew it was him. He just stared at me, the fires of my memories reflecting from his haunted eyes.

I stood there for a moment, my heart pounding and my sword at my brother's throat. A horse whinnied, somewhere in another street, and broke the spell. I sheathed the blade and pulled my cowl back up over my wet hair.

'What?' I said.

Jochan shook his head. He said nothing as he walked past me and out into the yard where the rain was falling harder now. He unlaced and took his piss out in the open, careless of the weather or anything else.

'Home,' he said, when he was done. He laced up and looked at me, the rain dragging down his wild hair. 'We're going home, then. You said Aunt Enaid has been holding the business?'

I shrugged. 'She told me she would,' I said. 'We'll see, won't we? When we get there. You and me, Jochan, and your crew and mine.'

'And if she fucking ain't?'

I gave him a look. 'Then we'll have two crews, and we'll take back what was ours.'

He nodded. That was the answer he wanted to hear. Jochan wasn't done fighting, I could see that much. The enemy might have been defeated, but that thing inside that drove him, that violence of the soul our da had left him with, that would never be overcome. We were different in that respect. Our da had left me with a cold devil inside, but Jochan's was hot and wild. He started to laugh. I don't know what at, but he laughed, standing there in that yard that was more horse-shit than mud.

'The lads are going to fucking love Ellinburg, ain't they?' he said.

I shrugged. I had to allow that they wouldn't, but they'd get used to it. City life had its advantages, after all, and it would be my job to make them see that.

'Fucking tell me something, Tomas,' he said, after a moment.

It was pouring now, and I took a half step back into the open doorway to keep the worst of it off me. I didn't think Jochan had even noticed the rain that was now plastering his wild hair to his face in wet straggles.

'What's that?' I asked him.

'How are you a fucking priest?'

'I said the words,' I told him. 'I took the vow.'

'And that's all there is to it?'

'Pretty much,' I said.

The ministry of Our Lady of Eternal Sorrows had little in the way of doctrine, or scripture. She wasn't a goddess for learned men, for mystics or merchants or politicians. She was a goddess for soldiers, and most soldiers can't even read.

It's funny how people always think soldiers worship a god of war. Do we fuck as like. The knights had one, of course. Real knights, that is, not frauds like our Sir Eland. They had an iron god of glory and honour, with a big long lance and a mighty beast between his legs. Us conscripts don't want glory or honour. We just want to not die today. That was what Our Lady offered, if you were lucky and you fought your balls off.

That was all we had, all we could hope for in this world.

Jochan shook his head, his wet hair showering droplets of water into the falling rain. *'Why?'*

I shrugged. 'Why not? The company needed a priest, once ours crossed the river with an arrow through his neck. A priest listens to people. A priest leads people. I can do that.'

'But you don't *care* about people,' Jochan challenged, taking a step toward me. 'You never fucking have!'

'No one ever said you had to,' I said. 'Listen and lead, the captain said. He never said care.'

Jochan laughed so hard he blew snot out of his left nostril. 'Fuck a nun, Tomas,' he said. 'You, a fucking priest?'

'Aye,' I said. 'Me, a priest.'

He looked at me then, sensing the change in my tone. I wasn't angry with him, but he was close to saying something that I couldn't let pass. I could tell he knew it too.

He pushed his sodden hair back from his face and shouldered past me into the inn without another word. I let myself relax against the doorway once he was gone, just breathing in the clean smell of the rain.

I was going to have to watch Jochan.

I gave him a minute or two and then followed him back into the common room. Most of the boys were awake now, his crew and mine, and there was an uneasy divide down the middle of the room. I strode straight into that empty space and stood with a wall behind me where I could see both sides of the matter. Jochan was sitting with his own lads, I noticed, dripping wet onto the floor.

'Right,' I said. 'Have a listen, my boys. For those as don't know me, my name is Tomas Piety. I'm Jochan here's big brother, and I'm a priest of Our Lady.'

I paused for a moment to let that sink in with the two or three of Jochan's lads who had been too drunk or too stupid to realise it last night.

'The war's done,' I went on. 'We won, for all that it doesn't feel like it. We won and now we're nothing, disbanded and unwanted. Well, I say fuck that.'

I paused again, watching the nods and listening to the grunts of approval from both sides of the room. I hadn't broached this with my own crew yet, but it seemed like now was the time. They might as well all hear it at once. The regiment would break up in this town, as I have written. Most of them would want to be off back to whatever was left of their past lives, but I needed to keep my crew with me. My crew and Jochan's as well, if I could.

'Three or four days north of here is Ellinburg,' I said. 'We grew up there, me and Jochan, and Fat Luka and Cookpot too. I've got a business in Ellinburg, a good one. Good money to be made. Lady knows the army don't want you no more, but I do. I'm no noble, to be looking down my nose at you, and I haven't always been a priest. The army made me that, but I came from the same place you did. My da was a bricklayer, and I was a bricklayer's 'prentice. That was until I decided breaking my back carrying a hod to build rich folks' houses was no way to live. Those who follow me to Ellinburg will have jobs when they get there, food in their bellies, and money in their pockets. Does that sound good, lads?'

I saw nods all around the room, nods from everyone but Sir Eland. He was just watching me, I noticed, his eyes narrow and weaselly. It would have felt like justice to kill Sir Eland, right then. I made myself ignore him, and carried on.

'Good,' I said. 'I welcome you all, my crew and my brother's. If you're with me, that pleases Our Lady and it pleases me. If you ain't, there's no bad feelings but the road's out there and you know the way back south. Best be going.'

I watched them, and nobody moved toward the door. That gave me just over twenty men, all told. Part of me wished Sir Eland had taken up his stolen shield and ridden off on his stolen warhorse, but he just sat there looking at me with a mug of morning beer in front of him. I nodded.

'Good,' I said. 'Have a drink and a piss and be ready to march in an hour.'

Chapter 4

We rode into Ellinburg three days later, as the sun was going down.

Jochan was at my right hand on his skinny rowan gelding, Bloody Anne at my left on her grey mare and Sir Eland behind on his stolen warhorse, leading a column of nineteen men on foot. The gate guards eyed us suspiciously as we approached the city walls at the south gate, but soldiers returning from war could hardly be turned away. Certainly not when they were led by a robed priest, they couldn't. The sound of our horses' hooves echoed in the gatehouse tunnel that cut through the wall, and then we were past the gate and into the city proper.

The smell hit me like a fist in the face. Ellinburg is an industrial city, home to tanneries and smelting works and forges beyond counting. The river that ran along the east side of the city was a polluted nightmare of effluent from the factories that lined its bank. I had grown up here, and yet during the three years of the war I had still managed to forget how it smelled. I patted my mare's glossy black neck to calm her. I had been given her by the captain when I took my holy orders. She was no city horse, and I could tell the noise and the smell were bothering her.

I glanced back over my shoulder at the column of men behind us. Fat Luka had a big grin on his face and Cookpot was staring with wide eyes in his round face, drinking in the familiar sights. Two or three of the other lads had gone a bit green, and one of Jochan's country boys was actually bent over and vomiting into the gutter.

I smiled. 'Welcome to Old Reekie,' I said. 'Welcome to Ellinburg.'

They didn't look too welcomed, most of them. Jochan and me, Fat

Luka and Cookpot, we were home. The rest of them looked like they were seeing the second worst thing of their lives. The very worst, of course, had been Abingon. We all had Abingon in common and that was what had forged the bond. That was what held us together. Men who have been through Hell together tend to stay together, if they can. The shepherds and pig farmers of the regiment might have left but these lads, these ones who had been made of the sort of stuff that held men together under Jochan's chaotic leadership or under my cold harsh justice, these were lads who would stay together through anything.

I hoped so, anyway.

We rode out from the long shadow of the walls and I looked around properly. The more I saw, the more I lost faith in the thought that Aunt Enaid might have kept things in her grasp for the last three years.

Ellinburg had never been a handsome city, it was true. This was no capital, and there were few grand buildings here. There was no palace, or great library, or theatre, or house of magicians, or any of the other things Sir Eland said he had seen in Dannsburg. If he had ever been there.

All the same, Ellinburg had been prosperous, before the war. There was a grand Great Temple of All Gods on the hill at the top of Trader's Row. That still stood, at least, but now half of the shops were boarded up, and I could see broken windows and alleys mounded with decaying refuse. There were beggars in the streets, far more than there should have been, displaying stumps of missing limbs or bandaged eyes to uncaring passers-by. Too many looked like veterans for comfort.

We turned our column off the main street and headed down into the Stink, the warren of slums that lay close to the river and the tanneries. This was our neighbourhood, this was home, and it was well named. The stench we rode into was like a living thing, cloying and vile. That was normal, but down here there had been life too. The narrow streets of close-packed homes had been alive with wives scrubbing their steps, unwashed children chasing each other and whooping and shouting in the gutters. Now there was barely a soul in sight, and those we did see looked starved to the edge of death. The streets smelled of bitterness and despair. It seemed every fourth door had the sign for plague on it in cheap, faded white paint.

'Lady's sake, Tomas,' Jochan said beside me. 'What the fuck happened?'

I squeezed my eyes shut and immediately I saw the flames leaping in the streets of Abingon, the diseased, starving people being dragged out of their homes and put to the sword. I remembered mounds of corpses shovelled into mass graves by soldiers with scarves tied over their mouths and eyes gone numb to horror.

'They brought it back with them,' I said, thinking of the veterans begging near the city gates. 'The wounded and the maimed. The plague followed them home from Abingon and Our Lady's face was turned to the south at the time.'

Jochan looked at me like he thought I was mad. Perhaps he did, but then it takes one madman to recognise another.

'If Aunt Enaid was running the business she'd have fucking sorted this,' Jochan said. 'These are *our* streets, Tomas.'

'How do you suppose she'd have sorted the fucking plague?' I snapped, as close to angry now as I dared let myself get with him.

'Aye, well,' he muttered. 'You know what I mean. There should be . . . I dunno. There should be food, at least. And doctors. And . . .'

He trailed off, and I knew he had remembered that every doctor who had less than sixty years to him had been forced into the army. Most of them died of plague in Abingon, and the country was the poorer for it.

'These are our streets,' he said again, and he sounded helpless now.

I nodded. That they were.

I owned a tavern half a mile away, and I led the column there. It was called the Tanner's Arms and it had been a fine old place, before the war. It wasn't looking so fine now, though. The windows had been the new sort – thick glass in square panes instead of the little leaded diamonds of older buildings – but now half of them were broken and boarded over. The sign was hanging at an angle and, most worryingly, there was no one on the door. All the men with less than forty years who could stand upright and hold a spear at the same time had been conscripted, of course, but Alfread had still been a fierce one at fifty-two and I had left him on the door when we went away. He wasn't there now.

I dismounted and hitched my horse to the dry, splintery rail outside, remembering when it had been smooth and gleaming with oil. The other three riders followed suit and I motioned Jochan, Anne and Sir Eland to come with me.

'The rest of you stay out here, for now,' I told the assembled crews. 'You'll know if we need you. Luka, you're boss.'

The fat man nodded and hooked his thumbs self-importantly into the top of his straining belt. I didn't really want Eland with me, but I wanted Fat Luka in charge outside, and if I had put him over the false knight there would have been trouble about it. A leader has to think of these things. Besides, Eland looked the part well enough in his stolen armour.

I led the three of them into the tavern. Any hope I might have had of seeing Alfread or Aunt Enaid or any familiar face behind the bar died as soon as the door swung closed behind us. The place was dim with half the windows boarded up and only a few lanterns lit against the gloom. The fireplace was cold despite the chill of the early evening. A man looked up at us from behind the bar, and his face went pale as I met his eyes.

'Who the fuck are you?' I demanded in the soft, flat tone of danger.

There was a big brass ship's bell hanging over the bar, something I had acquired from a merchant sailor years ago, and now this man who was standing behind my bar lunged for it and pulled the rope hard, making it clang fit to raise the gods.

Jochan lost his temper all at once. He picked up a chair and hurled it over the bar and into the man's face. The fellow went down cursing, smashing bottles and glasses as he fell. A door at the back opened and six ruffians ran in with knives and cudgels in their hands.

We drew steel, and Bloody Anne put two fingers to her mouth and whistled loud. The front door burst open as Fat Luka led his first charge, and a moment later there were nineteen men at our backs. The strangers froze, wild-eyed, as they stared at my crew spread out around them.

I took a step forward. 'My name is Tomas Piety,' I said, 'and you're in my fucking tavern.'

'I am Dondas Alman,' one of them said, 'and this is my tavern now.'

I looked at his men, then very deliberately turned in a slow circle to look at mine. Once I was sure I had his full attention, I smiled at him.

'Can you not count?' I asked him. 'This is *my* tavern.'

'I know people,' he said, and that sounded too much like a promise for comfort. 'I know important people.'

'We fucking *are* important people!' Jochan bellowed. 'We're the Pious Men, and we've come home!'

Chapter 5

Dondas Alman and his boys weren't stupid enough to try to fight us. We threw them out into the street, and then Fat Luka took half a dozen lads into the back and threw all of their stuff out into the street after them.

'There's a stable yard round the back,' I told Luka. 'Bring our horses off the road before it gets full dark and give them a rubdown and some oats.'

He did as he was told, and I sat at the bar with a glass of brandy and watched the room. The Pious Men. That was a name I hadn't heard since before the war. That was what we had called ourselves when we were up-and-coming young men, Jochan and me. I couldn't remember now which one of us first thought of it, but when your family name is Piety you might as well make something out of it. I'd never thought to become a priest as well, but it completed the picture nicely.

Once Alman and his meagre crew were out of sight I let the lads loose behind the bar. I hadn't paid for the stock, after all, and I thought some of them probably needed a few drinks to help them get over their first sight and smell of Ellinburg.

The tavern was a good size, with a kitchen and three storerooms out the back that would be large enough to sleep the boys, and a couple of rooms upstairs in the loft space too. I reckoned one of them would do for me. It's not like anyone in the crew was used to luxury.

Someone had got the fire going and lit a few lamps, restoring a little of the old cheer to the Tanner's Arms. I caught Bloody Anne's eye and motioned her toward me.

'Round up four lads and keep them sober,' I said. 'I don't want those fools coming back in the night and finding everyone passed out drunk.'

Anne nodded and turned away without a word. She walked across the room, picking men and taking the drinks from their hands with short, hard words. Anne had been a sergeant, and the boys in my crew respected her. I noticed she didn't choose any of Jochan's crew, and I thought that was wise. I didn't know them, and that meant I didn't trust them. Not yet, anyway. It looked like Bloody Anne thought the same way.

I poured myself another brandy and sat alone at the bar, watching the revelry. Jochan was drinking with his men, roaring with laughter, even louder than they were. We had different ways of leading men, Jochan and me.

I felt someone beside me and turned to see Billy the Boy staring at me.

'They're coming back,' he said.

I nodded. 'I guessed as much,' I said. 'When?'

Billy looked at my drink. 'Can I try that?'

I nodded again and poured a measure of brandy into a spare glass for him. He only had twelve years to him but he had fought in battles and he had killed men, so I didn't see why he shouldn't drink like a man too. He took a big gulp of the dark amber spirit and gasped, almost choking as it burned his throat.

'Do you like that, Billy?' I asked him.

'Beer's better,' he said.

'Then drink beer.'

'I just wanted to try it,' he said.

'And now you have. When will they come back?'

'Tonight,' Billy said. 'She didn't say when, exactly.'

She didn't say, exactly. Billy was touched by Our Lady and sometimes she spoke to him, or through him, or he thought she did anyway. Perhaps he was just mad, I wouldn't know, but he was right often enough that I wasn't about to reject the idea out of hand. He was *always* right, come to think on it. I reached across the bar and pulled the rope to ring the big brass bell.

'No more drinking,' I said when everyone turned to look at me. 'Those bloody fools will be back tonight, with their "important friends" no doubt. We need to be ready for a fight.'

'I'm always up for a fight!' Jochan bellowed, raising a bottle of brandy in his hand.

He took a long, deliberate swallow from the neck, as though to show me what he thought of my orders. His lads laughed. Mine didn't.

I couldn't let that pass, not now. Not when I needed them to be coming together, and Jochan seemed to be trying to keep them apart. We were brothers, after all, and we needed to stand as one on this.

I got to my feet. 'Listen,' I said. 'Most of you are new to the city, so you don't know how this works. We're the Pious Men. You're *all* Pious Men now. That means you do what I say, and you get rich. These are Pious Men streets, round here, and Pious Men businesses. I own taverns and boarding-houses and inns, racehorses and gambling houses and brothels and all the good fucking things in life. You can be a part of that, but you *do what I say*. Understand?'

Heads nodded, but not all of them. Sir Eland, I noticed, was just staring at me. Jochan was giving me that look of sullen resentment I knew too well, but I'd worry about him later. I met Sir Eland's eyes and held his gaze. He took his sweet time, obviously weighing his options, but eventually he nodded too.

'Good, that's settled then,' I said. 'Four-man watches, three-hour rotation. You know the drill, boys. It's just like the army. The rest of you get some sleep while you can.'

It was another three or four hours before they came, and by then I was dozing in a chair near the fire. The sound of shattering glass woke me. I opened my eyes in time to see something hurtle through the broken window and land in the middle of the tavern floor, fizzing.

'Flashstone!' I shouted, and dived off the chair and under a table.

That cry woke everyone, veterans all of them. A flashstone is like a hollow cannonball packed with blasting powder and nails. There's a fuse sticking out of it that you light, and then you throw the whole thing into a confined space. Most of us had used them in the war, and been on the receiving end of them too. I pulled the table over in front of me, putting a two-inch thickness of solid oak between me and the flashstone just in time.

It went off with an almighty noise, hurling shards of red-hot iron around the room and producing a choking cloud of acrid smoke. Someone screamed, hit by a flying chunk of metal, and then all Hell broke loose. The front door of the tavern exploded into splinters, and I could only guess that they'd put a charge of powder outside there as well. More smoke boiled across the room and flames licked at the door frame, lighting the face of Cookpot, who had been sitting nearest the entrance.

He went berserk.

I think only those who had not been at Abingon could fail to understand the effect that using blasting weapons on us would have. Cookpot wasn't even a fighter, not really. He had been in charge of stores and foraging and the cook fire, but he had been there. He had seen almost as much as the rest of us, and Lady knew he never wanted to see it again. The first of the attackers charged through the door, and Cookpot rammed his shortsword into the man's side with a bellow of tormented rage. He pulled the blade out and stabbed him again, and again. In that moment, Cookpot was back in Abingon.

'Breach!' Jochan roared, and then he was over the table where he had taken cover, an axe in his hand. 'Breach in the wall!'

Men stormed into the tavern over the body of the one Cookpot had stabbed, and Jochan met them with a bestial fury. We were all up now, steel flashing in the light of the fire in the grate and the other that was licking up the wooden door frame and trying to eat its way into the walls.

The Tanner's Arms was timber and daub at the front, and that fire could take with frightening ease if we didn't put it out soon. Smoke filled the room, and shouting, and the clash of blade against blade. I had the Weeping Women in my hands now and I slid into the battle beside my brother. I killed a man with a straight thrust of Mercy through his kidneys, then found myself driven back by a huge, red-bearded stranger with a battle-axe. I could only dodge and parry, unable to get inside the reach of his swings in the boiling, confused mass of fighting, cursing men. He forced me back almost to the bar before he went rigid, his face twisting in sudden shock. He dropped his axe and sagged to the floor with blood gushing from the inside of his thigh, and Billy the Boy grinned up at me.

'In Our Lady's name,' the lad said, a dagger dripping red in his hand.

Sir Eland ran a man through and kicked the corpse off the long blade of his sword. His eyes found mine across the room. Had he seen? Had he judged me weak, in that moment? I didn't know, but I would have to keep an even closer watch on him from now on.

The fire was threatening to take hold now, but we had won the fight. Jochan was holding the doorway, and all these *important people* were trapped inside the same as us. There were five of them on the ground, and eight still standing facing us. They slowly lowered their weapons in surrender.

'Put the blades down, all of you,' I told them. I pointed to a lad who couldn't have had more than eighteen years to him. 'You, come here.'

He dropped his shortsword and took a hesitant step toward me. I touched the point of Remorse to his throat.

'Kill the others,' I told the men.

It was butchery, but sometimes that's what harsh justice looks like. I held the lad in front of me at sword-point and met his terrified eyes with a level stare until all of his friends were dead on the ground.

'Now you,' I said, 'you I'll let go. You're going to go back to your boss, and you're going to tell him that the Pious Men are home from the war. If he sends any more fools into any more of my businesses, they won't come out again. You tell him Tomas Piety made that promise. You understand?'

He nodded, as much as he could with a sword under his chin.

'Kick him out,' I said.

Once the lad was gone into the night my boys set to putting the fire out, passing buckets down a line from the hand pump in the kitchen behind the bar. It was piped river water, too filthy to drink, but it served.

I stood in the sodden, smoky room and took stock. There were twelve men dead on the floor, and none of them were mine. Black Billy was holding a bloody rag to a wound in his bicep, the blood bright against his dark skin, but he'd live. One of Jochan's men didn't look too good, though – he was sitting slumped in a chair with both blood-slick hands clutching a cut in the top of his thigh. It wasn't in the killing place where Billy the Boy had got the axe man or he'd have been dead already, but it was close enough. His face was waxy pale and sweaty.

I went to him.

'What's your name?' I asked him.

'Hari,' he whispered.

'Keep the pressure on it, Hari.'

'There's metal sticking out of my leg,' he said. 'Please take it out.'

I shook my head. He'd been hit by a bit of the flashstone, and that meant the shard was in there good and deep. The lump of iron stuck in the wound was probably all that was keeping the rest of the blood in his leg, and taking it out would most likely have killed him.

'Leave it alone, and keep the pressure on it,' I told him.

I beckoned Fat Luka over to me.

'You remember old Doc Cordin, from Net Mender's Row?' I asked him in a quiet voice.

'Aye,' Luka said, trying hard not to look at Hari's leg.

'Right, go and find him and bring him here. Drag him out of his bed if you have to, but you bring him.'

Luka nodded and hurried out of the tavern. I sent Billy the Boy to find some rags to bind Hari's leg while we waited.

'Fuck a nun, can we have a fucking drink now?' Jochan shouted from behind the bar, and a couple of the lads cheered.

I ignored him the same way he was ignoring Hari. We had different ways of leading men. I looked at the bodies on the floor again. Only twelve of them, and the one I'd let go. They had obviously thought that their blasting powder would give them enough of an advantage to make up for the numbers, and no doubt they had expected to find us passed out drunk as well. I looked at Jochan, swigging from the neck of a brandy bottle. We would have been, I thought, if he had been the boss instead of me.

'We need to get rid of these bodies,' I said. 'Cookpot, you remember the short way to the river, don't you?'

Cookpot was staring blankly into space with a dazed look on his face.

He only came back to himself when I said his name a second time. He needed something to do, I realised. Something to bring his mind back from Abingon and into the here and now. After a moment he nodded.

'Through the alleys,' he said. 'There's steps down to the water.'

'That's right, Cookpot,' I said. 'I want you go and find a cart and hitch one of our horses to it. Not Sir Eland's monster, take mine or Anne's. Then I want you and Brak and Simple Sam to load these bodies into the cart and take them through those alleys and roll them down the steps into the river. Can you do that, Cookpot?'

He cleared his throat, licking his lips nervously. I didn't really think he could, but it would give him something to do. Once they had been shown the way, Brak and Simple Sam would take care of the rest of it anyway. Brak had never been one to be bothered by dead men, and nothing much of anything seemed to bother Sam.

'I can do that,' he said after a moment.

'Good lad,' I said. 'Best get on with it, then.'

Cookpot nodded again and headed out the back to the yard where Luka had stabled the horses. I knew there was a dray cart out there, to fetch the barrels behind the bar from the brew house. I'd let Cookpot find that by himself, and feel important for it. It would do him good.

I set a couple of the lads to boarding up the broken window and barricading what was left of the doorway. It would need replacing in the morning, but anything would do for now.

Fat Luka came back while Brak and Sam were dragging the bodies out of the tavern to the waiting cart, and he had Doc Cordin with him. Cordin was only sort of a doctor, more of a barber-surgeon really, and he had seventy years to him if he had a day. All the same, he knew how to clean and dress a wound. I'd seen him cut a crossbow bolt out of a man before; I couldn't think a shard from a flashstone would be much different. Cordin was wearing a nightshirt and a pair of old boots under a patched and grubby cloak, and he didn't look happy to be there. He looked even less happy to see me, truth be told, and he gave the dead men a hard stare.

'Tomas Piety,' he said. 'I never thought I'd see you again.'

I shrugged. 'It takes more than a war to finish the Pious Men,' I said. 'I've got a couple of wounded here for you.'

The doc crouched down beside Hari. He was now the colour of a cheap tallow candle, sick-looking and breathing in shallow gasps of shock and pain. Black Billy wasn't so bad off, so he'd have to wait.

'He's lost a lot of blood,' Cordin said, as though that weren't obvious. The left leg of Hari's britches was soaked with it, and it was pooling on the floor around his boot. 'Someone carry him into the kitchen and find him something to bite on.'

I looked down at Hari and saw that he had passed out in the chair. I let a couple of Jochan's lads see to him, and they disappeared into the kitchen with the doc. Jochan himself was still drinking. I went over to him.

'That's your man in there,' I said quietly. 'That's your man about to scream for his ma when the doc starts cutting. Maybe you should be with him.'

Jochan gave me a look, and I held his stare until he backed down and followed his lads into the kitchen. He took the bottle with him, I noticed.

Different ways of leading men, as I said.

Chapter 6

The next morning Hari was still alive, and I gave thanks to Our Lady for that. Black Billy was sporting a row of neat stitches in his arm, and in a few weeks he would have another fine scar to show the girls. Billy was a good man. He was the bastard son of a merchant trader from Lady only knew where, someplace across the sea where men are black as night. He grinned at me when I went to check on him.

'I'm fine, boss,' he said, flexing his muscular arm to prove it.

'Don't burst those stitches or they'll only have to be done again,' I warned him, and clapped him on the shoulder.

He was the first of my crew to be wounded as a Pious Man rather than as a soldier, and his lack of reaction was telling. That was a good sign – I didn't want anyone feeling like too much had changed, at least not yet. I went through to the kitchen to see Hari for myself.

He was lying on a straw-stuffed pallet bed on top of the long table, his leg swathed in bandages. He was breathing, but he was deathly pale and clammy-looking. There was blood soaking through the cloth, but not too much. Doc Cordin was still there, which surprised me. Jochan was passed out drunk in a chair, and that didn't surprise me one bit.

'Is he going to keep the leg?' I asked the doc.

Cordin pursed his crinkly old man's lips and drew his shabby cloak closer over his threadbare nightshirt. 'If the wound doesn't go bad, aye,' he said. 'If it does, he'll die. It's too high up for me to take his leg off. If that wound does go bad, Tomas . . . you might have to do him a kindness.'

I nodded. A quick death from a knife in the heart was better than a slow one from gangrene and madness, after all. If it came to it, that was what would be done. Sometimes a man needed help to cross the river peacefully. We had done it for friends before, in Abingon. It's a hard thing, but sometimes it's for the best.

'Aye,' I said. 'I know you'll want paying, and you will be paid. I just need to find my aunt.'

'Enaid?' the doc said. 'You'll find her at the convent.'

I gave him a look. 'Are you being funny with me?'

'No, Tomas, I'm not,' he said. 'Your aunt took holy orders a year ago.'

'Then who the fuck,' I said softly, 'is running my businesses?'

'I don't know,' Cordin said, 'but they ain't yours no more. You saw what happened here. The boarding-houses are still open, and the inns and the Golden Chains, but there's new faces in them. The brothel burned down, and traders are paying their taxes elsewhere now.'

'What about my fucking racehorse?'

'It broke a leg,' he admitted. 'They cut its throat. I . . . I'm sorry, Tomas.'

I stared at him.

Everything was gone, that was what he was telling me. That I had lost all my businesses, everything except this one tavern that I had just taken back. That was hard news, but what had been built once could be built again, to my mind. The Tanner's Arms had been the important one. This was the first business I had taken on, when I turned my back on bricklaying. The Tanner's Arms was special.

I left the doc watching over Hari and went to find Bloody Anne. She was in the main room where the crew were tucking into salt pork and breakfast beer, even Billy the Boy. At least Alman had managed to keep the place stocked during the shortages. That meant the black market was still healthy if nothing else, and that was good.

'Come with me,' I murmured in Anne's ear. 'Nice and quiet.'

She got up without a word and followed me through to the back, into the brick-built part of the building. I led her down the corridor to the smallest of the three storerooms.

'What is it, Tomas?' she asked.

I looked at her for a long moment, weighing her in my mind.

'I need to trust you with something,' I said at last.

'I was your second, before your brother came back. I'd like to think you can trust me with anything.'

In battle I could, I knew that. In the army I could. This might be different. This was vitally important.

'I want you to watch the door,' I said. 'Be subtle about it, but don't let anyone in here till I come out. Not even Jochan. Can you do that for me, Bloody Anne?'

She nodded. It was the measure of her that she didn't ask why, or for how long. She just stepped back out into the narrow corridor and closed the door behind her.

It was dim, with only one tiny window letting in grey light through its filthy pane, and I wished I had thought to bring a lamp with me. All the same I found what I was looking for, a pry bar of the sort used to open crates and dry storage barrels. It was covered with dust and cobwebs, but it would serve. I weighed the iron bar in my hand and turned to the back wall of the room. It was a good wall, that.

It ought to be; I had built it myself.

If the room was a little bit smaller than it should have been for the shape of the building then it would have taken a keen eye to spot it, and thank Our Lady no one ever had. I counted the bricks, twenty-three along from the door and sixteen up. That one.

I pushed the end of the pry bar through the thin skin of dry, crumbling mortar and wiggled it until I got some purchase. The brick started to move and I worked the bar back and forth, trying to be quiet about it. The crew were making plenty of noise over their breakfast beer out in the main tavern and I didn't think they'd hear me unless I started shouting, but I didn't want Anne hearing me either. I didn't trust her *that* much, not with this. If this went wrong, then I was done. I had promises to keep to the men, after all.

I worked the loose brick far enough out of the wall to get hold of it, then pulled it out and set it carefully down on top of a barrel of pickled fish. I stuck my hand into the cavity and stretched my arm down to the hidden shelf, feeling among the bags of coin.

The first I touched was gold, a bag half full of gold crowns. This was the secret of the Tanner's Arms. This was why I had led my crew straight there, why I had fought and killed to retake this business above any of the others, even the Golden Chains. I didn't trust banks. Banks came with tax collectors and questions, and so the Tanner's Arms had become the golden heart of the Pious Men. No one knew that but me.

I didn't want the gold, though. I groped blindly, my hand at an awkward angle, through the narrow gap in the wall. I could feel the thick weight of gold crowns through the leather bag, heavy and difficult to move with so little mobility. Eventually I wormed my hand around enough to find another bag full of thinner coins. Silver marks; those were what I wanted. I lifted the bag, worked it out through the gap, and weighed it in the palm of my hand.

There were between two and three hundred silver marks in that bag, by my reckoning. A skilled craftsman might earn two marks a month in Ellinburg, if he was doing well for himself and had steady work. I nodded and dropped the bag into the big pocket in the inside of my robe. It was heavy, but I reckoned it would be getting lighter soon enough.

I worked the brick back into the gap in the wall and smeared as much of the loose mortar as I could into the cracks around it, then swept the rest carefully out of sight with my boot. It wasn't perfect, but it would have to do. I hid the pry bar behind a cask of salt pork and opened the door.

Bloody Anne was leaning casually against the wall, picking her nails with a dagger and watching the corridor.

'Done?' she asked.

I nodded and reached into my robe. I took ten marks out of the bag and pressed them into her hand.

'You *are* my second, Anne,' I said. 'There's no *was* about it, and that means you get second's pay. Just, for the Lady's sake, don't let Jochan hear about it. He hasn't replaced you, but right now I need to let him think he has. You understand that, don't you?'

She looked down at the ten silver coins in her hand and back up at me. Her eyes narrowed. It took a sergeant a good long while to earn ten marks in the army, half a year or more. She pursed her lips like she was about to say something, then thought better of it. The coins disappeared into her pouch and she nodded.

'Appreciate it,' she said, and that was how Bloody Anne became my second for real.

I wanted a word with my aunt, but first there were things to take care of.

In the kitchen I paid Doc Cordin a silver mark. That was too much, but I didn't have anything smaller except a few coppers, which wouldn't have been enough. It wouldn't hurt to have him in my debt. Hari was staring up at me with a confused look on his death-pale face. I didn't think he knew who I was, right then.

'Go home and put some clothes on,' I told Cordin, 'then come back and look after Hari. I don't know him but he's my brother's man, and he got hurt fighting for me. That makes him *my* man.'

Truth be told, Hari had got hurt waking up when a bomb went off, but that wasn't the point. The point was, if he lived he'd be mine forever now. That would be one of Jochan's crew I had taken, at least.

I looked at Jochan, still slumped and snoring in the kitchen chair. The empty brandy bottle was on the floor beside his boot. He had fought well the night before and I knew I shouldn't take ill against him, but just having him back here under this roof again was reminding me of how little we got on. We had the horror of our childhood in common, but that had never made us friends as adults.

I went back into the common room and gave every man there three silver marks.

'Welcome to the Pious Men,' I told them. 'You did well last night, all of you, and I won't forget that. I told you there would be work for you here, and there is. It'll be harsh work sometimes, I won't lie to you, but harsh work pays well and it's no worse than you did in the army.'

There was a moment of stunned silence before grins started to spread across their faces.

'Thanks, boss,' a lad called Mika said.

He was one of Jochan's crew, and he had just called me boss. That was good. That might just have made it two. I clapped him on the shoulder and gave him another mark.

'Take that and find some tradesmen,' I said. 'I want a new front door by the time I come back, and those broken windows replaced too.'

He nodded. It was enough responsibility to make him feel trusted and valued, but not enough money to be worth running out on me for. That was how it was done, to my mind. A little trust, a little responsibility, increasing bit by bit until they were yours.

Cookpot and Brak and Simple Sam had been up half the night rolling corpses into the river and they were still snoring in the stable, so I let them be for now. I'd pay them later, and another mark each on top for losing those bodies for me. Once word got about that there was more money to be had for some of the harsher jobs, volunteers would be easier to come by. I knew I'd be needing them soon.

I gave Sir Eland a look.

'I'm going out,' I told him. 'Chuck a bucket of water over Jochan and tell him he's in charge till I get back.'

The false knight nodded, but I could see the resentment in his eyes. He thought *he* should be my second, I knew that. Maybe if I had trusted him then he might have been, but I didn't and that was because he had never given me a reason to.

Bloody Anne had saved my life more than once in Abingon, and I hers, and that had forged a bond between us. Anne was my right hand. Jochan was my brother, for all that we didn't get on, and that was a different sort of bond. Maybe it wasn't a good one, but it was a bond none the less. He would never be my second, whatever he thought, but I wouldn't see him without a place at my side. I owed him that much, at least. That put him at my left hand, then. That didn't leave Sir Eland a place at either of my hands, as far as I could see. He would follow behind a woman and like it or he could fuck off; it was all the same to me.

'Anne, Luka, come with me,' I said.

I led Anne and Fat Luka out into the yard behind the tavern. Anne and I saddled our horses, and Jochan's as well for Luka.

'Where're we going, boss?' Luka asked once we were done buckling the tack.

I shaded my eyes against the cold, watery morning sun and pointed to the hill that loomed over the west side of Ellinburg.

'Up there,' I said. 'There's a convent up there. Nuns of the Mother.'

'Why?' Anne asked.

'Apparently my aunt has taken holy orders,' I said. 'If it's true, that's where she'll be.'

'And you need a woman with you, to get you in,' she said.

'Maybe, maybe not,' I said. 'You're coming because I trust you, Anne, not because of what's between your legs.'

She gave me a sharp look. 'And that's why you're bringing me and not your brother?'

'I'm not bringing my brother because he's passed out drunk, and "fuck a nun" is one of his favourite expressions,' I said. 'He wouldn't be an asset.'

Fat Luka sniggered, and even Anne cracked a rare smile.

'All right,' she said.

She swung up into her saddle. Fat Luka and I followed suit, and the three of us rode out into a fine Ellinburg morning. A fine morning in Ellinburg means it's not raining yet.

'Keep your eyes open,' I said quietly as we rode out of the alley and onto the narrow street, into shadows cast by the overhanging upper floors of the houses. 'I can't say for sure if last night's message will have been understood.'

When I had given that message to the young lad I let go the night before, I had still assumed that I *had* other businesses. Now that I had discovered that apparently I didn't any more, I wondered if the threat might have sounded a bit hollow.

We were armoured, all three of us, and I was wearing my priest's cowled robe over my mail and the sword-belt that held the Weeping Women. Fat Luka rode like a sack of turnips, unused to the saddle, but he had a big axe at his belt, and Bloody Anne had her daggers and her crossbow. I didn't think anyone was likely to misunderstand our purpose that day.

'We're making a stop on the way,' I said.

'We are?' Anne asked.

'We are,' I said. 'Chandler's Narrow.'

I led them off the road and up a winding alley between two towering tenements, our horses picking their way over the wide, shallow steps. Most of Ellinburg is hills, with steps and narrow passages between dark, looming buildings that seem almost to touch overhead. Near the top of the alley was a courtyard, with a boarding-house on one side and a chandler's shop on the other. I cocked my head at the boarding-house.

'Anne, go in and see about renting a room for tonight,' I told her. 'I want to know who's behind the desk.'

She gave me a look. 'Why me?' she said. 'They'll only think I'm a whore.'

I didn't think they would. Anne was sitting on her horse like she had been born in the saddle, wearing mail over boiled leather with two daggers at her belt and a crossbow and quiver hanging from her tack. I didn't think anyone would be mistaking Bloody Anne for a whore any time soon.

'Because you're not from Ellinburg, and they won't know your face or your accent,' I said, and she had to nod at that. Luka and me were both Ellinburg men, after all.

She grumbled, but dismounted and pushed open the door of the boarding-house. Luka and I sat and waited, holding our horses and hers around the corner out of sight. When Anne came back she had a look like murder on her face.

'You're a cunt,' she told me.

I raised my eyebrows at that. Anne was my second and she could get away with it, but only just.

'Why's that?' I asked her.

'He thought I *wanted* a whore, and he told me I was too ugly for any of his girls. So thanks for that, boss. That's made me feel good about myself.'

That was a lot of words at once, from Bloody Anne. That told me she was upset, and I couldn't let that pass.

'Right,' I said. 'Stay here.'

I threw my reins to Luka and got off the horse.

'Wait—' Anne started, but I ignored her.

Anne was a good soldier, and a good woman, and this had been my place of business. Even if it wasn't mine any more – and we would see about that – I wasn't having her spoken to like that. She was my second, and I liked to think she was my friend as well.

I kicked the door open and marched into the dingy little room with my hands on the hilts of the Weeping Women, ready to deliver justice for the insult. There was only one person in there, a balding fat man of fifty or so years. He was face down over his desk in a spreading pool of fresh blood.

It looked like Bloody Anne had already pronounced her own harsh justice.

Very harsh, to my mind.

I turned and went back outside to where they were waiting.

'I can fight my own fucking battles,' Anne growled.

She turned her horse and rode up the alley without looking at me. I mounted up and followed her. She could, at that. Bloody Anne had earned her name at Messia, and I knew what she could do. Coming home, going back to my old ways, had perhaps made me forget who I was with. She had been harsher with the man than was deserved, and under other circumstances I might have been angry about that, but I had made her feel small and that was ill done of me. Fat Luka kept his eyes on his horse and held his peace, and that was wise of him.

We rode up through the Narrows, leaving the Stink behind us as we wound our way into the more affluent parts of the city. Even there it was obvious that hard times had come to Ellinburg. The market square had barely half the traders it should have done at that time of year, and the prices I heard being cried for simple food were ridiculous.

'The fuck has happened?' Fat Luka wondered aloud.

'War happened,' Anne rasped, and I knew she had the right of it.

'Aye,' I said, but she ignored me.

We carried on through the city and out of the west gate. We turned off the West Road and headed up the hill, the horses plodding as the way grew steeper. Anne's silence was a cloak of anger around her, and I knew better than to disturb her. Later I would have to apologise to make it right between us, but now wasn't the time. The convent loomed above us on its hill, and that was where my attention needed to be.

It was time to have words with my aunt.

Chapter 7

We were met at the convent gates. Those gates were never closed, except when there was rioting in the city, but that didn't mean all were welcome. There were two nuns standing guard, big burly women in grey habits with halberds in their hands. Their weapons moved together to bar the way ahead of us.

'What's your business here, Tomas Piety?' one of them asked.

It seemed I hadn't been completely forgotten in my own city, and that was good.

'I'm here to see my aunt,' I said.

The nun looked from me to Luka to Anne, assessing us and the weight of our weapons and armour. Her lips tightened into a hard line.

'Sister Enaid is doing penance and is not allowed visitors,' she said.

I couldn't help but smile. That didn't surprise me, knowing my aunt as I did. She had been a soldier in the last war, and she took no shit from anyone.

'Perhaps you could make an exception,' I said. 'Her favourite nephew has just come back from the war. She'll want to know I'm alive, if nothing else.'

'We'll be sure to tell her,' the other nun said, 'when she has finished her penance.'

Bloody Anne looked up then and took her cue. She was no fool, was Anne, and she had been right in part. There *had* been one reason in particular why I had wanted her along for this.

'I seek sanctuary, sister,' she said. 'I am a woman returned from war, and I wish to take holy orders. These men are my witnesses.'

The first nun scowled at her. She was obviously no fool either and could quite clearly tell that Anne didn't mean it, but those were the words and I knew she couldn't refuse them. This was a convent of the Mother of Blessed Redemption, the goddess of female veterans and the survivors of war. If Anne said she wished to take their holy orders, then they had to let her in, and her witnesses with her. Traditionally her witnesses were supposed to be women too, but nothing said they absolutely had to be, and Anne had known that. So had I, of course.

The nuns grudgingly uncrossed their halberds and allowed us through the gate.

'You'll have to put your case to the Mother Superior,' one of them called after us. 'That won't be so easy.'

Thankfully it didn't matter. Once through the wall we found ourselves in a wide open space where vegetable patches and fruit trees were laid out in front of the grey bulk of the convent itself, and there on her knees in the dirt was Aunt Enaid.

I dismounted and left Fat Luka holding the reins of my horse, still sitting his saddle like a sack of turnips with Anne beside him. I approached my aunt, who picked up her stick and got to her feet slowly and with obvious pain. Her grey habit was bunched up into her belt to spare it the worst of the muck, and her bare knees were muddy. She leaned on her stick and looked at me. I stared into her twinkling blue left eye, avoiding the stained brown leather patch that covered the missing one.

'Hello, Auntie,' I said.

She puffed her cheeks out with a sigh. She was a heavyset woman with some sixty years to her, short-haired and one-eyed and with a limp from a broken ankle that had never healed properly.

'You're dressed like a priest, Tomas,' she said, taking in my cowled robe.

'That's because I am a priest,' I said. 'And now apparently you're a nun.'

'I am a fat old woman being forced to weed a vegetable patch because the Mother Inferior can't take a fucking joke,' she said. 'How was the war?'

I could feel her weighing and measuring me, looking for the thing that I didn't feel. The battle shock. Jochan felt it, of course, and Cook-pot and maybe even Anne for all I knew. But I didn't.

'I came back, thanks be to Our Lady,' I said, and waved a hand toward the horses. 'This is Bloody Anne, and you might remember Luka.'

Enaid gave them a short nod. 'Well and good,' she said. 'You'll want to know what's happened.'

'Aye, I will,' I said. 'I'll want to know who these people are who are running my businesses. I'll want to know who we had to fight to take back the Tanner's last night.'

Enaid sighed again. 'It all went to the whores, Tomas,' she admitted. 'With you and Jochan and all the lads gone off to war. We found poor Alfread floating in the river. Your horse was nobbled in a fixed race. They took the boarding-houses and stormed the Golden Chains and burned the brothel, and I couldn't stop them. I held out for two years but . . . One fat old woman and a bunch of beardless boys and old men, what could I do?'

'Who?' I demanded.

Of course we Pious Men weren't the only businessmen in the city, but the other gangs had been dragged into the war the same as we had. No one should have been in a position of strength in Ellinburg for the last three years, and certainly not strong enough to overthrow Enaid. She might say she was a fat old woman, and perhaps she was, but she was also a veteran soldier who I had personally seen break heads open with a mace. Unseating Enaid hadn't been done easily, I knew that much.

She shrugged. 'Men from off,' she said, and spat on the ground. 'With all the fighters gone from the city, we looked a ripe old prize. They came down the road from some town or another, I suppose. I didn't really get the chance to ask, busy as I was not getting fucking killed.'

'Aye,' I said. I supposed it made sense, for all that I didn't like it. 'And now you're here, a nun.'

'Mmmm,' she said. 'A roof over my head, food in my belly, and strong walls around me looked appealing at the time.'

'And have they lost that appeal?'

'Oh, what do you think?' she snapped, gesturing irritably at her mud-spattered habit. 'Do I look like a fucking nun to you, Tomas Piety?'

'You most *certainly* do not sound like one, Sister Enaid,' a voice said, cracking like a whip across the open space.

I turned to see a thin, shrewish-looking woman in a white habit striding toward us with one of the nuns from the gate at her side. She had perhaps forty-five years to her, with a long, pointed nose and a thin-lipped mouth that looked designed to express disapproval. She was obviously the Mother Superior who couldn't take a joke.

Aunt Enaid turned to face her as she drew up. The woman in white was visibly quivering with anger.

'I don't know *why* you let them in, Sister Jessica,' she snapped at the burly nun beside her. 'Words or no words, this was quite obviously a falsehood. Sister Enaid is *not* allowed visitors while she is serving penance, and she will be serving penance for a *very* long time.'

'This is the Mother Inferior,' Aunt Enaid said to me.

'How *dare* you!' the other woman screamed at her. 'I'll have you switched to within an inch of your life for that!'

'Switch this,' Aunt Enaid said, and punched the Mother Superior full in the face.

The thin woman landed on her arse in the dirt, blood from a broken nose spattering the front of her habit. Anne snorted laughter and lifted the crossbow from her saddle. She pointed it at the big nun.

'Don't,' she said, covering Enaid as she hobbled toward them.

'Off the horse, boy,' Aunt Enaid told Luka. 'You might be fat but I'm sure you can run, and I can't.'

Fat Luka dismounted in a flustered hurry, and Aunt Enaid hauled herself up into the saddle and held her stick across her knees.

'Well?' she demanded of me as the Mother Superior struggled to her feet, spluttering with rage and streaming blood from her face. 'I think we should be going, don't you?'

I swung up into my own saddle and we spurred for the gates with Fat Luka panting along behind us on foot.

That was how Aunt Enaid left the convent.

Chapter 8

When we got back to the Tanner's Arms it was to find that Jochan had finally stirred himself from his stupor and there was a fight in progress. Cookpot was raging about how the others had been paid and him and Brak and Simple Sam hadn't, while Jochan was just raging because he could. Sir Eland was leaning back with both elbows on the bar, watching the scene with an amused smirk on his face.

We had already stabled the horses and left Fat Luka weeping and vomiting in the yard after his unaccustomed run, so it was Bloody Anne, Aunt Enaid, and I who came into the tavern through the back door and found the chaos waiting for us. Cookpot had a hand around Mika's throat and his fist raised, an uncharacteristic snarl on his round face.

'Oi!' Bloody Anne roared in her best sergeant's voice.

They knew that voice, these men of mine, and Jochan's lot might not have done but they recognised a sergeant when they heard one. The shouting stopped, and Cookpot let go of Mika's neck.

'What the fuck,' I said quietly, 'is going on here?'

'You're paying the men?' Jochan demanded. 'What fucking with?'

'With good silver, brother,' I said. 'And there's pay for you three too, and a mark on top for the night's work.'

Cookpot nodded at that, looking shamefaced at his outburst. Him and Brak and Simple Sam I gave four marks apiece, in full view of the others. Harsh work was well rewarded, and I wanted them all to understand that.

'Where the fuck did that come from?' Jochan wanted to know. 'Doc

Cordin's been telling me how the land lies out there, Tomas, and you haven't got it from any of our other places because they're all *fucking gone!*'

He was shouting again, at me this time, in front of everyone. I couldn't let that pass, and I could see that Aunt Enaid knew it.

'Haven't you got a hug for your fat old aunt, you silly drunken boy?' she said before I could speak, putting herself between Jochan and me with a practiced ease. 'Come on through to the kitchen with me and we'll catch up, my lad.'

She steered him deftly away from me and out of my sight. That wasn't the first time Aunt Enaid had rescued my younger brother from his own actions and the harsh justice they would have earned him, and I doubted it would be the last. Hari would still be in there, of course, lying unconscious on his pallet on the kitchen table, but I knew a thing like a near-fatal wound wasn't likely to bother my aunt. She had been a soldier herself, after all.

I took a breath, forcing my anger down. I looked around the tavern and for the first time I noticed the two carpenters who were bent over their work at the front door, their heads down as they tried hard to be invisible. I nodded at Mika.

'Well done,' I told him.

'They reckon it'll be done by sundown, boss,' he said. 'It'll be tomorrow before there's glass for the window, though.'

'That's good enough,' I told him. 'The door is the important thing.'

Truth be told, I was glad to be able to give them work. The streets around there had always been poor, but they had been my streets, Pious Men streets, and no one had gone hungry. That had changed while I was away at war, and I couldn't let that pass. I wasn't going to watch my people starve, whatever it took.

I went behind the bar and poured myself a brandy, and one for Bloody Anne as well. The crew were settling down now, going back to whatever they had been doing before the fight started. There were men sewing up holes in their clothes, while others sharpened weapons or cleaned rust from their mail. Brak was giving Nik the Knife a rudimentary haircut. Black Billy was arm wrestling with Will the Woman like a fool, his stitches standing out angry-red against his bulging bicep. Black Billy was proud of his arms and rightly so, but if he burst those stitches it would be his own fault. If it came to it, he'd have to pay Doc Cordin out of his own pocket to stitch him up again. I wasn't paying for stupidity.

Anne came to join me at the bar and nodded her thanks as she picked up her brandy. Some of the lads were shouting bets at each other over the arm wrestling match now, and Anne leaned closer to speak quietly under the noise.

'About the money,' she said, her voice a low rasp.

I gave her a level look. 'What about it?'

'I don't know what you were doing in that back room,' she said, 'and I know it's none of my business, but you went in with nothing and you came out with silver. Watch your brother.'

I drained my glass and poured another. 'What do you mean?' I asked her.

'You *know* what I mean,' she said. 'If you're hiding something, and I think you are, then Jochan will make it his business to find it.'

I nodded. 'Aye, I know my brother.'

I started to turn away, but she reached out and touched my arm to check me. 'And your aunt,' she said.

'My aunt?'

That made me pause. Aunt Enaid had all but raised the two of us.

'She's been in that convent for over a year, Tomas, and I doubt she's been enjoying it,' Anne said. 'If it turns out she needn't have been, I think she'll take it ill.'

That was as many words as I usually heard from Bloody Anne in a day, and they had all been said in the space of a couple of minutes. I looked at her, and took in the serious look on her face. She was worried, I could tell. Well and good, she was my second and worrying for me was part of her job, but she was wrong about Enaid. Jochan, yes. I didn't need her to tell me I couldn't put my faith in my little brother. That was why she was my second and not him. But my aunt?

'I found Alman's strongbox, that's all,' I lied. 'The takings from the tavern. My tavern, my silver.'

Anne nodded and turned away to watch the arm wrestling match, her brandy in her hand. It was obvious that she didn't believe me, and that she could tell that I knew she didn't. It didn't matter. That was the story, and that was what she would tell Jochan and Enaid if she was pressed. I could trust Anne, out of all of them. I sighed and touched her arm.

'About earlier,' I said. 'The boarding-house. I'm sorry, Anne. About what he said, and about not trusting you to make it right. That was ill done of me, and I apologise.'

She gave me a look, then nodded. The long scar on her face twisted as she turned the corner of her mouth up into a sour smile.

'If I want a whore I'll fucking well have one, ugly or not,' she said. 'I've got money now, and money beats looks every time.'

She got up then and walked across the room to join the men at the wrestling table. Black Billy had Will the Woman almost pinned, the back of his wrist barely an inch from the wood. I frowned after her. I had never known Bloody Anne to lie with a woman, but then come to think of it I'd never known her to lie with a man either. I supposed that was her business, either way.

I swallowed my brandy and went into the kitchen after my aunt.

Hari looked terrible but he was still alive, and the doc was with him. Jochan was pacing up and down with a bottle in his hand, and Aunt Enaid was slumped in a chair with her stick beside her, watching him.

I ignored them both and spoke to Cordin. 'How is he?'

Doc Cordin looked up at me and shrugged. 'The wound don't smell rotten, so there's that,' he said. 'He's in a bad way, though. Don't know who he is half the time, and every time I've tried to sit him up he's all but passed out. I'm giving him small beer and he's taken a few oats, but he won't be able to digest much. He lost so much blood, I . . . I don't know, Tomas. Truly, I don't.'

I nodded. Hari was ghost white and his breathing was shallow and uneven. There was a fresh bandage around his leg with a fresh stain on it, but the stain was red like good blood and not the greenish yellow that would have meant death. I'd seen wounds go bad before, and if it had I knew I would have been able to smell it from where I was standing.

'Captain?' Hari croaked. 'I'm so thirsty, sir. Is the oasis near?'

'He wants water, but that filth from the river will kill him quicker than the wound could,' Cordin said. 'It's small beer or nothing, but he's struggling with it.'

'Keep trying,' I said, and put a hand on the doc's shoulder as I passed him.

Cordin might not be a real doctor but he was a good man, and he was doing his best. I looked at Jochan, at the angry expression on his face and the brandy bottle in his hand, and I had to admit that neither of those things could be said of my brother.

'Jochan,' I said.

'Where the fuck is mine?' he demanded before I could say anything else. 'Everyone's paid, with silver you shouldn't have, but not me. Not your own fucking brother, Tomas.'

I held up a hand for peace, and took five silver marks out of my robe.

'Here's yours, brother,' I said. 'More than I paid any of the other men, so I didn't want them to see me give it to you. That's all.'

He held my gaze for a long moment, then took the money from my hand.

'Aye,' he said at last, and the anger drained out of him as it usually did.

More than I gave any of the other men, I had said, and that was true enough. Bloody Anne was no man, after all.

Jochan shoved the coins into his pouch and took a long swallow of his brandy. I gave another five marks to Aunt Enaid, out of respect and for her trouble. She sat there with the coins in her open hand and said nothing.

'Where did it come from, then?' Jochan said after a moment. 'You never answered me that one, Tomas.'

'Alman's strongbox,' I said. 'I found it, and I kept it. The silver he made from my tavern is my silver.'

'It's funny,' Aunt Enaid said, looking up at me.

'What is?' I asked her.

'It's funny that Alman had any money. This place wasn't his, the way I heard it. He was just running it for his boss. You wouldn't think there would have been much coin kept here.'

I shrugged. 'Then I suppose he was stealing,' I said, and I turned away to make that the end of it.

This wasn't going to do for long, I knew. I was going to need to spend more money soon, a lot more, to feed those streets outside my new front door. That meant I was going to have to be able to come up with an explanation for where it had come from, because Lady knew I couldn't tell them the truth.

There was no other way, to my mind. I was going to have to take back my businesses.

Chapter 9

The next morning I called a council of war. Bloody Anne and Jochan and Aunt Enaid joined me in the largest of the three storerooms, the big windowless room where most of the men slept. I had debated with myself whether I should invite Sir Eland as well, and decided against it. Part of me said I didn't trust him and that meant I should keep him close, but the bigger part of me said he thought too much of himself and needed reminding that he was just one of the crew. Maybe I was wrong about that.

'We need to talk,' I told them, sitting on a bedroll in the light of a flickering oil lamp. 'Jochan, you're my brother. Bloody Anne, you're my sergeant. Aunt Enaid, you all but raised Jochan and me after Da died. You're the ones I trust.'

They looked at me in that dim light, and no one said anything. I *didn't* trust Jochan, not nearly as much as I should have been able to, but he was my brother. I owed him a debt from the past, one I couldn't repay, and there wasn't anything I could do to change that. I sighed and pulled my robe around me against the morning chill. It didn't get warm in Ellinburg until later in the year, and it never stayed that way for long.

'Out there,' I said, 'on streets that belong to the Pious Men, there are people who don't have anything to eat. There are people who are sick and can't afford a doctor. On my streets, people are starving for want of work. I can't let that pass.'

'We grew up on those streets,' Jochan said quietly, a distant look on his face. 'You chased me down those alleys, when we were lads. People went hungry then too.'

'Aye, they did,' I said, 'and when we became Pious Men we put a stop to it. My streets, my people. My responsibility.'

'Our streets,' Jochan said.

I gave him a look, but nodded. 'Our streets, then,' I said. 'Pious Men streets. I lifted them up once before and I can do it again, if you're with me.'

I looked around at their faces. Bloody Anne had no history here, had never set foot in Ellinburg before in her life, but I knew she would be with me.

My aunt cleared her throat. 'The way I recall it, Tomas Piety, is that the way you lifted up these streets was to tax each house whether they liked it or not and spend the money as you saw fit on those you decided deserved it,' she said.

That surprised me, I had to admit. She wasn't wrong, of course, but I hadn't expected her to voice that opinion now.

'Aye, that's right,' I said. 'And for that they received my protection. No one robbed a house on Pious Men streets and got away with it, and after a while word went around and they stopped trying. Time was a woman couldn't walk alone after dusk, and I put a stop to that as well. I made these streets safe.'

'It wasn't too safe for anyone who didn't want to pay for your protection, though, was it?'

I stared into Aunt Enaid's single eye and wondered why she was going out of her way to make me angry. I was about to say something I probably shouldn't have done when Jochan did it for me.

'What the fuck is your point, old woman?' he demanded. 'Our streets, our fucking rules!'

'My point, Jochan, is that you can't do it again,' she said, still holding my gaze. 'You can't tax people who have got *nothing*.'

'I know that, Auntie,' I said. 'I've come back from war, not from the madhouse. I've got money all over this city, tied up in businesses that have been stolen from me. Well, I'm taking them back. We'll start with the boarding-house up in Chandler's Narrow. Bloody Anne showed her face in there yesterday morning and it's not held by anyone we know. I want it back.'

'Fucking right,' Jochan said. A slow grin spread across his face, and he slapped me on the shoulder like a real brother might have done. 'Fucking right, Tomas!'

I glanced at Anne, and she shrugged. 'I'll go where you lead,' she said.

Aunt Enaid slipped a finger under her eyepatch and scratched for a moment, sucking her teeth. She couldn't have looked less like a nun if she had tried, and it occurred to me that we'd need to get her some different clothes before anyone saw her in public.

'Do what you think is best, Tomas,' she said after a moment.

'Right then,' I said. 'That's good. Anne, get ten of the men together, and make sure the rest know they're to hold this place while we're about it. We'll go tonight.'

'Aye,' Anne said, and got to her feet.

She left us, and Jochan followed her a moment later. My aunt fixed me with that steel-hard glare of hers.

'This fucking tavern,' she said quietly, 'wasn't making a copper and you know it. You had that silver stashed somewhere, Tomas Piety, and don't you try to tell me otherwise. Your brother might be a fool, but I'm not. Is there more where that came from?'

'That's my business,' I said.

'If you've got money and you want to help those people, then just spend your bloody money,' she hissed.

Truth be told, there was enough gold hidden behind that wall to feed my streets for a year or more, but that was no more Enaid's business than it was Jochan's. If I started spending gold I would face hard questions about where it had come from, and I couldn't risk that. The gold had to stay my business and no one else's.

'I haven't got any more money,' I said. 'And even if I had, what would I do when it ran out? If people start to depend on me to feed them, I have to be able to *keep* feeding them, and that won't do. I need to give them work, not handouts, and to do that I need income. As you say, I'll not be taking it in tax for a good long while to come, so I need those businesses back. And I'm going to go out and fucking take them.'

Enaid didn't speak to me for the rest of the day, not even when I had Cookpot go out and buy her a woollen kirtle to replace her nun's habit. It was used, of course, but there would be time enough later to have new clothes made up for her. I was glad when night fell and I joined Bloody Anne and Jochan in putting our mail on, alongside Sir Eland and Fat Luka and Will the Woman and five of the others. Will was the only one of Jochan's old crew who looked to be coming with us, but that suited me fine.

'My aunt is in charge until we get back,' I told the others. 'No more drinking. I need this place held and held firm, understand me?'

There were nods and mutters, and I led my ten out through the new front door and into the street. We only had four horses between us, and they would have been in the way anyway, up in the Narrows. We went on foot.

It was full dark by then, and when we got to the top of the steps the chandler's shop was closed. The courtyard was thick with shadow, the only light coming from a single lantern hanging above the door of the boarding-house.

'How do we do this?' Bloody Anne asked me.

'We do it like Pious Men,' Jochan said, and before I could reply he lifted his axe and kicked the door in.

It looked like that was how we were doing it, then.

The others bundled in after Jochan, all except Bloody Anne and me. I kept a hand on her arm to hold her back, letting the crew follow Jochan's reckless charge.

'When you lead, Anne,' I told her, 'sometimes the front isn't the right place to be.'

I heard glass shatter inside, followed by a scream. There was a crash, and the sound of boots thundering up poorly made wooden stairs. I pulled Anne back into the doorway of the chandler's shop, and sure enough a moment later one of the second-floor windows of the boarding-house exploded into the courtyard in a shower of glass and broken lead as a body was thrown through it.

Whoever it was hit the cobbles in front of us with a wet thump. I could feel Anne's eyes on me in the gloom.

'Are we not fighting, then?' she asked me.

I shook my head. 'Not tonight,' I said. 'Tonight we are making a fucking entrance.'

I gave it another five minutes, until the sounds of chaos and violence had subsided. I could hear a voice from the lobby of the boarding-house, someone with a strange accent begging for his life. *Now* it was time.

'Come on,' I said, and stepped over the pool of blood that was leaking from the broken body on the cobbles.

I walked through the doorway with Bloody Anne at my side, my priest's robes drawn closed over my mail. There were three people on their knees inside, and blood and broken glass everywhere. Two men were dead that I could see, and neither of them was mine.

Jochan was standing behind his three prisoners with a mad grin on his face and an axe clutched in his hand, dripping blood on the floor.

'That's done then,' he said.

I nodded and looked at the three kneeling men. I didn't recognise any of them, but one of them was definitely not native to Ellinburg. He was too pale and too tall to have been from these parts, and he wore his hair long in a dirty blond plait. No Ellinburg man had long hair.

'My name is Tomas Piety,' I said, addressing them. 'This is Bloody Anne. And this, my friends, is *my* fucking boarding-house.'

The tall, pale man spat at me, and I kicked him in the face. Jochan's blade was at his throat a moment later, the broad shape of the axe forcing his chin up.

'How many of them did you kill?' I asked my brother.

'Four, in all.'

I nodded. 'Seven men,' I said to the pale man. 'Seven men to guard a boarding-house. That seems like a lot.'

'Someone killed our bookkeeper yesterday,' he said, his voice sounding thick through his split lips.

'So they did,' I said. 'Now, you're not from this city, so I'll do you the courtesy of explaining something to you. We are the Pious Men, and we're in charge. You're in one of my businesses, and I'm throwing you out. But first you're going to tell me who you work for.'

The blond man shook his head. One of his fellows looked like he was about to speak, then thought better of it.

'Well?' Jochan demanded.

He pressed his red blade to the kneeling man's throat but got no answer. Jochan growled and yanked the man's head back by his long plait of hair, the axe-head digging into his neck and drawing a trickle of blood.

'We can't,' one of the others said. 'Our families, please . . . he'll kill our families if we talk!'

'Shut up,' the blond one gasped. 'Say *nothing*!'

'Let him go,' I said, and Jochan reluctantly withdrew his axe from the man's neck. 'If that's the lay of things, then I understand. You're brave men, but know that you've crossed me. I'm not going to kill you, not tonight, but if I see you again I will. Do you understand me?'

The long-haired man gave me a sullen nod.

'Kick them out,' I told Jochan, 'and start making the place secure.'

'Aye, Tomas,' Jochan said.

Anne pulled me aside as the three men were booted out into the alley. Jochan disappeared into the back.

'Why did you do that?' she asked me quietly.

'Let them live?' I asked. 'Same as the one at the Tanner's – so that they can spread the word.'

'Not that,' she said. 'You come in like death walking, making your entrance like you said, and you gave your name and mine. You never mentioned Jochan, Tomas. You never named your own brother.'

'You're my second, not him,' I said. 'If he starts to realise that for himself, nice and slowly, maybe it's gentler than flat-out telling him.'

'And when he does?'

I looked at her and shrugged. It would be how it would be, to my mind.

Jochan blundered out of one of the back rooms just then, a bottle of brandy in his hand and his other arm around a half-naked woman.

'There's new whores, Tomas.' He grinned at me. 'We ain't killing them, I fucking hope!'

'No, we ain't,' I said, 'but we ain't taking advantage either. Round them up in the parlour.'

Anne gave me a look, but I ignored her. Business was business. A few minutes later, I went in to address them. There were seven women in total, most of them with no more than eighteen or nineteen years to them. They wore anything from thin shifts to demure kirtles, depending on what they had been doing when we burst in, I supposed, but each one had the bawd's knot on her left shoulder in yellow cord. There were city ordinances about that, after all, and any licensed whore had to show the knot. A couple of them saw my priest's robes and dipped clumsy curtseys. A redhead who looked to have a year or two more than the others laughed at them.

'He's no fucking priest,' she sneered. 'He's just another gangster.'

'I am a priest,' I corrected her, 'and I'm a businessman as well. You all worked here, and I assume you lived here as well?'

There were nods among the women, and some of them looked worried at my use of the past tense. That was good. That was the point I was making.

'My name is Tomas Piety,' I said, and I could see that more than a few of them knew that name. 'This was my stew, before the war, and now it's my stew again. Those that want to stay here and keep working are welcome to. Those who want to leave, leave.'

'Where would we go?' the redhead challenged me. 'We're not street scrubs. We're better than that. We all wear the knot, here.'

I shrugged. 'That's your affair,' I said.

I could see I was going to have to keep an eye on her. She was obviously the boss of them, and she had the look of trouble about her. She scratched her ribs idly and flicked her dirty hair out of her face, her insolent gaze finding Bloody Anne standing beside me.

'You his woman?'

'No,' Anne rasped. 'I'm my own woman.'

The redhead nodded, as though the answer pleased her. 'What terms?' she asked me.

Truth be told, Aunt Enaid had always run this side of Pious Men business, but she wasn't there and I was. I didn't know how high my terms of commission should be. I was about to say something to stall her when Will the Woman spoke up.

'I'll take care of it if you want, boss,' he said. 'I used to run a bawdy house back home, before the war. I know how it's done.'

I gave him a nod. I wasn't too sure how far I could trust Will, not yet anyway, but he had fought for me and when Black Billy had beaten him at the arm wrestling he had taken it good-naturedly enough. Those things went a way toward building that trust, to my mind.

'Aye,' I said. 'This is Will. He's the boss here, now. You do what he says and everyone will get along.'

I left the men to get acquainted with the Chandler's Narrow girls and walked back out into the courtyard. One of the lads would have to stay there with Will, of course, to keep the place guarded. I was sure none of them would mind that duty, but Sir Eland would be ideal for it. He might give the place a bit of fake class, for one thing, and more importantly I knew he didn't like women in that way so at least he would leave the girls alone. The duty would keep his sneer out of my face as well.

I stood in the gloomy courtyard and stretched my back under the weight of my mail. That body would need shifting before long, I thought. I was aware of Bloody Anne standing beside me.

'Thank you,' she said.

I glanced at her. 'For what?'

'For not assuming I know how to run a bloody bawdy house just because I'm a woman,' she said. 'I wouldn't know where to start.'

I shrugged. It had never crossed my mind that she would. 'Help me with this?'

Anne nodded, and between us we dragged the body back into the boarding-house and threw it in a corner with the others. As my memory served, there was a dirt-floored cellar under the building. Some of the lads would be digging graves down there tonight.

Anne looked at the pile of bodies and shook her head. 'I need some air,' she said. 'Coming?'

We went back out into the courtyard again. Eleven men were out there waiting for us. Anne was about to yell for the crew when I held up a hand to say be quiet. This lot were from the biggest, best-armed and meanest gang in Ellinburg – the City Guard.

I knew the one who led them. Captain Rogan was the city governor's chief thug. I should have been honoured to warrant a visit from him in person, I supposed. He had almost fifty years to him, and was a strong, solidly built man who wore a plain steel breastplate over his mail, with a gold star on each shoulder to show his rank. It was a running street joke that those stars looked like the bawd's knot, but it would be a brave lad who called Rogan the governor's whore in the hearing of a guardsman. Heads had been broken for less, and sometimes people just disappeared and weren't seen again.

'Captain Rogan,' I said. 'What a pleasure.'

He met my eyes and scowled. 'Piety,' he said. 'You're coming with us. Hauer wants a word with you.'

I had thought he might, sooner or later. Looked like it was sooner.

'It's all right, Anne,' I said. 'Tell Jochan I've gone to see Grandfather.'

'Right,' she said.

She didn't move, though. She just stood there with her hands hanging by her sides, near the hilts of her daggers. There were eleven of the Guard, but I knew she would have waded in if she'd had to, buying me time until the crew could get to us. Bloody Anne was the best second a man could want and no mistake.

'It's all right,' I said again, and let Captain Rogan and his men lead me away.

Chapter 10

The governor of Ellinburg wasn't really my grandfather, of course – that was just street cant. 'Going to see Grandfather' meant you had been taken in, but it wasn't bad. If it was bad you were 'going to see the widow', and that was a different matter. If I had said that, there would have been a pitched battle between my crew and the Guard, and I wasn't sure how that would have ended. Our numbers were roughly even, but the guardsmen were sober and well fed and their mail was in good order, and each one carried steel along with his club, as well as a whistle that would bring more men running.

No. All in all I was glad to be going to see Grandfather.

'I wasn't sure you'd be back,' Rogan said as we marched through the narrow by the dim light of a couple of lanterns. 'I heard it was rough, down south.'

'Aye, it was rough,' I said.

Rogan had fought in the last war, in Aunt Enaid's war, and I knew his understatement wasn't meant as an insult. It was just how veterans spoke of things, in terms that made them seem less than they had been. You don't dwell on the memories so much, that way.

'Aye,' he said. 'Well, here you are, Tomas Piety, and the big man wants to see you.'

Of course he did. Word travels fast on the streets of Ellinburg, though, and my face was remembered.

'And see me he shall, Captain,' I said. 'I've no quarrel with the Guard, you know that. I'm just finding my feet and putting my house in order. Then regular payments will resume, and we'll all go back to how we were.'

Of course I'd had an arrangement with the City Guard, one that had involved my silver in exchange for their blind eyes. A fair quantity of that silver had gone to Rogan himself.

'We'll see,' he said, but I could see the corner of his mouth curling slightly with avarice.

Captain Rogan was a hard man and a ruthless bully, but he was also greedy and he had his vices. Gambling was chief among them – before the war, on a good week at the racetrack, I could take back the bribes I had paid him and more besides.

'I hope we will, Captain,' I said. 'I hope we will.'

I let them lead me out of the narrow and on up the hill toward the governor's hall that lay in the shadow of the Great Temple of All Gods. There was no castle in Ellinburg, but the governor's hall was the closest thing to one that a building could be. A great lump of grey stone with narrow windows and iron doors, it squatted near the end of Trader's Row like a war elephant from Alaria.

Lanterns on iron hooks projected from the walls, casting a yellow glow on the ground outside where the uneven cobbles gave way to good flagstones. A single royal standard flew from the rooftops, the red banner looking almost black in the darkness. There were two of the City Guard stationed at the front doors at all times, and regular patrols around the building day and night.

Rogan greeted the men on guard duty, and they opened the heavy double doors to admit our party. We trooped up the steps and into an echoing stone hall. Lamps burned in there, but not many. The hour was late and the governor was a frugal man, or so he let it be thought.

'You know the drill,' Rogan said.

I unbuckled my sword-belt and handed over the Weeping Women, Remorse and Mercy heavy in their scabbards as I held the belt out to Rogan. He passed it to one of his men and looked at me with narrowed eyes.

'Is that everything?' he asked me.

'I was out on business, not riding to battle,' I said. 'That's everything.'

They searched me anyway, but I hadn't been lying. Eventually Rogan grunted and sent half his men back to their barracks. The other five escorted me down a long corridor and up a flight of narrow stairs meant for servants. The grand staircase in the main hall wasn't for the likes of me; that message was plain enough.

Governor Hauer was in his study on the second floor, sitting behind a large desk with a glass of wine in his hand. He looked paunchy even in his expensively tailored clothes, and he was already half bald. The governor lived well, whatever he liked to put about regarding his frugal ways. He lived to excess, in fact, and his health was the poorer for it. He looked like he had ten more years to him than he actually did.

Rogan bade his men wait outside and followed me into the study alone. The look on the governor's face gave me pause. I had thought I knew what this meeting was about – bribes and taxes and how they had no doubt gone up while I was away. Now I wasn't so sure.

'Tomas Piety,' Hauer said.

'Lord Governor,' I replied. 'This is an unexpected pleasure.'

'No, it isn't, unexpected or a pleasure,' he said. 'Give me one reason why I shouldn't have Rogan break your neck.'

'And why might you want to do that?'

He glared at me. 'You're only a few days back in Ellinburg, and the place is already a charnel house. Corpses found floating in the river, a disturbance at the convent – and don't think I haven't heard all about *that* from the Mother Superior – and now a battle in Chandler's Narrow. You're more trouble than you're worth, Piety.'

'I've been to war to fight for queen and country, and I come home to find myself robbed blind and my people starving in their own homes. You think I can let that pass?'

'You've been to war because you were conscripted and forced to go, so don't give me all that horseshit,' he said. 'Queen and country mean no more to you than they do to me, and we both know it.'

He was wrong about that, to an extent anyway, but I didn't see a need to tell him so. Not yet, anyway.

'I see,' I said instead. 'Do you expect me to sit meekly by and watch while other men profit from the businesses I built with my own hands?'

'No,' Hauer said. 'No, I don't, and that's why you're still breathing. Sit down, Tomas. Have some wine.'

I sat in the chair across the desk from him, all too aware of Rogan looming behind me. Rogan's big, callused hands were made for wringing necks, and I was there unarmed. Not defenceless, no, but I've never been as good with my fists as Jochan was. If it came to it, I knew I'd struggle against Rogan. I sat and offered a silent prayer to Our Lady that tonight wouldn't be the night I crossed the river.

I reached for a goblet and the flagon and poured myself a drink. I prefer brandy to wine, but hospitality extended should never be refused. The wine was strong and cloying, too sweet for my taste, but I drank it anyway.

'You've something on your mind,' I said.

The governor took a long draft from his own goblet and cleared his throat. 'What've you noticed, about these people you've been killing?'

'They're scared,' I said, thinking of the three in the boarding-house. 'Whoever's in charge of them, they're more scared of him than they are of me and my crew. One of them said something about their family being held hostage. That and I've lived in Ellinburg all my life aside from the war years and I don't recognise a single one of them.'

'Someone's got a knife held to their children's throats,' Hauer said.

'Who?'

He ignored the question. 'Have you seen any foreigners among them?'

'One,' I said. 'Long haired and blond and tall. Not from these parts.'

'From Skania,' Hauer said.

'If you say so,' I said.

I had only spent a few years in school; enough to learn my letters and how to figure simple accounts, but that was all. History, geography, those were mysteries to me. I knew Skania was somewhere across the sea to the north, but no more than that.

'I do say so,' he assured me. 'Most of the men you're fighting are petty scum like you, little people made to feel big by violence and stolen silver. Men from country towns by and large, and a few billy-big-bollocks they've brought up from Dannsburg to stiffen them. They've been careful not to recruit any Ellinburg chaps, who might have other loyalties. A man called Bloodhands leads them, so folk say, and where he came from is anyone's guess. No one even fucking knows who he is.'

I let the insults slide and thought about it. 'What about the other crews?'

The Pious Men had been influential in Ellinburg before the war, but of course we hadn't been the only street crew doing business or paying off the Guard. The Gutcutters, the Alarian Kings and all the other crews had seen their men dragged off to war just like we had.

'Much the same,' Hauer told me. 'Our northern friends have been busy, while Ellinburg men have been at war.'

The governor hadn't been at war, I noted, for all that he was of an age. He might not look it, but he only had a few more years than me. Not too old to fight. No man with less than forty years to him was called too old to fight when the recruiting parties came calling.

'And who are they then, these mysterious northern friends?' I asked him.

He paused to refill his goblet, and all the while Captain Rogan stood just behind my chair with his big, hard hands not so very far from my neck. This was the point of the interview, I realised. This wasn't about the violence I had caused, or even about the bribes I owed. Whatever the governor really wanted to say to me was about to come out.

'Foreigners, as I say,' Hauer said. 'From Skania like the one you met, although he sounds like he was no one. They're not people like you, Tomas; don't ever make the mistake of thinking that they are. No, they're people more like me. They're people like the Queen's Men, in their own land. And now they're here.'

That gave me pause. The Queen's Men were a semi-secret part of the royal government. They were *nothing* like the governor, and he was flattering himself if he thought otherwise. They were a particular order of the knighthood whose weapons were not sword and lance but diplomacy and gold and a knife in the dark. The Queen's Men were subtle, unseen and officially non-existent. They were the thing businessmen like us frightened our children with. Never mind the boggart with its long twisted fingers, that was just in stories – the sort of scary stories that children enjoy because they know they're not real. Do what your father says or the Queen's Men will come and take you away. Now *that* was something to be frightened of.

'Is that right?' I said.

'It is,' Hauer assured me. 'I need to be honest with you now, Tomas, and to trust you with something. Can I do that?'

I looked at him for a moment, at his drooping jowls and the faint sheen of sweat on his broad forehead. I doubted very much that he was going to be honest with me, and I knew that he didn't trust me any more than I trusted him. All the same, this was a change from the way our conversations usually went, and that held my interest if nothing else.

'Of course,' I said.

'There's a Queen's Man in the city right now,' he told me. 'Well, a Queen's Woman, I suppose you might say.'

'Is there, now?'

'There is,' he said.

'And why's that, then?'

And why are you telling me that, more to the point?

'There are things afoot, Piety. Political things, which I can't expect a cheap thug like you to understand,' he said. 'That's all right, you don't have to understand. You just have to do what you're told. When the Queen's Men say jump, you jump, you understand me? You'll do what she tells you, if you're wise.'

'Why me?' I asked him.

I had a strong suspicion I knew exactly why me, but I wanted to find out if *he* did.

He shrugged. 'I was told to put them in touch with the first gang boss who made it home from the war,' he said. 'That would be you.'

I wasn't sure how far to believe that. From what I had seen of Ellinburg, I probably *was* the first boss to make it home, but it sounded thin to me. I thought this might be more to do with history than anything else. History that the governor still didn't seem to know about.

'All right,' I said. 'Who do I expect, and when?'

'I don't know,' he said, and for the first time he sounded shaken. 'A woman, that's all. She's a Queen's Man, Tomas – for the gods' sake, I never saw her face. She'll find you.'

I could see the fear in his eyes now and couldn't help wondering if he had woken one night to find this woman in his bedchamber, holding a knife to his balls while she made her demands. From what I knew of the Queen's Men it wouldn't have surprised me.

Not one bit it wouldn't.

Chapter 11

It was late when I got back to the Tanner's Arms. Most of the men were asleep by then, but Simple Sam was on the door and Bloody Anne was inside waiting for me.

'What in the Lady's name happened?' she asked me.

'It's all right, Anne,' I said. 'I got taken to see Grandfather, that's all.'

'Taken in,' she said, and I knew someone had explained what that meant, 'but they let you go again. Why, and what for?'

I sighed and poured myself a brandy. 'The governor wanted a word,' I said. 'You have to understand the way this works, here in Ellinburg. We're a crew and I'm a boss, and the City Guard are a bigger crew and the governor is a bigger boss. I have to pay him taxes, the same way my people pay me taxes. It's just business.'

Anne frowned at me. 'The governor is corrupt?'

'He's a businessman,' I said. 'We're all businessmen, Anne.'

Bloody Anne was a soldier, not a criminal. I didn't know much about her past, where she had lived or what she had done before the war, but she was honest and she was faithful. Those were admirable qualities in a sergeant, but now she was my second in the Pious Men and it was time she learned how things really worked.

'I'm not a fucking idiot, Tomas,' Anne said. 'A bribe is a bribe, so call it that.'

'All right, we'll call it that,' I said. 'I bribe the Guard to keep them out of Pious Men business, and so do the bosses of the other crews in the city. Captain Rogan gets a cut of that money, the guardsmen get a pittance and the governor keeps the rest of it for himself. That's just how it works.'

I shrugged, making light of it, and looked around the room. Mika and Brak were sitting by the fire playing cards and looking reasonably sober, but everyone else appeared to have turned in for the night.

'Where's Jochan?' I asked.

Anne was my second but Jochan still thought that *he* was, so by rights it should have been him waiting up for me and not her. But it hadn't been. That said a lot, to my mind.

'Asleep out the back,' she said. 'He's had a drink.'

He'd had a bottle of brandy or more and passed out, was what she meant.

I nodded. 'How's Hari?'

'Better,' Anne said, and now she looked uncomfortable. 'Much better.'

'That's good,' I said.

She stared down at her boots and didn't say anything for a long time. I knew that face. She had looked like that in Abingon, when she had needed to tell me someone else had died. That was the face Anne got when there was hard news, but if Hari was getting better then I couldn't see what that news would be. I sipped my brandy and waited, giving her the time she needed to put her words together.

'He's a lot better,' she said at last. 'Doc Cordin had to leave, so Billy the Boy sat with him a while, and then he was sitting up and eating and he seemed to know who he was again. Tomas, this morning he called me Colonel and asked how far it was to Abingon. He was so far gone, so nearly dead from all the blood he'd lost, and now . . . he isn't.'

'Well, that's good,' I said. 'Isn't it?'

I gave Anne a look, and she nodded.

'Aye, it's good,' she said. 'I know he's not part of our crew but he seems like a good man.'

'He *is* part of our crew,' I said. 'Now, he is. They're all Pious Men, Anne.'

'Aye,' she said again. 'Just like Billy the Boy is.'

I nodded. I could tell that Anne was scared of Billy the Boy, and that didn't surprise me. I knew that Sir Eland certainly was, and had been ever since that first night in the woods outside Messia. Sometimes I was scared of him too, although I'd have been hard pressed to put my finger on exactly why.

Touched by the goddess, I thought.

No twelve-year-old child should be a confessor and a seer, but Billy was.

'Is there something you're not telling me, Bloody Anne?'

'Maybe you ought to see for yourself,' she said.

I followed Anne through to the kitchen and there was Billy, watching over Hari as she had said. Hari did look better, I had to allow. He was asleep again now, but that awful waxy sheen was gone from his face and he almost had some colour back in his cheeks. Billy was sitting cross-legged on the table staring at him, unblinking. Billy had an intense way about him sometimes, and this was nothing out of the ordinary for him.

'What am I not seeing?' I asked her.

'Tomas,' Anne said slowly, 'he's not touching the table.'

I looked again, and realised that she was right. There was a good inch of clear space between Billy's arse and crossed legs and the top of the table.

He was floating in the air.

'By Our Lady's name,' I whispered.

I swallowed. Billy was touched by the goddess, I knew that. I knew that, but knowing it and seeing it weren't the same thing.

Billy didn't look like he realised we were in the room. He just floated there, staring at Hari, and he gave no sign that he could see or hear us. Perhaps he couldn't. He was in some sort of trance, to my mind, although how and why were anyone's guess. Was the goddess really working through him, healing Hari? Perhaps. I didn't discount the idea, but if that was the case then I had no explanation for it. Our Lady didn't heal men, that I knew of.

'We should send for a priest,' Anne said.

I gave her a look. 'I *am* a fucking priest,' I said, 'and it's more than I can explain. We'd need a magician to explain this.'

Of course I didn't know a magician, no more than I knew a real doctor. There was Old Kurt, though, who people called a cunning man.

He was to a magician what Doc Cordin was to a doctor, I supposed. Not book-schooled, maybe, but what he did worked well enough. Most of the time, anyway. Perhaps *he* could explain it.

Still, if Billy the Boy had done something to Hari, or if Our Lady had done something through Billy, then it didn't seem to have caused anyone any harm. Quite the opposite, to my mind. A man of mine who had been dying wasn't any more, and I wasn't going to argue with that.

'It's late and I'm tired,' I said. 'If Billy wants to float in the air, then I can't see it's hurting anyone.'

'You're just going to let it pass?' Anne asked.

I shrugged. I couldn't see what else I could do about it, short of getting hold of him and physically dragging him down onto the table. I had a feeling that wouldn't have been wise.

'It's witchcraft, Tomas.'

'I'll pray on it,' I said. 'Then I'm going to sleep.'

I left Anne in the kitchen, watching Billy the Boy while he floated above the table and stared down at Hari, never blinking.

I wouldn't pray on it.

Our Lady didn't answer prayers, after all, and I had more pressing things to concern me than Billy the Boy.

I made my way up the rickety stairs to the garret room I had claimed as my own, and shut the ill-fitting door behind me. I could hear my aunt snoring in the next room.

Billy the Boy would keep, I told myself, whether it was witchcraft or not and how the fuck was I supposed to know either way? I was a priest, not a mystic, but the last thing I wanted was Anne worrying about witchcraft in our crew. I took my sword-belt and mail off and flexed my shoulders, aching from the weight of the armour. She would have to keep as well; other things wouldn't keep at all.

There were Queen's Men in the city, and they wanted me to work for them.

Again.

I woke early the next morning, despite not having laid my head down much before dawn. I needed to piss. I kicked my bedroll open and got up, feeling the cold morning air around my bare shins. I found the pot and stood over it in my smallclothes, thinking while I did my business. There's nothing like a good piss in the morning to clear the head. That was better than prayer any day, to my mind, and certainly more productive.

The Queen's Men.

I thought I had seen the last of them, but it seemed like I had been wrong about that.

I have written that I'm a businessman, and I am. I'm a priest as well, and that's true enough. But perhaps I'm something else too. That gold hidden in the wall of the storeroom downstairs hadn't come out of thin air, after all. I had earned that gold, and no one knew about that. Not Governor Hauer, not Jochan, not even Aunt Enaid.

No one.

I had earned that gold from the Queen's Men, before the war. That was what I had been worried that Governor Hauer might have discovered. From what he had said last night it seemed that he hadn't, and that was good even if nothing else was.

They paid well, the Queen's Men, I had to give them that. They had paid me very well indeed, to spy on the governor. Oh, he thought he was untouchable, did Hauer, here in his reeking industrial city where none of the fine lords and ladies of Dannsburg would ever want to set their silken feet.

Incomes were what he said they were, to Hauer's mind, and taxes were paid accordingly. He never thought anyone in the capital would trouble themselves to question his accounts, but then of course at the time he didn't know there was a war brewing. Wars need to be paid for, in gold as well as blood. Blood might be cheap but gold had to be wrung out of the provinces, by force if necessary. I'm no politician, but even I knew that.

A man contacted me maybe a year before the war broke out. He was no one I knew, just a trader from the east offering good terms on tea and silk and poppy resin. We made some deals, that man and I, and once he had my trust he showed me the Queen's Warrant and offered me another deal – work for the Queen's Men or face the queen's justice for the dodged tea taxes and the unlicensed poppy trade.

I knew the queen's justice was even harsher than mine, so of course I agreed.

I never thought I'd be a spy for the crown, but then I never thought I'd be a priest either. Working for the crown had stuck in my throat like a fish bone, though, and it almost choked me. To work for the crown, to be an informer and a spy, that went against everything I believed in, and I hated it.

Better that than hang, though, or so I told myself so I could sleep at nights.

I worked for that man for five months, passing him information on everything from the bribes that the Pious Men paid the City Guard to the number of boats that came down the river and how many bales and barrels each unloaded and what each one had contained.

It cost me silver to find those things out, of course, but for every mark I spent it seemed the Queen's Man was happy to repay me with a gold crown. I was careful, and circumspect, and I made sure that my eyes and ears were no one that we knew. This wasn't Pious Men business; I had known that from the start. If I had made it Pious Men business, then Jochan would have known about it and got himself involved, and it would all have gone to the whores. Even then, I realised as I finished my piss and buttoned my smallclothes, even before the war I had known I couldn't trust my brother.

That was over and done, or so I had thought, but it looked like I had been wrong about that. It seemed that the Queen's Men weren't done with me yet. I've heard it said that the only way to leave the service of the crown is at the end of a rope, and it seemed that that might just be true after all.

I splashed water from the basin into my unshaven face. I needed to see a barber, I thought. It wouldn't do to greet a representative of the queen with a rough chin.

I got dressed and headed downstairs to the kitchen, buckling my sword-belt as I went. I found Hari sitting in a chair with a bowl of oats in his hands and a mug of small beer on the table in front of him. He was spooning oats into his face like he hadn't eaten in a month. He was still a bit pale, but otherwise his recovery was nothing short of miraculous. I wasn't sure that I believed in miracles, but I believed what I could see with my own eyes.

'Morning, boss,' Billy the Boy said from beside the fireplace.

I gave him a look, noting how pale and drawn he seemed.

'Morning, Billy,' I said. 'Hari, it's good to see you up and about again.'

'Aye, boss,' Hari said. 'I'm feeling a lot better. Just needed some sleep, I reckon. I've been awful tired, of late.'

I wondered how much he remembered but decided to let it pass.

'You take it easy,' I said.

I reached into my pouch and gave him four silver marks. He stared at me in open astonishment.

'You missed out on the accounting,' I told him. 'It's three marks a man for joining the Pious Men, and there's another for you on account of being grievously wounded in my service. I look after my crew, Hari, and I reward loyalty. You remember that.'

'Yes, boss,' he said, making the money disappear swiftly into his sweaty shirt. 'Thank you.'

The men would need new clothes, I thought. They were all filthy and ragged, every one of them, and I wasn't much better myself. Conscripts usually were, of course, but that wouldn't do any more. Not now we were home it wouldn't. The Pious Men had a certain appearance to maintain, after all.

'Billy,' I said, and the lad looked up at me with expressionless eyes.

'Boss?'

I didn't want to do this, I realised. Not now, anyway. It would keep, as I had told myself the night before.

'Stay out of Bloody Anne's way today,' I said. 'I'm going out.'

I went back into the common room and found Fat Luka returning from the shithouse in the yard.

'You're coming into town with me,' I told him.

He just nodded and went to get his weapons. Luka was a good Ellinburg man, and he knew how things worked. Bloody Anne was my second, no mistake about that, but I had known Luka a lot longer and he knew the city. There were some tasks he'd be better suited for.

I knew I could trust him.

Chapter 12

I put Luka on Jochan's horse again and the pair of us rode up out of the Stink toward Trader's Row. I didn't need anyone with me, not really, but a man in my position should never ride alone. If nothing else there are expectations to be met, and it wouldn't look right for Tomas Piety to be about in Ellinburg without at least one bodyguard.

Three years of war was a long time, and if people had started to forget about the Pious Men, then it was my job to remind them who we were. We were back, and I needed the whole city to know that. These Skanians that Hauer was so worried about were only half the problem, to my mind. I needed my own people, the people of Ellinburg, to respect me. That wasn't going to happen while my men and I looked like vagrants.

Many of the streets in Ellinburg were named after the trades that had first claimed them, hundreds of years ago. Net Mender's Row, where Doc Cordin lived, was what it sounded, a squalid street near the river in the heart of the Stink where the poor worked on the nets with their gnarled and arthritic hands until they could no longer afford to feed themselves. It backed onto Fisher's Gate, where the river water seeped into the foundations of the houses and men pulled sickly fish from the polluted river to feed their equally sickly wives and children. Trader's Row, half a city away and near the governor's hall and the Great Temple, was another matter.

Trader's Row was home to the halls of the guilds, and there was money there. Even these days, even with how the city was now, there was money on Trader's Row. There was a barber's shop near the hall of spicers that I had frequented before the war, and that was where we went first. It was expensive, of course, but as I say, there were expectations to be met. Doc Cordin had always been a better surgeon than he was a barber, and I wasn't letting him near my face with a razor.

We hitched the horses outside and Luka pushed the door open for me. An elderly, aproned man was halfway through shaving a well-dressed stranger, and he gave Luka a disdainful look before his eyes found me. A look of shock blossomed on his pink face.

'Mr Piety,' he said, and if his hand trembled on the razor just a little it wasn't enough to cut his customer's throat, so there was that.

'Hello, Ernst,' I said. 'I'm home, and I need a shave and a haircut.'

I have never seen a barber finish a shave so fast. Ernst had sixty or more years to him, but he could work quickly when he needed to. Whoever the man in the chair was, he was smooth and dry and out the door in less than five minutes.

'Sorry to keep you waiting, Mr Piety,' Ernst said, wringing his plump, pink hands. 'So sorry. It's just me here now, you see. My apprentice boy went off to war and he hasn't come back, not yet he hasn't, so I'm rushed off my feet all day. Sit down, sir, sit down.'

I shrugged out of my robes and he ushered me into the chair in my shirtsleeves, all the while fussing around me like he had a prince of the realm in his shop. Good. That was what I wanted.

I was Tomas Piety, and in Ellinburg I *was* a fucking prince.

Luka stood by the door while Ernst worked, keeping guard. Before long I was shaved smooth and my hair was cut short and neat, the way it should be. Ernst passed me a moist towel, the water scented with rose petals. This water hadn't come from the river, that was for sure. There were good wells around Trader's Row, for the servants of the rich folk to draw their water.

'I'll take tea while you see to my man,' I said.

Ernst nodded and bustled into the room behind the shop, returning a few minutes later with a shallow, steaming bowl cradled in his hands. Ernst loved his tea, and there was always a pot ready. Tea was expensive, though, very expensive, and he didn't make a habit of offering it to customers. Only princes don't wait to be offered, do they? Princes demand what they want, and are given it. Expectations to be met, as I have said.

I stood by the window and sipped my tea while Luka had his shave and his haircut. He looked better for it, I had to admit, although he was still fat. There was little enough to be done about that – if he had managed to stay fat on army rations then it was just his natural shape and he'd be fat for life, to my mind.

When we were done, I paid Ernst and told him to expect my brother and some of my friends over the next few days. He looked uncomfortable about that, but he nodded anyway. Jochan frightened him, I knew, but then Jochan frightened most people. That was what he was best at.

We left the barber's and headed farther up Trader's Row, past the hall of mercers and the temple of the Harvest Maiden to the shop of a tailor I knew. He looked a good part more pleased to see me than Ernst had, and he took our measurements and showed me the bolts of cloth without any unnecessary conversation. A good tailor has to be discreet, after all, and Pawl was certainly that. He was old too, older than Ernst, and he had seen enough of life to understand how it worked. I thought Pawl might have been a soldier once, but if so he had never spoken of it in my hearing. He agreed to come by the Tanner's Arms the next day and measure up the rest of my crew. I wasn't having any member of the Pious Men seen looking like that lot did, not now things were starting to happen.

They might not like it, but they had money now and they were going to start spending it in the right places and on the right things. Soon enough they would learn what those were.

I would insist on it.

Luka and I returned to the Tanner's Arms shortly before noon, and I found there was a whore waiting for me. She stood at the bar chatting to Bloody Anne, her back to me and her long red hair loose, but I could see the bawd's knot on her shoulder clear enough. We didn't run whores from the Tanner's. We never had done, and I wasn't about to start now.

'Who's this then?' I asked.

Anne was about to speak when the other woman turned around and gave me an insolent grin. It was her, I realised; that redhead who seemed to be the boss of the Chandler's Narrow girls. I had known that one was going to be trouble the moment I first saw her.

'Well now, don't you smarten up fine-looking?' she said.

She tossed her hair off her shoulder, proudly displaying the bawd's knot. Her hair was clean now, I noticed, which was probably why I hadn't recognised her at first. That and she was wearing a kirtle that looked new. Will the Woman had obviously started spending money on his girls now that he was in charge up there, and that was good. That was investment, and it showed initiative and that he knew what he was doing. Maybe he was one to watch.

'What do you want?' I asked her.

'He's a silver-tongued devil, ain't he?' the redhead said to Anne, and I noticed my second's scar twitch as she tried not to smile. 'What a charming man! My name's Rosie, Mr Piety, seeing as you didn't ask before.'

'And?'

'And I'm here to see you.'

She held my stare bold as brass and gave her hips a suggestive wiggle, and a thought struck me.

There's a Queen's Man in the city right now, the governor had told me. *Well, a Queen's Woman.*

It wasn't impossible, I realised, that I was looking at this Queen's Woman right now. The bawd's knot would make a fine disguise for a spy. A licensed whore comes and goes where she pleases, just about, and is seldom questioned. How far did duty to queen and country extend? I wondered. Enough to wear the knot, and do what that entailed? Perhaps it did. I wouldn't know.

'Then see me you shall,' I said. 'I think I'll see you in my chambers, Rosie. As I'm such a charming man.'

Bloody Anne gave me a look, but I ignored that and ushered Rosie up the rickety stairs and into the room I had taken as my own. I closed the door behind us and turned to face her.

'You'll have been spoken to,' Rosie said, and all the flirting ended. This was *her* talking now, not what she wore on her shoulder. 'I don't know by who, but someone's told you.'

'People tell me a lot of things,' I said. 'I'm a priest, after all.'

She snorted. 'You're a thug and a gangster,' she said, 'but someone's got your balls in a jar, haven't they, Mr Piety? I don't know who and it's none of my affair, but here's what I'm to tell you: she'll give her name as Ailsa. She'll be here tonight, and you're to give her a job when she asks you for one.'

'How do I know she's the one?'

'She'll say she can be trusted with money and with words alike. You hear her say that, she's the one.'

'Is that all?'

She shrugged. 'It's what I was told to tell you. Don't know what it means, and I don't much care.'

So this Rosie wasn't the one, then. I was glad about that, although I couldn't have said why.

'Told by who?'

Rosie sucked her teeth for a minute and shook her head. 'I ought to get back,' she said. 'Will don't want us being out and about on our own.'

I blocked her way. 'You'll tell me if I insist,' I assured her.

'Do you hit women, Mr Piety?' she asked me, and I saw a sudden flash of anger in her eyes. 'You probably do, but never the merchandise, I'm sure. That'd be bad for *business*, wouldn't it, and you wouldn't never want that. Get out of my way.'

Chapter 13

Rosie shoved past me and out the door, a furious set to her shoulders. She might not be the Queen's Man I had been told to expect, but I didn't think she was quite an ordinary whore, either. Someone important trusted her enough to carry messages, anyway. I followed her down the stairs and reached the common room in time to see her pulling a good woollen cloak around her. It seemed new as well, and all in all she made Bloody Anne look like she had just escaped from the poorhouse. That wouldn't do, not for my second it wouldn't.

'That was quick.' Anne smirked when I came into the room.

'I'll be seeing you,' Rosie said to Anne, and blew her a kiss. 'I hope.'

She ignored me completely and stalked out of the tavern, letting the new door swing shut behind her.

I looked around the common room, at the general state of the men in there, and shook my head. I rapped my knuckles on the bar to get their attention.

'We've been to see Ernst the barber, Fat Luka and me,' I said.

'Ain't he pretty now?' Black Billy laughed, reaching out to pinch Luka's smooth-shaved cheek.

'He's presentable is what he is, unlike you lot,' I said as Luka slapped Billy's hand good-naturedly away. 'Ernst is expecting the rest of you, so you'll get yourselves up there and get made presentable too. Jochan knows the way. And there'll be a tailor calling by tomorrow to measure you all up for some proper clothes. You're paying for your own, but old Pawl discounts deep when he's stitching for the Pious Men, so treat yourselves to something nice.'

'I ain't wasting my beer money on clothes,' Simple Sam complained. 'I'm all right how I am, like. I ain't naked, Mr Piety.'

'Not this time,' someone said, and got some laughs for his trouble.

Simple Sam might not be naked but his britches had holes in the knees and it was a wonder I couldn't smell his shirt from where I was standing. I shook my head.

'Listen to me,' I said. 'You're Pious Men now, and in Ellinburg Pious Men look and act a certain way. When word gets around who you are, you'll be treated like lords, mark my words. That comes with some expectations, one of them being that you look and act like fucking lords. Isn't that so, Jochan?'

'Fucking right it is,' my brother said, and treated the men to his grin. 'You won't be paying for your own beer, my boys, not on our streets you won't. The Pious Men get the finer things in life.'

I nodded. 'That's settled then,' I said, making an end to it. 'Go five at a time; I don't want to frighten Ernst too bad all at once.'

Hari would have to wait, of course – he might be better than he had been, but he was still a long way from healed, and I knew he wouldn't be walking more than a few steps at a time on that leg for a long while yet. I'd have Cordin give him a shave, at least; that would have to do.

I went behind the bar to get myself a drink while the men argued over who was going first and with who, and I found Bloody Anne waiting for me. She put her thumbs through her belt and hitched up her britches.

'Don't think I'm wearing a dress, because I'm not,' she growled. 'I can't fight in a dress or ride in one neither, so I've no use for them.'

I shrugged. What she chose to wear was her business, to my mind, so long as it wasn't what she was standing in now.

'So have Pawl make you up some new britches and shirts, then,' I said. 'I don't think a woman in britches will bother him any.'

I started to turn away before she got to what she really wanted to say, but she put her hand on my wrist and stopped me.

'We need to talk about last night,' she said in a low voice. 'About Billy.'

'No, we don't,' I said.

I shook my hand free and poured myself a brandy. I hadn't had time to think about it, or rather I had but I had chosen not to. Something about Billy the Boy had always made me uneasy, but all the same I had accepted him as my confessor. I tried to remember why I had done that, back in Abingon, and found that I couldn't. It was a long time ago now, lost in the mists of blood and smoke and horror.

Eventually five of the crew got themselves out of the door with Jochan in the lead. He was busy telling them tall tales about the high life the Pious Men had lived before the war. There was some truth in his words, but I noticed that he hadn't mentioned that by the time war came there had only been him, me, Enaid, Alfread and Donnalt left. Pious Men lived well, it was true, but not necessarily for very long.

'Come and see Hari with me,' Anne said.

She wasn't going to let it pass, I could tell that much. I followed her through into the kitchen, where Hari was eating another bowl of oats and a hunk of salt pork, a fresh mug of small beer on the table in front of him.

'How are you, Hari?' she asked.

He looked up and grinned around a mouthful of pork. 'Good, Sarge,' he mumbled, and stuffed oats into his face to follow the pork.

'That your fourth bowl now, Hari?'

He shrugged, his brow furrowing in thought for a moment before he nodded. 'Aye.'

'That's good,' I said. 'You eat if you want it, there's plenty. Get your strength back.'

'Where's Billy?' Anne asked.

Hari jerked his head toward the fireplace, where the lad was curled up asleep on a threadbare rug by the hearth. For a moment I thought he was dead, he was so pale.

'He looks tired,' Anne said.

I shrugged. Perhaps he was. If he had been awake all night watching over Hari then it wasn't surprising, to my mind. I steered her out into the corridor to let Hari eat in peace and leaned close to speak to her.

'Is there a point you're getting to, Bloody Anne?'

'You know what point I'm getting to,' she hissed. 'Yesterday Hari was almost dead and today he's sitting up and eating enough for three men, and now Billy looks like he's crossed the river himself. Last night, Tomas, we saw him doing *witchcraft*!'

'No, we didn't,' I said, for all that I had no idea what we had seen. 'We saw him floating in the air, and who's to say how and why that happened. Do you know what witchcraft looks like, Anne? Because I don't. Maybe we saw a miracle.'

'Does Our Lady work miracles now, Tomas? *Does* she? Because we could have fucking done with some in Abingon, and I never saw any.'

I took a breath. Anne was making me angry, and I didn't want to get angry with her. I looked down the corridor into the common room and frowned.

'Where's my aunt?'

'Gone home,' Anne said. 'Jochan took her and a couple of the lads to her house this morning while you were out making yourself beautiful. They were going to see who was living there now, and to kick them out.'

'Right,' I said. 'Well, that's good.'

It was. It wouldn't have been good for whoever had decided they could help themselves to Aunt Enaid's house, I was sure, but whatever Jochan had done to them was deserved, to my mind. No one stole from the Pious Men, or from their families. Not in the Stink they didn't, not if they knew what was good for them. And this way I wouldn't have Enaid under my feet, with her looks and her awkward questions, and that was good too.

Jochan and I had never bothered getting homes of our own, even once we had enough money. It was easier to just live out of one of our boarding-houses, but for a long while after our da died we lived with Aunt Enaid in that house. I was glad she had it back now.

'I trust someone's staying with her, in case they come back,' I said.

Anne nodded. 'Brak is,' she said, 'and stop trying to change the subject.'

'What do you expect me to do about it, Bloody Anne?' I snapped. 'I'm an army priest, not a fucking mystic. I don't know what he was doing.'

'There must be someone,' she said. 'You said we'd need to talk to a magician.'

'There aren't any magicians; this isn't Dannsburg,' I said. 'There's no house of magicians here. As far as I know they never stir themselves far from the capital and the queen's favour. The closest thing I know to a magician is Old Kurt. People call him a cunning man, but he's about as much a magician as Doc Cordin is a real doctor.'

Magicians were very respectable, of course, whereas witches were to be hated and feared. The cunning folk fell somewhere between the two, but I wasn't sure I could see the difference. Magic was magic, whoever did it.

'Cordin knows what he's about,' Anne said, and from the stubborn set to her jaw I understood we weren't going to resolve this without shouting. 'I'm not letting it pass, Tomas.'

I could see that she wasn't. I had never thought Bloody Anne to be a particularly superstitious woman, no more than any other soldier is, anyway, but this idea she had got into her head that Billy the Boy was a witch was obviously troubling her more than she wanted to let on.

'All right,' I said. I'd let her have this, to keep the peace if nothing else. 'All right, Bloody Anne, if it'll make you happy we can go and talk to Old Kurt.'

'It would ease my mind some,' Anne admitted.

Old Kurt lived down in the Wheels, north of us between the Stink and the docks, on the edge of the river where the great waterwheels turned day and night. The waterwheels powered bellows in foundries, churns in tanneries, grinding stones in mills, anything that could be hooked up to gears and spindles. With most all the men of working age in the city dragged off to war at once, it was those wheels that had kept Ellinburg alive for the last three years. Those wheels, and women and old men. Ellinburg men age tough, like old roots, and if you ask me our women are born that way.

Ellinburg owed its life to the Wheels, but that didn't make it a nice part of the city.

'You and me, then,' I said. 'We'll go down to the Wheels and find Old Kurt. You'll want weapons and mail, and we'll be going on foot.'

'Should we take a couple of the crew with us, for guards?'

I shook my head. 'Old Kurt wouldn't like that,' I said. 'Me he knows, although we're not friends. You he'll tolerate just because you're a woman, and he likes women. All the same, he doesn't like strangers, and the Wheels is the sort of place where a band of armed men will draw more attention than we want.'

'I thought these were your streets?'

'*These* are,' I said. 'The Wheels ain't. I don't own all of Ellinburg, Anne. The Wheels is Gutcutter territory. I don't think their boss is back from the war yet, and Our Lady willing she won't be *coming* back, but even so it's no place for the Pious Men to go in force until we mean it.'

Bloody Anne nodded thoughtfully and went to don her leather and mail. She was still learning the city, I reminded myself. Yes, we were the Pious Men who were treated like lords, but only in the right places. The Stink was my territory, and the Narrows. Trader's Row and the wealthy streets around it were neutral ground, under the control of the City Guard, and western Ellinburg belonged to the Alarian Kings and the Blue Bloods. They were no one much and too far away for our territories to overlap, so we left each other alone. The Wheels, though, that might as well have been a foreign country. One that we weren't quite at war with, not at the moment anyway, but we seemed to be always on the brink of it. The Wheels belonged to the Gutcutters, and they were no friends of mine.

I got into my own leather and mail and buckled the Weeping Women around my waist. I looked at my priest's robe and decided against it. I told Fat Luka he was in charge until Jochan got back. Anne and me went out the back way, through the stable yard and along the alleys that led toward the river. We found the steps down to the water, where I had sent Cookpot with the cart and the bodies that first night back in Ellinburg.

The steps were stone, so old each one was worn into a shallow bowl by the passing of thousands of feet over more years than I knew how to count. Those steps were death in winter, I knew that much, when the hollows filled with water and froze into ice, and a careless man could slide all the way down into the merciless cold of the river.

'Right here,' I said to Bloody Anne, 'this is the edge of Pious Men streets. South of us is the Stink, and that's mine. Southwest is the

Narrows, and that's mostly mine too up as far as Trader's Row. That way, north, that's the Wheels, then the docks, and it ain't.'

Anne followed me down the steps to the narrow stone path that edged the riverbank and looked the way I was pointing. Upstream, the great waterwheels ceaselessly turned, dozens of them, casting their long afternoon shadows across the water. Most of the city's industry lay that way, all those lovely factories with all their profits, just waiting to be taxed. The filth they pumped into the river ran downstream into the Stink and gave the place its name. The Wheels wasn't going to stay Gutcutter territory forever. Not if I had my way.

Before the war, Ma Aditi had run the Gutcutters, and moving into her territory was unthinkable. But Ma Aditi had gone off to war with the rest of us, leading her men like some sort of empress. Women didn't get conscripted, but they could volunteer and she had, just like Bloody Anne, and so far she hadn't come back. I would be very happy if it stayed that way.

Ma Aditi was Ellinburg-born, but her skin was the same deep brown colour as the men off the tea ships. Her parents must have been from somewhere in Alaria, I could only assume, not that it really mattered. Ma Aditi was very clever and very cruel, and to my mind Ellinburg was better off without her. I knew *I* was, anyway.

'Are we safe then, going up there?' Bloody Anne asked.

I shrugged. 'Are you ever safe, Bloody Anne?' I asked her, and I was mocking her now even though I knew better. 'A Pious Man lives life on the edge. You could get run over by a cart tomorrow. You could get a curse put on you by a witch.'

I don't think I've ever seen Bloody Anne move so fast.

Before I could draw breath I was up against the slimy stone wall with her hard hand around my throat and the point of her dagger pressed into the corner of my eye.

'You take that back!' she hissed in my face, and I could see she was pure fucking furious. 'You take those words back, Tomas Piety, or I'll fucking blind you, I mean it!'

I didn't move a muscle.

'All right, Bloody Anne,' I said, offering a silent prayer to Our Lady that I wouldn't cross the river today. 'It's all right. I'm sorry, and I take my words back. I didn't mean anything by it.'

'No,' Anne said, and she eased the dagger back from my eye and took a step away. 'No, I know you didn't. I'm sorry. It's . . . doesn't matter. It's a long story, and not for telling now.'

She looked shaken, though, and it takes a lot to shake Bloody Anne. I blew out a breath and straightened my mail where she had grabbed me.

'Right,' I said. I'd let it pass, but I was curious all the same. Still, that would keep for later. 'Shall we?'

Anne nodded without speaking, and followed me along the path beside the river and into the Wheels.

Chapter 14

The Wheels was squalid and damp, but then it always had been. Although this was one of the worst parts of Ellinburg, it was also one of the most profitable territories to control. No one wanted to live near a tannery, no, but they might well enjoy the money from one.

Ma Aditi and the Gutcutters owned the Wheels, but I knew that she wasn't back from the war yet, so I hoped that meant most of her boys weren't either. Even so, we went carefully, keeping our hands close to the hilts of our weapons as we made our way along the treacherous path with the oily-looking river lapping at its bank a few feet below us.

It was quiet down by the water, and as we drew closer we could hear the great wooden wheels themselves turning on their axles, groaning rhythmically. Scummy white froth drifted downstream toward us where the river had been churned up by the movement, and in places I could see things floating in it. Turds, mostly, but there was the odd dead rat too.

We were in the Wheels all right.

'Keep your eyes open,' I said quietly, 'and don't draw attention.'

I could feel eyes on me like the flies on a hot Abingon night, making my skin crawl. There were high buildings on our left, their damp timber flanks rearing above the path and keeping us in shadow. Across the water to the east was nothing. It was just open marshland stretching into the distance. The river formed the fourth wall of Ellinburg, and they would be desperate raiders indeed who tried to cross the marshes, and then that wide expanse of flowing filth.

'Someone's watching us,' Anne said.

'I know,' I murmured. 'Someone always is, in the Wheels. It's probably just children.'

It probably was, but even children are dangerous if there are enough of them and they're armed. I didn't know how many there were, but they would be armed all right. You could bet on that. The path ended in a sheer drop down to rotting wooden pilings that had once supported a jetty, but on the left there was a cobbled alley leading up between two buildings. About twenty feet ahead of us was the first of the great wheels.

'There's folk up there,' Anne said.

I turned and looked up the alley toward Dock Road, where three cloaked figures were hiding in the shadows at the top in a way that said *murder* as loud as if they had been shouting it.

'Stinkers and Wheelers don't get on,' I explained. 'We didn't come along the riverbank for the fresh air. Going through the streets wouldn't have been good for our health. I don't think those fine fellows know who we are, but they're giving us the hard eye just because of which direction we've come from. The river path is all right, though, usually – Old Kurt insists there's free access to his door for everyone, wherever they're from.'

'And these Wheelers listen to him, do they?'

'Yes, Anne, they do, and more to the point so do the Gutcutters. Old Kurt is . . . well, I told you that people call him a cunning man. He's that all right, in both senses of the word. He knows how to win respect and get his own way, and I admire that. Whether he knows how to do magic, though, that's another matter.'

'I don't want him to *do* magic,' Anne said, somewhat sharply. 'I just want him to tell us about it.'

'Aye, well, he can do that,' I said. 'Some of what he says might even be true. I wouldn't know.'

I led the way into the alley, keeping my eyes on the fellows at the far end. Halfway along the narrow cobbled space, set into the side of an otherwise blank brick wall, was Old Kurt's door.

The building he lived in had been a workshop of some sort once, but many years ago Old Kurt had paid my da to brick the frontage up for him and seal it off from the street. He'd had Da bash a hole through the alley wall and make a new entrance there instead, so that Wheelers and Stinkers alike might have access to his door without having to fight their way there.

That was how I had first met him: as a ten-year-old 'prentice boy mixing lime mortar in this alley for Da and trying not to get my head kicked in while I was doing it. Kurt had made a point of picking a Stink man to do the work instead of a Wheeler, although that had caused some hard words at the time.

Kurt had been old even then, or had looked it to my young eyes anyway, and I had over thirty years to me now. Old Kurt was still there, though; I could tell that from the rat that was nailed to the outside of his front door.

He always nailed a fresh rat to his door every fifth day, and this one didn't look to be more than two or three days old. As to why he did it, well, I supposed that was his business, but it told folk he was still alive if nothing else.

I rapped on the door and called out the words. 'Wisdom sought is wisdom bought, and I have coin to pay,' I said loudly.

A moment later the door creaked open and Old Kurt's face peered out at me from the shadows inside.

'You'd better have, Tomas Piety,' he said. 'Oh, and this fine lady too! Welcome, welcome. Come you in, and mind your heads.'

I looked at Bloody Anne with her scar and her daggers and her stained, dirty men's clothes, and wondered if Old Kurt had ever seen a fine lady in his life. Probably not, I thought. We followed Kurt into his house, which was dimly lit with lamps on account of most of the windows having been boarded up. The place was squalid and it stank, but there were treasures in there too. Odd things, things you wouldn't necessarily notice if you didn't know to look for them.

The sword hanging over the mantel, its scabbard thick with cobwebs, had once belonged to a king. The skull on the windowsill, the one with its temple bashed in, had supposedly belonged to the same king. That brass candlestick with dried crusty tallow all over it was really solid gold. Or so Old Kurt had told me when I was a boy, anyway.

I smiled at the memories. He was a horrible old man with a house full of shit, to my mind, but he had been the one who had chased those Wheeler boys off me while I had been mixing my mortar in the alley outside. Not my da. Old Kurt had done that. Da had thought fighting was good for a boy, that it made a man of him. Although considering what went on in our house at nights I'd have thought that was the last thing Da wanted. I didn't want to think about that now, though. Or ever.

There had been three boys, and all of them old enough to shave, but Da hadn't stirred himself while Kurt chased them away. I had told Anne that Old Kurt and me weren't friends and that was true enough, but I would always have time for him, for that.

He took his chair by the fireplace and waved us to a pair of rickety stools.

Kurt must have had almost eighty years to him, by my reckoning, but he still looked the same as I remembered him from when I had been a boy. He was a narrow, spare man, his pointed face and whiskered chin making him look much like the rat nailed to his door. His thin white hair was short but dirty, pushed up in all directions by his darting, ratty hands.

'Show me your silver and tell me your troubles, Tomas,' Kurt said.

I looked at Bloody Anne. 'This is your question, not mine,' I said to her. 'It'll be your silver that buys an answer to it.'

She took a mark out of her pouch and put it in Old Kurt's grubby outstretched hand. He looked down at the coin, back at Anne, and grinned.

'Fine silver from a fine lady,' he said with a leer. 'I'm a lucky boy, ain't I?'

She cleared her throat. She looked uncomfortable, did Bloody Anne, and I noticed her eyes kept wandering to the skull on the windowsill, the bound herbs that hung in bunches from the ceiling, the thick dusty books that were scattered around the room. Some of the books had rat shit on them, I saw.

'There's this boy,' she started. 'He—'

'A boy, is it?' Kurt interrupted. 'Might have known you'd be wasting my time, Piety. I don't do love spells, nor potions neither.'

I said nothing and let Anne speak for herself. The lesson of the boarding-house was still fresh in my mind, and I don't believe in making the same mistake twice.

'I don't want a fucking love spell,' Bloody Anne snarled at him. 'I've paid you silver for wisdom, so you'll have the good grace to shut up and listen to the fucking question without interrupting me again or I'll nail you to your door with your fucking rat, you understand me?'

Old Kurt stared at her for a moment, then laughed his thin, reedy old man's laugh. 'That's me told, ain't it,' he said. 'I'll listen, my fine lady. I'll listen to you.'

He was quiet then, but something in his eyes and the way he was looking at Anne made me wary. You didn't cross Bloody Anne, not if you knew what was good for you, but you didn't cross Old Kurt either.

No, you didn't do that.

'This boy,' Anne started again. 'He's an orphan, with twelve years to him. We found him near Messia, after the sack. In the war, this was, way down in the south. A strange boy, but he wanted to join up and the regiment took him and any others they could get. He's touched by the goddess.'

'Which one?' Kurt asked. 'And who says so?'

'Our Lady of Eternal Sorrows. Tomas is her priest, and *he* says so.'

Old Kurt turned a stare on me. I wasn't wearing my robes that day, and this was obviously the first he'd heard of it.

'A priest, is it?'

'It is,' I said. 'This boy, Billy. He's a confessor and a seer. The goddess speaks to him, or through him. I don't know which.'

'Well and good,' Kurt said, 'if a *priest* says so.'

He smirked when he said it, though, and I remembered why Old Kurt and me weren't friends.

'One of our crew was wounded,' Anne went on. 'He nearly died from all the blood he lost. *Should* have died, to my mind, but he didn't. He didn't because Billy sat up all night floating in the air and staring at him, doing magic at him. Now he's awake and alive and eating for six men, and I want to know if we have a *witch* in our crew.'

Her scar tightened and twisted when she said *witch*, I noticed.

'Witches now, is it?' Old Kurt said. 'Messia, is it? Well, what could that mean?'

'You tell us,' I said. 'You're the cunning man.'

Old Kurt thought on it for a moment, then got up and went over to a big chest by the back wall. He rummaged inside for a moment, then straightened up and handed Anne a long iron nail.

'You put this under where the boy sleeps at night,' he said, 'and we'll see.'

'What is it?' Anne asked.

'A nail,' I said.

'It's a witchspike, you ignorant thug,' Old Kurt snapped. 'Priest my hairy arse, or you'd know what it was. That there's a witchspike, and if he's what you fear he'll feel it. Put that under his blankets and wait. If he wakes screaming in the night then he's a witch, and you can deal with that as you see fit. If he doesn't, though, then you bring him here. You bring him to see Old Kurt and I'll have a look at him. Is that a deal, my fine lady?'

Anne nodded and slipped the nail into her pouch.

'Deal,' she said.

Chapter 15

We left Old Kurt's after that, having no reason to linger. I stepped back out into the alley and there were the three cloaked figures waiting for us.

'You're away from your streets, Piety,' one said to me.

I nodded slowly. 'That I am,' I said. 'I've been visiting with the cunning man, as you can well see. All have free passage to Old Kurt's door. You know that.'

The man stepped closer to me, and I could see the jut of an unshaven chin poking out of the hood of his cloak. He looked to have perhaps thirty years to him and he sounded like an Ellinburg man, and those things together made him a veteran.

'How long have you been back?' I asked, before he could say anything else.

He paused, looked at me. I heard his sigh and knew I had found common ground. Men who had shared the Hell of Abingon would always have that in common, if little enough else.

'Three days,' he said.

'And no Ma Aditi,' I said.

'Not yet. She'll come.'

'Will she?'

I was conscious of the other two, who had the back of the one I was talking to, and of Bloody Anne, who as always had *my* back. Common ground or no, that made us three to two, and we were on their streets where they might have mates just a shout away. I didn't know what they were carrying under those cloaks, but I wouldn't have bet a clipped copper against it being steel. We might have shared the same horrors, but that alone wasn't going to make us friends. That was three to two against us at the very best, then. Not good odds, not when we'd be betting with our lives.

'She will,' he said.

I nodded at that, and decided that honour would keep for another day.

'We'll be on our way, then,' I said.

'Back to the Stink.'

'Aye, back to the Stink,' I agreed. 'The Wheels belong to the Gutcutters, everyone knows that.'

'That it does, Piety,' he shouted after us as we walked back down to the path at the riverside. 'That it does, and see you remember it!'

When we returned to the Tanner's Arms it was starting to get dark and we were both hungry. I found Hari limping around in the kitchen, leaning on a stout stick he had picked up somewhere. He was tidying cupboards and taking what looked like an inventory of what he found in there.

'How're you feeling?' I asked him.

'Not so bad, boss, thank you,' he said, although I could see the pain and weariness etched in the lines of his pale face.

'You look at home, in here,' I said.

He shrugged. 'Just trying to keep busy,' he said. 'I want to be useful to you. I . . .'

I don't want to be thrown out into the streets to starve because I can't fight no more, his face said.

'You're all right, Hari,' I assured him. 'Don't you worry. Have you seen young Billy?'

Hari shook his head, but some of the tension went out of his face at my words and he allowed himself to sink into the chair with a wince of pain.

'I think he went in the back to sleep some more,' Hari said.

I nodded and helped myself to something to eat, then left him to it. I dumped my mail and leather upstairs in my room but buckled the Weeping Women back around my waist again over my shirt tails.

I didn't think the Gutcutters would bother us, not on our own streets. Not without Ma Aditi here to say so, anyway, but one of them had seen me and by now they'd all know I was back in Ellinburg.

The war in the south might only just have ended, but all that meant was that the war in Ellinburg was about to start up again. It was a quiet sort of war, by and large, but it was a war all the same, and now we had this man they called Bloodhands and his Skanians added to the broth. If Hauer was to be believed we did, anyway, and I couldn't think that he wasn't. He had no reason to lie about it, that I could see.

I went back down to the common room and found Bloody Anne waiting for me behind the bar with two glasses of brandy already poured for us. She nodded to me cordially enough, but I couldn't help noticing the way her fingers kept touching her pouch. Billy the Boy was going to come between us if I wasn't careful.

'You're going to use that, then?' I asked as I picked up my drink and leaned forward with my elbows on the bar opposite her.

'The witchspike? Yes, Tomas, I am.'

I nodded. 'Well, that's your affair,' I said. 'Your silver bought you wisdom from Old Kurt, so it's up to you whether to believe what he told you.'

'Don't you?'

I shrugged and took a swallow of brandy. 'People call him a cunning man,' I said, 'and that has two meanings, like I said before. Maybe he knows about magic and maybe he doesn't, but he's the other sort of cunning too. Old Kurt is very good at making people believe in him, Anne. Very good indeed. He's *that* sort of cunning, you mark me.'

'I'll put it under Billy's bedroll,' she said, sounding firm about the notion, 'and then we'll see.'

I just nodded. If that made Anne happy, then who was I to judge, but to my mind all that would prove was that a boy who was exhausted and would probably go to bed drunk anyway wouldn't notice that there was a lump under his blankets.

The front door creaked behind me, and I turned to see who it was coming back from wherever he had been. My eyebrows rose as I realised that this wasn't one of my crew at all. I leaned back with my elbows on the bar behind me and my hands hanging loose within easy reach of Remorse and Mercy.

She walked into the tavern with her hood pushed back to bare thick dark hair and a face the dusky brown colour of an Alarian's. A patched and frayed green cloak hung from her shoulders, open over her white linen shirt and servant's skirts. There was a leather travelling bag in her hand.

'How do?' I said.

She smiled shyly and bobbed a clumsy curtsey. 'Good evening, sir, Mr Piety,' she said. 'My name's Ailsa. I heard the tavern was opening again, under new management as you might say, and I wondered if you had any work going? I need the coin and I ain't afraid of hard work, with my hands nor my head. I can keep a bar and I can tally books, or I can scrub a floor and wash glasses, and I can be trusted with money and with words alike.'

She had perhaps twenty-five years to her and she looked like a trader off one of the tea ships, but I realised she wasn't. Oh, she was young and very pretty, but I wasn't fooled. Her dark eyes met mine and I knew *exactly* who she was.

She'll give her name as Ailsa, Rosie from Chandler's Narrow had told me. *She'll be here tonight, and you're to give her a job when she asks you for one.*

That had sounded a lot like an order to me, the sort of order that I knew I had to obey. I didn't fucking like it, but then I hadn't liked it the last time either. Serve the crown or hang; that had been the choice before me, and to my mind that was no choice at all.

She'll say she can be trusted with money and with words alike. You hear her say that, she's the one.

I nodded. 'Aye,' I said. 'The Tanner's Arms is back under its rightful management, to set the matter straight, but aye. I reckon there might be work going, as you asked so nicely.'

I heard Bloody Anne draw breath to speak, then obviously think better of it. She poured herself another brandy, and if she put the bottle down harder than was strictly called for then that was her affair.

Ailsa bobbed another curtsey and showed me a smile that was a little bit more than friendly. 'Thank you, Mr Piety, sir,' she said. 'You won't regret it.'

I wasn't too sure about that, but I knew what the choice was. Ailsa might appear common and clumsy, but she was a Queen's Man and I was swimming out of my depth in dangerous waters.

Billy the Boy came through from the back just then, and he stood there staring at Ailsa with his mouth open. I frowned at him, and he looked at me and nodded.

'She'll be staying,' he announced.

'Aye, Billy, she will,' I said, but it hadn't sounded to me like he was asking a question.

'Who's this young man then?' Ailsa asked.

'I'm Billy,' he said.

'Billy the Boy, we call him,' I said, 'and this here's Bloody Anne.'

'A soldier's name,' Ailsa said, giving Anne a long look.

'What of it?' Anne snapped.

'Nothing at all.'

'There's a room upstairs, next to mine,' I said, cutting in before the two of them fell to hard words over nothing, as strangers sometimes can. 'My aunt doesn't need it any more so you might as well take it.'

Ailsa nodded. Jochan and Anne were both happy enough sleeping with the crew, but obviously I couldn't put Ailsa in there with that lot. That wouldn't have ended well, for someone. Whichever of my boys stupid enough to put his hands where they weren't welcome, I suspected, but I knew someone would have been bound to try it. Best if that didn't happen.

'Much obliged,' Ailsa said.

I had Billy show her up to the room, and the lad even took her bag for her like a proper young gentleman. Anne waited until they were gone before she rounded on me.

'What in Our Lady's name are you doing, Tomas?' she demanded.

'I need a barmaid,' I said. 'It's time we opened the Tanner's to the public again. I've a mind to put Hari in charge of the business as he seems to have a feel for it, and he can't do much else. Even so, he can't be behind the bar all night on that leg of his. She can keep the bar and he can run the business side, with one of the others on the door.'

'And where are we supposed to sleep, and live?'

'We'll fit round it, for now,' I said. 'Later on, we'll have more places to choose from.'

'Billy likes her, I see,' Anne noted, and something in her tone made me give her a look.

'You haven't proved anything about Billy yet,' I reminded her, 'and I don't believe that you will. Don't jump to justice until you know if it's deserved, Anne. That's no way to lead.'

She patted her pouch, the one that held Old Kurt's witchspike.

'I'll know tonight,' she said. 'And then we'll see.'

I supposed that we would, at that.

Chapter 16

I let Ailsa settle in, and told Hari and Jochan what I had in mind. Hari was overjoyed, obviously glad to feel useful and even more glad to know he'd be keeping a roof over his head. Jochan just leered at me.

'The room next to yours, is it?' he said. 'Boss gets first go, is that the way of it?'

I snorted. If he wanted to think that, if all of them wanted to think that, then it made my decision to hire a stranger at a moment's notice a lot more believable. I'd rather they believed I was keeping Ailsa as my fancy woman than that they started wondering who she might really be. That way she'd be left alone too. It was for the best, to my mind, and I can't say that the idea was without its charms. You didn't see many women who looked like her, not in the Stink you didn't.

'If you want a woman, you know where Chandler's Narrow is,' I said. 'But see that you pay for it.'

Jochan winked at me. 'Might be that I will, Tomas,' he said.

I made a mental note to check with Will the Woman that Jochan and any of the others who went up there had paid their way. You can't keep a stew and tell men like these they're not to visit it, but they were going to pay full price like anyone else. Taking for free was stealing from the girls, and indirectly it was stealing from me as well. There would be harsh justice for anyone who thought he could do that and look me in the eye afterward.

Ailsa was in the kitchen with Hari now, being shown the ropes. Hari had even found himself an old stained white apron in one of the storage chests out the back, and made himself look like a proper tavern keeper. He could hobble about on his stick for a few minutes at a time but that was all, and I knew I'd have to make sure there were always a couple of the crew on hand once we opened up properly.

These were my streets but that didn't mean there was never trouble, and when folk have beer and brandy inside them and dice or cards in front of them the chances of that always go up. Hari wasn't going to be stopping any fights by himself. That was for sure.

I was standing at the bar thinking on who might be best for that job, who looked the part and who I could trust not to get too drunk of a night, when Fat Luka strolled over.

'The new lass seems nice,' he said, drawing himself a beer from one of the big barrels behind the bar.

'Aye,' I said.

Luka wouldn't do – he drank too much, and besides as an Ellinburg native he would be more useful doing other things for me. I didn't want him stuck in the Tanner's every night.

'She knows her figures too, and she can read well enough,' he said, sounding impressed. 'She could do the books and that.'

Luka hadn't even spent as long in school as I had, and while he could read after a fashion it was hard work for him. All the same, apart from me and Jochan, he was the only one of the crew who could read and figure at all, to my knowledge. I knew Cookpot couldn't, school or not. Sir Eland said he could, of course, but no one had ever seen him do it. I think Luka had been dreading being asked to keep books.

'She could,' I agreed. 'Tell me something, what's your opinion of Mika?'

Mika was one of Jochan's original crew and I didn't know him well yet, but he was the one I had sent to find carpenters when I had needed them and he had managed that all right.

'He can think for himself, which is more than some of the lads can,' Luka said.

I nodded. That was what I had thought too.

'Him and Black Billy, then,' I said, thinking out loud. 'They can keep the peace here when the Tanner's opens for business again.'

Black Billy was a big lad and he was good with his fists. Black faces weren't unknown in Ellinburg, but they were a lot rarer than brown ones, and certainly not so common that he wouldn't be noted. I'd put him on the door where he could be seen, I decided, and have Mika inside keeping a quiet eye on things. That would work.

The right man for the right job, that was how I led men.

Luka took a long drink and put his tankard down on the bar. 'Can I say something?' he asked.

'What?'

'It's Jochan,' he said.

I had thought it might be.

'What about him?'

Luka had another drink while he picked his words carefully. 'Well, he ain't said anything, not to me,' Luka said, 'but I've known him since . . . ever. You too, of course.'

I nodded. 'Out with it, Luka,' I said. 'I know what my brother's like, and I don't think you're about to tell me anything I'd call a surprise.'

'The Tanner's Arms,' Luka said. 'He'll think it should have been his. You've put Hari in what he'll think was his rightful place, and Hari's crippled as well so you've got to set another two men to mind the place where one would have done. He'll think that, is all I'm saying.' Luka coughed and gulped beer, looking worried that he'd said too much.

'I'm disappointed that you think I don't know that, Fat Luka,' I said. 'Jochan all but has brandy for breakfast, these days. Lady knows the last thing he should be doing is running a fucking tavern.'

'I know, boss,' Luka said, 'and I didn't mean you wouldn't, like. I'm just saying, is all.'

I nodded, and looked at Fat Luka. I had known him since we had all been in school together, him and me and Jochan and Cookpot. He hadn't been a Pious Man before the war, but he had been around, on the fringes of our life. He had done bits and pieces of work for me even back then, and I knew I could trust him. I wondered if perhaps he was working around the edges of saying he thought *his* part in things should be bigger now, and maybe he had a point about that.

I considered that for a moment, and I made a decision.

'I want to ask you to do something for me, Luka,' I said. 'I won't take ill against you if you say no, but there's silver for you if you'll do it.'

'Course,' he said. 'I'm a Pious Man now, ain't I?'

He was, and he knew better than most of the others what that meant. He had seen enough of how things worked before the war to know what he was getting into, and he had been happy to join us just the same. Luka was greedy, I knew that, but he could be trusted. To a point, anyway. Knowing your men, knowing which levers move them, is a big part of leadership, to my mind.

Fat Luka was moved by silver.

'You are,' I said. 'You're all Pious Men now, but you're an Ellinburg man too and you know how things work. How they *really* work, I mean, which might not always be how I explain things to the rest of the crew. They're still learning the city, all except Cookpot anyway, but he was never one of us before the war. He doesn't know how business is done any more than Simple Sam does.'

'That's true enough,' Fat Luka said. 'What do you need, boss?'

'Eyes and ears, and a supportive voice,' I said. 'I want you to watch the men and listen to them when I'm not here. I want you to listen to their talk over dice, and when they're in their cups. If anyone starts disagreeing with me or questioning my orders, I want you to explain to them why they're wrong. Then I'll want to hear about it, and who said what. Can you do that, Fat Luka?'

He took a moment, and a long swallow of beer, then put his empty tankard down on the bar and nodded.

'I can do that,' he said.

I took a silver mark out of my pouch and slid it across the bar to him, and he made it disappear.

The right man for the right job, as I said.

It was late by the time I had the chance to talk to Ailsa in private. There had been enough nudges and winks and gossip exchanged throughout the evening that no one passed further comment when I went up to her room, and by that time half the crew had taken themselves off to

Chandler's Narrow to find a girl of their own. Bloody Anne had gone with them, I noticed.

Ailsa opened her door at my knock and let me in. She turned a smile on me as I stood leaning against the inside of the door with my arms crossed. She had unpacked her few things, hung some spare clothes from nails in the beams and spread herself a bedroll on the floor. There was a neat row of little bottles and small flat cases lined up on the windowsill above the washbasin.

'Welcome to the Pious Men,' I said. 'We live in luxury, as you can see.'

'You did before and you will again,' she assured me as she sat in the room's only chair.

She sounded completely different than she had earlier, I noticed. Her voice now carried the inflections of Dannsburg aristocracy instead of a common girl from the countryside, and if she had seemed clumsy before, then that was gone too.

'What do you know about me?' I asked.

'Everything,' she said. 'Assume that I know absolutely everything, and you will never be surprised or caught in a lie that you would regret.'

'Well, I don't know the first thing about you, so there you have me at a disadvantage.'

'Yes.'

'Tell me this, then,' I said, lowering my voice. 'How does a slip of an Alarian girl become a Queen's Man?'

She smiled, and this time it was without warmth. 'I was born and raised in Dannsburg,' she said. 'My parents may have come from Alaria, but I have never set foot in the place. And "a slip of a girl", Tomas? Is that what you think?'

'You've what, twenty-five years to you?'

She snorted. 'Paints and powders are worth their weight in gold,' she said, and showed me that humourless smile again. 'I'm a good deal older than I look, and if you're underestimating me based on my face and the colour of my skin then you are a fool and I am pleased, because that means it's working.'

'I'm not a fool,' I said. 'This is new to me, that's all. I only saw a Queen's Man once before, and he had over sixty years to him.'

'Had he? Paints and powders, Tomas. False hair and mummer's scars. Perhaps he was your age. Perhaps you and Luka walked past him on Trader's Row this morning on your way to the barber's and the tailor's, and you never knew him.'

I shrugged. I supposed she had a point, but that didn't matter. She was telling me that she knew where I had been that morning, before I even met her, and who I had been with and what I had done. That wasn't lost on me.

'Perhaps,' I admitted.

'You didn't, he's dead.'

'Those are the times we live in.'

'One of his informers betrayed him a year ago,' she said. 'Someone sent him back to Dannsburg on four different trade caravans, a piece at a time. This is "harsh work" we do, as you would put it, and our enemies are every bit as harsh as we are.'

I cleared my throat and looked at her. Now that she had told me, I could almost see her age. There was something in the way she held her head, keeping her neck out of the light of the lamp with an ease that spoke of practised skill. Something in the way her hands were neatly folded in her lap that was helping her hide the telltale signs of age on the backs of her knuckles. She was good, though. She was very, very good, and I would never have guessed if she hadn't told me and I hadn't been trying hard to look for those signs.

'Tell me about the Queen's Men, then,' I said. 'I thought you were supposed to be knights.'

'We are,' she said. 'A particular order of the knighthood, one that answers directly to the crown. You won't have seen any of us on the battlefield, though, not and known who we were. The sort of knight you're thinking of, their weapons are the sword and lance and battle-axe. My weapons are gold and lace, and paints and powders. And the dagger, when it's needed. You can hide a dagger very well indeed, behind enough lace.'

I supposed that you could, at that.

The right man for the right job, I thought. I wondered exactly what job Ailsa was here to do.

Chapter 17

I was still awake and sitting in the common room with Black Billy when those of the crew who had gone out came blundering back from Chandler's Narrow in the small hours of the morning, drunk and looking pleased with themselves. Bloody Anne looked the most pleased with herself of all, and I hoped that she had found what she was looking for up there. I remembered how her and Rosie had been talking in the Tanner's, and I thought that she probably had. It was only then that I noticed Billy the Boy was with them.

I snagged Jochan's arm as he swayed past.

'Tell me you didn't get Billy a woman,' I said.

Jochan laughed. 'He's too young for that,' he said. 'He'll have a pecker like your little finger. He said he wanted to come with us so I let him, but he just sat there staring at Sir Eland all night while we had our fun. Fuck knows why. The lad's strange in the head, Tomas.'

I saw Anne's scar twitch at that, and her hand go to her pouch again. She'd be putting that nail under Billy's bedroll tonight. I knew she would. I just hoped that Our Lady was kind and Billy didn't wake up screaming from some nightmare, or I dreaded to think what Anne was likely to do.

'Eland must have been pleased to see him,' I said, knowing he would have been nothing of the sort. 'How's Will the Woman getting on?'

Jochan shrugged. 'He knows what he's about,' he said. 'The place is the cleanest I can remember it, and the girls too. None of them have taken ill against him, anyway, so he must be doing right by them.'

'Good,' I said.

Licensed whores don't grow on trees, and you have to keep them happy. Rosie might have said they had nowhere else to go, but I knew Ma Aditi's Gutcutters would have taken them in tomorrow, and I thought that she probably knew that as well. The bawd's knot has to be earned and paid for, and it's what sets them apart from common street scrubs. That meant higher prices and more money all round. It sounded like Will was working out well up there in Chandler's Narrow.

'Go to bed, the lot of you,' I said. 'It's Godsday tomorrow, and I'll be taking confession from those that want to give it.'

Godsday fell every eighth day, the day when all the temples were opened and the priests of the various gods held confession and gave absolution to their faithful. Traditionally, no one worked on Godsday. When times were as hard as they were now in Ellinburg, though, and folk had to work if they wanted to eat, most priests let that pass. In the army it had been irrelevant anyway, and sometimes it had been hard to even keep track of what day it was.

At Abingon I had taken confession whenever someone wanted to give it. There was no saying they would still be alive come the appointed day, after all, but now we were back home it seemed only right that I put some formality into it. People expect certain things from a priest, in the same way they expect things from a businessman. They expected certain ways of being, and of acting. I'd need to remember that. Being a priest in a city in peacetime was different to being one in the army during a war. I knew that much, and I had never done it before.

I shrugged and finished my brandy as the crew jostled their way through to the back to wait their turns at the shithouse and get into their bedrolls. Black Billy was on the door, his new post, and I gave him a nod.

'You can lock up for the night now,' I told him. 'Get yourself a drink, if you want one.'

'Thanks, boss,' he said.

He seemed pleased to have a regular posting, and had taken to wearing a big wooden club at his belt that left no one in any doubt that the door was his.

Things were starting to come together quite well, to my mind. I thought of Ailsa, asleep upstairs in the room next to mine, and I frowned.

She was a Queen's Man, and sleeping under my roof at that. What did that make me? I wondered. An informer, I knew, and the very word made my tongue curl up in my mouth like I wanted to spit at someone.

You've no choice, I told myself. *It's this or hang, and that won't help those streets outside your door. It's just business.*

Perhaps not quite everything was coming together, but most things were.

The next morning Bloody Anne had a sore head and dark circles of tiredness under her eyes.

'All night I sat up, and he never screamed,' she said. 'The lad slept like a fucking baby on top of that witchspike.'

'Told you so,' I said, while Ailsa brought us mugs of small beer and hunks of black bread to break our fast.

She had donned a clean white linen apron that put Hari's to shame, although where hers had come from was anyone's guess. I could only assume she had brought it with her in her bag.

'You did,' Anne admitted. 'I was wrong about him, Tomas.'

I just shrugged. A nail from a crazy old man didn't prove water was wet, to my mind, but if it quietened Bloody Anne down on the subject then I would take that and be grateful for it.

'No shame in that,' I said. 'Magic is a tricky thing, so I hear.'

'We saw what we saw,' she said, and I could see she still wasn't going to let it pass. 'If he's not a witch, then what?'

'I don't know, Anne. Old Kurt said to bring Billy to him, if he slept on the nail and didn't wake, so I suppose we'll be doing that. But not today. Today is Godsday, and I'll be busy and so will Kurt.'

'He's no priest,' Anne said.

'No, he ain't, but he's the closest thing a lot of folk have, especially down in the Wheels. He hears confession too. He shouldn't, to my mind, but he does.'

'And you'll be taking confession today?' Anne asked. 'Here, I mean?'

'I could throw open the doors of my magnificent golden temple and do it there instead, but it's a long fucking walk to dreamland,' I said. 'Aye, I'll be doing it here.'

There was no temple of Our Lady in Ellinburg, but she had her shrine in the Great Temple of All Gods along with all the others. That wasn't my place, though, I knew that. My place was here in the Stink, with my crew.

Anne cleared her throat. 'Aye,' she said. 'I . . . I might speak to you, then.'

'As you like,' I said. 'Our Lady listens to everyone.'

Anne had never come to me before, and I had always assumed she had some other god she held to, but perhaps not. She nodded and left me there, thinking on the day ahead.

When I had finished my breakfast I put it about that I would be hearing confessions, and I went up to my room. I put my robe on and sat in the chair under the small window, and waited.

Cookpot was first.

He came into the room, looking nervous for all that he had said confession to me enough times before. Perhaps it felt more formal like this, alone in a room together on Godsday instead of in a tent behind the lines whenever the chance came up. Whatever it was, he couldn't meet my eyes as he shuffled into the room and knelt awkwardly at my feet with his round face cast to the ground.

'I wish to confess, Father.'

They only used the title when I was hearing confession, but it still sounded strange in my ears. 'Father' was Da, to my mind, and Our Lady knew I wasn't him.

Anything but that.

'Speak, in the name of Our Lady,' I said.

'I killed a man,' Cookpot said. 'I never done that before, not ever. That night, here, when they came. The flashstone went off and then the door blew in right beside me and I . . . I . . .'

He choked into silence. I waited, giving him his moment. That was how this was done. Some men found confession easy and some found it hard, and some treated it like a joke. It was all the same to me. They were speaking to Our Lady, not to me, and it was on their consciences how they went about it. Every man in his own time and his own way. That was how I held confession.

'I ain't a fighter,' Cookpot said at last. 'I was at Abingon with everyone else, but I never killed no one. That doesn't mean I never saw it, though, or heard it. I'm just a fucking cook, but I remember when they brought Aaron back on a stretcher with his guts hanging out all blue and slimy and him screaming for his ma. I remember when the surgeon took Donnalt's arm off at the shoulder and he still went mad and died from the rot in his blood. I remember the noise, Tomas. The fucking *noise*! Them cannon, all fucking day, and the walls coming down, and the smoke and the dust.

'When that door blew in, I just . . . I thought we was done with it, you know? I thought it was over and I weren't dead after all and it might be all right now, but when that door came in I was right back there and Aaron was screaming again and I could hear the cannon roar and that man come through the door and I just . . . I just had to stab him. I *had* to, do you understand?'

Cookpot was weeping now, and I reached out a hand and put it on his head.

'It was his time to cross the river, and Our Lady forgives you,' I said. 'In Our Lady's name.'

Truth be told, I didn't know what Our Lady of Eternal Sorrows would have thought of that. Not much, I suspected. She had decreed that that wasn't Cookpot's day to die, and that had been the end of her part in the business, to my mind.

Cookpot wiped a sleeve across his eyes and nodded, still sniffling. 'In Our Lady's name,' he repeated. He got to his feet and looked at me, snot running out of his left nostril. 'I don't know that I can do this,' he said. 'Be a Pious Man, I mean.'

I nodded slowly. 'Well, you think on it, Cookpot,' I said. 'If you can't, then I won't take ill against you for it, but I'll need to know soon.'

'Aye,' he said. 'And thank you, Father.'

I would have to have Luka keep a close eye on him until he made his choice, I thought. Cookpot left, and I had Simple Sam after that.

Simple Sam grinned and confessed that he had pissed in Jochan's brandy bottle one night when Jochan had passed out, then Jochan had woken up and drank it and not noticed the difference. Simple Sam held that that was funny, but he felt he ought to confess it anyway, and I told him that I thought it was funny as well, but he didn't ought to do it again or Jochan would hurt him, and I forgave him and sent him on his way.

Most of the others came, one after another, to confess to cheating at dice or stealing something they shouldn't have done, and I forgave them all in Our Lady's name. Petty crimes from petty criminals didn't interest me, and I dare say they interested Our Lady even less.

Grieg from my original crew confessed that he had hurt his girl last night, in the house at Chandler's Narrow, and that was how he liked it. I stood him up and I belted him in the face, and felt his nose shatter under my knuckles.

When he stopped choking on the blood, he admitted he didn't like it when someone did it to him, and I forgave him and sent him on his way. I made a mental note to have Will the Woman find out which girl that had been and make sure she was all right, and to pay her a week off by way of apology from me.

That was how I held confession that day, until at the very end Bloody Anne came to my room and knelt in front of me.

'I wish to confess, Father,' she said.

'Speak, in the name of Our Lady,' I said.

Anne spoke, and what she told me wasn't what I was expecting to hear.

'Last night I lay with a woman,' she said, and that part I had been expecting, at least.

'I don't think Our Lady cares who we lie with, so long as both are willing,' I said. 'There's no need to confess that, Bloody Anne.'

Her head snapped up, and there was a look of fury on her face. 'Don't tell me what I need to confess!' she snarled. 'A priest listens to people, so you'll fucking well listen to me.'

That made me blink, but I nodded. 'As you will,' I said. 'Confess, then.'

Bloody Anne drew a shuddering breath and lowered her head again. 'I grew up in a little village in some hills, northwest of here,' she said. 'Nowhere you'd have heard of. We raised sheep and traded wool, and we held to the Stone Father there, not Our Lady, and we didn't have no priest. There was just Mother Groggan.'

I sat quiet and waited for her to work her way around to her point.

'Mother Groggan very much cared who lay with who,' Anne went on. 'One day my brother caught me and Maisy the cooper's daughter out in Da's barn together. He raised the gods over it, and we were both dragged in front of Mother Groggan to confess how we had sinned with each other in the Stone Father's eyes.'

I nodded, understanding. I didn't know this Stone Father, but a god who had nothing better to worry about than who you might choose to fuck didn't sound like he was worth much, to my mind.

'It was Mother Groggan,' Anne went on, her voice going very quiet. 'She was the one.'

'The one what, Anne?'

'The witch!' she spat. 'How do you think I got *this*, Tomas?'

She threw her head back and gestured angrily at the long scar on her face.

I had never given it any thought. Anne had been at war for a year before I ever met her, and a lot of soldiers had scars. I shrugged.

'Fighting, I'd always thought,' I said. 'The road to Messia, maybe.'

'Being held down by my own brothers and cut by a witch called Mother Groggan, when I had only sixteen years to me,' she said, and now her voice was flat and quiet. 'Cut open for the crime of being in love with a girl. She cut my face, and she cut me in the other place too. Me and Maisy, both. I was pretty once, Tomas. Can you believe that?'

I nodded slowly. I could.

'She cut my face so I wouldn't be pretty enough for anyone to want me no more, and she cut me down below so I wouldn't be tempted even if they did. She did the same to Maisy and she put her witch's curse on us so we wouldn't never love again. Love another woman, Mother Groggan cursed us, and she'll die. Only I never stopped loving my Maisy because how could I, and then her wound went bad and she died from it and that was my fault.' Anne paused to choke back tears before she could go on. 'Last night I . . . it was the first time, in all those years. I lay with Rosie, from Chandler's Narrow, because I like her a lot. I can't . . . with a woman, or a man neither. Not since Mother Groggan cut me. But I can touch someone, and take pleasure from doing it. And now I think it's going to happen to her too, like it did to Maisy, and it will be my fault again. I shouldn't have done it, put her at risk like that. So I'm confessing that, whether you think Our Lady cares or not.'

I swallowed. I had never known, never even suspected, what Bloody

Anne had been through. She was my second and my friend, and I had never had the slightest idea. I found that I didn't have any words to say to her, and that shamed me.

'I never,' Anne said, like she had to fill the silence somehow. 'I never lay with anyone else, after Maisy, not until last night. I was a long time healing from what Mother Groggan did to me. Once I was healed I went back to the fields and I watched the sheep like I was supposed to, but I was dead inside just like my Maisy was dead, because what right did I have to be alive when she wasn't? Even with my scar, a boy from the village tried to court me, once, very properly, and I said I'd kill him if he touched me and I meant it and he knew I did. When the recruiters came through our village I almost begged them to take me off to war.'

'Did you expect to die, in Abingon?'

'I did.'

'Did you hope to?'

She shrugged. 'Perhaps. To start with. But you see things, in war. I don't have to tell you, Father, you were there. Among all the pain and the suffering, you see things that give you hope.'

You did, at that. I remembered witnessing acts of bravery and of kindness that you'd never see in Ellinburg if you lived there your whole life. I just nodded. That wasn't something we needed to talk about.

'So you found hope,' I said. 'And you came back to life.'

'I did,' Anne said. 'I came back to life, and I came back to the world, and then I saw witchcraft in our own fucking crew and then I broke my promise to myself and I lay with Rosie. Now I'm terrified I've brought it down on her too, what happened to Maisy.'

I reached out and put my hand on Bloody Anne's head.

'What happened to Maisy wasn't your fault, and it won't happen to Rosie,' I said. 'I promise, Anne. Our Lady forgives you your guilt. In Our Lady's name.'

Bloody Anne looked up at me, and there were tears in her eyes. 'And that makes it right, does it?'

'No, Anne,' I had to admit. 'It doesn't, but it's all I have to offer.'

Chapter 18

Bloody Anne's confession was the hardest I'd ever heard, and I'd heard confession from rapists and murderers and men so battle-shocked they couldn't do more than stare into space and cry. I could see now why she was scared of Billy the Boy, but I knew the lad wasn't a witch. Not the way Anne thought of witches, anyway. If he could do magic, and perhaps he could, then he wasn't doing it in the name of any cruel god who wanted to maim and mutilate folk for who they loved.

I thought that one day, once I had time and money and resources again, I might find out where Anne had been born and head up there with her and some well-armed men. I thought Mother Groggan and I might have some points of theological difference to discuss, priest to witch. I thought Bloody Anne might like to settle those points.

All told I was glad Anne's was the last confession I heard that Godsday.

It doesn't sound difficult, being a priest of Our Lady, not when the captain knows he needs a replacement and he's talking you into it. Listen and lead, the captain said, and he never said care. He never said it, but sometimes I did, whatever Jochan might think of me. Not often, no, but sometimes. If I had been hearing the confession of strangers in a temple, then no, he was right.

I wouldn't have cared.

Why would I care about people I didn't know? But these were my crew and some of them were my friends, like Bloody Anne. Some like Cookpot I had known most of my life, and if we weren't friends then we were at least a part of each other's lives. That goes a way to building a trust, to my mind, if not necessarily a friendship.

I took my priest's robe off and hung it up, and only then did it occur to me that Fat Luka hadn't come to say his confession. That was his affair and I never insisted any of the men came to me, Godsday or otherwise, but Luka had often knelt in front of me in Our Lady's name before. Not today, it seemed.

I shrugged the thought off and headed down to the common room, where Pawl the tailor was just finishing taking measurements while his boy made notes of who wanted what. The tavern was open by then, open to the public for the first time since I had kicked Dondas Alman and his boys out into the street and put his 'important friends' to the sword. Trade was slow, as might be expected after that, but there were a few folk in there from the surrounding streets. No one had much coin to spend, I knew, and I had Hari selling beer below cost just to get bodies through the door. I was still selling Alman's stock, of course, so I could do that for a while and not show a loss, but I knew it wouldn't do forever. Not at the rate my own lads were getting through the taproom it wouldn't, anyway.

Black Billy was on the door how he should be, and I could see Mika at a table in the far corner with two walls at his shoulders where he could keep a watchful eye over the whole room. Ailsa was a vision behind the bar in her clean white apron, smiling and flirting and sweeping coppers into the lockbox as she served mugs of beer and the occasional glass of brandy. I kept an eye on those who were buying brandy. They were the ones who had coin to spend, and on these streets that made them conspicuous.

Hari limped out of the kitchen on his stick and smiled at folk, shaking the hands of those he didn't know and introducing himself. He looked the part as the tavern keeper, and word soon got around who he was and who he worked for.

When I made my entrance and Ailsa brought me a brandy I didn't pay for, everyone in there knew *exactly* who I was.

It might be Godsday but everyone who was likely to visit a temple and say their confession would have already done so by then, and I had put away my priest's robes for the day. Father Tomas was done, for now, and it was time to be Tomas Piety again. I stood up, the glass in my hand, and cleared my throat.

'Everyone shut up!' Jochan roared.

Silence fell over the room, and I took my moment.

'Welcome to the Tanner's Arms,' I said. 'Most of you here know me, but for those who don't my name is Tomas Piety and I own this place, among others. I've been away to war but now I'm back, and the Tanner's is back to being how it should be.'

'And are taxes back to being how they were?' someone said, his voice carrying more than I thought he had meant it to.

'Taxes are suspended,' I said. 'I know times are hard. The war has been hard on everyone, those who fought and those who stayed behind alike. Whatever you were paying Alman is gone now, and what you paid me before the war we can discuss later. For now there are no taxes on these streets, and if anyone comes asking for them you come and tell me or my brother about it, and we'll make them go away.'

There was a cheer at that, albeit a half-hearted one. I doubted that anyone there had much of anything to pay taxes with, other than the few conspicuous brandy drinkers. I watched each of those carefully, noting their faces, and I hoped Fat Luka was doing the same. There were some I knew by sight, and if they were doing that much better than their fellow men then I wanted to find out how and why.

I remembered what Governor Hauer had told me about this mysterious Bloodhands and his Skanians, who had supposedly overrun the city while we had been at war, and about how they had gold to spend. I remembered the men in the house at Chandler's Narrow too, and how they had been scared for their families. These men with brandies in their hands were playing a dangerous game, to my mind.

Ailsa stood behind the bar, drawing tankards of beer and smiling and flirting, but I would have bet a gold crown to a clipped copper that she was noting who had money for brandy too. Oh, she was no fool, that one, that was for sure.

No, Ailsa was nobody's fool, and whatever tricks she could perform with paints and powders and lace, I was sure that the Queen's Men didn't take in anyone who wasn't shrewd at business as well. I gave her a look and she nodded back at me, and I could see that we understood each other.

She had a way with people, I could see that too. Upstairs in her room she had spoken to me like a Dannsburg aristocrat, with her accent like cut glass and always making me feel like she was looking down her nose at me. Down here behind the bar she was everybody's sweetheart, common and charming and funny with a wink and a smile and a joke. Oh, yes, she was good. A spy has to blend and mix and mingle until they could have been anyone, and no one thinks anything of a flirty barmaid, do they? Flirty barmaids are two a copper penny, and who's to remember which tavern they know her from?

I sat and watched the room for an hour or so, then told Ailsa to take her break in the kitchen and had Fat Luka stand a turn behind the bar while I went after her. We were left alone to talk in peace, which was another advantage of having the crew think she was my fancy woman.

'The ones with money for brandy are spies, more than likely,' she said as soon as we were alone, 'or at least in their pay. Do you recognise any of them?'

'A few faces I've seen before, but not to put names to them,' I said. 'I thought you might have noticed that.'

'I notice everything, Tomas, it's my job,' she said. 'You realise the one the men call Cookpot has battle shock, don't you?'

'I know,' I said. 'He's having a think about whether he wants to stay.'

'You'd be better off without him,' she said. 'He'll be unpredictable.'

I knew that. Jochan was unpredictable too, but then he always had been.

'He's my man, and he stays my man unless he chooses otherwise,' I said. 'I'll take your say on whatever your business here may be, but don't you tell me how to lead my men.'

She held my gaze for a moment, then nodded. 'Very well,' she said. 'We'll keep to the subject of the spies, the Skanian agents. That should interest you well enough. The Skanians are the ones who have taken over your old business interests. It's high time you started taking them back again.'

'I know that,' I said. 'What I don't know is why they're doing it.'

'Ellinburg is corrupt to the core,' she said. 'From Governor Hauer on down, the city all but stands on the shoulders of its underworld. People like you and Ma Aditi are key to the real economy of this city, or at least you were before the war. The bulk of the gold might be in the hands of the merchant guilds and the factories, but they survive only so long as they have a workforce. Those who control the streets control that workforce, in the main. Hauer managed to get a little of that control back during the war years, but then he lost most of it again to the Skanians. If they were to take over the street economy of Ellinburg, they could be in a position to break Hauer's authority and the wealth of the merchant guilds together. With control of the city in their hands, they could prepare an advance staging point here, ready and waiting for a possible invasion that might threaten Dannsburg itself. We won the last war but only just, truth be told, and the country is weak and ripe for invasion. They keep slaves in Skania, Tomas, did you know that? Do you have any idea what it is like, to be a Skanian slave? If we fail here, you could well find out.'

I looked at her and frowned. I'd die before I would be any man's slave, but, that aside, it seemed to me she had told me much that was supposition and little that was certain.

'That's an awful lot of *could* and *might* and *possibly*, to my mind,' I said.

'Yes, it is,' she agreed. 'You'll find that we deal mostly in *could* and *might* and *possibly*, Tomas. By the time something becomes a certainty it is often too late to do anything about it.'

'So you could be wasting your time with—' I started, before she interrupted.

'And don't be shy about it, my handsome,' she giggled in her barmaid's voice just as the door opened and Mika stuck his head into the room.

'Sorry to interrupt, boss,' he said. 'Only there's an old geezer in the bar asking for you. Says his name's Kurt.'

I frowned at that, but I got up. 'Keep it warm for later,' I told Ailsa, following her lead and wondering just how good her hearing must be to have known there was someone outside the door.

Hearing that wasn't deadened by years of cannon fire was bound to be better than mine, I supposed. She giggled again and I followed Mika into the bar. Old Kurt was there right enough, leaning on a gnarled length of wood and with a shabby cloak around his shoulders. I gave Luka the nod.

'Give him a beer on the house,' I said.

I let Kurt have a sip of his beer, then took him by the elbow and steered him to a table in the corner. Mika came and stood with his back to my table and his arms crossed in front of him, sending a clear message that we weren't to be disturbed. Mika could think for himself, as Fat Luka had said, and that was good.

'What are you doing here?' I asked the old man.

'Having a drink' – Kurt grinned at me – 'and I thank you for it. I came to see how this boy of yours slept last night, of course.'

'Well enough,' I said, and Old Kurt nodded his narrow, ratty head.

'I thought as much,' he said. 'You'll want me to look at him, then.'

'I will,' I said, 'but not here. Never here, Kurt. This is Anne's worry and only her and I know about it, and I want it kept that way. I don't want you at the Tanner's, spreading fear and superstition among my men.'

'So Old Kurt's not welcome among your finery, is that the lay of things?'

'It is,' I said. 'I have respect for you, to a point, but these are simple men and if they get wind of magic in their midst they'll raise the gods over it, and then there's bound to be trouble. I don't want that.'

Kurt shrugged. 'That's your choice, but if you keep it from them and then they find out for themselves, you'll be sorry, you mark my words.'

He drained his beer in one long, greedy draft, the lump in his scrawny neck working as he swallowed. He thumped the tankard down on the table and got to his feet.

'Thank you for your hospitality,' he said.

With that he picked up his stick and left the Tanner's Arms, leaving me to think on what he had said.

Chapter 19

By the next day I had made a decision on that.

Old Kurt was right, I knew. If I hid Billy's gift from the crew and something gave it away, then all my attempts to instil order and discipline would have been wasted. There would be panic, and anger, and then there would probably be blood. The men knew Billy was touched by the goddess, and that was one thing, but it would only take someone else to say 'witch' and it would all go to the whores in a heartbeat.

These were religious men, in their way, and acts of the goddess were all well and good, to their minds. I doubted a single man of them had ever seen a magician, but they knew they existed and they were well and good too, and even folk like Old Kurt got a wary sort of respect. Breathe the word *witch*, though, and there was fear and violence. I wasn't sure I could see a difference, myself, but then it wasn't something I much cared about. Priest I might be, but if I'll confess anything it's that I'm a sight less religious than most of my crew were.

Of course, if we had been in Dannsburg this would have been easy. I could have taken Billy to the house of magicians and told them he had the gift, let them test him, and paid them for his schooling. Talented children were always in demand in Dannsburg, so I had heard, but we were in Ellinburg and there was no house of magicians here. There was just Old Kurt, and I knew that would have to be how I sold this to the crew.

I took Fat Luka out to the stable for a quiet word. Cookpot was grooming the horses and Simple Sam was mucking out, so we kept on walking until we were in the alley behind the tavern. I was starting to feel how cramped it was at the Tanner's with so many men sleeping there, and it was chafing at me. Will the Woman and Sir Eland were living in the house on Chandler's Narrow now, of course, and Brak was with my aunt, for which I could almost feel sorry for him. Even with that, though, we were still too many under one roof.

'What's the lay of things?' I asked Luka once we were finally away from listening ears.

'Jochan's brooding, like I said he would, but he hasn't made trouble yet,' Luka said. 'Grieg had some hard words to say about you breaking his face until some of the others got to the truth of why you did it, and now he's got more bruises than he can count. Everyone took that ill, I reckon, and he got a good kicking. You shouldn't ought to hit whores, and I reckon even Grieg knows that now.'

I nodded. That was well enough.

'How's Cookpot?'

'Fat-faced and stupid, same as usual,' Luka said. 'He's been a bit quiet, though.'

'You keep a close eye on Cookpot,' I told him. 'He's got the battle shock worse than he lets on. I'm not sure he's suited to this life.'

'Right,' Luka said. 'Anything else you need?'

'There is,' I said, 'and this is important. It's about Billy the Boy.'

'What about him?'

'You know Billy's touched by the goddess,' I said, and Luka nodded. 'Well, I think he has a bit of the cunning in him, too, and that's good. It's good but it's not something I know how to help him learn. So Old Kurt, the man who came to see me yesterday, he's a cunning man. You remember Old Kurt from back when we were boys, Luka?'

'I know the name,' Luka said, and now he looked a bit uncomfortable. 'Can't say I've had anything to do with him. People say . . . well, you know how folk are. People say things.'

'He's a cunning man,' I said again, 'and all that means is he's a magician who hasn't had the schooling. Like Doc Cordin is to a doctor, you understand? There's nothing wrong in it.'

'I heard he did witchcraft, down in the Wheels,' Luka said.

I leaned very close to Luka, and put my hand on the back of his neck while I spoke softly in his ear. 'If I hear that word again, Fat Luka, I won't be able to let it pass,' I said. 'That's the very word I don't want to hear spoken, not by you or anyone else, do you understand me? Billy is touched by the goddess and he might have it in him to become a magician if he gets some teaching, and those are good things. Those things are good for Billy, and they're good for the Pious Men too. I need to know that you understand that.'

I heard Luka swallow, and he nodded.

'Right, boss,' he said.

'Good,' I said, and let go of his neck. 'Now, Billy is going to learn from Old Kurt, and he might have to go to the Wheels to do it. I know that isn't ideal, but there it is. If there were a house of magicians in Ellinburg he'd be going there, but there's not and that's not something I can change. What I need from you is to make sure everyone in that tavern understands what a good thing this is, and how nobody wants to make any fuss over it. Can you do that for me, Fat Luka?'

Luka nodded, and I patted him on the shoulder and pressed a silver mark into his hand. Luka might fear magic, but he loved silver more.

We went back through the yard as Cookpot and Simple Sam were finishing up in the stables. I put my hand on Cookpot's shoulder to keep him back.

'A little word,' I said.

The others left us in peace, standing there among the smell of freshly raked stables and clean horseflesh, and I looked into Cookpot's round, sweaty face.

'I set you something to think on, yesterday,' I reminded him. 'Have you made a decision yet, Cookpot? Only I can't have a man here who's not committed to what we do, I'm sure you understand that.'

'I . . . I don't know that I can do it,' he admitted, 'but I don't want to leave, neither. I went to war and back with you and Jochan and Luka, and we met Anne and all the lads. You . . . you're all I've got, Mr Piety.'

I knew Cookpot didn't have any family. His ma had died just before we went off to war, and it had only ever been the two of them since we were children. I could understand what he was getting at. All the same, he wasn't from my streets and if he couldn't be a Pious Man, then why should I feed him? I thought on that for a moment, and I looked around the yard. My gaze settled on the stables, and Our Lady gave me my answer.

'I saw you grooming the horses earlier,' I said. 'It needed doing but I never told you to do it, so that was well done. Do you like horses, Cookpot?'

'I do,' he admitted. 'I've never rode one, but I like them all the same. They're noble beasts, are horses.'

I wasn't sure about that, but I nodded to keep him happy. I had seen enough horses torn to pieces by cannon to think that they were no nobler than men were, and that was to say not very. That wasn't anything Cookpot needed to hear, though.

'Might be I need a groom,' I said. 'That could be you, Cookpot. You won't be a Pious Man, and you won't earn silver like those who are, but you'll have a place here and a job and a roof over your head. Does that sound good?'

He looked up at me, and there were tears in his eyes.

'It does, Mr Piety,' he whispered. 'It sounds very good indeed.'

'That's done, then,' I said. 'Be sure to tell the crew, so everyone knows the lay of things.'

Cookpot nodded and hurried off into the tavern, and he looked like a great weight had been taken off his shoulders.

The weight of a cannon, maybe.

I looked at our four horses and I knew very well that I didn't need a groom. Not for four horses I didn't. I was being soft on Cookpot, I knew I was, but then I felt like he had earned it. He had kept us fed at Abingon, when the supply lines were cut and some companies were starving. A forager like Cookpot had been worth five fighting men, to my mind, and I owed him for that. He was hurt because of it, hurt in the mind where it doesn't show to a casual eye.

He had made it all the way home and then he had killed a man, because of a situation I had put him in. I knew that had hurt him even more. I owed him a soft job, and some peace.

That was how I made it right with Cookpot, the only way I knew how.

*

The tavern was open again that evening, but we didn't have so many customers as the day before. The brandy drinkers were all gone, no doubt having seen what they needed to see and gone off to whisper in their masters' ears. The few patrons left were all faces I recognised from the surrounding streets.

Sir Eland came to see me that night, and that surprised me. I still didn't trust Sir Eland, and truth be told, I had been greatly enjoying his absence. The false knight joined me at my table and I could feel his narrow, weaselly eyes on me.

'Can we talk?' he asked.

I nodded.

He had something on his mind, I could tell.

'A bunch of the crew came to Chandler's Narrow, night before last,' he said.

'Aye, I know.'

'Billy the Boy was with them.'

Again I nodded, and waited for him to work his way around to his point. If he had some sort of complaint about the crew, then he should be taking it to Bloody Anne, to my mind, not bothering me with it, but he was there now so I'd hear him out.

'What of it? Jochan said they didn't get him a woman anyway.'

'No, they didn't,' Sir Eland said. 'They left him with me.'

'And?'

The false knight swallowed, and looked down at the table, and I could see the fear in him.

'You can trust me,' he said, so quiet I almost didn't catch his words. 'I know you think you can't, but you can. Maybe I was jealous when your brother came back, I'll admit that. Maybe I haven't shown you as much respect as I should have done, and I apologise for it. I might not be a real knight, I'll accept that you know that, but I'm a real Pious Man now. I'll prove it to you somehow, when I get the chance. Just . . . just don't send that boy to me again.'

I frowned at that, and wondered what the fuck Billy the Boy had said or done to Sir Eland that night, while Anne and the men were whoring. Whatever it was, Sir Eland seemed to be of the mind that it had been my doing. Billy seemed to have frightened some honesty into him anyway, and that was good. Whether it would last remained to be seen.

I nodded slowly, and fixed him with a look. 'I appreciate your words, Sir Eland,' I said, 'and I hope you get that chance soon.'

He sighed and got up. 'I'll prove it to you somehow,' he said again. He turned away then and left the Tanner's Arms, alone.

I circulated after that, shaking hands and listening to what people had to say for themselves while Hari played dice with a couple of local men at another table. I heard nothing new, by and large, but folk appreciate being listened to. There wasn't enough work to go around, and some of their neighbours were going hungry. They'd like to help, of course they would, but they had families of their own to feed, surely I understood that.

The streets weren't as safe as they had been before the war, when the Pious Men were running things properly. I heard that as well, and I knew it was meant to carry my favour. There was still disease. They weren't ill, oh no, not them, so no need to be throwing them out of the tavern, but they'd heard of people who were. No one they knew, though, of course, but they'd heard things.

Sometime in the middle of the evening when trade had all but died and I was sitting at a corner table with Mika, Ailsa came over to speak to me.

'Quiet night,' I said.

She nodded, still wearing her barmaid's face for the sake of the remaining men in the common room.

'There's sickness in the streets again, so I heard,' she told me. 'The plague all but burned itself out these last few weeks, but people are saying how maybe it's coming back again. A lad on Sailcloth Row come down with a case of the boils, and there's all but panic. Folk don't want to mix too much, if you take my meaning, Mr Piety.'

I frowned at that. 'The plague we had doesn't give you boils,' I said. 'The lad's probably just been washing in bad water.'

'Or he's caught the pox off some street scrub,' Mika put in, and immediately looked like he wished he hadn't. 'Begging your pardon, Ailsa.'

'I hope that's true, sir,' she said, and gave me a look that said she knew very well that it wasn't.

The plague was all but gone from Ellinburg, and thank Our Lady for that, but folk were bound to still be nervous at the first sign of disease of any sort. It was the same sort of nervousness they got at the first sign of magic, too, and that made me think of something.

'Have you seen Billy the Boy tonight?' I asked her.

'He's away in the back, with some of the lads,' she said. 'Luka's been telling them all about how the lad's going off to learn to be a great magician, and now they can't get enough of looking at him. I've never seen so many men look so impressed about something that weren't a horse or a woman.'

Luka was good at this sort of thing, I was coming to realise, very good indeed. He was good at making people see what I wanted them to see and in the right way, a way that meant them never getting around to thinking there might be a different way to see a thing. They'd had a word for that in the army, but I couldn't remember what it was. This was the same sort of thing, to my mind, and it seemed Fat Luka had the knack for it.

'That was skilfully done,' she whispered to me in her own voice.

She was right, it *had* been well done. I had chosen very well, giving that task to Luka.

The right man for the right job, always.

She gave me a knowing tip of the head and sauntered off back behind her bar.

It was only later that night, when I was lying in my blankets trying to sleep, that I realised I had never spoken to Ailsa about Billy's magic.

Not even once.

Chapter 20

I spent the next morning thinking on what I had heard the night before. A lot of it had been what folk thought I wanted to hear, I knew that, but some of it hadn't. The streets really weren't safe at night, and there was nothing like enough work to go around and keep everyone fed. Those things were true enough, and I needed to do something about them.

Finding work for all those people was out of my reach, at the moment anyway, but the other thing wasn't. To my mind the Pious Men streets weren't safe because there were crews other than the Pious Men operating on them. That was something I could change, and it suited me well enough to do so. If I had to do other things later, to feed and employ people, I would need gold.

Ailsa would have gold, or at least access to it, and of course there was the fortune I still had bricked up in the back of the small storeroom from the last time I had worked for the Queen's Men. That was the problem in front of me, of course. I hadn't been able to spend much of that gold back then and I couldn't spend *any* of it now, not without facing too many hard questions about where it had come from.

I needed to get my businesses back and push some of the gold through them to make it look like it had been earned in commerce and honest crime and wasn't the queen's money, dirty money that I should never have taken. Then things could be different. There was little enough I could move through the Tanner's Arms, not with trade how it was at the moment.

I thought on what I had owned, where each business was in relation to the Tanner's and how I needed to consolidate my strength into one area to keep it defensible. I wanted the Golden Chains back, but that was out of the question for now. The Chains was a gambling house, a very private one, where only the wealthiest of the city were welcome. The place made a fortune, but I knew it was guarded hard and I didn't have the strength yet to take it. That and it was almost on Trader's Row, too far away from my other businesses.

That brought the decision down to a simple one. There was another boarding-house I had owned, in Slaughterhouse Narrow. That one was an actual boarding-house, not a thinly disguised stew, a legitimate place that mostly took in travelling slaughtermen and the labourers and skinners who followed them. It wasn't the Chains, but it made money well enough. If I started with that one, I could use the Chandler's Narrow house as a staging point, with an easy supply line back to the Tanner's if needed. I had learned a thing or two in the army, I realised, even if I hadn't much appreciated it at the time.

Jochan was happy with the idea when I told him, and Bloody Anne still looked preoccupied but she nodded agreement anyway. The three of us were in the back room, having our council of war while Luka kept the door and listened in.

That was good. He'd need to know what the plan was anyway, so he could explain to the lads why it was a good one that would see everyone make money and not get hurt in the process. He knew his job, did Fat Luka, and if I hadn't quite explained to Jochan and Anne what that job was then I think they had mostly worked their way around to figuring it out for themselves by then.

'Slaughterhouse Narrow it is, then,' Jochan said, and his face twisted into a savage grin that put me in mind of a wild animal. 'We'll make it a fucking slaughterhouse all right, Tomas. These pricks think they can steal from us? Well, they fucking can't!'

'Well said, brother,' I said. 'Well said.'

I tasked Jochan with picking the men for the job, and Luka with putting some fire in their bellies. I kept Anne back for a moment as the two men left the room.

'I have to ask you something, and I hope you won't take it ill,' I said.

'Go on.'

'When you went to Chandler's Narrow the other night, did you talk much with Rosie? Afterward, perhaps?'

Anne shrugged. 'Some,' she said, looking uncomfortable.

'Did you tell her about Billy the Boy?'

'I . . . I might have done,' she said. 'I was drunk and happy and scared, Tomas. I can't rightly remember what I said. Why do you ask?'

'No matter,' I said, shrugging it off as a casual thing, but I had learned something.

Rosie hadn't just been a messenger – she was actually working for Ailsa and the Queen's Men. That might matter or it might not, but it was a good thing to know. It stood to reason that Ailsa wouldn't be alone, not in a nest of vipers like ours. Oh, I was sure she could take care of herself and then some, but she had to have some way of passing information back to Dannsburg. No spy works truly alone. I had learned that much in the army. Of course she had someone else attached to my business, and now that I knew who it was I felt a little bit more secure. Once you know who the spy is, you're halfway to controlling the flow of information.

I'd have to keep a close eye on Rosie from Chandler's Narrow from now on.

We went that night. Ten of us rallied at the Chandler's Narrow house, slipping through the darkened streets between the Tanner's and the stew two and three at a time until we were all together. Everyone had their leather and mail on, and weapons hidden under their cloaks. Sir Eland was ready and waiting for us in the parlour of the boarding-house. He was wearing his stolen armour, with his long sword hanging at his belt.

Jochan and I disagreed over this, but I had made it his business to pick the men for the job and he had chosen Sir Eland as one of them, so I had to let it pass. I still didn't trust the false knight and I wouldn't until he gave me a reason to, but Jochan didn't know him the way I did and he didn't know about the words we had exchanged in the Tanner's Arms the previous night. All he saw was a fighting man with good harness and a keen blade and nothing better to do with his night.

Truth be told, I think Sir Eland was getting bored at Chandler's Narrow. Women didn't interest him, and to hear him tell it there had only been three fights, all of which he had ended in seconds with his usual arrogant ease. Will's version of events differed slightly, but not enough that I had to make something of it. Nothing was ever as easy as Sir Eland made it sound to people who hadn't been there to see, and that was another reason I still didn't trust him, but he had done what was needed all the same and that was good. So was the house, I had to admit.

The house at Chandler's Narrow was spotless, in fact, well repaired and all the furniture polished while the women walked around clean and neatly dressed. Will admitted to me that he had sunk all the money I had given him into the business, but when I offered to cover his expenses he shook his head.

'I'd like to think we were partners now,' he said. 'I've made my investment, and I think a quarter of the returns for me would be a fair deal on that.'

I looked at him for a long moment. Will the Woman was more shrewd than perhaps I had given him credit for, I realised. He said he had run a bawdy house before the war and I believed him, but now he was talking about moving out of working for me and into working with me, and they were very different things. That showed ambition, and ambition is always to be admired.

Within reason.

'We'll see,' I said. 'If you can show me you've taken five marks by next Godsday and turned at least a mark profit on it, you can keep a quarter of that profit. Any less and I'll cover your expense but take all your profits. Does that sound fair, Will the Woman?'

He nodded. 'That sounds fair,' he said. 'Do me a favour, though, boss?'

'What's that?'

'Stop calling me "the Woman". Your brother Jochan came up with that name and I've never cared for it. Maybe I wept when I done hard things, but who hasn't? It ain't only women who weep.'

I nodded. He was right about that. All the same, names were given, not chosen, and they weren't always given kindly. That was the way of soldiers, and he knew that as well as I did.

'Will the Wencher, then. Does that suit you better?'

He snorted. 'I'll take what I can get,' he said. 'Suits me now, I suppose.'

It did, at that.

Jochan hadn't picked Grieg for tonight's work, and I thought that was wise. I doubted he was welcome at Chandler's Narrow at the moment. I spoke to Will about that while I was there, and he agreed to make it right with the girl that Grieg had hurt. The crew had already made it right with Grieg, with their boots by the sound of things, and I didn't think he'd be doing it again.

That done, I gathered the crew together in the parlour. Jochan and Bloody Anne were both there, and Sir Eland and Fat Luka and Nik the Knife and the others.

'You know what we're doing and why,' I said. 'Slaughterhouse Narrow belongs to the Pious Men, and we're taking it back. The slaughterhouse itself is at the bottom of the narrow. We'll go around the side and up the steps there toward the boarding-house. It'll be dark behind the slaughter yard, so watch your footing.'

'And it fucking stinks,' Jochan added with a grin. 'I hope none of you ladies has a dainty nose.'

There were a few half-hearted laughs, but that was it. Men were checking weapons and mail, preparing to fight and kill for me, and few were in the mood for humour. I caught Luka's eye and looked at Jochan. Luka gave me a nod. He would keep an eye on my brother, that nod said.

We headed out, me and Jochan at the front and Bloody Anne keeping the rear of our column with Sir Eland beside her. Our route led us down Chandler's Narrow to the main street, then through the shadows of an alley and into the darkness behind the slaughterhouse. Jochan had been right, to be fair; the stench was appalling even by the standards of the Stink. I heard someone gagging, and a muffled thump as someone else hit them to tell them to shut up.

Slaughterhouse Narrow itself led up the hill between two tenement buildings, the steps steep and in utter darkness at that time of night. The blank sides of the buildings loomed over us, robbing us even of moonlight. I felt my way along the damp wall beside me, aiming for the dim glow of a single lantern hanging outside the entrance to the boarding-house in the small courtyard. As I climbed I realised I could see a shadow under that lantern where a shadow shouldn't be.

I stopped and put a hand on Jochan's arm to hold him.

'There's someone on the door,' I whispered, right close into his ear.

Jochan looked, nodded. He turned and picked a man out of our group, one of his old crew, who I had only ever heard called Cutter. This fellow was lean and wiry, dark haired and bearded, and he hardly ever spoke. He slipped through the men and joined Jochan and me at the front. Jochan pointed to the shadow under the lantern and made a hand gesture that I didn't recognise, some sign cant of their crew. Cutter nodded. He had a shortsword hidden under his cloak, but he ignored that and produced two small knives from his belt. He held them backward, to my mind, one in each hand with the top under his thumb and the flat of the blade against the inside of his wrist. When he lowered his hands, the knives were invisible.

I watched as he slipped past us and up the steps. He stumbled drunkenly, although he wasn't drunk.

'Fuckin' steps,' he slurred, loud enough to be heard. 'I fucking hate these . . . fucking steps.'

The shadow under the lantern moved, became the shape of a man.

'Who's that?'

'Wha'? I'm fucking lost, pal. How d'you get to fucking Trader's Row from here? I gotta . . . got a woman waiting for me and I can't . . . fucking find the place.'

The man who should have been on the door laughed and pointed, half turning away from Cutter to indicate the way up through the narrow. Cutter moved fast, his hands crossing the sides of the man's neck in a blur of movement and steel. Blood sprayed black in the dim light, and Cutter lowered the dead man silently to the cobbles.

'Thanks, pal, you're . . . you're a pal,' he said, and stumbled on a few steps farther for the benefit of anyone listening.

That done, he crouched down at the edge of the light and beckoned us on.

I didn't know this Cutter but it seemed that he had his talents, for all that he hadn't really made any friends among the men. We hurried to join him. A man on the door meant they were expecting trouble, but after what we had done at Chandler's Narrow that wasn't a surprise. I searched the blood-slick body and came up with a key, and I smiled.

'I'm first in,' Jochan whispered. 'I'm always first in.'

I nodded. I remembered Kant from my old crew, who I had killed with my own hand before we even reached Ellinburg. He had always been first too, leading his squad with his mace in hand, crushing and bludgeoning and forcing his way forward. Bludgeon and force, that was how Kant the Cunt had made his way in the world, and I couldn't think that my brother Jochan was much different. Still, it was good, for now.

We'd do this the same way as last time, then. What had worked once would work again, to my mind. I gave Jochan the key and stepped aside as he unlocked the door to the boarding-house.

'The fuck are you—' someone started, and Jochan's axe rose and fell.

He charged into the house with Sir Eland and the others at his back. I kept Bloody Anne with me in the narrow until they were all inside, and then we dragged the dead body farther into the shadows and followed a minute later.

There were five of them already dead in the main room, and I could hear fighting from upstairs and in the back. Too much fighting. Nik the Knife was slumped on the floor with his back against the wall, white as a sheet and clutching his stomach.

'How bad is it?' Anne asked him.

He heaved in a breath, and when he exhaled blood ran out of his mouth and down his chin.

'Bad enough, Sarge,' he said, and I saw that it was.

His mail was slick with blood around his hand, where a sword-thrust had gone straight through it and deep into his guts. A man doesn't survive a wound like that, not without a surgeon and usually not even with one. He looked up at me.

'I wish to confess, Father,' he whispered.

I nodded and turned to Anne. 'I'll stay with him,' I said. 'Go and help the others.'

She drew her daggers and followed the sounds of violence into the boarding-house, a hard set to her scarred face. It would go badly for the first stranger Bloody Anne laid eyes on.

I crouched down beside Nik. 'Speak, in the name of Our Lady,' I said.

'I'm dying, I know that,' he said. 'I'm dying and I'm scared, Father. I've done wrong in my life, and I ain't always confessed it. I . . . I don't know that I've the time or the strength to confess it all now, and I'm scared what that means.'

'It's your time to cross the river, and Our Lady forgives you,' I said. 'In Our Lady's name.'

'In Our Lady's name,' he repeated.

I reached out to put my hand on his head, but he had already died.

I stood up, and drew Remorse and Mercy.

I started up the stairs.

Chapter 21

I met a man on the first landing. He was no one I knew, so I rammed Remorse into his groin even as I took the last step. He screamed and fell, clutching at himself, and I gave him Mercy through the throat.

'Pious Men, call out!' I bellowed.

I heard a shout from the room ahead of me, followed by a curse and the sound of a crash. I kicked the door open and found Fat Luka hard-pressed by a stranger with a mace. Luka dodged and ducked as best he could, keeping his blade up, but it's a difficult thing to fight a mace when you've no shield. The man swung again and Luka dodged, and the weapon smashed into the door I had just thrown open, splintering it.

Remorse slashed out and up, and took his hand off at the wrist. The mace tumbled to the floor with the severed hand still gripping it, and Luka lunged with his sword and that was done.

'Fuck, but there's a lot of them,' Luka panted, red-faced and sweating from the unaccustomed exercise. 'This ain't like the last bunch of cunts – these are fucking soldiers.'

I nodded. That had been my thought too – no civilian carried a mace, or would have much idea what to do with one if they did. This Bloodhands or whoever he was had obviously started recruiting from among the veterans who were beginning to trickle back into the city. That was bad, but it gave me an idea.

'Where's Jochan?'

'He took the top floor, with Sir Eland,' Luka told me.

That was as I had hoped.

'Hold here,' I said. 'You'll know what do when the time comes.'

I bolted back down the stairs and into the back room. I found Bloody Anne working one of her daggers out of a dead man's eye socket. She was red to the elbows, and there were three corpses in the room with her. Anne always had preferred the close work. That was how she got her name in the first place.

'Call the hammer,' I told her. 'How we took the east cloister at Messia, remember?'

Bloody Anne nodded and pulled her dagger free with a satisfied wrench. She marched into the main room with me beside her, and she threw her head back and took a great breath.

'Company!' she roared, her leather-lunged sergeant's voice filling the building with ease. 'The hammer!'

Anne was no tactician but by Our Lady she was loud, and on the battlefield a loud commander is worth two clever ones any day. What's the point of clever orders if no one can hear them?

Three of the lads rushed out of other downstairs rooms and joined us, red blades in their hands. From upstairs came an answering roar, Sir Eland's war cry. I heard boots stamping on wooden floors, thundering down the stairs toward us.

There were six of them left and they fled down the narrow corridors before Jochan and Sir Eland's insane charge, and as they passed his door Fat Luka leaped out to join the pursuit. They were the hammer. The enemy had thought to make a stand in the main room where they'd have space to make their numbers count, but they found our steel waiting for them. We were the anvil that the hammer met, with those men between us.

It was bloody slaughter.

We had used the tactic before, in the sack of Messia, and I couldn't take the credit for it. It was the captain's design, but what had worked then would work again. In narrow spaces, such as corridors or cloisters or tunnels, numbers count for little. It's ferocity that matters, and when two men decide to charge like wild beasts they can drive a whole squad before them. That was what Jochan and Sir Eland did, and the enemy panicked and ran, looking for space enough to spread out and fight as a group. The trick was to have that space prepared for them, with armed men waiting. Drive them into the trap, and you'll crush them between your two forces.

The hammer and the anvil, that was how we took back the house on Slaughterhouse Narrow.

It was a victory, but not without its cost. Nik the Knife was already dead on the floor behind me, and in the melee another of our men had joined him on his river crossing. He was one of Jochan's, and to my shame I didn't even know his name.

'Ganna's done,' Cutter said, not sounding like he cared one way or the other about it.

Jochan looked at his fallen man, lying prone with a shortsword still lodged between his ribs and his mail drenched in blood.

'Aye,' he said, and it seemed like that was all the opinion he had on the matter.

Jochan's crew had never seemed close like mine had been, but that felt cold even for his way of leadership.

'Who was he?' I asked.

Jochan shrugged. 'A soldier, a conscript. They only sent me the shit-heads, by and large. Cutter here's a good man, and Will the Woman can handle himself, but the rest of them aren't worth spit.'

I thought of Mika and Hari back at the Tanner's, both men from Jochan's original crew, and found that I disagreed with him on that. All the same, I held my peace on it. That wasn't the time to debate the merits of men, after all. There was one thing, though.

'I gave Will a new name,' I said. 'Now he's running the stew, he won't be weeping any more. He's Will the Wencher now.'

Jochan laughed at that, and Cutter turned and spat on the floor to show what he thought of it, but it broke the mood as I had intended. I was pained by the death of Nik the Knife, but I hadn't known Ganna, and Jochan obviously hadn't cared about him, so grief for him was a waste of emotion, to my mind. There was work to be done.

There was a good deal of work, to remove the bodies and secure the house on Slaughterhouse Narrow before dawn came. Moving bodies was harsh work, but Fat Luka said he had heard where there was a plague pit not far away that hadn't been filled in yet. A few more corpses stripped and shovelled in with the others would never be noticed.

Harsh work, as I say, but we had done worse before.

Every one of us had done worse.

When it was done, I turned the house over to Jochan to see to. It was time he had some responsibility, and I still remembered what Luka had said to me about his views on Hari running the Tanner's Arms. He had fought well, too – being the hammer is hard and dangerous, and Jochan had stepped up and done it the same as Kant had back in Messia.

There was a good deal of likeness between my brother and Kant, but he was still my brother all the same. He chose Cutter to stay with him, which didn't surprise me, and Sir Eland as well, which did. Eland had been part of the hammer too, I reminded myself, and I wondered if perhaps him and Jochan might be starting to find a trust between them. We could see to a more permanent arrangement in the morning, so I just nodded and let him have it his way.

Anne and I led the rest of them the quiet way back to the Tanner's Arms.

Ailsa was waiting up for us with Mika and Black Billy when we came in, although she'd had the sense to close up for the night before then. That was good. We shed our cloaks to reveal clothes and hands almost black with blood, although little of it was our own.

'You've had a night of it, Mr Piety,' Ailsa said, in her barmaid's voice.

She went to pour brandies without being asked. There was a look of approval on her face, although I was sure she could see we were fewer than we had been. We were fewer than we should have been, even accounting for setting guards at Slaughterhouse Narrow, but she didn't mention that. She took it in her stride like any businessman's woman would have done, and that was good. I respected her for that.

Anne set Simple Sam to heating water in the kitchen for washing, and we drank in the sort of shaky silence that always follows harsh work. There would be jokes and boasting in the morning, and tales grown tall in the telling of who had killed the most men and how, but that was for later. These were hard folk used to hard deeds, but shock is shock and no one is immune to it. Not even Jochan, for all that he might pretend otherwise.

Perhaps it's different for archers, or the crews who work the great siege cannons, men who barely see the faces of the people they kill. I wouldn't know. What I do know is how it feels to look into the eyes of a man not a foot in front of you as you pull a length of sharpened steel out of his guts and take his life away.

You don't feel like joking about it afterward.

I sat at my usual table in the corner with my brandy and nodded at Mika across the room. He hadn't been with us, of course. His place was in the Tanner's with Billy now, but he had been at Messia, and at Abingon. He knew what harsh work felt like, and he knew I'd want leaving alone. He nodded back and left me be.

Bloody Anne joined me a minute later, a brandy of her own in her hand. Now we were in the light I noticed she was walking stiffly, favouring her right leg. She lowered herself into the chair across from me with a grimace that made her scar writhe.

'It's a sad thing to lose Nik, and Jochan's man,' she said. 'We're spreading thinner.'

I nodded. That was true enough. With Will and Sir Eland and now Jochan and Cutter holding the boarding-houses, Nik the Knife and Ganna both dead and Brak still guarding my aunt, Hari wounded, and Cookpot effectively retired, I was down to eleven men stationed at the Tanner's Arms, not counting Billy the Boy or Anne herself.

That was enough, for now, and it was still a lot to have sleeping under one roof. All the same, the more businesses I took back the thinner I would be spread, and a business once taken had to be held or I wouldn't keep it for long.

'Those are the times we live in,' I said. 'We'll do, for now. Later, perhaps I'll put the word about the streets that there's work for likely lads who can follow orders and know which end of a blade to hold.'

'How will the others take that?' Anne asked. 'We have a trust, a comradeship. Losing comrades is hard, and Nik at least was well liked. Bringing new faces into that . . . I don't know, Tomas.'

I shook my head. 'I don't mean as Pious Men,' I said. 'Not straightaway, certainly. Perhaps in time, but that would have to be seen. Door guards and runners and watchmen, though, they can be hired lads.'

'I suppose they can,' she said, obviously giving the matter some thought. 'It'll be like Messia. We took in new men there, to fill the holes in the line.'

She frowned, and I knew she had remembered that we had also taken in Billy the Boy at Messia. She winced again, rubbing her leg under the table.

'How bad are you hurt?' I asked her.

She shrugged. 'I got clipped in the thigh with a mace,' she said. 'It only got the meat, though. Nothing's broken. I'll heal.'

'You'll have a good black bruise to show Rosie tomorrow.' I smiled, but when Anne looked up at me I wished I had held my peace about that.

'I don't . . .' she started, and trailed off.

'Our Lady forgave you your guilt,' I reminded her, keeping my voice low. This was a private matter, after all, a matter between a priest and one of his faithful, and nobody should be overhearing that. 'You didn't cross the river in Abingon, and you didn't cross it tonight, but I can make no promises for tomorrow. Live, Bloody Anne, while you have the chance.'

She put her head down and took a long, shuddering breath. 'Aye,' she said after a moment, and lifted her face again. 'Perhaps I will.'

She drained her brandy in a single swallow and went through to the kitchen to wash the blood from her hands at last.

Chapter 22

Things settled down after that, for a few days. Anne wasn't the only one who'd been hurt at Slaughterhouse Narrow, and everyone needed time to rest and heal. There was grief for Nik the Knife, but he wasn't the first friend these men had lost, and they knew he wouldn't be the last. Pawl the tailor and his boy came by again, with a cart this time, and everyone collected their fine new clothes. With that, and regular trips to Ernst the barber up on Trader's Row, I had the lot of them looking like proper Pious Men. That was good.

We had taken back the two boarding-houses, in addition to the Tanner's Arms, and money was starting to come in. I had fresh supplies brought into the Tanner's, food and beer and brandy, and Will the Wencher kept good on his promise; when Godsday came around again and he presented me with his accounts, I had to admit that he had done what he said he would do. He had taken six marks, not five, and turned a good profit on them. A quarter of that profit was his, then.

I heard confessions in the morning, and that afternoon I made Will a partner in the Chandler's Narrow house. Anne hadn't come to say confession, but I knew she had been up to Will's place every day since the battle at Slaughterhouse Narrow and she looked the better for it. I was pleased to see her happy.

All was well, except one thing.

I had told Old Kurt that I would bring Billy the Boy to him, and I hadn't done that.

Billy seemed happy enough, and he and Hari had found a friendship somewhere. Whether it was born that night when Billy floated over Hari's dying body and done whatever it was he had done, or whether it was rooted in the extra treats that Hari produced for him in the kitchen I didn't know, but then I dare say it didn't matter either. It was good to see and I didn't like to take it away from either of them, but I knew the thing had to be done.

The day after Godsday, Anne and I took Billy the Boy through the stable yard and along the alleys to the path beside the river. Anne was still limping from the blow she had taken at Slaughterhouse Narrow and I had suggested that she didn't need to come, but to her mind I was wrong about that.

That made the going slow, but we walked to the Wheels anyway with Billy the Boy between us. We might have looked like a family, if Anne had been wearing a kirtle under her cloak and not the men's britches and shirt and coat that she insisted on. I looked down at Billy, and thought that perhaps it would be no bad thing, to have a family. Not with Bloody Anne, though; I knew that could never happen and truth be told, I wouldn't have wanted it to. We were friends, and that was all. My thoughts wandered to Ailsa, and I thought perhaps that might be a different matter.

That was a fool's thinking and no mistake. Working for the crown sickened me enough without starting to think about a Queen's Man in that way. It was out of the question, I knew, yet I seemed to keep doing it. I turned my attention to the alley that led up to Old Kurt's door. There was a fresh rat nailed to the door, I noticed, not more than a few hours old by the look of it.

'He's in, then,' I said, nodding to the rat.

'Aye,' Anne said.

I knocked on the door and called out the words. 'Wisdom sought is wisdom bought, and I have coin to pay.'

Old Kurt opened the door and grinned at us. 'Tomas Piety and the fine lady,' he said, 'and this young gentleman too!'

Billy the Boy watched Old Kurt, his face expressionless. After a moment he turned and looked up at me. 'I'll be staying here,' he announced.

I blinked at him. That was the same way he had decided in his mind that Ailsa would be staying at the Tanner's Arms. He had been right about that, but this might be a different matter. It wasn't something I had intended to bring up so soon, or quite so abruptly as that.

'I said I'd have a look at him,' Old Kurt said. 'No more than that, Tomas.'

'The lad needs teaching,' I said, 'and he's keen to get started, that's all. You know how boys are when they've an idea in their heads. Can we come inside?'

Kurt nodded and led us through to his dusty parlour where the sword of a king hung over the fireplace. So he said, anyway. Billy sat down on a low stool in front of the cold grate and drew his knees up to his chin. He looked at home there.

'Hmmm,' Kurt said, looking down at the lad.

'We proved he's not a witch,' I said, although to my mind we had proved nothing of the sort, 'but he's something. Touched by the goddess, aye, but Our Lady doesn't heal men. Apparently Billy does, and that must mean he's got the cunning in him.'

'Perhaps he has,' Kurt admitted. He sat down and looked at Bloody Anne. 'What does the fine lady say?'

'She says she'll stab you if you call her that again,' Anne growled. 'My name's Bloody Anne.'

Kurt snorted but made no more of it. 'Well and good,' he said. 'And what do you say, Bloody Anne?'

She took a breath and shook her head. This didn't sit well with her, I knew that, but she knew what needed to be done.

'Teach him,' she said.

'This is no house of magicians,' Kurt said. 'He won't learn no philosophy from me, nor mathematics beyond his 'rithmetic. I don't scry the stars like they do in Dannsburg, nor summon up demons and make pacts with them neither. That's high magic, and I don't do that.'

I doubted that the magicians in Dannsburg did that either, but then I wouldn't know. I nodded and held my peace about that.

'What *can* you teach him, Old Kurt?'

Kurt snorted again and waved at the fireplace. There was a sharp crack, and the coals in the grate caught and burned with an acrid smoke that his chimney did a poor job of removing. Anne hissed and took a step back, her hands going to her daggers.

'Easy, Bloody Anne,' I cautioned her. 'This is what we're here for.'

'I can teach him the cunning, if he has the wits and the will to learn,' Kurt said. 'Cunning is about real things in the real world, not stars and demons and debating high ideas. Sorcery, the magicians call that. Low magic. They look down their noses at it as being beneath them. Maybe it is, with all their money. A man as rich as a magician has servants to lay his fire for him, but a cunning man don't so he makes his life easier the best way he can. A cunning man can set fires and quench them, mend hurts and cause them. A cunning man can tell you things you've forgotten you knew, and divine what tomorrow might bring.'

'What do you think, Billy?' I asked the lad. 'Do you want to learn from Old Kurt here?'

Billy glanced at the fire and it abruptly went out, the last of the smoke curling slowly into the room.

'I'll be staying here,' he said again, and it seemed his mind was set on it.

I nodded and looked at Kurt. He had a frown on his face and was staring hard at Billy. It occurred to me that perhaps it hadn't been Kurt who put the fire out. The old man cleared his throat like he was about to say something, perhaps change his mind, and I couldn't have that.

'You'll want paying,' I said.

'I will,' Kurt agreed, and maybe it was talk of money that swayed him in the end. 'A silver mark a week, for my time and his keep. Not a copper less, and I won't dicker on this. If I'm teaching the lad I'll have little time for anything else, and why should I be short of pocket? A mark a week, Piety, and I'll take six weeks up front or you can fuck off.'

That was a lot of money, but I had it. The price wasn't something anyone else needed to know about, which meant I could draw on my hidden coin for it and no one would be the wiser. I nodded.

'All right,' I said. 'But you keep this between us, Old Kurt. The Pious Men know Billy is coming to learn from you, but the price has to be kept a secret and it has to stay that way. Does that sound fair?'

Kurt nodded. 'That's fair,' he said.

He stood and spat in his palm, and I spat in mine and we shook hands on it, the old way. I dug in my pouch and took out six silver marks, and gave them to him. He nodded again, and it was done.

That was how Billy the Boy started on the path to becoming a magician.

Chapter 23

When we got back to the Tanner's Arms my aunt was waiting for me, sitting in the common room with a mug of beer in her hand. She had the same look on her face that she had always got when I was a child and about to receive a switching.

'Aunt Enaid, what a pleasure,' I said.

Brak was standing behind her chair like a bodyguard, and his expression said he felt somewhere between proud and foolish to be doing it. I hadn't seen him since Enaid had got her house back, and I could only wonder what old stories she had been filling his head with of an evening.

'Come and sit down, Tomas, and talk to your fat old aunt,' she said, and it wasn't so much an invitation as an order.

I did as she said, while Bloody Anne disappeared into the back to put her weapons away.

'How are you, Auntie?' I asked her. 'I hope the house is adequate.'

'My house is fine and never mind that,' she said, fixing me with a glare from her one bright eye. She lowered her voice and leaned forward across the table toward me. 'Who is that tart behind our bar, and where the fuck did she come from?'

I cleared my throat and offered up a silent prayer to Our Lady that Ailsa's hearing wasn't good enough to catch Enaid's words.

'Ailsa is a barmaid, not a tart,' I said. 'She's working here, and she's doing a good job.'

'That's not all she's doing, to hear your men talk,' Enaid said.

She grabbed her crotch for emphasis in a way that immediately reminded me that she had been a soldier herself. All the same, that wasn't what I wanted to see from my own aging aunt.

'Men talk,' I said, trying to shrug it off. 'What of it?'

'I'm disappointed in you, Tomas Piety,' she said. 'I thought perhaps you and Anne, yes, but this? You and some foreign tart off the tea ships?'

'She's not a tart,' I said again, starting to get angry with her now, 'and she's not off the tea ships. And you thought it would be Anne? No, Auntie. Never Anne.'

'If you can't see past a scar, then I raised you wrong, Tomas,' she growled at me. 'Anne's a good woman, I can see that.'

'Aye, she is,' I agreed, 'and she's a good friend too. Anne doesn't enjoy male company, Auntie, not in that way.'

Aunt Enaid looked at me for a moment, then turned and spat on the floor. 'Bugger,' she said.

'The fuck is it to you, anyway?'

'I know how strange women can get to a man,' she said. 'I don't want that one whispering ideas into your ear on the pillow at night and making you soft in the head.'

My head had never been on the same pillow as Ailsa's, but as I watched her serving drinks and moving among the men I had to admit to myself that I wished it had. There was something about her that fascinated me, and it wasn't just her looks. I was impressed by the way she had adapted so smoothly to our way of life, and by the easy way she had with the crew and the customers alike. All the lads seemed to love her, and that was how it should be. If she were really my woman, I thought, that would be a good thing for me and for the Pious Men. She would make any boss a fine wife. It was out of the question, I knew that, but that didn't stop me wanting it to be otherwise.

It was a long while before I got rid of Aunt Enaid, nearly midnight, and by then Brak was having to help her walk. She had one hand on her stick and the other on his arm, and she was still swaying visibly as she tottered toward the door. It was amazing how much one old woman could drink, when she put her mind to it and it was free.

As the door started to close behind them I saw Enaid's hand move from Brak's arm to his arse, but I pretended that I hadn't. She was almost thrice his age, but that was between them, to my mind, and none of my business. I knew what my aunt was like, and I just hoped that Brak understood what sort of woman she was. I sighed and looked around the room. There were no customers left in there now, just Pious Men and Ailsa. I nodded to Black Billy and told him to close up for the night.

Ailsa was racking dirty glasses and taking them through to the kitchen, and I got up and followed her. When I came in Hari picked up his stick and limped out, giving us our privacy.

'Your aunt doesn't like me any, Mr Piety.' Ailsa giggled.

I kicked the door shut behind me and looked at her. 'No,' I said. 'She doesn't, but she'll learn to live with it.'

'She had better,' Ailsa said, using her own voice now that the door was closed – or at least what I assumed was her own voice. Perhaps it was another act. I didn't know. 'The last thing I need is that old war-horse making trouble. Everybody else has accepted our pretence, and she needs to learn to do the same.'

'She will,' I said.

'Never mind that now,' Ailsa said. 'There's news. The Skanians have noticed your return, which by now is hardly surprising. I don't think they'll try to retake the boarding-houses, but only because they don't care about them and you've chosen too good a defensive position for them to do it easily, which I'm pleased about. They still hold the Golden Chains and I think that's the only one of your businesses they really wanted. They'll try to draw you out, though, to stretch you and force you to overreach until your supply lines break and you suddenly find you haven't got enough men to hold your territory any more.'

I nodded. 'I worked that out for myself,' I said.

'What are you going to do?'

'Consolidate,' I said. 'Build up the three businesses that I have, maybe recruit some more men if I think I'll need them. Now that there's income again I can start to trickle some of my stored funds through the businesses, make the money look legitimate. It's a slow game, but I know how to play it.'

'No,' Ailsa said, her voice turning sharp and cold. 'You really don't.'

That made me look at her, and I noticed the hard set to her jaw as she sat down at the kitchen table. She waved me to a seat as though she were receiving me in her own parlour. *This* was what working for the crown was like, being fucking bossed around and made to feel small in my own place of business, and a pretty face didn't change that.

It was this, or hang.

I swallowed it like bitter medicine, but that didn't mean I liked it.

'How so?'

'You think small, Tomas, but then you're a small man,' she said. 'We play on a greater stage than you can imagine. The *last* thing you should do is consolidate. You need to expand, fast and hard, while they don't expect it.'

'Which is the opposite of what you just said,' I pointed out.

'No, it isn't,' she snapped. 'What I said was that they will *try* to draw you out and overstretch you, not that you should allow it to happen. Let them think you're playing into their hands. Take back everything you had, as hard and as fast as you can. I have the means to fund it, if you need to hire men and buy weapons. I have access to men, for that matter, trained men we can slip in among the new recruits if we have to. *Dangerous* men. The Skanians must be stopped, Tomas.'

I like to think that I'm not a fool, but Ailsa seemed to be trying to make me feel like one. I didn't care for it. Not at all.

I leaned across the table until I was very close to her. 'I hate to tell you this,' I started quietly, 'but I don't give a *fuck* about your Skanians!'

She didn't even blink when I shouted in her face. She just held my gaze and slowly put a finger to her lips. 'Shhhhh,' she said, as though she were speaking to a child. 'I understand, Tomas. This is my business, not yours, and you've been dragged into it against your will. But know this – things have changed, and we have moved beyond *could* and *might* and *possibly* and into uncomfortable certainty. If we cannot stop this infiltration, there will be another war and *we will lose*. There will be another Abingon, right here in our own country. If you think that what you did in the south was harsh work, you have no idea what the Skanians would do to *us* in war. In war, and after they have *won* that war.'

I swallowed, my mouth suddenly gone as dry as dust.

I would never forget Abingon, but it was over and done with and it had been so far away it almost felt like a dream now, some nightmare from which I had awoken. I looked into Ailsa's dark eyes, and it seemed I could see the flames of battle reflected in them, the mouths of the cannon looking back at me from her inky pupils.

I reached out for my brandy.

I managed to stop my hand from shaking, but only just.

'Tell me what you want me to do,' I said, 'and I'll think on it.'

Ailsa started to talk, and I to listen.

I couldn't sleep that night. My thoughts kept going back to what Ailsa had said. *There will be another Abingon, right here.* I couldn't allow that, not if it was in my power to help stop it. These were my streets and my people, and I wouldn't see them reduced to the smoking rubble and rotting corpses that we had left behind us in the south.

That was well enough, but I knew my crew wouldn't agree.

These weren't imaginative men, and to their minds they were good and done with this queen who had dragged them off to war against their will. When the time came for me to announce that we would be taking back another business, I knew the crew would set to it. If word got out we were doing it because an agent of the crown said so, though, then they'd raise the gods over it and I would lose half of them at least. These men weren't patriotic, or overly concerned with what the law might or might not say. They'd have been little enough use to me as Pious Men if they had been. No, these were men out for themselves, trying to put the war behind them and make something fresh of their lives.

I had promised them they would get rich and have all the good things in life. Perhaps I could still keep that promise, but if they thought I was working for anyone but myself they would come to doubt my words, and fast. People expect things of a businessman. One of those things is self-interest, and if I did this I would have to make sure it looked like I was acting for myself and the Pious Men, and no one else.

Whatever happened, this wasn't a decision I could share with Anne or Jochan or anyone else, not even Aunt Enaid. Sometimes a leader has to keep things to himself and make the hard decisions alone. We had come together as soldiers, and in the army you don't get to vote on decisions. Orders come down the line and they are obeyed, and that's just the way of things.

It was nearly light. I kicked my blankets off and padded to the window, looking out into the pre-dawn grey of the street below. Dew glistened on the cobbles, making them shine like dark pearls. I leaned forward and rested my forehead on the inside of the pane, feeling the cold glass against my skin.

Abingon.

I remembered smoke and dust and noise, the siege cannon firing day and night to bring down the great walls. There had been flames everywhere, in the city. Disease was rampant. Wounds got infected and men died screaming in their beds. Supplies were lost or looted, and men starved. Even Cookpot couldn't produce forage from thin air, but he had caught rats for us to eat rather than see us go hungry. The water was almost always bad, and it wasn't uncommon to see men fighting with liquid shit running down their legs from their poisoned guts.

Abingon, where I had seen men driven so mad by the constant noise of the guns that they didn't know their own names any more. I remembered a fellow brought before me for confession, dragged between two of the colonel's bullyboys. He was a man broken with battle shock who had fled the field the day before when he simply couldn't stand it another second longer. They brought him to me to say his confession, but all he could do was weep.

Afterward, they executed him for cowardice.

No, there couldn't be another Abingon. Not here, not now.

Not ever.

It had been horrific and yet we had been on the winning side, those of us who had laid siege to Abingon. What it had been like for the defenders, the besieged, I couldn't even bring myself to imagine. They were eating their own dead in Abingon, before it was over, and we'd heard tales of children being killed for meat by the starving soldiers.

We will lose.

You haven't truly known Hell until you have seen a city under siege. *That* was what would happen here, if the Skanians got their way.

I would do *anything* to prevent a repeat of Abingon, especially here in my own city. Sometimes a man has to balance two evils in his hands, and choose the lighter one. If that meant working for the crown, then so be it.

Those were the times we lived in.

The decision made, I went back to my blankets and I managed to sleep at last.

That was how I gave my loyalty to the Queen's Men.

Part Two

Chapter 24

Winter had come to Ellinburg, and brought bitterness with it. It was six months since we had returned home from the war.

I was sitting at one end of a long table in the private dining room of a fine inn on Trader's Row. That was neutral territory, outside of my streets and anyone else's bar the governor himself. At the other end of the table, staring back at me, was Ma Aditi.

She was a fat woman with perhaps forty years to her, richly dressed with thick black hair that framed her dusky brown Alarian complexion. She styled herself Mother, but if she had ever borne a child I didn't know of it.

Bloody Anne sat at my right hand and Jochan at my left. The arrangement wasn't lost on him, I knew, but he was becoming used to it. Bloody Anne had earned her place ten times over, these last six months. Fat Luka stood behind my chair, draped in his fine new clothes, and he leaned forward to whisper softly in my ear.

'The one in the purple shirt,' he said. 'Gregor.'

I nodded without taking my eyes off Ma Aditi, and Luka straightened again and rested his big, strong hands on the back of my chair.

I glanced at the man he had indicated, the one seated at Ma Aditi's left hand. He was the one who was taking Luka's bribes, then. Our man inside the Gutcutters. I wondered if Aditi had anyone inside the Pious Men yet, although I was sure she must have. More to the point, I wondered who it was.

One of the new recruits, I was certain. The old crew was getting thin now – we had lost another three men in the bitter fighting to reclaim my businesses, and those who were left were loyal to the bone. Even Sir Eland the false knight had finally proven himself when an agent of the Gutcutters offered him gold to betray me. Sir Eland had brought me his head in a wet sack, and when I clapped him on the shoulder and thanked him for his loyalty he almost wept. I thought that perhaps all Sir Eland really wanted was a place in the world, and to my mind now he had found one.

To date we had had no open blood on the streets with the Gutcutters, though, and I wanted to keep it that way. For now, at least. I tried to gauge Ma Aditi's mind on that and found that I couldn't. Her face was expressionless, her plump hands folded on the table in front of her, where the light of the oil lamps made her many golden rings shine softly.

'Ma Aditi,' I said, breaking the silence at last. 'I am glad to see you returned safely from the war.'

I was glad of no such thing, of course, and truth be told, I had prayed that she had died in Abingon. Our Lady doesn't answer prayers, though, and Ma Aditi had returned to Ellinburg a month after I had, riding in at the head of her surviving men. This was the first time we had spoken, in a carefully brokered meeting that had taken Fat Luka three months to arrange to his satisfaction and that of her agent.

She nodded slowly. 'Mr Piety,' she said. 'I give thanks to the Many-Headed God for your life.'

I showed her a thin smile. The Many-Headed God was an Alarian god, not one I knew, but there was a temple to him up by the docks that served the traders off the tea ships. Perhaps Aditi held to him. I wouldn't know, but I doubted it somehow.

'Let those be the last two lies we tell each other today,' I said. 'Are we not both people of business?'

Aditi frowned, her fleshy face creasing until her small black eyes seemed almost to disappear into the folds that surrounded them. 'We are,' she agreed.

I could feel her thinking, trying to work out my intentions. The form of these rare meetings between rival bosses was usually to tell pleasant lies while each plotted how best to stab the other in the back. I had come close to being candid, then, and I think that surprised her.

'Then let us speak like people of business,' I said. 'We are no nobles of the court, you and I, to be hiding our knives behind smiles and sharp courtesies. I have my interests and you have yours, but as long as they don't conflict, then I see no reason why we can't exist together in Ellinburg. Do you?'

'The Stink is yours, the Wheels is mine,' she said. 'That hasn't changed.'

'No, it hasn't,' I agreed. 'But tell me this – how many of your businesses did you find had been taken away from you when you returned from the south?'

Her mouth tightened in an angry line and the man seated to her left, this Gregor, who was wearing a purple shirt under his fine black coat, leaned close to whisper in her ear. She thought for a moment, then nodded.

'I know the Pious Men weren't to blame in that,' she said.

'No more than the Gutcutters were to blame for the businesses *I* lost during the war,' I said. 'We have a mutual enemy.'

'Hauer,' she spat. 'Always that fat slug wants more, and more. Taxes and bribes, permits and inspections and fees for this and fees for that. Always more, every year.'

I shook my head slowly. 'The governor is the same man we knew before the war,' I agreed, 'but why would he take businesses away from us that he would then have to staff and run himself? Far easier to just tighten the screw on taxes, instead. Hauer isn't behind this.'

'Then who?'

I recited the carefully prepared speech Ailsa had given me before the meeting. 'There are new people in the city,' I said. 'Opportunists, from far northern towns that the recruiters never got to. They're backed by someone else, though, someone big from outside Ellinburg who wants to take our livelihoods away from us.'

'Do you know who?'

'No,' I lied. 'But that doesn't mean we can't hurt them. I've taken back all but one of my businesses now, and from what I hear you have been doing much the same thing. How have you fared with that?'

Ma Aditi narrowed her eyes, as though she suspected a trap. Again, the man in the purple shirt leaned close to whisper in her ear, feeding her the version of the truth that Fat Luka had bought and paid for with my gold.

'I have lost men,' she admitted, after a moment. 'You?'

I nodded solemnly. 'There have been deaths,' I agreed. 'Too many Pious Men have crossed the river this last six months.'

I had lost five men since my return to Ellinburg, all told. Six, if you counted Hari, who would never fight or walk properly again. From what Luka's whisperers told me, Ma Aditi's losses had been heavier, though. Much heavier, I suspected.

The Skanians had concentrated their efforts more in her territory than mine, in the Wheels where the factories and the tanneries were. They wanted the infrastructure of the city, Ailsa had explained to me, and they wanted its workforce. They had taken my businesses because they could, but they never much wanted them. Except for one, anyway. The one they still held.

Ma Aditi sat back in her chair and gestured to the man at her right hand, a big scarred brute in a voluminous coat and silver-studded black leather doublet whom I didn't recognise. He was new to the Gutcutters, Luka had told me. I could only assume she had brought him back from Abingon with her, a recruit from whatever crew she had ended up in charge of down there, but I didn't know for sure.

Strange that he should be at her right hand, if so.

He reached into his fine coat and produced a long clay pipe, passing it to her. She lit a taper from the lamp on the table between us and puffed her pipe into life, and the sickly sweet smell of poppy resin reached my nose.

The man obviously wasn't the only thing that had come back from Abingon with her. I saw Bloody Anne's eyes narrow with disapproval. Poppy resin had been a problem in Abingon, and we all recognised the smell of it.

It had been known in Ellinburg before the war – I had traded in unlicensed resin myself, of course, with the first Queen's Man I had known, which was how the bastard snared me in the first place – but it had been rare, and I had only sold it to doctors who used it for treating those in unbearable pain. In Abingon it had been used for the same purpose, to start with, until men discovered that smoking it when you weren't half dead from wounds made you feel good.

Men smoked resin to make themselves feel good, to escape the horrors in their minds, to let them sleep at night. Eventually they discovered that once you start smoking poppy resin, you can't stop.

Then there had been problems.

Since the war we had been seeing more and more of it in Ellinburg, and seeing what it did to people. There were resin smokers driven onto the streets, having sold everything they owned to feed their habits. Petty crimes were the highest I had ever seen them, and even on my own streets my newly recruited watchmen were hard-pressed to keep honest households safe.

Those who smoked resin and turned to crime to feed their habits, I ejected from the Stink.

Those I caught selling it, I killed.

I looked down the table at Ma Aditi, at the tendrils of blue smoke curling up from her nostrils, and I knew this meeting had been a waste of time.

'She wouldn't have helped us take the Golden Chains even if I could have brokered a truce between the Pious Men and her Gutcutters,' I explained to Ailsa that night, in her room next to mine above the Tanner's Arms.

It was after midnight by then, and the tavern had closed over an hour ago. Snow swirled over the stable yard below Ailsa's window and settled gently on the wooden frame.

'So what did you say to her?' Ailsa snapped in her cut-crystal Dannsburg accent. '"I'm terribly sorry but you seem to be a poppy smoker so we can't work together, goodbye"?'

She was sitting in the only chair in the room, knitting by the light of an oil lamp on the windowsill.

I took a swallow from the brandy bottle in my hand and glared at her.

'No, Ailsa. I didn't,' I said. 'I spoke the platitudes to her, how I was supposed to. I used the backup speech you gave me in case it all went to the whores, which it fucking well did. "Yes, Ma Aditi, we're all friends and fellow businessmen. No, Ma Aditi, I'm not looking to take over the Wheels. Thank you, Ma Aditi, it was an honour. Bend over, Ma Aditi, and I'll kiss your fat fucking arse." When I think how much Luka paid that purple-shirted bastard Gregor and he never mentioned she was a *fucking* resin smoker . . . !'

I turned and slammed a fist into the wall beside the door, cracking the plaster and hurting my hand with equal success.

'Be calm, Tomas,' Ailsa said, which irritated me so much I could almost have thrown the bottle at her.

Almost.

Her knitting needles clicked together, the sound boring through my head and making me feel like live things were crawling around inside my ears. I took a long swallow of brandy and a shuddering breath.

'It wouldn't have worked. You see that, don't you?' I said. 'She's probably their best fucking customer by now.'

'Yes, of course I see that,' Ailsa said. 'I'm thinking, that's all.'

'Well, think quickly,' I said. 'We're supposed to be taking the Chains back next Godsday, and now we've no Gutcutters to support us and no fucking plan.'

'Godsday is still five days away,' Ailsa said. She sighed and put down her knitting. 'Without the Gutcutters, an all-out assault like we had planned is out of the question. We simply don't have the numbers for it.'

I clenched my teeth. I knew by then that Ailsa often thought out loud, but to my mind a lot of the time that sounded like she was explaining my own business to me as though she were addressing a simple child. I knew that was just her way, but all the same I had to remind myself not to take ill against her for it.

'I realise that,' I said, forcing my voice to stay calm.

'There are ways and means, Tomas. There always are,' she said. She looked up at me then, and smiled brightly in the way that she did when she was about to change the subject with a lurch so hard it gave me a headache. 'You should go and see Billy tomorrow.'

'Aye,' I said, happy for anything that steered the conversation away from the evening's failure of a meeting with Ma Aditi. 'Perhaps I'll do that.'

'Take him seriously, Tomas,' Ailsa cautioned me. 'You haven't seen him since he began his time with the magician and he may seem different to you now, but see that you take him seriously. The time may come when we might need him.'

We were back to *may* and *might* again, I noticed. The habit of the Queen's Men of never speaking in certainties was chafing at me, I had to admit.

I said good night to her and went to my own room to sleep.

That wasn't easy, but with the help of the rest of the brandy I managed it in the end.

Chapter 25

I don't know why I took Bloody Anne with me the next morning, but it seemed like the right thing to do. She was the one who had a problem with Billy the Boy in the first place, of course, and without her worries he would never have ended up at Old Kurt's.

Going alone was out of the question, especially after my useless meeting with Ma Aditi the day before, but I could have taken any of the men with me as a bodyguard. I didn't, though. I brought Bloody Anne and no one else.

That was risky, these days. The last time we had trod the riverside path into the Wheels I had only been back in Ellinburg a short time and word about that had yet to completely get around. That was then, though. Anne and I had managed to pass for any scruffy returning veterans wandering the bad parts of the city, but I couldn't do that any more.

Now I was Tomas Piety again, head of the Pious Men, and *everyone* knew who I was. By rights I should have had six armed men at my back wherever I went, but we were heading into Gutcutter territory and it wasn't on official Pious Men business. I had told Anne once before that the Pious Men wouldn't enter the Wheels in force until we meant it, and that was still true. All the same I could feel the eyes on us, watching us from the grimy windows of the wooden tenements we passed.

The river path was treacherous in the winter, and thin skins of ice floated downriver past us. It was freezing down by the water, and despite our fine coats, cloaks and gloves, both of us were chilled to the bone by the time we reached Old Kurt's front door. The rat nailed to it looked to be frozen solid.

I raised a hand to knock, drawing breath to call out the words, but the door opened before I touched it. Billy the Boy stood in the entrance looking up at us.

'Tomas,' he said. 'Bloody Anne.'

I nodded. 'How are you, Billy?'

He had the first fluff of a moustache on his upper lip, I noticed, and he looked to me as though he had grown almost an inch for each of the months he had been with Old Kurt. Not literally perhaps, but truth be told, the lad wasn't all that far off my height already. All the same he looked to be painfully thin under his loose shirt and britches. I thought perhaps his thirteenth nameday had come and gone unmarked while he was away, and it pained me to have missed his coming of age.

'Well enough,' he said. 'You'll be coming in.'

As always with him it was a statement, not a question, and I wondered just how prescient Billy the Boy was. Did Our Lady truly speak to him, telling him what was to come? I wouldn't know. Perhaps it was the cunning in him, or perhaps he was just a good judge of human nature, or just mad. Whatever it was, he was right.

'We'd like that, Billy,' I said.

He nodded and stepped back to let us into Old Kurt's house.

He led Anne and me through into Kurt's parlour, where the old man was sitting in his chair close to a fire that burned fiercely in the grate. Kurt looked older than I remembered, pale and drawn. That was passing strange, to my mind, as he seemed to have aged little in the years between my childhood and my return to Ellinburg. Life catches up with all men in the end, I supposed.

He looked up at us and grinned his ratty grin.

'Tomas Piety and the fine . . . and Bloody Anne,' he said, and I knew that he had remembered Anne's words. 'How fare you?'

'Well enough,' I said.

I took the stool across from him, there being no other chair in the room, and Anne stood behind me with her hands never far from her daggers. I knew she didn't trust Kurt even now, and I thought she still wasn't easy in her mind with what was being done in this house.

Kurt laughed, a sound full of phlegm and age. 'Well enough,' he repeated. 'Well enough that you're dressed like a lord and have the whole of the Stink bowing and scraping to you again. You and Aditi both, back from your war, and it's as though nothing ever happened.'

I thought of Jochan, and Cookpot, and my own bleak memories, and I shook my head. 'It happened,' I said. 'We survived it, that's all.'

'Well and good,' Kurt said. 'You look rich. Maybe I should put my prices up.'

'We agreed on the price,' I said. 'A mark a week for his tuition and keep. That's more than fair.'

'Well, growing boys eat a lot,' Kurt said, and he looked evasive now. His gaze shifted from the fire to his boots to me to the door, his eyes moving like restless animals.

'What is it, Kurt?'

He coughed, and I realised Billy was standing in the doorway listening to us.

'Boy,' Kurt said, his voice quavering a little despite his attempt to put authority into it. 'Go upstairs and fetch your notes.'

Billy nodded and left the room, and a moment later I heard his footsteps on the stairs. I looked at Kurt and raised my eyebrows as he beckoned me close with a surprising urgency. I leaned toward him to listen.

'Three marks a week or you're having him back.'

'What's the problem?' I asked him.

Kurt grabbed me by the back of the neck and dragged me closer, so he could whisper in my ear. I held up a hand to tell Bloody Anne to be calm, and I listened.

'Touched by a goddess, my wrinkly cock,' Kurt hissed in my ear, so quiet I was sure Anne couldn't hear him. 'He gives me the fear, and I don't say that lightly of anyone. No unschooled lad should be that strong. The boy's fucking *possessed!*'

I remembered the day we had first brought Billy to Kurt's house, how Kurt had lit the fire with cunning and a gesture and how Billy had put it out again with just a look. I hadn't known he could do that, and it had been clear that Kurt hadn't expected it either. I wondered what Billy could do now, after half a year of teaching.

I had always been a little bit scared of Billy myself, truth be told, although I could never have clearly said why. I knew Sir Eland walked in fear of him too, even more so after Billy's visit to Chandler's Narrow, but I didn't know what had happened that night and I never expected to learn the answer. I had said my confessions to Billy, during the war, and that was because one night in Abingon after I had done things that troubled me he had come to me in my tent and told me that I would confess.

He had *told* me.

There was never any question, with Billy. If he said a thing would happen, it did. He said I would confess to him, and I did, and I still didn't know why. Touched by the goddess, I had thought. That was how I had explained it to myself, and to the men, and that was well enough. That made Billy holy, in their eyes.

Holy and possessed were perhaps two sides of the same coin, but one was acceptable, laudable even, and the other very much wasn't. I knew I couldn't let this pass, not when that would mean the risk of others hearing it.

'I don't want to hear that word again,' I whispered in Kurt's ear. 'Three marks a week if that's what it takes to keep your mouth shut but not a copper more, and that price will never go up again, whatever he does. Don't test me on this, Old Kurt. The boy is *holy*, you mark me on that, and that's the way it's staying. Understand?'

Old Kurt nodded sharply and let go of me just as Billy started back down the stairs. Three marks a week was enough money to make me wince. All the same it was coin well spent, to my mind. I turned to see Billy standing in the doorway clutching a great black leather book in his arms, his unblinking stare taking in the three of us.

Where is the difference between holy and possessed? I wondered. When does miracle become magic, magic become witchcraft? Is it in the nature of the deed itself, or in the eye of the beholder? Is it decided in the telling after the fact, and if so does it depend on who does that telling? Magic was magic, but then I wouldn't know. That was a philosophical question, I supposed, and this was no time for philosophy.

'What have you got there, Billy?' I asked him.

'Show your Uncle Tomas what you've been working on, boy,' Kurt said.

Uncle Tomas. That was something I had never been called before. Jochan was my only sibling and he had never fathered a child, any more than I had myself. It sounded well to my ears, I had to admit. It would be a good thing, to be an uncle. Perhaps a better one, to be a father.

I got to my feet and Billy opened the book and held it for me to see. The thick vellum pages were covered in his childish handwriting, scrawled with notes and diagrams that I didn't have time to read before he turned the pages. All I could think was that that book must have cost a pile of silver, even unprinted. A book like that was well out of the reach of a common man, that was for certain. It was the sort of book that guildmasters wrote in, and that I supposed nobles did as well. Perhaps Old Kurt wasn't overcharging me all that much after all, if he was giving Billy things like that.

I nodded as though I knew what I was looking at, wanting to please Billy. The lad had obviously been working hard, although I couldn't divine what at. The cunning was as far beyond me as it was most other people and I've no shame in admitting it.

Maybe one person in ten thousand has it in them to learn the cunning, if that. There had been sixty-five thousand of us at Abingon and we had had two cunning men and three women among us that I knew of. The magicians of Dannsburg hadn't gone to war, of course. War magic was sorcery, and as Old Kurt had said, they looked down on that as beneath them. Our five cunning folk had all died in battle, fighting for their country. It hadn't been beneath *them* to serve the crown, I noted.

'Look at this one, Uncle Tomas,' Billy said, turning the page to show me a diagram of almost impossible complexity.

I stared at it, trying to work out exactly what I was looking at. I found I couldn't really focus on it. Billy had just called me Uncle like it was the most natural thing in the world. I kept hearing that word in my head, rolling over and over like distant thunder. The image on the page seemed to squirm and shift even as I looked at it. I blinked and put a hand to my head.

Uncle.

The image moved, the lines redrawing themselves across the vellum before my eyes. I saw words I couldn't pronounce, fading as fast as I made them out. I saw maps, contours and hills and buildings, lines of supply and attack and defence. I saw strategic plans and armies arrayed across sketched terrain. I saw Ailsa's face, staring up at me. I saw a bird's-eye view of the Stink, of the Narrows and the houses that bordered them.

I saw cannon, positioned on the hill by the convent.

I saw what would happen to Ellinburg, if Abingon came here.

Ailsa.

Cannon.

Smoke boiled across the page, lit red from within by the cannon's murderous roar.

Uncle, they bellowed.

Uncle!

I saw the face of Our Lady, looking back at me.

Merciless.

Uncle!

Anne caught me before I hit the floor, her strong hands in my armpits. She lowered me back onto the stool by the fire and crouched down in front of me, looking intently into my face.

'Tomas? Can you hear me?'

I shook my head and blinked. I could see Anne's face, her scar puckering as she frowned with concern. I pinched the bridge of my nose between thumb and forefinger, squeezing my eyes closed for a moment before I opened them again and nodded at her.

'I hear you, Bloody Anne,' I said.

I looked up at Old Kurt and saw him staring back at me, a bleak look on his face. 'Billy drew that one himself,' he said. 'I never showed him how.'

'What is it, Billy?' I asked.

The lad shrugged. 'A picture,' he said. 'I drew it.'

'It's a wyrd glyph,' Old Kurt said. 'In three years, maybe a bit less if he was clever and learned fast, it would have been time for me to have started teaching him how to draw those. He done that one himself, two weeks ago, and I never showed him how.'

Old Kurt swallowed, the lump in his scrawny neck working up and down, and he said no more on the subject.

'Well done, Billy,' a man said, but his words sounded hollow, as though he was a long way away, at the end of a tunnel. 'It seems like you're ahead of your studies. I was never very good at school, myself, but it looks like you're making up for my failings there.'

Had *I* ever been to school? I couldn't remember. Perhaps that man had been, but I wouldn't know. I didn't know who he was.

Billy just looked at me. 'You fell down,' he said, after a moment. 'I knew you would.'

He turned and walked out of the room then, his book under his arm, and I heard his footsteps climbing the rickety wooden stairs.

Had I fallen down?

I had no idea.

I stared into the fire and shivered. I was frozen to the bone. I pulled my cloak around me, huddling for warmth in my coat and all my fine warm clothes as sweat ran tickling down my back.

I was so cold.

I leaned closer to the fire, until I could feel its heat making my cheeks tighten.

So.

Fucking.

Cold.

'What is it?' Someone said that, somewhere. I think it was a woman's voice, but it was so raspy it was hard to tell. I wondered who she was. 'What's wrong with him?'

'Battle shock.'

That was a man's voice, an old man by the sound of him.

I wondered who they were talking about, but my thoughts were drifting now and I found that I didn't really care.

I was so cold, and the fire was so far away. Why were they keeping the fire so far away from me when I was so cold?

'He's never shown signs of it before.'

'Sometimes it comes out later. Sometimes, when it's bad, it takes a long time.'

'And you'd know about that, would you?'

She sounded aggressive now, the raspy woman. Challenging.

'Aye, I would,' the old man said, and the sorrow in his voice told me that he knew from bitter experience.

I wondered who he was.

Chapter 26

'We had to come and fucking get you,' Jochan said.

I blinked up at him. I was lying in my bed above the Tanner's Arms, and Jochan was standing over me. Cold morning light was shining through the window, and my little brother was giving me a telling.

'Bloody Anne sent a runner, some Wheeler girl she found and paid,' he went on. 'I dunno who she was. Urgent it is, she said. Send men and a cart. Well, fuck that, we both know you being carried through the Wheels in a cart would have been the end of the Pious Men. Me and Black Billy and Fat Luka came for you, and we waited until it was full dark, and then we carried you back between us down the river path where no one could see, with Bloody Anne watching our tail. So you're home now, Tomas. It's all right. It's over. You're home now.'

I looked up into Jochan's face, and I could see from the pain in his eyes that he understood.

Battle shock.

That thing that I didn't feel, or so I had thought. I never had felt it, not until Billy the Boy had shown me his drawing or his glyph or whatever it had been. I had . . . lost my way, for a while there.

I knew that, but this was no time to show weakness.

'I'm well,' I said, and sat up in my blankets. 'I'm well, Jochan, and don't let anyone think otherwise of me.'

'It was me and Luka,' he said, 'and you know you can trust Black Billy. We won't say anything, none of us.'

I nodded, but it left a sour taste in my mouth all the same. Was it a secret that needed keeping, that I had been affected by the war like every other man who had fought? I had been strong all the way back from Abingon, keeping my crew together until we reached Ellinburg. I had been strong for the last six months, leading them and taking back my businesses one by one, watching men die and still doing what needed to be done.

I had been strong right up until I just couldn't do it any more.

Billy the Boy had done something to me, I knew that. Something that had opened the strongbox in the back of my mind where I kept the horrors locked away. That was the place where I never went, the part of my mind where I had parcelled up the memories called *Abingon* and vowed never to look again.

Whatever Billy had drawn in that book, it had been something magic. Ink on vellum can't do that to a man, not by itself. There was magic woven into the picture Billy had drawn. I knew that much, and I was starting to understand why Old Kurt had looked so scared of the lad. They were living under the same roof, after all.

But of course, Billy had been at Abingon too.

Billy had killed men in battle under the crumbling walls of the citadel. Billy had endured the noise of the cannon the same as the rest of us. Billy had done his part when it came to giving mercy to the wounded and shovelling corpses into the plague pits.

I wondered how much of what I had seen in that picture had come from my mental strongbox, and how much from Billy's own. Of course the lad was scarred by what he had seen, and by what he had done. We all were, but the rest of us were grown men.

Billy was a child. A scared and scarred and broken child, who was touched by a goddess and learning magic at a frightening rate.

I got out of my bed and took a long and deliberate piss into the pot, to show Jochan that I could. We all start the day the same way, after all, and once you've seen that you might not notice the otherness in someone quite so much.

'Right,' I said as I buttoned my smallclothes. Someone had obviously undressed me and put me to bed the night before, but I didn't know who. 'Let me get dressed, and then we'll see how the land lies.'

'No better than it did yesterday,' Jochan said. 'The Chains is still held like a fucking fortress, and without the Gutcutters we still ain't got the men to take it.'

No, we hadn't, but I remembered one thing from yesterday. When Old Kurt had greeted us he had almost made the mistake of calling Bloody Anne a 'fine lady' again, and that had given me an idea.

'Are you taking the piss?' Anne demanded when I told her.

We were sitting in the kitchen of the Tanner's Arms, and Ailsa was washing glasses and listening.

'No, Anne, I'm not,' I said. 'I need the Chains back, you know that. We've been planning this for weeks.'

'We've been planning to do it with the Gutcutters' help, and that's in the shithouse now,' she said. 'What makes you think we can still do it at all?'

'You remember what the captain told us about battle, don't you, Bloody Anne? "Always cheat, always win," he said. Well, if I haven't got the men to do this in an honest fight, then I'm going to fucking cheat.'

'And even supposing I say yes, which I haven't, how would this make us look to the other gangs?'

I shrugged. The only unfair fight is the one you lose, to my mind. In a year's time nobody would remember the details of what had happened or how it was done. They would only remember who had lived and who had died.

'It'll make us look like the people who own the Golden Chains,' I said. 'This will work, Anne.'

She fixed me with a stare and jabbed a finger pointedly at the long scar on her face. 'What sort of "fine lady" has a face like mine, Tomas Piety?'

'We might be able to do something about that,' I said. 'Ailsa? Come here a minute.'

Ailsa came over to the table and put her hand on my shoulder as naturally as if she really were my fancy woman and not just playing a part. She was very convincing, in everything she did. I had to keep reminding myself that playing a part was *all* she was doing.

'What can I do for you, my handsome?' she asked, and giggled.

Anne gave her a look but held her peace.

'How good are paints and powders, really?' I asked her.

'Oh, but they can work wonders,' she said. 'And there's other things too. Resins and dyes and . . . oh, oh, I see! Oh, why Anne, I can make that scar go away, my lovely, if that's what you're asking me. For a little while, at least. It'll take a bit of filling so you didn't ought to be smiling or you might crack, but Ailsa can make that look just—'

'What about everyone else?' Anne interrupted.

She thought Ailsa was no more than a foolish barmaid and my bit of fancy, and she made no pretence at liking her. Ailsa took that in her stride, of course, like she did washing glasses and flirting with drunks and everything else needed to keep up her false face.

'These lovable louts?' she said. 'Oh, I can make them look like new men, with a little touch of this and that. If that's what you're wanting, Tomas?'

I nodded. It was.

I hadn't had the chance to discuss my plan with Ailsa yet, but I could tell she had already worked out what I had in mind. She was no one's fool, whatever Bloody Anne might think.

'That's good, then,' I said. 'We stick to the original plan. Godsday evening. That gives us enough time to get clothes and things bought as well. Can you do everyone in a day, Ailsa? It'll be Anne, me, Jochan, Grieg, Cutter and Erik.'

Ideally I would have liked to have had Black Billy with us, but black faces weren't so common in Ellinburg that someone wouldn't have recognised him whatever Ailsa did. Grieg and Erik from my old crew were both good at close work, though, and Jochan's man Cutter was a devil at it. More to the point, no one would know them.

'What about Luka?' Anne said. 'He's hardly the only fat man in the city, and he plays the lute. That might be useful.'

He did, at that.

Luka had played before the war, and once he had some coin in his pocket again he had bought himself a beautiful instrument that he kept in a big leather case. It was that case that interested Anne, I realised, not the lute itself. I gave her a nod of approval. She was no one's fool either.

'Aye,' I said. 'Luka too, then.'

'Well, I'll be busy, but I can do it,' Ailsa said. 'For you I can, Tomas.'

I patted her on the arse, something I could only get away with when she was playing her part, and smiled at her.

'You're a good lass,' I said.

She went back to her glasses and I pursed my lips in thought.

'We'll need to get you a proper dress,' I said to Anne. 'Something fine, like a real noble lady would wear. Footmen's outfits for the men, I think, and finery for Jochan. I'll be your consort.'

'Oh, will you?' Anne said, but smiled to take the sting out of it. 'That'll be the day, Tomas Piety.'

I returned her smile. We understood each other, Anne and I. She was still one of the best customers of the house on Chandler's Narrow, and I think Rosie seldom saw anyone but her these days.

'Is that a yes, Bloody Anne?'

She sighed. 'I suppose so,' she said, 'but don't expect miracles. I'm no actress, and I've told you before I can't fight properly in a fucking dress.'

'Keep Luka close and you won't have to,' I said. 'If we do this right, and we will, they won't know what's fucking hit them.'

Chapter 27

Godsday came at last, and I held confession upstairs in the Tanner's Arms while Ailsa worked her magic on Bloody Anne in the room next to mine. I had been cultivating a moustache for the last week, and it finally looked almost presentable. As presentable as a moustache can ever look, anyway. I had kept it thin and neat, the way nobles wore them. I hated it, but it was the last thing that Tomas Piety would ever have chosen to wear on his face.

Tonight I didn't want to look like Tomas Piety.

When Simple Sam had finished telling me how he had farted on Erik's face three nights ago while he was sleeping and I had forgiven him for it, I took off my priest's robe and went down to the common room. The Tanner's was closed today, as there was too much happening to have people from the neighbourhood coming in and maybe carrying tales away with them.

Grieg was already dressed in his footman's clothes, prancing about the room and making a fool of himself practising his bow. If Pawl the tailor had been surprised by my request for three sets of footman's livery, a fine lady's dress and the clothes of a Dannsburg dandy he had kept it to himself, and he had delivered exactly what I wanted. A good tailor should be discreet, as I have written, and Pawl was certainly that.

Grieg just looked like himself in foolish clothes, but that was well enough. No one at the Golden Chains would know Grieg, after all, or Erik or Cutter. It was Jochan and me, and maybe Luka, that someone might recognise. I would be dressed as a lord and I had clothes enough for that already. Jochan was to be the dandy, and posing as my friend. Grieg, Erik, and Cutter had footman's livery, and Fat Luka was to be a bard.

Ailsa came down after a while with her pots of paints and powders in one hand and a bag in the other.

'Now, my lovely boys, who's first?'

I went first, to show them there was no shame in it.

Ailsa could have opened a theatre company with the things she had in that bag. Two hours later I had greying hair, a faded scar on my cheek and lines around my mouth and eyes that made me look like I had twenty more years to me than I had in truth. She held the looking glass up for me and smiled.

'You look like some old duke, with a boyhood duelling scar,' she said.

I did, at that.

'Thank you,' I said. 'That's fine work, Ailsa. Very fine.'

'Oh, I have my talents, Tomas. You of all people should know that,' she said, getting a laugh from the men for her sauce. 'Now then, my lovelies, who's next?'

Jochan went next. Yesterday he'd had Ernst style his wild hair into a pomaded swirl that the barber had assured us was how the fine gentlemen of Dannsburg were wearing theirs this season, and he had grown a fashionably thin strip of beard on his pointed chin. He looked ridiculous, to my mind, but more importantly he looked like a different man. Ailsa didn't have to do much work on him, just some darkness around the eyes that somehow made him look like he lived an overly dissolute lifestyle and slept for too few hours a night, which wasn't all that far off the truth. She was so skilled with her paints and powders it was almost witchcraft.

Luka was the hardest.

He had always been fat but he had got even fatter over the last six months, and there was no hiding that. He had tried to grow a beard but with little success, and the patchy stubble on his plump cheeks just made him look like there was something wrong with him. Ailsa tutted and fussed and opened her bag, and started to work with a pot of glue and a little brush.

I watched, transfixed, as Luka's beard took shape. She had all the tools of the mummer's trade in that bag, false hair and glues and dyes and things I couldn't even put names to, things to hide scars and things to raise them, things to make beards and to cover baldness.

When she was done with Luka I could have walked past him in the street and not known him. He now had a thick, full beard, and he looked older and somehow more important than he had before. He looked ready to take the stage at a grand theatre in Dannsburg and act a part from one of the great tragedies. How do you make a man look like an actor? I wouldn't know, but Ailsa obviously did.

By the time the painting was done it was dark outside so the rest of us got into our clothes, and then Bloody Anne came down the stairs and joined us.

I was pretty once, Tomas, she had told me, and I saw now that it was true. Her hair was still short, but Ailsa had styled it with wax so that it curled around her face, and she was wearing the magnificent green silk gown that I had paid Pawl a small fortune for. Her scar was invisible, and if the side of her face didn't move much then I doubted anyone would notice. Noble women weren't renowned for smiling, after all.

'Fuck a nun,' Jochan said when he saw her. 'Is that really you, Bloody Anne?'

'Fuck yourself, Jochan,' she said. 'It's me, all right, and bugger if this dress isn't sending me half mad already.'

If I looked hard, *really* hard, I could just about see the line of her scar under the thick coating of powder on her face. Anyone who didn't know it was there would never have noticed, I was sure of that. I had no idea what Ailsa had used to fill it with but I only hoped it wouldn't fall out before the evening's work was done.

'Right,' I said. 'Listen to me. You all know the plan, but now it's time to put it into action so we're going to go over it one more time. The captain always said you can't be too prepared, and he had the right of that. Just remember that no plan survives first contact with the enemy, and tonight we're going right into the heart of them. The Golden Chains was my business before the war, but these bastards who've stolen it from me have made it their stronghold. There's money in the Chains, not just silver marks but real gold crowns money. This is where the rich folk go to play their games of cards and smoke their fucking poppy resin, and it's guarded tight as a virgin's arse. We stick to the plan, boys, but as soon as it goes off we take them hard and fast. They'll have the numbers but we'll have surprise, so we've got to be quick and brutal about it. You understand?'

Heads nodded around the room, and that was good. Brutal was something these men understood, I knew that. Jochan flourished what he thought was a courtly bow, lace spilling from his cuffs as he moved his arm.

'My dear sir, we shall kill them all most terribly fucking politely,' he said, and the men laughed.

'Just remember who you're supposed to be, and try not to say *fuck* too much,' I said. 'The carriage will be here in a minute. Luka, have you got your lute case?'

'Yes, boss,' he said, his expression serious under his mummer's beard as he picked up the heavy instrument case and hefted it in his hand.

Jochan might not be taking this very seriously, but I could tell that Luka was, and that was good. I could see that this felt like a grand caper to Jochan and Grieg, an excuse to dress up and play the fool, but it wasn't. The Golden Chains was important to me, and more than that it was important to Ailsa.

There were actual Skanians there, she had told me, not just their hired agents. This was the one business of mine that they had really wanted: the place where the rich folk went. The Golden Chains was a gambling house just off Trader's Row where hands of cards were played for more money than a working man made in a year, and now it was a place where aristocrats smoked the finest poppy resin to escape the tedium of their privileged lives.

The place had always been strong, but since the poppy trade began the Skanians had made the Golden Chains into a fortress, beyond my means to simply storm. I wouldn't be doing this the way I had taken back my other businesses, I knew that. My original idea had been to make a deal with the Gutcutters, to take it between us through sheer force and split the business, but when I had seen Ma Aditi smoking resin I had known that idea had gone to the whores. The Chains was the centre of the resin business in Ellinburg, everyone knew that. Aditi would hardly be likely to want to kill her own supplier, after all.

No, that plan was dead and in the shithouse, as Anne had said. That left cheating, and the captain had taught me well how to cheat.

Chapter 28

'Lady Alicia Lan Verhoffen,' Anne announced herself to the five guards on the door of the Golden Chains. They looked frozen, all of them huddled in heavy cloaks against the winter night. 'My consort, Baron Lan Markoff, and his friend the honourable Rikhard Spaff. My bard, and three footmen of no account.'

Ailsa had coached her well, for all that Bloody Anne had struggled to take instruction from a barmaid she regarded as no more than a tart. Her accent was passable Dannsburg, if nowhere near as sharp as Ailsa's was when she spoke with her own voice. I nodded to the head doorman and palmed a silver mark into his hand by way of introduction.

My own accent is so strongly Ellinburg that there was nothing to be done about it, so we had agreed that I would say as little as possible. *Keep a disdainful silence,* Ailsa had advised me, and from what I knew of nobles that didn't seem so far from the truth.

'Your bard?' the man asked, his breath clouding the air in front of him. 'It's not usual to bring your bard to a gaming house.'

'I enjoy music,' Bloody Anne said, her mouth held in the tight line that was all that the filler Ailsa had set into her face would allow. 'I may wish for a tune, later, after I have wiped your tables clean of coin.'

I could see the doormen looking at us, obviously scanning us for weapons. Of course, there was nowhere to hide anything larger than a pocketknife in any of the ludicrous clothes we were all wearing.

'My lady enjoys music,' I repeated, giving the man a look.

I was dressed in my finest clothes, and the grey in my hair and the false duelling scar on my cheek made me look every inch a Dannsburg noble. If my accent was wrong then surely that only spoke of a man widely travelled, or so I hoped. I was very cold, and standing out in the street wasn't helping.

The doorman fingered the coin I had given him and nodded. 'As you will, my lord baron,' he said, and finally let us in.

'Wait by the door, boy,' I told Cutter. 'My lady may wish for something from her carriage during the evening.'

Cutter nodded, and loitered in his footman's costume next to the two men on the inside of the great oak-and-iron front door. They exchanged the sympathetic looks of put-upon servants.

The remaining six of us walked down the corridor and into the warmth of the main gaming hall. There were no more guards along the way, as I had suspected there wouldn't be. I knew the Golden Chains, and I knew how it was run. I used to run it myself, after all.

There was only one way in or out, and that was the door we had just come through. There used to be a tradesman's door at the back, once, but I had bricked that up myself. One door is easier to guard than two, and guarded it was. There were five men outside that door, as I said, and from what Ailsa's spies had reported there were another five patrolling around the building, watching the narrow windows.

The whole idea was to keep prospective threats out of the business. Once inside, the wealthy patrons didn't want a horde of thugs with weapons standing over them. There were only five men in the gaming hall who were conspicuously armed, although I suspected the card dealers and footmen probably had blades of some sort hidden about their persons as well. Storming the Golden Chains by brute force would have been virtually impossible even with the Gutcutters' help, I realised now.

This way was better.

The warm air in the main room was thick with the sickly smoke of poppy resin, and the light was dim. There were maybe a dozen patrons at the gaming tables, all of them playing the same complicated game with cards and stacks of wooden counters. I understood nothing of it, but Jochan had assured me that he knew how the game was played.

'Cards,' he announced with a joyful smile that I didn't think he had to feign.

'Not for me,' I said, taking a glass of wine from a tray held by a footman in the livery of the house.

'My friend the Baron Lan Markoff is a terrible bore,' Jochan went on as he drew up a chair at one of the card tables, pushing his way between a man in elegantly cut grey wool and a woman in a russet silk dress. He was affecting a ridiculous accent that made him sound somewhere between a rich drunk and a simpleton. 'Never plays a bloody hand. Name's Spaff, the honourable, et cetera. I bloody love cards. No good at it, though, but it's only money and I've got shitloads of that. What's the buy-in?'

One of the other players grinned at him and silver moved from Jochan's purse to the banker's box to be replaced by a small stack of wooden counters. Why they didn't just play for coin I didn't know, but I suspected they may have regarded it as being beneath their honour or some such nonsense. One thing I have noticed in life is that the men who speak the most of honour are usually those who have the least of it.

'How very tedious,' Bloody Anne said loudly, in her best Dannsburg accent. 'All these silly people, playing games with cards. It pleases me that you do not indulge, my lord baron.'

I made a noncommittal noise, looking out the corner of my eye at a tall man in an extremely expensive-looking coat who was heading our way. This was the one, I was sure. This had to be the Skanian who Ailsa had told me was running the Chains.

'Baron . . . ?' he asked, letting the question hang in the air.

'Lan Markoff,' I said in as gruff a tone as I could manage without sounding too Ellinburg.

'A pleasure,' the man said, although I noticed he offered no name of his own. 'I cannot place your accent, my lord baron.'

'The accent of ships and caravans,' I said with a shrug. 'I am a merchant speculator. My home is Dannsburg, although I've not seen the city in years.'

I had no idea what a 'merchant speculator' was, but Ailsa had assured me it was a plausible occupation for a minor noble such as a baron.

The man's smile widened a little, and I could only assume she had been right about that.

'Have your travels taken you to Skania, my lord baron?'

'Not as yet,' I said, 'although who knows what the future may bring? I'm not here to discuss business, not tonight.'

I looked around the gambling house, affecting boredom in an attempt to steer the conversation away from this supposed occupation of mine that I didn't know the first thing about. The Skanian obviously caught my mood.

'If cards are not to your liking, Baron,' he said, 'perhaps I might offer you and your lady something . . . a little more relaxing?'

He meant resin, of course, and I wanted no part of that. All the same, we had to stick to the plan. I turned away and coughed into my fist, taking the opportunity to glance over my shoulder. Fat Luka was two paces behind me, where he should be, with his heavy lute case in his hand. He met my eye and nodded a fraction.

'A pipe would be most soothing,' Bloody Anne said. 'Don't you think, my dear?'

'Aye,' I agreed. 'Pipes it is.'

The man turned away from us and clicked his fingers at a footman, and I shot Jochan a look.

Now, I mouthed at him.

'Fucking *cheat*!' Jochan bellowed.

He surged to his feet with a roar and flipped the card table over, scattering drinks and counters and cards all over his astonished fellow players.

That was the signal.

I heard a grunt from down the corridor as Cutter's tiny blades, no larger than pocketknives, sent the men inside the door on their way across the river. I could only offer up a prayer to Our Lady that Cutter could get the key turned in the lock and the heavy beam down across the inside of the door before the men outside stormed in to see what the shouting was about.

If not, we were done.

Jochan punched the man next to him full in the face, sending him reeling backward into his fellows. Anne yanked up the skirts of her dress to reveal her daggers, one sheath strapped to each pale thigh. She drew her blades and hammered one into the Skanian's chest without word or hesitation.

Fat Luka flipped open his lute case, took out a compact crossbow and shot the nearest guard through the gut even as he tossed my sword-belt to me with his free hand. I grabbed it out of the air and drew the Weeping Women, letting the leather fall to the floor as the armed men in the room charged us with bared steel in their hands.

I was hard-pressed for a moment before Jochan vaulted the overturned card table and grabbed his axe from Luka's open case. We felled three men between us. Grieg and Erik took up their weapons and waded in. Even Luka wasn't strong enough to have carried enough weapons for everyone in one hand, so this had been the plan. The surprised guards fell before us.

Our Lady smile on me, it was working.

It kept working until another Skanian came out of the back room. This one was older than his dead fellow, his long blond hair bound back from his gaunt face with a silver clasp. He was wearing robes not unlike my priest's garb, but I knew this was no priest. His eyes were as hard as any soldier's, his thin lips drawing tight with fury as he saw his countryman lying dead on the floor in a spreading pool of blood.

Grieg took a step toward him with a guard's shortsword held ready to do murder, and the Skanian raised his hand. A great gout of fire burst from his fingers and took Grieg full in the face.

He fell shrieking, the meat cooking from the bones of his skull even as the rest of us hastily took cover behind overturned tables. A moment later Grieg exploded as though he'd had a flashstone sewn up inside him.

'Lady save us!' I gasped, although I knew She wouldn't. 'Magician!'

Sudden panic gripped the room. The other patrons had seemed almost bemused by the earlier violence, as though armed men fighting were beneath them and none of their affair, but now they were cowering along with the rest of us and that was good. That added to the confusion.

The magician, who hadn't seen the initial eruption of violence and didn't know who was who, wasted precious moments burning a young man with foolish hair who had nothing to do with anything.

Anne took aim with one of her daggers and let fly in a long overhand throw, but the blade seemed to swerve in the air as it neared the Skanian magician. The dagger made an impossible turn and ended up embedded harmlessly in the wall behind him.

'Bloody witchcraft!' Anne spat.

Something moved behind me, just outside my vision. It seemed to scuttle along the wall like an oversized rat, but it was gone before I could take it in. I had to duck again as a new blast of flame washed across the room from the magician's hands, setting a tapestry on fire behind me. I didn't have time to think about what the moving thing might have been. There was only one way in or out of the Chains, as I have said, and I could hear the guards outside pounding on that door even now. If the fire took we would all burn alive in there. It could be minutes before the second half of my plan bore fruit, and I didn't think we had minutes to spare.

'Reload the crossbow and give it to Anne,' I hissed at Luka. 'It's the only way we'll get that fucking—'

I stopped in astonishment as the sides of the magician's neck burst open in a spray of blood that decorated the wall beside him and the low ceiling over his head. He twisted and fell with a gurgling rattle, blood still gushing from his neck, and I saw Cutter standing behind him with his tiny knives dripping gore.

'Fuck a nun, you took your time,' Jochan said. 'Scuttle quicker next time, you little bastard.'

Oh, yes, Cutter had his uses all right. I could see that now.

Jochan got to his feet and laughed. There was a single guard left alive in the room with us, white-faced with fear. Jochan planted his axe in the man's head without comment and showed me his savage grin. I could still hear pounding on the front door, and however strong it was I knew it wouldn't hold forever.

'Where have those fuckers got to?' Luka wondered aloud, voicing my own thoughts.

A moment later there was a thud, then a scream, and I heard the thump of crossbows and the sound of more impacts. The ten lads I had hired from around the Stink and armed with crossbows had finally come out of the alleys they had been hiding in, then.

Thank the Lady for that.

Someone pounded on the door and called out, 'Pious, in Our Lady's name!'

Those were the right words. I nodded to Luka. 'Go let them in,' I said. 'Erik, get that fucking fire out before it takes in the plaster and we all burn to fucking death.'

Bloody Anne was staring at the dead magician, and at the tattered shreds of cloth and flesh and the huge red stain on the floor that had once been Grieg.

'I don't . . .' she started to say, before Jochan kicked a table back the right way up and jumped up onto it.

'We're the Pious Men!' he roared, arms outstretched and his axe in his hand with bits of the guard's head still clinging to the blade.

I counted eleven of the wealthy patrons left alive, all of them staring at Jochan as though he were some sort of devil, escaped from Hell. This wouldn't do, I realised. I picked up my sword-belt and buckled it on, sheathing the Weeping Women as the first of the hired crossbowmen came into the room with reloaded weapons in their hands. Luka was still outside in the cold, directing the defence of the building. I took a step into the centre of the room and gave Jochan a look that said to be quiet.

'My name is Tomas Piety,' I said. 'I don't normally look like this, but I'm sure you'll make allowances under the circumstances. I am a businessman, and I own the Golden Chains.'

'Gangsters,' a woman said, fanning herself rapidly with her hand.

'Businessmen,' I corrected her. 'The Chains was mine before the war, and now it is mine again. This has been a business disagreement, no more than that, and now it's settled.'

'That man *exploded*!' a weak-chinned fellow shouted, waving vaguely at the stain where Grieg had been.

'Aye, he did,' I said. 'They had a magician, and I didn't expect that. It won't happen again.'

'I dare say it won't,' the woman said. 'The magician appears to no longer be with us.'

She tittered, then giggled, then fainted into the arms of the man beside her.

'For fuck's sake,' I heard Bloody Anne mutter to herself.

Still, it was done. Not done easily perhaps, but as I had told the men, no plan survives first contact with the enemy.

Chapter 29

There was no chance that an assault with crossbows would have gone unnoticed in the middle of the city, especially not so close to Trader's Row. I let the patrons go and sat down with a drink to wait for the City Guard to arrive. There were far too many bodies for us to attempt to hide them, so we didn't bother.

Captain Rogan came in person, as I had thought he might, leading a full troop of twenty men armed with crossbows as well as their shortswords and clubs. I was paying taxes to Governor Hauer again by then, of course, large ones, so I wasn't overly concerned what Rogan might think of the evening's events.

All the same, he was furious, and he made no attempt to hide it.

'What in the name of all the gods do you think you're doing, Piety?' he demanded. 'I know who you are, all of you. No amount of mummer's paint will change that.'

He was standing in the main gaming hall with ten of his men around him while the rest of them dragged corpses out into a waiting cart, and he was far too close to me for my liking. I looked into his ugly, brutish face and held his stare.

One thing you didn't do in front of a bully like Rogan was back down or show weakness, not ever. Back down once and you'd never stop doing it, I knew that. My da had taught me that much, at least.

'I am conducting a business takeover, Captain Rogan,' I said. 'The Golden Chains is now back under its rightful management and will be open for business again in a few days' time.'

'You've conducted a fucking massacre, in full view of half the city!' he roared at me. 'Take him in.'

We had done it in view of some of the city's nobility was what he meant, of course. Now he had to be seen to do something, and that inconvenienced him. Being inconvenienced meant having to do some work, and that put Rogan in a foul temper at the best of times. I had been expecting this.

'I'm going to see Grandfather,' I told Jochan, who nodded back at me.

'You're too sure of yourself by far, Piety,' Rogan growled at me, but I ignored him.

I was untouchable, and we both knew it.

'We'll be open for business again soon,' I said instead. 'I don't recall that you used to be a member here, Captain. Perhaps that could change.'

Rogan shot me a look. He had his vices, as I have written, and none so strong among them as gambling. He was a regular face at the racetrack, where I had often won back the bribes I paid him, but he had never had enough social status to earn an invitation to the Golden Chains. Letting him in might slightly lower the tone, I knew that, but after what had happened there this evening I thought the reputation of the Golden Chains might have suffered somewhat already. At least I knew he had plenty of money to lose.

'That . . . that would please me,' he said. 'I still have to take you in, you know that.'

'I know,' I said.

He nodded, and led me from the Golden Chains with his men surrounding me, but I wasn't in irons and I knew I'd be out again by morning.

That was how business was done in Ellinburg.

I had expected to be thrown into one of the cells under the governor's hall, for appearance's sake if nothing else, but instead Rogan brought me before Governor Hauer himself once more.

It was late, but the governor was still up, although obviously much the worse for wine. He received me in his study on the second floor as he had six months ago when I was newly returned to Ellinburg. He looked even more unhealthy than I remembered, florid of face and fat, with ugly pink patches on his scalp that showed through his thinning hair.

'Business is going well, I see,' Hauer said.

He was all but reeling in his chair, and wine sloshed from his goblet onto the polished wooden surface in front of him as he gestured at me.

I pretended not to notice that.

'The Pious Men have always paid their taxes, Governor,' I said.

'Not for three years they didn't,' he said, and laughed.

The war was nothing to make jokes about, to my mind, not by a man who hadn't even been there. I held my peace, but I think he could see in my eyes that I had taken that ill. He cleared his throat with obvious embarrassment, and I was aware of Rogan moving that little bit closer to the back of the chair I had been pushed into.

They had taken the Weeping Women from me when I was brought before the governor, of course, and once again I wondered if I could best Rogan in a bare-handed fight. He had ten or more years than me at least, but still I doubted it. With swords perhaps, but not fists.

'This evening's events were regrettable, but necessary,' I said. 'The Golden Chains was mine. The last time we spoke, you said you didn't expect me to sit meekly by while men stole my businesses from me, and I haven't. That's all this was.'

'You really haven't, have you, Tomas?' the governor said, and laughed into his wine. 'Oh, no, not at all you haven't. Between you and Aditi, we've never had so many murders in Ellinburg in less than half a year.'

'I pay my taxes,' I said, 'and I assume Ma Aditi does the same. I wouldn't know, but that's between you and her. What I *do* know is how our arrangement works, and I can't see that I've broken the terms of that arrangement.'

'Perhaps not,' Hauer said. 'Perhaps not the letter of them, anyway, but certainly the spirit. No amount of taxes can allow you to conduct open warfare on my streets.'

'Tonight was an exception,' I assured him. 'A regrettable one, as I said. I don't intend for it to happen again.'

'It had better not.'

He thumped his goblet down on the table, spilling more wine, and put the elbow of his expensive silk shirt in the resulting sticky mess. His doublet strained over his gut as he leaned toward me.

Here it comes, I thought. *This is why I'm here, not just to take a telling. There's something he's been working his way around to saying to me.*

'Did she come to you?' Hauer asked, his voice dropping to a hoarse whisper. 'The Queen's Man?'

I nodded, seeing no gain in lying. 'She came,' I said.

Hauer's complexion visibly darkened as he realised I wasn't about to say anything more on that. I remembered our previous conversation, and the fear I had seen in his eyes when he had spoken of the woman I knew as Ailsa.

That gave me an idea.

'And?' he demanded. 'What did she want? What did you do for her?'

'I did what she wanted,' I said, and forced myself to swallow. 'I don't know if I'd still be here if I hadn't, Governor, do you?'

'And where is she now?'

'I really couldn't say.'

I really couldn't, I knew that.

If Hauer realised I had a Queen's Man living in my tavern, serving behind my bar even, then Lady only knew what he would do. So far I wasn't doing anything that he hadn't expected, and the fact that I had only struck as hard and fast as I had on Ailsa's insistence wasn't something that he needed to know, to my mind. All the same, I wondered how well he knew me, and whether he might be working it out for himself.

'It seems to me that you've taken your businesses back very quickly,' Hauer said.

I nodded. 'I won't sit meekly by and be robbed,' I said. 'My men are soldiers, and they know what they're doing. I have men under me who fought at Messia, and at Abingon, and came home to tell of it. They are trained, experienced, *ambitious* killers. Men like that need to be paid, to keep them at heel. They need to be paid well. You realise what would happen if I couldn't pay them any more, don't you?'

Hauer coughed and gulped his wine. I thought that we understood each other now. The thought of my crew unleashed on the city, leaderless and feral, was enough to give the governor pause.

'And the Queen's Man isn't behind this?'

I met his eyes. 'I don't even know her name,' I said, and that was true enough.

She called herself Ailsa, but I could call myself the Baron Lan Markoff and that didn't make it true. I knew nothing about her, I realised, not even her real name. I was the only one of the crew who had heard her speak with that beautiful Dannsburg voice, but who was to say that was really her own and not just another act? I had never seen her without her paints and powders, and I didn't even know how old she really was.

I had to admit to myself that that bothered me.

Hauer sighed and looked over my shoulder at Rogan.

'Who saw?' he asked.

'Hard to say, my lord governor,' Rogan admitted. 'The patrons were gone by the time my men arrived so I don't have their names, but nobles aren't like to gossip about something that would mean admitting they had been there with resin pipes in their hands. It's the fight outside that's likely to have been seen, but there's no way of knowing by who.'

'What to do?' Hauer wondered aloud. 'I should lock you up and leave you to rot, Piety.'

'An imprisoned man pays no taxes and earns no money to pay his men,' I said.

'I *fucking well* know that!' Hauer shouted. 'You're a thorn in my side, Piety, you and Aditi both. The gods only know what will happen when the rest of your sordid peers finally drag themselves home from the war.'

I held my peace at that.

To date, Ma Aditi and me were still the only bosses to have come back from Abingon, but the rest of them led only minor gangs anyway. The Pious Men and the Gutcutters were the main businesses in Ellinburg, as the governor well knew. He was drunk, I could see that, but I could also see that he was scared.

His grip on order in the city depended on maintaining good relationships with people like me, and he knew it. If he lost that grip, then Dannsburg would notice and they would send people to help him regain control. The sort of *help* that a failing governor would get from the Queen's Men was probably the stuff of his nightmares, and I knew I could make something of that.

I looked at him, and I could see he was measuring me with his bloodshot eyes, trying to work out through the haze of wine how much of what I had told him was true. I prided myself that I hadn't told him a single lie that night, although of course many truths are open to interpretation.

I should know.

I'm a priest, after all.

It was fear of the Queen's Men that drove him, in the end, as it had driven me. For him it was fear of failure, and of intervention from the capital. Fear of an investigation that would expose his accounts and the queen's ransom in taxes that he had withheld from the crown over the years. For that he would hang, just as surely as I would for the poppy trade. Under that, I could see, was a deep-rooted fear that perhaps there was still a Queen's Man in Ellinburg.

No, he didn't know that I was working for Ailsa, but I thought that he might be beginning to suspect it.

I would have to do something to change that.

Chapter 30

I spent the night in a cell, as I had expected. There were appearances to be kept up, I understood that, and I didn't take it ill. Rogan made sure I was fed, at least, and that I was brought drinkable water from the good wells off Trader's Row and not the river filth that they gave to normal prisoners. I used most of it to wash the paint and powder from my face until I looked like myself again. Apart from that hideous moustache, anyway.

I had been in the cells before, but not since I was a young man. I hadn't missed it. The room was two floors below the entrance to the governor's hall, a cramped and windowless stone space lit by a brazier in the corridor outside that shed a feeble light through the bars of the door. It stopped me from freezing to death, too, but only just. There was a straw pallet on the floor, crawling with lice, and a wooden bucket already half full of someone else's shit. It stank down there.

I ignored the pallet and sat on the cold, damp floor with my back to the wall, huddled in my coat, and waited. Hauer would have to let me go in the morning, I knew, and anything can be endured for a little while. It can when you know there will be an end to it, anyway. Every soldier knows that.

My chin sank down onto my chest, and I started to think on what the governor had said.

At some point I must have dozed, and after a few hours Rogan came and shook me awake.

He looked tired, with dark circles under his heavy eyes, and I didn't think he had slept at all. He told me that the workings of the governor's operation had spread the word that we were honest businessmen who had been attacked and robbed and had merely been defending ourselves within the extent of the law.

I just nodded.

Stories like that didn't have to be true, or even particularly believable, so long as they came from the right source. If the governor said a thing was so then it was so, as far as the majority of the population were concerned.

The nobility simply didn't care.

I knew there would be trouble over the young dandy who had died, but luckily it had been the Skanian magician who had killed him and not one of my crew. That meant that the outrage of society was directed toward the mysterious foreigners who had so imposed themselves on a fine and upstanding member of the Ellinburg business community like me, and that was good.

I was fed again, and come the dawn the Weeping Women were returned to me. I was released from the cells with the governor's official apology and his public vow to maintain the peace in Ellinburg against the corrupt influence of foreigners.

That was how business was done.

Captain Rogan himself showed me from the governor's hall that morning, and I got a surprise when the doors opened. I was cramped and cold and dirty from my night in the cells, but I found Bloody Anne waiting for me in the packed square outside. The mummer's paint was gone from her face and she looked herself again, in her men's coat and britches with her scar standing out against her pale face. She had Jochan and Fat Luka and five of the lads with her, and a crowd of perhaps two hundred Stink folk around them. Two hundred or so people from my streets, all turned out in the cold to see me walk free with the governor's pardon.

There was a cheer when the morning sun touched my face, the face of a good Ellinburg man who had been wronged by outsiders and had put matters right for himself. A truth can be interpreted in many ways, and the people from my streets had obviously chosen the way in which they would hear this one.

That or they had been told.

Rogan looked at them all, counting heads and not liking what he saw. I could tell he was wondering what might have happened if I hadn't been released. Riots are ugly things, and far from unknown in Ellinburg.

If that gave Rogan something to think on, then that was good.

Business in Ellinburg is one tenth violence to nine tenths posturing, and it was in everybody's interest to bring down the ratio of violence. Blood is bad for business, everyone understood that, but all the same sometimes it's necessary. The threat of it, at least, can be a strong bargaining tool.

Bloody Anne stepped forward from the crowd and clasped my arm as I walked down the steps from the governor's hall. We shook hands in that manner, each holding the other's wrist in the traditional greeting between second and boss. I squeezed her arm for a moment and nodded to her in appreciation.

I wondered who had taught her that.

Ailsa, I assumed, or possibly Fat Luka.

I looked over her shoulder and my eyes found Jochan in the crowd. He knew that Anne stood above him in the Pious Men, and if he hadn't fully accepted that truth before, then now there was no way he could avoid it any longer. She had publicly greeted me as my second, and I had returned the greeting in front of too many people for it to be undone.

That might make trouble later, but I knew it had needed to be done. Anne had obviously known that too, or more likely Ailsa had.

I walked out into the square with Anne at my side, and accepted claps on the shoulder and pats on the arm from my men. Only Jochan hung back, a brooding hurt in his eyes that I knew I wouldn't be able to ignore for long.

Luka had brought the fine carriage we had hired the previous night, and I can only think that we made a lordly sight as I stepped up into it with Anne and Jochan behind me. Luka got in after us and closed the door. He thumped on the roof, and the carriage driver flicked his reins, and then we were moving. I sat back against the padded leather bench and sighed.

'Well done,' I told them. 'Bringing the common people with you was a good touch, and not one that the governor will be able to ignore.'

'They came by themselves,' Anne said. 'Perhaps Luka put the word around, but we didn't force anyone.'

I nodded. That was good, better than I had expected, in fact.

Luka just smiled and said nothing.

He had removed his mummer's beard and shaved at some point in the night, I noticed, and his eyes crinkled in his smooth, plump face. I would have bet good silver that he had been behind the enthusiasm of the common folk, and I wondered how much that had cost me. Still, it was coin well spent, if only to see the look on Rogan's face.

'How are the men?' I asked Anne.

'There was some grief for Grieg,' she said, 'although in truth less than there might have been before word got around about what he did in Chandler's Narrow back in the spring.'

I nodded. Grieg had lost a lot of friends over that, I knew, and never recovered them. Now he had crossed the river that was between him and Our Lady, to my mind.

'Aye,' I said, and left it there.

'The foreign witch has some of them worried,' she went on, 'but Cutter proved that witches can die like everyone else, so it isn't panic. Mostly they're just glad to see you released unharmed.'

'Everyone fucking loves you, Tomas,' Jochan said, but he was looking at his boots as he said it and I couldn't read the expression on his face.

When we got back to the Tanner's Arms I found Aunt Enaid there waiting for me, with Brak beside her. Ailsa was behind the bar, and there was a hostile tension in the air between the two women that I could feel the moment I walked into the tavern.

Mika and Black Billy led the boys in a cheer when I walked in, and I grinned and sketched a mock bow that got a laugh.

'The Golden Chains is ours again,' I said to my aunt, and got another cheer for my trouble.

My aunt was not cheering.

'I hear you're quite the hero,' Enaid said. 'The local boy who stood up to the villainous outsiders and won. What a load of fucking *horseshit!*'

The room went quiet when she shouted at me, and I narrowed my eyes as I met my aunt's piercing one-eyed glare.

'Of course it's horseshit, Auntie,' I said. 'Horseshit makes things grow, and the legend of the Pious Men is even now growing, out there on our streets. That's good.'

'Is it?' she snapped. 'Is it good, Tomas? The Pious Men are *businessmen*, but you've turned them into soldiers. A pitched fucking battle on the streets, with crossbows? On the edge of Trader's Row, of all places? How's the governor supposed to take that?'

My aunt was giving me a telling in front of almost my entire crew, and I couldn't let that pass.

I slammed the flat of my hand down onto the table in front of her to shut her up. I leaned over her and I spoke quietly but in a voice that I knew the whole room could hear.

'He'll take it with his taxes and keep his nose out of my business, like he always has,' I said. 'Do not, my dear aunt, tell me how to run my business. Don't ever do that.'

I stood up and straightened my coat, and I walked across a tavern that was utterly silent.

I went upstairs to my room, and Ailsa followed.

She closed the door behind her and stood there looking at me as I stripped off my coat. It was stained and damp from the cells, and it smelled of shit. I tossed it on the floor and turned to face her in my shirtsleeves.

'What was that all about?' she demanded in her sharp, Dannsburg voice.

Just then I would have welcomed common, funny, flirty Ailsa, but it seemed I was getting the other one. I was getting Ailsa the Queen's Man whether I wanted her or not.

I met her dark eyes and had to admit that I *did* want her. There was no fooling myself on that score any longer, however far out of the question it might be. Ridiculous, I know, but there it was.

'I can't have my aunt give me a telling in front of the men, you understand that,' I said. 'I have—'

'Certain expectations to meet, yes, I grasp that,' she interrupted. '*Why* was she giving you a telling, I mean? I thought that old harridan was part of your operation, before the war?'

'Aye, she was,' I said. I sat down in the chair and sighed. 'Things are different now, Ailsa. Before the war . . . Aye. The Pious Men were businessmen, as she said. Jochan and me, her and Alfread and Donnalt and the others. Me and Jochan were the violent ones, when we had to be, and that wasn't often. Since we came back things have changed, and not to her liking.'

'Your business was built on violence,' she said.

'No, it wasn't,' I said. 'It was built on the *threat* of violence, and the capability for it, but very seldom the reality of it. In Ellinburg it is enough to be seen as violent, as *potentially* violent. People are weak, Ailsa, and the poorer and more oppressed they are, the weaker they become. When I gave up bricklaying and became a businessman, me and my brother and two friends walked into this tavern and we made them an offer. We offered to protect them from having their business burned down, in exchange for a weekly tax. They paid. So did the baker, so did the chandler, so did the cobbler. Soon half the Stink was paying us to protect them.'

'To protect them from yourselves, yes, I understand that,' she said. 'And when someone else threatened them?'

'Aye, then we did what we had said we would do. Protection is protection, after all. The Gutcutters were a new outfit then as well, down in the Wheels, and when they sent lads down the river path to try their luck in the Stink, we showed them how unwise that was. Twice that happened, no more, and then a border was drawn up and everyone went back to doing business in their own neighbourhoods and leaving each other alone. That was just how it worked. When I had enough money I came in here and I told the owner I was buying his tavern, and he didn't refuse me. No violence was done. It wasn't necessary. Do you see what I'm saying?'

'That the past was glorious, that the sun always shone, and you were firm but fair and you never really hurt anyone,' Ailsa said, the sarcasm dripping like venom from her beautiful lips. 'Yes, Tomas, I know very well what you're saying and it's about as true as the face I gave Bloody Anne last night. The past is as scarred and bitter and ugly as your second is, and you know it.'

That was going too far.

I was on my feet in a moment, my hand around Ailsa's throat as I forced her back against the wall.

'Don't you *ever* insult Anne like that,' I hissed in her face. 'Don't you *fucking* dare!'

I felt the unmistakable pressure of steel against the inside of my thigh, in the killing place.

'It would be very wise of you to take your hands off me, and never put them back,' Ailsa said.

We stood there for a moment, me with my hand around her throat and her with a dagger I hadn't even known she had, held a whisker away from taking my life. She had me at the disadvantage there, I had to admit.

I let go and took a step backward, and Ailsa made her blade disappear again.

You can hide a dagger very well indeed, behind enough lace.

I remembered her telling me that, once, but it seemed a barmaid's apron served well enough. I had underestimated her, and I wouldn't make that mistake again.

Chapter 31

I slept for a few hours after Ailsa stalked out of my room, making up for the fitful night I had spent in the cells. When I woke I shaved with the cold water in my washbasin, which was uncomfortable but better than wearing that moustache any longer. By the time I went back downstairs my aunt had left, for which I was glad. I didn't want more harsh words between us, but I could see no other way it would have gone that day. I had a late breakfast in the kitchen with Hari, who fussed around me as though being taken in by the Guard and released the next day were some great event. Perhaps it was, to him. I had no idea where Hari was from or what he had done before the war, and I was happy to keep it that way. He was a Pious Man now, to my mind, and that was all that mattered. The past was the past, and it was best for everyone to leave it there. Some things in the past didn't want looking at too closely. I knew that all too well.

When I returned to the common room, Ailsa was there waiting for me.

'You look brighter for some sleep, my poor lovely,' she said, wearing her barmaid's face in front of the other men in there.

No one would ever have guessed we had been moments from killing each other just a few hours before.

'I feel it,' I admitted, and it was true.

I leaned closer to her, hiding my thoughts behind a smile. She smiled back up at me and ran a flirtatious hand along my arm until Mika looked away and Simple Sam went bright red and left the room.

'I'm sorry if I spoke harshly to you before,' I murmured. 'Not enough sleep, and after a fight . . . no one's quite themselves.'

'Oh, don't you worry, my handsome,' she said, 'it takes more than hard words to upset Ailsa.'

I thought perhaps a hand around the throat might do it, though, and I felt bad about that now. All the same, if I had pressed it I knew she would have killed me and disappeared without a backward glance, and no one would ever have found her even if they had been of a mind to look. I had to remind myself who I was dealing with here.

Do what your father says or the Queen's Men will come and take you away.

This was a Queen's Man right here, her hand lying seductively on my arm, and I knew she was one of the most dangerous people I had ever met in my life.

'Aye,' I said, and cleared my throat. 'We'll say no more about it, then.'

'Let's not,' she whispered, her own accent cutting me across the face sharp as a whip.

'I can take the bar, boss,' Luka volunteered. 'If you two want to, you know, have some time.'

I looked at him for a moment and nodded. Fat Luka was a good deal cleverer than I had ever given him credit for before the war, I had to admit. He saw things that other men didn't, and he knew how to use the things he saw, and that made him useful. It made him dangerous too, in his way, but I knew I could trust him.

'That sounds good,' I said, and caught Ailsa's eye.

She giggled on cue, and let me chase her up the stairs to my room.

'What?' she said once we were alone.

'Ailsa, I've said I'm sorry and I meant it,' I said. 'Let's not have harsh words between us.'

'That's done,' she said dismissively. 'There's something on your mind, though.'

'Aye, there is,' I admitted. 'Hauer is suspicious. He thinks I've done too much too fast, and he's right. I was thinking on it in the night, and he *knows* me, Ailsa. He knows that my instinct would have been to consolidate, the way I told you I was planning to, but I didn't. I went all out, and he'll know that idea didn't come from me. He doesn't know who you are but he knows you came to me, and I think he suspects that you're still here.'

Ailsa frowned, and for a moment she looked much older. 'That is not acceptable,' she said.

'No, I know,' I said. 'There's more too, although it's more my problem than yours. My brother. Anne openly declared herself my second this morning, in front of half the Stink. That's how it is and it's well and good, but Jochan's taken it ill. I haven't seen him since we got back, and come tonight I dare say I'll have to send the lads out to pour him home from some tavern somewhere. He'll make trouble, if I'm not careful.'

'Then *be* careful,' Ailsa said. 'Your brother is your problem, not mine, but the governor worries me.'

I nodded. I had given this a lot of thought during my night in the cells.

'I need to fuck something up,' I said. 'If I do something rash, something poorly planned that fails, then Hauer will know you weren't behind it. That would work, but I also can't be seen to look a fool when I'm just now winning the common folk over to my side.'

Ailsa smiled at me then, a smile that was neither the barmaid's nor that of the Dannsburg aristocrat. It was truly beautiful, that smile. For one brief moment, I thought perhaps I had seen her real face.

'Well, that's simple, then,' she said, and all at once the aristocrat was back. 'Put your brother in charge of something, and let nature take its course.'

I stared at her.

Of course, I could see the sense in her words. Everything Jochan touched with an unguided hand went to the whores, just about. Could I hang him out like that, though? Could I give him a job just to watch him fail, because it would put the governor's mind at ease?

I knew I had to. This was war, and in war sometimes sacrifices have to be made. Again I felt my respect for Ailsa growing. She had the ruthlessness of a businessman, I had to allow. I liked that about her.

I liked it a lot.

I wouldn't see Jochan get hurt, of course, but people knew what he was like and I knew he could fail without making me lose face. It would still be a failure for the Pious Men, though, and no crew with a Queen's Man backing them would ever make mistakes. Yes, it made sense, for all that it left a bad taste in my mouth.

'Perhaps that's the answer,' I admitted.

Jochan rolled into the Tanner's late that evening, after we had closed. I was in the middle of saying a few words to the men in memory of Grieg.

My brother was stinking drunk, as I had expected, but I had sent Fat Luka out to find him an hour earlier and Luka had at least brought him home unbloodied. Jochan shoved his way through the circle of men in front of me, reeking of brandy and vomit, and he leered at me with mad eyes.

'Grieg was a cunt!' he shouted. 'Fuck him. Fuck anyone who hits whores.'

'We've covered that,' I said. 'He said his confession and we made it right with him, in our way.'

'We kicked the fucking piss out of him,' Jochan slurred, and laughed. 'Fucking right we did.'

'We did, and now that's done,' I said. 'Grieg has crossed the river. May he sleep in peace.'

'May he sleep in peace,' the men echoed.

'May he fucking rot,' Jochan muttered, but Luka was steering him away toward the door behind me now, and I don't think anyone else heard.

I turned to Bloody Anne to say something, I don't remember what, when Jochan suddenly lurched around in the doorway, almost dragging Luka back with him.

'That's another fucking thing!' he bellowed, his words so thick with drink he was barely intelligible. 'You fucking . . . your own fucking brother, Tomas. We always stuck together, didn't we? We fucking used to, anyway. When Da was . . . when . . .'

'Go to bed, Jochan,' I said, lowering my voice into the tone that always got through to him whatever state he was in. He didn't want to argue with that tone, I knew, and he *really* didn't want to bring up our da in front of everyone. That wouldn't have been fucking wise. 'Go and sleep it off, before you say something you'll regret.'

He glared at me, his bloodshot eyes wide and staring. No one spoke.

Anne was by my side, and I didn't think that was helping. This was about that morning, I knew it was, and how Anne and me had greeted each other in front of hundreds of the common folk from our streets. This was about him feeling betrayed, although if he couldn't see why he wasn't suitable to be my second, then I wasn't sure I knew how to explain it to him.

It was about all that, and about the past. About Da.

Luka whispered something in Jochan's ear and put an arm around his shoulders that was part comforting, part restraining. Luka knew what would happen if Jochan pushed this too far in front of the crew, I realised. He was a clever man, and he had known us both for a very long time. He might not have grasped the truth of the matter, but he understood all too well what was happening between the Piety brothers.

'Go to bed,' I said again, in the quiet tavern.

'Our own da . . .' Jochan said.

A sob caught in his throat, but he said no more and I gave thanks to Our Lady for that. He slumped against Luka's chest as his knees buckled. The big man tightened his grip around my brother's shoulders to keep him from falling on his face and all but dragged him out of the room.

I turned away.

Anne kept a distance between us, perhaps sensing something private between brothers, something painful, and she made sure the others kept their distance too.

I needed some air.

I headed for the front door, which Black Billy hastily unlocked and opened for me without a word. I shouldered past him and stepped out into the freezing cold darkness of the street, out of sight.

Only then did I allow myself to weep.

I have written of the strongbox in the back of my mind where I keep the horrors locked away, the place where I never go.

Part of that box is called *Abingon*, but part of it has another name. Part of it is called *Da*.

Chapter 32

I stayed out in the street until I had myself under control again. Fifteen, perhaps twenty minutes had passed by the time I went back into the tavern, red-eyed and shivering with the cold, and with flakes of snow in my hair. I found the common room empty except for Bloody Anne.

She was sitting at a table in the middle of the room, a bottle of brandy and two glasses on the scarred wood in front of her. She didn't speak, just lifted the bottle in her hand and raised her eyebrows in a silent invitation.

I locked the door behind me and took the chair across the table from her. She poured for us both and pushed a glass toward me. I drained it in a single swallow, and she poured again. I lifted the glass and stared into the dark amber spirit, avoiding her eyes.

'I don't want to talk about it,' I said.

'Then don't. Just drink.'

'Aye.'

We drank together, neither of us speaking, until the bottle was half empty. It had been like that in the war, sometimes. When we had managed to get our hands on some drink, anyway. At first you think you want to pour out your feelings into the bottle, but you come to realise that you don't. You just want to drown them, to burn them away with alcohol until it stops hurting.

Anne knew that. She had been there.

It had been like that after Messia, I remembered. We had sacked the city when it fell and we looted what little they had had left. I remembered sharing a bottle with Anne and Kant, in the ruins of the great temple. None of us had said a word all night, just passed the bottle back and forth between us until it was done. After what we did that day, even Kant's bravado had deserted him. For a little while, at least. There's a comradeship in that, in drinking together and saying nothing, because no words need to be said.

'I think,' Anne said at last, when the bottle was half gone, 'I think I'm in love with Rosie.'

I looked up at her, at the expression on her face. That expression was half joyous, that she had someone she could tell, and half terrified by what she was saying. I nodded.

'That's good,' I said.

'Be better if she felt the same,' Anne said, and swallowed her drink. 'I'm still fucking paying for it.'

I shrugged. 'There's no shame in that.'

'There's no future in it either, though, is there?'

'Who can say? Perhaps there is.'

Anne nodded, and poured again. She could drink, could Bloody Anne, I had to give her that.

'Perhaps,' she said. 'She's got to make a living, I understand that, and time she's with me is time she's not with anyone else, earning. I have to . . . cover her lost income, I suppose.'

'That's between you and Rosie,' I said, 'but you don't have to justify it to me, Anne. If she makes you happy, then it's good.'

'She does,' Anne admitted. She swallowed her drink and looked at me. 'What about Ailsa, Tomas? Does she make you happy?'

I dare say she could have done, if she had ever shown the slightest interest in trying. I felt things for Ailsa that I knew were foolish and unwise, but knowing that a thing is foolish and doing something to change it are different matters. Ailsa thought nothing of me, I knew that. She was my fancy woman as far as everyone in the crew was concerned, though, including Anne. I didn't want to lie to her about this, not after she had opened up to me, but I knew I had to.

'She's a good girl,' I said, and forced a smile I didn't feel.

'She's got more to her than I thought at first, I'll admit that,' Anne said. 'I haven't been kind to her, and I regret that now. She's no fool, Tomas.'

'That she's not,' I agreed. I reached for the bottle and poured us both another drink, emptying it. 'I don't enjoy the company of fools.'

Anne laughed and swallowed her drink. 'Your brother must chafe you some,' she said.

I stopped the glass halfway to my lips and bit back a harsh reply that Anne didn't deserve. Jochan *was* a fool, I knew that, and Anne certainly wasn't, so of course she knew it too. I put the glass down again, untouched, and looked at her.

'It's difficult, sometimes,' I said. 'With Jochan. He's my little brother. Our childhood was . . . difficult too. I looked after him, in my way, as best I could.'

I remembered what Anne had told me about her own youth. What Jochan and I had suffered didn't compare to that. Not quite, anyway.

'I never meant—' Anne started.

She looked embarrassed now, and I didn't want that.

'No, it's all right,' I said. 'He *does* chafe me, you've the right of that. I . . . I owe Jochan a debt I can never repay, Anne. From the past, from when we were children. I should have done a thing . . . I did do it, but not soon enough, and he suffered for that. He suffered a great deal, and I could have stopped it and I didn't until it was too late. I'll always owe him a place at my side, for that. Not at my right hand, no, that's your place, but *a* place none the less.'

Anne just nodded.

'I'll get another bottle,' she said.

The next morning I had a headache like all the guns of Abingon were firing in the back of my skull. I lay in my bed with an arm over my eyes and suffered it. I had earned that sore head, I knew. I think Anne and me had almost emptied the second bottle before we finally admitted defeat and crawled to our respective blankets. *Crawl* was right, as well. I still had the splinters in the palms of my hands from dragging myself up the rough wooden stairs to my room on all fours, like an animal.

I groaned, and tried to remember where the conversation had gone once the second bottle was open. I know from experience that I'm a quiet drunk, not a talkative one, so I could only hope I hadn't said anything that I might regret. I didn't think I had, and even if so I doubted Anne would remember any better than I did.

Snatches of memory floated back to me as I lay there in my sweaty bedding. Anne had opened up to me, I recalled. She *was* a talkative drunk, which made me think again about what she might say to Rosie of an evening. I'd have to keep that in mind, I knew. She had told me more about what went on in their bed than I had really wanted to know, I remembered now, but I supposed it was no more than any other soldier boasts about their woman.

That made me smile despite the pain in my head, and I forced myself to sit up. Bloody Anne was a good friend, and I'll not record what she told me that night. Those things were her business, to my mind, and no one else's.

I made myself have a wash and a piss and put some clothes on, and I headed unsteadily down the stairs to the tavern. Mika and Hari were sharing small beer and black bread in the common room, and I joined them.

'Late night, boss?' Mika asked.

'Aye,' I said.

Hari picked up his stick and limped off to fetch me a mug of small beer, and I sipped it reluctantly. It would do me good, I knew, but truth be told, it was a struggle.

'Where's Ailsa?' I asked, after I had choked down half the mug.

'In the kitchen,' Hari said. 'She's got a visitor. That Rosie, from up Chandler's Narrow. I think they're friends, like.'

That gave me pause. I was certain by then that Rosie was Ailsa's contact in the Queen's Men, and I wondered what business they could have together at that time in the morning.

'I hope Bloody Anne don't take it ill,' Mika said, and I could see that he had a point there.

Mika could think for himself, as I have written, and Ailsa's tastes were something I had never even given thought to. Just because Ailsa had shown no interest in me didn't mean she preferred women, of course, but I had never even considered the possibility until then. I didn't want to see Anne hurt, I knew that much.

'Course she won't,' I said, making light of it. 'I know my Ailsa, and Anne's got no worries there.'

The lads gave me a laugh for that, and I excused myself and went through to the kitchen to see for myself.

'Oh, he's a devil, ain't he?' Ailsa was saying when I opened the door, and I knew she had heard someone coming and switched to her barmaid's voice without a second thought.

She giggled, and I gave her a look that said I knew very well what she had done. Rosie was sitting across the table from her, chewing on a hunk of bread.

'Good morning,' I said.

'Oh, you do look rough, you poor thing,' Ailsa said, and laughed her barmaid's laugh. 'You will sit up drinking with other women, my lover, you ought to expect to suffer for it in the morning.'

I closed the door behind me.

'Drinking's all we were doing,' I said, more for Rosie's benefit than hers.

'I know that,' Ailsa said in her sharp Dannsburg voice. 'Sit down, Tomas. We need to talk business.'

I looked at Rosie, and her gaze was like razors.

Chapter 33

'If you haven't worked it out for yourself yet,' Ailsa said, 'Rosie works for me.'

'Aye,' I said. 'I'd just about found my way to that.'

'Well and good,' she said. 'Now be quiet and listen, there's news.'

'There is,' Rosie said. 'Ma Aditi's pure furious with you, Mr Piety. Her new second had ties to the Golden Chains, and now it's yours again he's raising the gods over it. Well, I say he's her second but I'm not so sure that's even the lay of things down in the Wheels any more. From what I hear, Ma Aditi's a slave to the poppy now, and he's where her resin comes from. He's only been with them a couple of months but it might be he has more influence over the Gutcutters than she does, these days.'

That made me think. I remembered the man who had been sat at Ma Aditi's right hand. He was a big brute of a fellow, with the scarred face of a soldier. Someone she had found in Abingon, I had assumed, as he was no one I knew from Ellinburg. How he had ended up her second I still didn't know, but I suspected that the poppy had a good deal to do with it. I wondered who he was, and where his allegiances really lay. To the north, if I was any judge. To Skania.

The Skanians wanted the infrastructure of the city, as I have written, and they wanted its workforce too. Perhaps, it came to me, instead of continuing to fight the Gutcutters as they were fighting me, the Skanians had simply found the means to take them over from within. That would make sense – no general would choose to fight a war on two fronts if he didn't have to, and if the Skanians had truly taken over the Gutcutters, then that was a lot more soldiers they had at their command.

'And what does she mean to do?' I asked.

Rosie snorted. 'Aditi means to smoke her poppy resin and fuck her young lads and get even fatter, the way I hear it. It's this man of hers you want to be thinking on, Mr Piety. What he wants is the Chains, and he's making no secret of it. There's a good deal of gold to be had from the Chains these days, selling poppy resin to nobles and those who deal down the line and onto the streets. Ruthless bastard he is, too, from what I hear. Bloodhands, they call him, though I've not managed to hear why.'

I almost fucking choked, and Ailsa's face told me this was news to her too.

'I *beg* your pardon?' Ailsa said.

Rosie gave her a blank look, and I realised she wasn't privy to all of Ailsa's business after all. So she was just a spy then, and not a Queen's Man herself. For Anne's sake, I was glad about that.

'What I said, ma'am. They call him Bloodhands, but—'

'Never mind.' Ailsa cut her off, but her eyes bored into mine across the table and I knew that we were thinking the same thoughts, but I wasn't to speak them in front of Rosie.

Ma Aditi's new second was Bloodhands, the boss of the Skanians in Ellinburg. Bloodhands, who commanded the loyalty of his men by threatening their children's lives. Bloodhands, who had murdered a Queen's Man and sent him back to Dannsburg in four fucking pieces on four separate trade caravans.

I had been sitting at the same table with the cunt, and I hadn't known him.

'We must take the poppy trade before he does,' Ailsa announced.

I shook my head. 'I'm not doing that,' I said. 'Not resin.'

'You sold resin before the war,' she said. 'That was how we approached you the first time. Tea taxes alone wouldn't have done it.'

Fucking *approached* me? *Blackmailed* was the word for it, to my mind, and whatever I felt for Ailsa I still took that extremely ill.

'Aye, I did,' I said through clenched teeth. 'I sold it to doctors who couldn't get it any other way, so they could help desperate people who needed it to ease their suffering. I'm not supplying the street trade. Lady's sake, Ailsa, I'm doing everything I can to *stop* the fucking street trade.'

'There's gold to be made,' Rosie said again.

I thumped the flat of my hand down on the table and glared at both of them. 'I don't give a *fuck* if there's gold to be made,' I said. 'I've *got* gold, and I can't spend half of it. Poppy resin is ruining my people. I won't have it.'

Ailsa ignored me. 'Thank you, Rosie,' she said. 'I think it's time for Tomas and me to speak alone.'

Rosie nodded, dismissed, and got up from the table. We sat in silence while she put her cloak on, and then she was out of the kitchen and the door closed behind her.

'Bloodhands is Aditi's fucking second?' I said, once we were alone.

'So it would appear,' Ailsa said.

'I was sat at the table with the fucker,' I said. 'I could have—'

'But you didn't,' she interrupted me, 'because we didn't know. Now we do, and we must use that knowledge and move on. By its very nature the battlefield is ever shifting, Tomas, and it's no good dwelling on what *didn't* happen. The poppy trade is what matters now.'

'I'm not having that filth around my people.'

'Not your people, then,' Ailsa said. 'Forget the street trade. You're right; that causes more problems than it solves. The nobility, though, think on that. They know what they're doing, and they don't need to turn to crime to feed their habits.'

I put my head in my hands and drew a long breath. My head was still pounding from last night's drink and I was struggling to make sense of what Ailsa was saying.

'If you don't supply them they'll simply go to someone who will,' she went on. 'They'll go to Bloodhands, and through him to the Skanians. Do you want to put gold in his pockets so he can buy more soldiers and threaten more children?'

'I won't have it on my streets,' I said. 'I won't have it near working people, nor children either.'

'The nobles,' Ailsa said again. 'The nobles who come to the Golden Chains, at least. They expect it, Tomas. They *need* it.'

'I don't know anything about the fucking poppy trade,' I said. 'Where would I even get poppy resin to sell to them?'

'From me, of course.'

It took me two days to come up with a job that I could be confident Jochan would botch, but not badly enough to get himself hurt. By the time I was satisfied with my plan, I didn't need it any more. The Gutcutters broke the peace themselves.

Rosie had all but told us that they would, of course, but I hadn't expected it so soon. This Bloodhands wasn't a man to take his time, it seemed.

I was in the kitchen at the Tanner's after closing up for the night. Ailsa and me were having another argument about selling poppy resin through the Golden Chains when Simple Sam burst in on us. Thank the Lady he was too worked up to have overheard anything he shouldn't have done.

'Boss! Quick!'

I hurried after him into the common room to find a breathless Aunt Enaid leaning heavily on the bar, her fallen stick on the floor at her feet and snow melting from her cloak. Brak was slumped in a chair, his right hand clutching his left shoulder. Blood seeped between his fingers, and his sleeve was soaked with it. He had a long cut on his face too, and burns on both hands.

Jochan was there before me, reeling drunk and shouting.

'What the fuck happened?' he demanded.

'Gutcutters,' Enaid wheezed. 'I can't . . . curse it to the whores, I can't run on this fucking ankle. They stormed my house, four of them. Brak tried to fight them, bless his silly young heart. They—'

'Cunts!' Jochan bellowed.

He grabbed his axe from behind the bar and was off and running out the door a moment later, his mail forgotten and his shirt tails flapping behind him in the freezing wind and blowing snow of the winter night.

'Sam, Billy, Mika, get after him,' I snapped. 'I'll see to my aunt.'

The boys hastily grabbed weapons and set off after my brother's reckless charge. Ailsa was helping Enaid into a chair now, and I had a proper look at Brak.

'I'm sorry, boss,' he said. 'I tried me best.'

'I know,' I said, and frowned. 'How are you burned?'

'They had blasting powder,' he said. 'That's how they took the front door off. There was a fire. I couldn't . . . I tried.'

His face and hands were a mess, but a few more scars wouldn't kill him. It was that shoulder I was worried about. The cut was deep, right through the meat and almost to the bone. That's not a killing place, not in itself, but if it went bad he'd be done.

'Ailsa, rouse Cookpot out of the stable and send him to get Doc Cordin,' I said.

She nodded and went, and by then Anne and Erik had joined us. I put Erik in Billy's place on the door to watch for more trouble, with Stefan and Borys in the alley behind the stable yard. That was it; that was all the crew I had left at the Tanner's, what with the men I had off guarding my other businesses. I didn't count Hari in that, but he could still barely walk. I found I actually missed Sir Eland, which wasn't a thought I'd ever had before. He was a Pious Man in truth now, and his heavy armour and long sword would have been welcome if the Gutcutters came in force. I considered sending a runner to Chandler's Narrow to fetch him back, but what if they struck there instead? Will couldn't hold the place alone, and Cutter was still at Slaughterhouse Narrow.

'Cookpot's off on his errand,' Ailsa said.

I looked around and saw her standing there with my sword-belt in her hand. She passed it to me and I nodded thanks as I buckled it on.

'Keep the pressure on that shoulder,' I told Brak. 'The doc's on his way.'

Brak nodded, pale now with shock.

'Fucking blasting powder,' he whispered, and I could only nod.

It seemed to me that if Ailsa could supply me with poppy resin, then she ought to be able to get her hands on powder too. That was a thought for later, though. I turned to Anne.

'I need to go after my brother before he gets himself killed,' I said. 'Can you hold the Tanner's with just three men, if it comes to it?'

'Aye,' Anne said. 'If it comes to it.'

'I can work a crossbow,' Ailsa said, and smiled at me. 'If it comes to it.'

I was sure she could, at that.

'My thanks,' I said. 'Anne's in charge.'

With that I threw a cloak around my shoulders and headed out the door in pursuit of Jochan.

Chapter 34

Aunt Enaid's house wasn't far from the Tanner's Arms, and by the time I had run the length of three streets I could hear fighting. It had stopped snowing by then, but as I dashed around a corner my feet still almost slipped on the wet cobbles. I drew the Weeping Women. The house was on fire, the house that I had mostly grown up in, and Black Billy and Mika were back to back and fighting three men in the street outside. There was no sign of Jochan or Simple Sam anywhere. I stepped up behind one of the Gutcutters and rammed Mercy through his left kidney, dropping him to ground. Billy pressed the advantage and finished his man with a swing of his heavy club that smashed the fellow's head like an egg.

'Where the fuck's my brother?' I demanded.

Billy jerked a thumb toward the burning house and turned to help Mika. I left them to it and ducked through the shattered doorway, where a charge of blasting powder had torn half the front wall down. Inside was chaos.

Enaid had said there were four of them, but either she had been wrong about that or more had followed – there were two Gutcutters dead on the floor in the main room, and Sam and Jochan were fighting another three who were holding them off while one of their fellows wrestled a barrel upright in the space under the stairs.

Jochan had cuts and grazes and blood all over him, one sleeve of his shirt torn off and a long sooty burn up his exposed arm. He was roaring like a madman as he fought. Sam was favouring his right leg and had a hand held to a bloody gash in his thigh as he slashed wildly about him with the shortsword gripped in his other.

The damn fool had obviously charged straight into the house in his rage, and poor, faithful Sam must have followed him. I coughed in the thick smoke and joined them in the fray. Now we were evenly matched, Pious Men and Gutcutters. Cinders fell from the ceiling as we fought, and the wooden stairs were on fire. It felt like Abingon in there, choking smoke and flames all around us, the desperate clash of steel in the firelit darkness.

I parried a cut with Mercy and took my man through the throat with Remorse. A moment later Billy and Mika joined us, and the last Gutcutter still fighting chanced a desperate look over his shoulder at the man with the barrel.

A barrel.

A burning building, and a barrel . . .

'Run!'

I grabbed Jochan by the shoulder and almost dragged him after me as I sprinted for the hole in the wall. The others followed, trusting my instinct and the voice of command that they remembered from Abingon. When I saw that the two Gutcutters were fleeing with us, I knew that my instinct had been right.

We all but threw ourselves into the nearest alley, and a moment later the house exploded with a deafening roar as the barrel of blasting powder went up. A great rush of hot air and dust and smoke burst past the mouth of the alley, choking us even as we covered our heads against the rain of shattered timbers and burning laths.

The last timber clattered to the cobbles, the following silence broken only by the faint crackle of flames.

'Fuck a nun,' Jochan whimpered. He was slumped on the ground with his back against the wall, visibly shaking. His breath came in short gasps that spoke of a violent bout of battle shock. 'Oh, fuck a nun, Tomas, when will it ever end?'

He put his head in his hands and started to weep.

I rubbed a hand over my face and it came away black with soot and sweat. Billy and Mika were both obviously shaken too, and I saw Sam hurrying down the alley away from us.

No, that wasn't right – Sam was wounded in the leg but he wasn't limping. This man was balding on the crown of his head, too, and Sam wasn't.

'Oi!' I shouted.

Billy's head whipped around and he took off on his powerful legs, quickly running down the Gutcutter whom I had taken to be Simple Sam in the dark confusion of the alley. There was a thud and I saw Billy's knife rise and fall once, twice, and it was done.

'Where the fuck's Sam, then?' Mika asked.

I doubted Sam could have run, not on that wound. I swallowed bile and looked away.

'Stay here,' I said. 'Watch my brother.'

I ducked out of the alley and back into the street, Remorse in my hand. The house was gone, and only flames and a few of the heavier timbers remained of the place I had called home after my da had died. People were out of their houses now that the fighting had stopped, passing buckets from their pumps and trying to keep the flames from reaching their own homes. Everything was still wet from the earlier snow, thank the Lady, and I didn't think the fire would spread.

There were two bodies lying on the cobbles.

No one paid me any attention as I stood over them. These were my streets, the heart of the Stink, and if anyone there saw me they would know well enough to pretend that they hadn't. One man lay on top of the other, his back raw and blackened with burns. He was quite dead, but he was no one I knew. I rolled him to one side and bent over Simple Sam. He was breathing, at least, and with no time for niceties I slapped his face until his eyes opened.

'Come on, Sam lad, up with you now,' I said.

Sam grinned up at me. 'Hit me head, boss,' he said. 'I knew I couldn't run none so I stabbed that arsehole and pulled him down over me, but I hit me head on the cobbles.'

'Aye,' I said. 'You're alive, thank the Lady, but we need to go.'

Simple Sam was alive because he had had the good sense and the plain ruthlessness to use the fleeing Gutcutter as a shield from the explosion, even if he had managed to knock himself out in the process. I wondered if Sam was quite as simple as we all thought.

Mika and Billy helped Sam back to the Tanner's between them. He had both his arms over their shoulders, and his wounded leg dragged behind him in the patchy snow as the three of them walked awkwardly down the road. I led Jochan, my hand on his arm to steer him. He was meek as a child now, his eyes downcast and his breathing steady once more.

As we approached the tavern I caught a glimpse of Ailsa at my upstairs window, with Bloody Anne's crossbow in her hands. Erik let us in and locked the door again behind us as Anne hurried over to help the lads get Sam into a chair.

Doc Cordin was there, finishing sewing up Brak's shoulder.

'I brought you another one, Doc,' I said.

The doc just sighed and nodded, and I sat Jochan down and put a bottle of brandy on the table in front of him. I thought he had earned it.

'What happened?' Anne asked.

'We killed them,' I said, and that was enough. I looked up and met my aunt's flinty stare. 'Your house . . . I'm sorry.'

She shook her head and said nothing.

Jochan had the bottle open now and was drinking straight from the neck, the lump in his throat working as he swallowed brandy like it was beer. I saw Ailsa come down the stairs with the crossbow still in her hands. It looked at home there.

'We blew your fucking house up, Auntie,' Jochan said.

He laughed, brandy dribbling from the corner of his mouth. He laughed, and once he had started he didn't seem to be able to stop. I helped him out of the chair, and as I did I saw that he had pissed himself. I picked his bottle up for him and led him through to the back where the others couldn't see him any more. Hopefully he'd drink himself to sleep soon enough.

When I came back Ailsa had put the crossbow down on the bar and donned her barmaid's face.

'Are you hurt, my lover?' she asked, fussing around my sooty face with a damp cloth.

'I'm fine,' I said. 'Doc, how's Sam and Brak?'

'I'm all right, boss,' Brak said, but he was ghost white and clutching a brandy bottle so hard with his good hand that I thought the glass might shatter. Enaid was sitting with him now, her hand resting on his knee.

Sam was biting down on a folded belt while the Doc sewed up the long gash in his thigh, but to my mind he'd got off lightly. It's not often a man walks away from an explosion like that.

'This isn't too deep,' Cordin said. 'Keep it clean and he'll be all right. Your other man's shoulder worries me, though.'

'I'm all right,' Brak said again, but he obviously wasn't.

'The silly boy's being strong for me,' Enaid said.

'I'm not a boy,' Brak said, for all that Enaid must have had forty more years than him. 'I'm your man.'

'Hush now,' she said, and I realised she thought I didn't know.

'Auntie,' I said in a low voice, taking a chair beside her, 'who you choose to bed is your affair, not mine. Brak, you're *not* all right. You need to rest. Take my room tonight, you and Enaid. I'll sleep with the men.'

'You can sleep with me, my handsome,' Ailsa said, putting a hand on my shoulder.

It must have looked like an affectionate gesture to anyone watching, but I could feel the strength in her grip and I knew it wasn't meant that way. Ailsa wanted words, I could tell.

'Aye,' I said. 'Aye, why not.'

Mika and Black Billy hid their grins as best they could, and I let it pass. Ailsa was supposed to be my fancy woman, after all, so why not indeed?

Chapter 35

Borys and me helped Brak up the stairs to my room, and we left him there with Enaid looking after him. Alone together at the top of the stairs, Borys gave me a level look. He was older than most of the others, a big, thoughtful man who said little. He looked like he was about to make up for that, to my mind.

'It's going wrong, boss,' he said in a low voice. 'We're running out of men in a fit state to fight. They've got blasting weapons and we ain't. What's going to happen if these Gutcutters come at us in force?'

'I can get blasting weapons,' I said, and thought on what Ailsa had told me. 'More men too. Trained men, who can handle themselves. This is my city, Borys. I can get men.'

Both those things were true, if unrelated. I had raised the crossbowmen we had used at the Chains myself, admittedly, but they wouldn't do. They weren't men I knew and they weren't veterans, and I wouldn't trust them with anything more than a simple ambush. Ailsa's men, though, I thought they would be useful.

'Are you lovely boys having a private chat, or can anyone join in?' Ailsa said, startling me.

The stairs were old and splintery and creaked like a sign in the wind, but I hadn't heard her climb them. That explosion obviously hadn't done my ears any good.

'Sorry, Miss Ailsa,' Borys said, moving out of the way of her door.

'How many times do I got to tell you? Just Ailsa's fine,' she said, and showed him her barmaid's smile.

She went into her room and beckoned me to follow with a saucy wink. Borys nodded and clumped off down the stairs, leaving us alone in her bedroom.

I closed the door behind me and turned to face her.

'Well, you said you wanted to fuck something up,' Ailsa snapped at me. 'Blowing up your own aunt's house certainly qualifies.'

'That's not . . .' I started to say, and sighed. I slumped against the wall and put a hand over my eyes. 'That's not exactly what happened. They had a whole fucking barrel of powder in there, Ailsa. Blowing the house up was what they intended. They were making a statement, going after my family to show me that they can.'

'And you just didn't stop them, is that it? Oh, it's well and good, Tomas. Hauer will never believe *I* orchestrated a disaster of that magnitude, so at least your brother's incompetence should have thrown him off my scent. That is what we wanted, after all.'

'I didn't want Jochan to get hurt,' I said.

'He's in a better state than Brak and Sam are.'

'No, he's not,' I said. 'I saw him in that house, fighting in the flames. He was back in Abingon, Ailsa, back there in truth. When the blast went off I think he nearly lost his mind.'

'Tomas,' she said, and came to me. She took my hand and looked into my eyes. 'Your brother's mind is probably beyond your power to save, you have to realise that. You can't cure him, but you do have to control him.'

'I know,' I said.

'He can still be useful,' she went on. 'He fights like a wild animal, and he's dangerous, and men fear him. Those traits can be used, but they must be used *carefully*.'

'I know,' I said again, and sighed. 'He's my brother, Ailsa, not a war dog.'

'The right man for the right job, isn't that how you lead men?'

It was, but I couldn't recall ever having said it to her. I supposed I must have done, and forgotten it.

'Aye,' I admitted.

'And how are *you*?'

'Well enough,' I said, although I wondered if I really was.

I still remembered what Billy the Boy had done to me at Old Kurt's house, and I wondered if my own mind was so very much stronger than Jochan's. I walked over to the window and stared out of it, into the stable yard behind the tavern. Stefan was keeping watch at the alley gate, wrapped in two cloaks over his heavy coat. Bloody Anne was coming out of the shithouse, hitching her britches up with one hand and trying to hold her cloak around her with the other against the freezing night air. It might be cold, but other than that Ellinburg didn't feel so very different to Abingon, that night.

That was the very thing I was trying to avoid, and it seemed to my mind that I was failing at it.

'You need to sleep,' Ailsa said.

'Aye,' I said, but my voice sounded hollow in my own ears.

'Tomas,' she snapped. 'Look at me.'

I turned from the window and tried to focus. Lady knew Ailsa was beautiful, but I was struggling to see her face. The shadows in the room looked all wrong, and that was making me nervous. Anyone could be hiding in those shadows. My hands went instinctively to the hilts of the Weeping Women and I bent my knees into a half crouch, my gaze darting around the room. I felt exhausted but too alert, my senses stretched taut yet at the same time also strangely numbed. I drew a sharp breath.

I was ready.

Ready to kill.

'It's all right, my handsome,' Ailsa said in her barmaid's voice. 'There's no one here but Ailsa.'

She came and took my face in her hands, and looked deeply into my eyes. She breathed steadily, slow and deep, and unconsciously I found my own breaths matching her rhythm. My hands slowly relaxed, slipping off the hilts of my swords until they hung limp at my sides. That awful tightness of the senses drained away and I felt myself calming.

I was so tired.

She backed up a step and I went with her, feeling the warmth of her hands on my face. She held my stare and never broke it until we were right beside her bed. She breathed slow and deep, and so did I. Just then I was fighting to keep my eyes open, as though I hadn't slept in days. I wondered if perhaps she was doing something to me, some magic, but I was too tired to think about it.

'You need to sleep,' she said again, her voice low and soothing.

My knees buckled and I slumped sideways onto the mattress. She stroked my forehead with her fingertips and my eyes closed. Her touch lulled me like . . . a charm.

I was dimly aware of her pulling her blankets over me. As sleep took me, I wondered just what hidden skills the Queen's Men had.

When I woke it was to see Ailsa dozing in her chair with a spare blanket wrapped around her. I took care to be still, not wanting to wake her. She was sitting under the window, and the dawn light lit her face in a way that she would never have chosen. Some of her paints and powders had rubbed off in the night, and I could see then that she had a good many more years to her than I had first thought. She had forty, perhaps forty-five years to her, I could see now, and not all of them had been kind. It made sense. I had thought when I first met her that she was too young for the position she held, and she had told me herself that she was a good deal older than she looked. But I didn't recall her ever telling me that she was a cunning woman.

Perhaps she wasn't that, not exactly anyway, but she had done something to me the night before. Some sort of magic, I was sure. Truth be told, I was glad that she had. I had been slipping, I knew, starting to lose my way again. Perhaps my battle shock wasn't the same as Jochan's, or Cookpot's, but it was there all the same. Men could react to a thing in different ways, to my mind.

I eased the blankets off and Ailsa's eyes snapped open at once.

'Morning,' I said.

'How do you feel?' she asked, and it was the Queen's Man talking again now.

'Better,' I said, and it was true. Whatever had started to take hold of me last night had gone, or at least faded away in the night. 'What did you do to me?'

'I just helped you to sleep,' she said. 'You needed some rest.'

'Was that magic?'

'No,' she said. 'No, not in the way you mean it. I'm not a magician, Tomas, nor do I have what you would call the cunning. There are things that can be learned, though. Ways of speaking, rhythms of breathing and tones of voice that can make a person . . . receptive to suggestions, shall we say.'

I didn't really understand what she meant, but I couldn't see that she had reason to lie to me about it. Making a man 'receptive to suggestions' had obvious uses when it came to asking questions, and it was common knowledge that the Queen's Men asked questions on behalf of the crown.

'I see,' I said.

I sat up and swung my feet out of bed. She had taken off my sword-belt and boots at some point after I fell asleep, but other than that I was still dressed in the soot-stained clothes I had fallen down in the night before. I had left a fair amount of that soot in her bed, I realised.

'Sorry about your blankets.'

'The washerwoman can see to them,' she said. 'Never mind that now. I need to repair my face – go downstairs and see who's awake. Hopefully your brother is still unconscious, but if not you may need to keep an eye on him this morning.'

'Aye,' I said, biting back my irritation at being dismissed from her room like a servant.

I put my boots on and left her to her paints and powders, buckling on my sword-belt as I headed down the stairs. It was early but Bloody Anne was up, taking the morning watch in the common room.

'Who's about?' I asked her.

'Borys has the back,' she said. 'I let the rest sleep. It seemed to me that as you slaughtered the lot of them at Enaid's house last night they might not be in a hurry to try again.'

I nodded. I had the same hope. The Gutcutters might have succeeded in destroying my aunt's house, but it had taken them nine men to do it and we had left no survivors. That wasn't a good result for them, to my mind, and I doubted that this Bloodhands thought otherwise. He was ruthless, yes, but as the governor had told me he was something like a Queen's Man himself so he must understand strategy, and when losses were acceptable and when they very much weren't.

'That's good,' I said, and took the seat opposite her. 'I hope you got some sleep yourself.'

'Aye, some,' Anne said. 'I'm working the men on short watches, like we did in the mountains. It's too cold out there for a man to stand a full watch in the yard and not freeze to death.'

'Aye,' I said.

Bloody Anne knew what she was about. This was sergeant's work, not Pious Men business now, and Anne had been the best sergeant in our regiment.

The Pious Men are businessmen, but you've turned them into soldiers.

I remembered my aunt telling me that, and I knew then that she was right. These *were* soldiers, every one of them, so why not use them that way? The right man for the right job, always.

'Word will have got round the streets about last night,' I said, after a while. 'If you need to go up to Chandler's Narrow and show Rosie that you're safe, I'll understand. Once some of the men are awake I'll send a bodyguard with you.'

Anne gave me a bleak look. 'I don't know that she's been up all night worrying,' she said. 'I'm her best customer, but I'm not fooling myself that I'm any more than that to her.'

I shrugged and looked away. I wouldn't know, and I didn't want to say the wrong thing.

'Ailsa couldn't wait to get you in her bed last night,' Anne went on, a bitter note in her voice now. 'That must be nice, to have someone who wants you back.'

'She doesn't,' I said, although I hadn't meant to. I was supposed to be keeping up a pretence that Ailsa was my fancy woman, after all, but I was sick of lying to the only real friend that I had left. 'I slept in her bed, that's all. She didn't join me.'

'I thought you two . . . ?'

'No,' I said. 'No, but that's between us, Bloody Anne.'

'Of course.' She surprised me by putting her hand on mine, on the table. Her scar twisted as she formed a wry smile. 'Who'd want either of us, Tomas?'

I returned her smile and gave her hand a squeeze. In a different world, perhaps one where Anne liked men and I didn't regard her almost as a brother, we might have been good for each other. Not in this world, though; we both knew that.

A knock on the front door had us on our feet and sent my hands to my sword hilts. I shot Anne a questioning look. She frowned and slipped one of her daggers from its sheath and into her sleeve, then got up and went to the door. She pushed back the small sliding hatch that let her see outside, and then her face split into a wide grin and she hastily unlocked the door and threw it open.

Rosie was in her arms a moment later.

'Thank the gods,' Rosie gasped, visibly out of breath. 'I just heard what happened. I ran all the way here from Chandler's Narrow.'

I turned away and found that my eyes were stinging.

Chapter 36

After a week of arguing, I made a deal with Ailsa.

The Gutcutters had caused no more trouble, and according to Luka's spies they were barricaded in the Wheels awaiting my reprisal for the attack on Aunt Enaid's house. They could wait, to my mind, although I thought my aunt disagreed on that. Jochan was still in a bad way with the battle shock, drunk every day and barely coherent. That, and I had too many men wounded to be able to move against the Gutcutters yet, whatever Enaid said. Brak was healing slowly, and I had temporarily moved the two of them to the house on Slaughterhouse Narrow where they would be out of my way. Cutter had the guard there, and I didn't think anyone would get past him easily.

'It won't do, Tomas,' Ailsa said, yet again. 'You have your old businesses back, but that isn't enough. It won't be enough for the Skanians to merely control the Gutcutters and their part of the city. They want all of it. They will come after you again, and still you sit here and do nothing.'

'I know that,' I said, pacing to her window to stare down into the stable yard. 'I know that, and I've told you that I don't have the men or the weapons to attack the Wheels. If you want me to expand, I need blasting powder, and flashstones, and men who know how to use them. I need crossbows and bolts and swords, and skilled hands to wield them.'

'Men and swords are easy to come by; military weapons are not. Flashstones are illegal outside of the army.'

'So's fucking poppy resin!'

'That's different,' she said, although I couldn't see how. She sighed and sat down on her bed. 'A stalemate is no use to me; I need to drive the Skanians from the city completely.'

'Aye,' I said, 'and if you want me to do that for you then I need the fucking weapons to do it *with*.'

'Then you'll do what I ask,' she shot back at me. 'You're asking me for a miracle, Tomas. Well, miracles are not free, and this is the price.'

I had been hiring staff, mostly through Fat Luka, and I was about ready to open the Golden Chains again. Ailsa's price was that I continue the poppy trade through the Chains, selling to the nobility and rich merchants who would be my customers there. She wanted the lever that moved them, of course, and addiction is a strong enough lever to move anyone. With her hand controlling the supply of poppy resin that these powerful people were becoming dependent on, she would gain a great deal of influence in the upper levels of Ellinburg society. I knew that, but that didn't mean that I liked it. I didn't like it one fucking little bit, truth be told, but I couldn't see that I had a choice. It seemed I seldom did, where the Queen's Men were concerned.

All the same, I couldn't see any other way to break the deadlock between us. Ailsa owed me nothing. I knew that. Our relationship only stood while we were useful to each other, for all that I would have had it be otherwise. I hated what she represented, it was true, but I had to allow that I was a long way from hating *her*.

'Aye,' I said at last. 'I'll make a deal with you, then. You bring me the weapons and men that I need to take the fight to Ma Aditi and the Skanians who move her, and I'll sell your filthy poppy resin for you. Only through the Chains, mind, and only to the rich folk. I'm not having it on my streets, Ailsa. I mean it.'

'Well and good,' she said. She sighed. 'You're a stubborn and difficult man, Tomas Piety.'

I supposed that I was, at that.

'How long?' I asked her.

'To bring you men and swords and crossbows, blasting powder and illegal military weapons? Do you think I have them under my skirts?'

I cleared my throat and turned back to the window. I had been giving too much thought of late to what lay under Ailsa's skirts, and I knew talk like that wouldn't help.

'I accept it may take time,' I said.

She laughed. 'A week to send a rider to Dannsburg, perhaps two for the wagons to make the return trip with what you ask. No more than that.'

I stared at her, and realised she had been making fun of me.

'So simply?' I asked.

'If I want men and weapons, I will have them,' she said. 'I have the Queen's Warrant, Tomas. I can do anything.'

'Not so much of a miracle, then, is it?'

'Is it not miracle enough that the crown is prepared to give you the means to take over almost the entire underworld of Ellinburg? "When you are gifted a horse, count not its teeth". I believe that is the expression.'

I didn't know much about horses, or their teeth. I could ride one, but that was it. I was no idle noble, to have time on my hands to spend on horse breeding, and I had hired the people who used to look after my racehorse. Again, I suspected she was making fun of me, and I didn't care for it.

'Three weeks, then,' I said, pushing the conversation back to where I wanted it. 'In three weeks I'll have the men and weapons to take the Wheels?'

'Three weeks or thereabouts,' she said. 'My rider might be waylaid on the road. There could be a shortage of blasting powder in Dannsburg. We deal mostly in *could* and *might* and *possibly*, as you may recall. Nothing is certain in this life until it is too late, but yes. Plan for three weeks, and be prepared to hold off if required.'

'Aye,' I said, and started to turn to the door.

'Oh, and Tomas? Have someone run up to Chandler's Narrow and bring Rosie to me, would you?'

Of course it was Rosie she would give this request to, and Rosie who would no doubt pass it to someone else, some other agent of the Queen's Men in Ellinburg. That person would set a rider on their way to Dannsburg, and soon enough what I had asked for would arrive. I had no idea who Rosie might speak to, and I wondered if Ailsa herself did. From what I had seen of the Queen's Men, it wouldn't have greatly surprised me if she didn't.

The day before Godsday, Old Kurt came calling at the Tanner's Arms.

He had Billy the Boy with him, and the lad had a bag in his hand.

It was a little after sundown, and snowing outside. The tavern was busy, full of local men drinking away their wages or gambling them on the turn of the dice. That was how life was lived, in the Stink. Godsday was traditionally a day of rest, as I have written. Even where that rule wasn't strictly observed, the night before was usually the night when men did most of their drinking. The day before Godsday was Coinsday, and it was when working folk who were paid by the week received their wages. A man might give two thirds of his pay to his wife, to keep their house, but the rest was his and it was usually gone by Godsday morning. People are weak, as I had told Ailsa, and the poorer and more oppressed they are, the weaker they become. Working men, above all others, have a weakness for drink.

The Stink was a good place to keep a tavern.

I was sitting at my corner table in the common room, with Simple Sam standing between me and the customers to keep folk away from me. His leg was mostly healed by then, and since the night of the explosion he had taken it upon himself to become my personal bodyguard. I think he felt indebted to me for bringing him home that night. Sam was a slow lad but a faithful one, and he certainly had a good size to him. No one bothered me without an invitation, not with Sam standing in front of my table.

The job suited him, I had to admit. I believe in putting the right man in the right job, but if a man chooses that job for himself and is suited for it, then I won't argue with him.

I poured myself another brandy from the bottle on the table in front of me and was just raising the glass when Old Kurt walked into the Tanner's. Black Billy had the door, and he shot me a look as the old man shambled into the common room, leaning heavily on his stick. I saw the boy beside him, in a hooded cloak that was too big for him and flakes of snow melting off the thick wool around his shoulders. I nodded to Billy to let them in and reached out to tap Sam on the arm.

'Let those two join me,' I said. 'And they drink on the house.'

Sam nodded and ushered Kurt and Billy the Boy to my table. A moment later Ailsa was there with mugs of beer for them both, without needing to be asked. She missed nothing, I had to admit, however busy the tavern might be.

'Kurt,' I said. 'This is an unexpected pleasure. And young Billy, how are your studies progressing?'

'Well, Uncle Tomas,' Billy said, pushing his hood back from his head.

He needed a haircut, but the fluff on his upper lip was gone, I noticed, and he had a faint shadow on his jaw that said he had started shaving.

'That's good,' I said, and caught Kurt's eye.

The old man had a bleak expression on his face, and I could tell that he wanted to speak to me alone.

'Billy, why don't you run into the kitchen and see if Hari can find you something to eat?'

The lad grinned at me and nodded, and did as I said. He took his beer with him, I noticed, as a grown man would have done. I raised my eyebrows at Old Kurt.

'You're having him back,' the cunning man said.

'Pardon?'

'You heard me. I can't handle him no more, and that's that.'

'Three marks a week and not a copper more, that's what I told you. I said that price would never go up again whatever he does, and I stand by those words.'

Old Kurt turned and spat on the floor beside his chair. 'You could offer me ten marks a week and I'd turn you down,' he said. 'I don't want him in my house no more. The boy's fucking possessed, like I told you.'

'And I told you, the boy is *holy*.'

'No,' Old Kurt said. 'He fucking well ain't.'

He met my stare without blinking, and I saw that he meant it.

'What did he do?' I asked at last.

'I came down one morning and there must have been fifty rats in my parlour,' Kurt said. 'Not running around, mind, nor nibbling on nothing. Just sitting there, they was, staring at me with their little ratty eyes. Accusing, like. Billy said it was on account of the rats I nail to my door, and how they didn't like it when I did that. I allowed that perhaps they didn't, and asked him if he knew how they had got there.'

'And?'

'Well, he didn't say he had brought them, but then he didn't say as that he hadn't, either. He just sort of smiled at me. That smile made me feel cold, Mr Piety, I have to admit. I asked him if he could get rid of them, and he nodded. I went through the back for my morning piss and when I come back . . . when I come back they was all dead. Fifty dead rats lying on my parlour floor and all of them with their backs broken, and your Billy didn't look like he'd moved an inch. He shouldn't . . . he shouldn't ought to be able to do that. Not yet. Maybe not ever.'

'And you didn't teach him how?'

'I don't fucking *know* how,' Kurt hissed at me.

I nodded slowly. Old Kurt couldn't keep Billy the Boy any longer, I could see the truth of that. Not now he was this afraid of the lad. Besides, it seemed to my mind that Billy might have outgrown his teaching already.

'All right,' I said. 'I'll have the lad back and we'll call it square. What else can he do?'

Kurt just shrugged. 'He learned the basic things fast enough,' he said. 'The quenching of fires he had before we even started, and he picked up the setting of them fast enough, and then the calling of them. He can mend hurts, but you knew that, and now he can cause them too. Divination's a strange one, with him. Sometimes he knows a thing will happen, however outlandish it may seem, and the thing happens just how he said it would. But ask him what time the sun will rise in the morning and he has no answer to give you. He can write and he can draw a glyph, but he seems unable to read any hand but his own, and he can't read a printed book at all. How you can learn to write when you can't read is beyond me, but there it is.'

'The goddess moves through him,' I said, thinking out loud.

'Something does, aye,' Old Kurt said. 'Whether it's your goddess or some devil from Hell is another question.'

'You be quiet with that,' I said, sharply. 'You listen to me, Old Kurt, and you mark me. The boy is *holy*. Do you understand me? If you've a different opinion, you'd be wise to keep it to yourself. Very wise indeed.'

'Aye,' Old Kurt muttered, and took a long swallow of his beer. 'Aye, I mark you, Tomas Piety.'

I nodded. 'Well and good,' I said. 'See that you do.'

Chapter 37

Billy the Boy seemed happy enough to move back into the Tanner's Arms, and he took to Ailsa immediately. Once word reached him that she was my woman, he took to calling her Auntie.

For all that that caused some merriment among the crew, she didn't seem to mind it any. I was glad about that. I remembered walking along the river path with Anne and Billy on our way to Old Kurt's house, back in the spring. It had seemed to me at the time that we might almost have been a family, and I remembered that I had thought then that perhaps it would be no bad thing. Not with Anne, no, but with Ailsa I thought it might well be a different matter. I was being a fool there, I knew that, but still the thought lingered.

Aunt and Uncle, I would take that if it was offered.

Hari and Billy renewed their friendship, largely based on pastries though it may have been, and a few days passed merrily enough. Jochan still worried me, but there was little I could do about that. He would come out of it or he wouldn't, I supposed. Fat Luka was away a lot, out in the streets doing what he did best.

'The Gutcutters are laid in for a siege,' he told me one night, sharing my table in the Tanner's while Simple Sam loomed in front of us and kept flapping ears away. 'I think they don't understand why there's been no reprisal for Enaid's house. Some of them say it's because you're too weak to strike back, but the prevailing word is otherwise. I've paid well for that word, and so far it's working. Our man Gregor sits at Ma Aditi's left hand, and he whispers in her ear whatever I tell him to.'

I remembered that man from our sit-down with the Gutcutters, sitting there in his purple shirt and whispering to her as Luka said. Whether or not Bloodhands listened to him remained to be seen. I nodded.

'Well and good,' I said, 'but it won't do forever, will it?'

'No, boss, it won't,' Luka said. 'Is there any word on the . . . the thing we talked about?'

'It's coming,' I said, and I hoped that was true.

Ailsa might well like to deal in *could* and *might* and *possibly*, but I preferred cold certainties. I needed those weapons and men, and I needed them soon. It had been over a week now since I had made my deal with Ailsa and sent a boy to fetch Rosie to her, so I could only hope that her rider had already reached Dannsburg. All being well, there were wagons rolling up the West Road toward us even as we spoke, laden with trained men and army weapons.

If not, then there would be hard times ahead. Luka's gold could only keep the Gutcutters sitting tight for so long, and if they came at us again I knew we would be sorely pressed. They had blasting weapons and I didn't, and through Bloodhands they had the backing of the Skanians.

If the Skanians had had one magician then I dare say they had another. I didn't have a magician, but perhaps I had something else. I had Billy the Boy, and from what Old Kurt had told me I thought that might be a good thing.

It may seem harsh, to use a boy so young in battle, but he had fought and killed men in Abingon, and before that. We had found him as an orphan in Messia, but he was alive and unharmed and that meant he had fought there, too, alone among the ruins. He'd have been dead if he hadn't.

Billy the Boy was a soldier, in his way, and he was of age now. Aye, if it came to it, Billy would fight. Whether his cunning was strong enough to defeat a Skanian magician was another matter, of course. I remembered the one we had faced in the Golden Chains and how flames had sprung from his fingertips like living things. I remembered how Grieg had burned and then simply exploded before my eyes. Could Billy really stand up against that?

The boy's fucking possessed, Old Kurt had said. *Whether it's your goddess or some devil from Hell is another question.*

If those weapons didn't arrive soon, I would take whichever I could get.

Another week went by, and I knew it wouldn't keep any longer.

Luka's spies reported that the Gutcutters were restless, and nothing that his man said could keep them in fear of us now. I had sat too long without acting, and I knew that I couldn't wait for Ailsa's men. I had to do something, and at once.

'Word is, they'll try us tomorrow,' Luka told me that morning. 'Something to test our defences. Bloodhands has Aditi's ear, and he controls her poppy supply. I don't know where he's getting it from so I can't cut it off, but he has more say over her now than my man does.'

I would have bet good gold that Bloodhands was getting that resin from his Skanian masters the same way I was getting mine from Ailsa, but I couldn't tell Luka about that. He certainly wasn't getting it through the Golden Chains, I knew that much. We were open for business again by then, but the membership list was small and select and drawn only from the upper class of Ellinburg, such as it was. And Captain Rogan, of course. I had had to honour that agreement, although all he did was play cards and lose money. Rogan wasn't the type to smoke the poppy, whereas Ma Aditi very much was.

I was sitting with Luka and Bloody Anne at my table in the common room, keeping our voices low although we weren't open for the day yet. I hadn't invited Jochan to this council of war. He was my brother, yes, but he was still too far gone from himself to be of much use at the planning table.

'Very well,' I said. 'Then we hit them tonight, while they're busy planning for tomorrow. That should put them off the idea.'

'Boss,' Luka said, and shifted his bulk in his seat the way he did when he was about to say something he thought I might take ill. 'I don't know that we can. The new men are untried and I don't trust a one of them, not yet. Sam's only just fit, and Brak's still useless with his shoulder. We could swap out Cutter and Sir Eland for a couple of the new lads just for a night, I suppose, but you need four to hold the Tanner's and that still only leaves us . . .'

His brow furrowed as he tried to figure it, and I cut him off.

'I know how many men I've got, Fat Luka,' I said. 'You're right, it's not enough for a frontal assault on the Wheels and that's not what I'm suggesting.'

I turned to Bloody Anne and noted the thoughtful expression on her face.

'You remember the road from Messia, when we were ahead of the main march of the regiment and we caught up with the enemy baggage train?' I said. 'Well, the captain didn't have us attempt to storm it, did he? That would have been madness, and the captain was no fool. Small raiding parties, coming in the night from all directions, that was how we did it. Hit and run and hit again, until they thought we had ten times the numbers that we did. Do you remember that, Bloody Anne?'

She nodded. 'Aye,' she said. 'I remember.'

'Well and good,' I said. 'What worked once will work again, to my mind.'

Anne nodded, and even Fat Luka started to smile.

'Who, and where?' Anne asked me.

I trusted Sir Eland enough to have him running security at the Golden Chains now, where his airs and graces could be put to good use, while Will the Wencher was breaking in a couple of the new lads for me in his place up at Chandler's Narrow. That was good and Eland needed to stay there, but Cutter was wasted babysitting a boarding-house full of harmless slaughtermen and skinners.

'Jochan, with Stefan and Erik,' I said. 'Leave Sir Eland where he is, but take Cutter and put him with Jochan's crew. Some of the new boys can look after Slaughterhouse Narrow for a bit. Me, with you and Borys. Mika, Billy and Luka with Sam to hold the Tanner's.'

'Which Billy?' Luka asked.

I blinked at him. 'Black Billy, you fool. The door's his, and he won't want anyone else taking it. Billy the Boy . . .' I paused for a moment, and remembered my thoughts of the previous week. 'Aye, I'll take Billy the Boy with me.'

Anne gave me a look, but I ignored that.

'A bit of experience will do him good,' Luka said.

I nodded, but that wasn't what I had meant.

Not at all.

Chapter 38

That night we didn't open the Tanner's to the public, and I assembled the three crews in the common room to address them.

Jochan, Stefan, Erik, and Cutter made up one raiding party. Me, Bloody Anne, Borys and Billy the Boy were the other, leaving Fat Luka, Simple Sam, Mika and Black Billy to hold the Tanner's. Sir Eland and his squad of hired men had a good grip on the Golden Chains, I knew, and I could only hope that Will the Wencher had his new lads in good enough shape to keep the house on Chandler's Narrow safe. Slaughterhouse Narrow wasn't likely to be at risk, to my mind, being the farthest from the Wheels and the least valuable. The rest of my businesses just paid me protection and weren't permanently guarded. That was well and good, then.

Everyone was mailed and fully armed, and Bloody Anne had made sure no one was drunk. Except for Jochan, of course. There was nothing to be done about that.

'Right,' I addressed them. 'Tonight we take the fight into the Wheels. There's two ways up there from here, the river path and Dock Road. Jochan, I want your squad to head along the river path. Slip up the alley past Old Kurt's house and come out at the top of Dock Road where they won't expect you. Kill anyone who tries to stop you. I'll lead my lot right up the road from here, where they'll see us coming. That should put the fox in the fucking henhouse, and once they're up and at us you can come running and take them in the rear. Everyone clear on that?'

There was a chorus of grunts and ayes, and I nodded. Ailsa was standing behind the bar, for all that we weren't open. I looked over and caught her eye. She gave me a short nod, and it was done.

We pulled up the hoods of our cloaks and set off into the blowing snow.

Dock Road was a good mile long, from the edge of the Stink to the top of the alley that ran past Old Kurt's house, but no one had noticed that flaw in my plan. Not that it was a flaw, as such, not if what I believed turned out to be true. Expecting Jochan's crew to creep along the river path and join up with us before we were overwhelmed would have been a fool's thinking, of course, if it had just been the four of us with blades marching into Gutcutter territory. I had hoped for it to be the four of us with a cart full of flashstones, and another five men who knew best how to use them, but it seemed that wasn't going to be the case tonight. I had something almost as good, though.

I had magic, or so I very much hoped.

'How do you feel, Billy?' I asked the lad as we approached the edges of my streets.

'We're going to fight,' he said. 'Good fucking deal.'

'Aye, we are,' I said. 'We're raiding tonight, though, not going into battle. Do you know what raiders do, Billy?'

'Strike fast, strike hard, burn everything and run away afore we're caught,' Billy recited, quoting the captain's words from memory.

'Good lad. That's right,' I said. 'That's exactly what raiders do. They strike fast, and they burn everything. If I ask you to burn something, Billy, can you do that for me? A workshop maybe, or an inn?'

He looked up at me, although truth be told, he wasn't all that much shorter than I was, by then.

'With the cunning?' he asked.

I nodded. 'Aye, lad, with the cunning.'

'I can do that,' he said, and he grinned at me. 'Old Kurt never let me burn nothing big, but I know I can if I try.'

'Good lad,' I said again.

I could feel Bloody Anne giving me the hard eye in the darkness, but I had to ignore it. Billy the Boy was of age now and he was one of us, whether Anne liked it or not. If I was right, he was the most dangerous man I had.

Apart from Cutter, perhaps. I remembered the fight in the Golden Chains, and how the Skanian magician had sent us all cowering behind tables. I remembered how Cutter had crept up behind him and opened his neck, magic or no fucking magic. Cutter was very dangerous too, I had to remind myself.

That, and he was still Jochan's man, not mine.

All my attempts to build a trust with Cutter had fallen on stony ground. He had been content to move into the house on Slaughterhouse Narrow and I had seen little of him since. The man said next to nothing, and I had no idea what levers moved him. Something tied him to my brother, some bond of loyalty forged in the war, although I hadn't managed to find out what it was. I didn't even know where he was from, but he had skills that conscripts don't get taught.

I would have bet a gold crown to a clipped copper that Cutter had been a professional killer before the war, but where and for who remained a mystery. So long as he was a Pious Man, that was well and good, but I trusted him even less than I had trusted Sir Eland before he proved himself to me, and that was quite some statement to be making.

'Right,' I said, and squared my shoulders under my cloak. I could feel the weight of the mail dragging against them, over the thick layer of leather beneath. 'This is the last street of the Stink. Up there is Dock Road, and that runs all the way through the Wheels to the docks. That's Gutcutter territory, all of it. What we're going to do is walk up that street, nice and slow. Billy, I want you to leave the houses alone but burn every business I tell you to. Anne, Borys, we're going to kill every bastard who comes out and tries to stop us. When we meet up with Jochan and his lads, we're going to turn and run back to the Stink like the very gods of war are behind us. Everyone understand?'

They all nodded, and the smile on Billy the Boy's face told me how much he was looking forward to it.

'Yes, Uncle Tomas,' he said.

We set off up Dock Road, and the first place we passed was a baker's that I knew paid protection to Ma Aditi. I pointed to it, and Billy's smile widened. He stopped in the street and stared at the shop front, the snow settling on his cloak. A moment later a dull glow began to light the windows from within. It brightened by the moment, until I could see flames licking at the inside of the panes.

'It's done,' he said.

I nodded, and we moved on.

'Witchcraft,' I heard Bloody Anne mutter under her breath.

'Magic,' I said, correcting her. 'It ain't the same thing, Anne.'

I wasn't sure I could see a difference, but I needed *her* to.

There was shouting behind us, the crash of breaking glass and the sound of panicked voices as the baker and his family fought the fire. They weren't my enemies, no, but then the people of Messia had done nothing to me either. This was war, the same as Messia had been.

The same as Abingon.

Civilians suffer in war, and there was nothing to be done about that. I couldn't meet the Gutcutters in formal battle any more than our generals had been able to draw the garrison at Abingon out from behind the city walls. Instead we had smashed those walls with our cannon and stormed the city, killing and burning as we went. This was the same thing, to my mind.

'There,' I said, indicating a chandler's shop.

That went up even better than I could have hoped, and it took the tailor's shop next door with it. A lot of Ellinburg is timber and daub, and even in the cold wetness of winter that burns well. We hurried on, hearing the shouts and chaos building behind us. These were just protected businesses, though, and for all that we were making a nuisance of ourselves in the Gutcutters' eyes, we hadn't really hurt them yet. To do that, we had to reach the Stables.

The Stables was nothing to do with horses.

It was Ma Aditi's favourite place in all of Ellinburg: a brothel that specialised in boys. She liked young lads herself, and there were enough men who felt the same way for it to be a lucrative business. The Stables was near the top of Dock Road, where it could attract incoming sailors who had got too used to their cabin boys while aboard ship.

I wanted to burn the Stables to the ground.

We had to be careful about it, though, I knew that much. Those lads hadn't hurt anyone, and for all that civilians have a hard time in war I wouldn't see it happen to them. Those boys had seen enough hardship.

This was where the second part of my plan came to life, the part I hadn't shared with anyone.

Chapter 39

I led my raiding party through the alleys, leaving Dock Road behind us. The Gutcutters would be out in force now, with fires burning the length of their main street, and I wasn't looking for open battle. Not with only two soldiers and a boy at my back I wasn't.

I knew the Wheels better than most Stink men did, and I had my da to thank for that if for little enough else. He had worked for Old Kurt when I was a boy, as I have written, and had taken me up there with him. I had been chased by Wheeler lads more times than I could remember, and I had learned those alleys while fleeing for my life. Memories like that stay with a man, it has to be said.

Anne, Borys and Billy followed me through the narrow ways, keeping quiet and listening to the din of fires being fought on the main street. I led them roughly parallel to Dock Road, through the twisting wynds behind workshops and between tenements. Only once did we stop, when I pointed to the back of a cobbler's shop and had Billy set it alight from the rear. We hurried on after that, until our alley opened up onto the courtyard behind the Stables.

'Right,' I said. 'This is it. This is Ma Aditi's favourite business, and I want it burned down. But first, there's work. There are lads in there, and we need to get them out.'

'What lads?' Borys asked.

'Boy whores,' I said. 'Young ones. Too fucking young for whoring. We're getting them out.'

'How?' Anne asked.

I looked at the back of the Stables. There was a single guard outside the back door, leaning against the wall and picking his nose with obvious enthusiasm. With him gone, we could slip inside and up the stairs to the rooms where the boys worked, and lead them out before anyone knew what was happening.

'The man on the door,' I said to Anne. 'Can you drop him from here?'

Anne lifted her crossbow and sighted along the bolt, her eyes narrowed against the snow that was blowing into the mouth of the alley.

'Perhaps,' she said. 'It's dark and the angle's for shit. I can't make any promises.'

That wasn't what I wanted to hear. If she missed he would raise the alarm and then it would all be in the shithouse, I knew that much. I was about to speak when Billy beat me to it.

'I can, Uncle Tomas,' he said.

I frowned at him. 'I need him dead, Billy, you understand?' I said. 'Fast and quiet, without anyone seeing.'

The lad nodded. 'I know,' he said. 'He'll die.'

Anne and me exchanged a look, but I knew that when Billy said a thing would happen he was always right. If he said he could do this, then . . .

I knew I had to trust him.

'Do it, then,' I said.

Billy narrowed his eyes and stared at the man outside the door. He was maybe thirty yards away, and as Bloody Anne had said the angle was for shit and that was without the dark and the wind and the snow. I couldn't have made that shot with a crossbow, I knew that much, and if even Anne doubted herself then it was a difficult shot indeed. Billy didn't have a crossbow, though.

He didn't need one.

Billy's fists clenched at his sides, hard and sudden, and he made a sharp hissing noise like he had pushed all the air out of his lungs at once. The man on the door jerked forward, one hand scratching desperately at his throat, then pitched onto his face on the icy cobbles. He kicked once and was still.

I waited for him to rise, but he didn't. Falling snow settled on his back as he lay there under the glow of the single lantern above the door.

'What did you do, Billy?' I whispered.

'I crushed his lungs and took his breath,' Billy said. 'All of it. He don't need it no more, Uncle Tomas. He's dead.'

'Aye,' I said. 'Aye, that he is.'

We slipped through the shadows to the back door of the Stables. The snow was falling heavier now, already beginning to cover the body of the fallen man. I eased up the latch and opened the door an inch, putting my eye to the gap. There was no one in sight, just a patch of bare wooden floor at the bottom of the stairs that led to the upper floor.

The Stables was a tavern, officially, and only a certain few knew what was upstairs. The way up was in the back, and when there were no ships in and no sailors to entertain like there weren't at the moment, the back was kept curtained off.

I could hear laughter and revelry coming from the common room, but the back of the building was quiet. That was how I had hoped it would be. I eased Remorse out of her scabbard and pushed the door open.

Bloody Anne followed with her crossbow slung and her daggers in her hands, and Billy came behind her. Borys brought up the rear, closing the door silently behind us. He could move quiet when he wanted to, for a big man, and I didn't think anyone had heard us. I made my way up the stairs as softly as I could, trying to figure how long it had been since we all set off from the Tanner's Arms.

Jochan would be making slower time than us, I knew. The river path was treacherous in the snow and they would have had to take it carefully, and I was sure they would have met at least some resistance coming that way. I thought I had perhaps ten minutes until they reached the alley beside Old Kurt's house. They would have to fight again there, as that way was always guarded.

Then they'd be out onto Dock Road, only a hundred yards or so north of the Stables. I had to have the place burning by then. I hadn't explained this part of my plan, as I said. I should have done, I knew that, but I just couldn't bring myself to speak of it in front of the men. All the same, Jochan would know what to do. Once he saw the flames at the Stables he would realise that I had set them, and why. That would bring him running, and his men with him.

We slipped into the corridor at the top of the stairs and I paused outside the first door. I eased it open and saw the lad inside. He had perhaps twelve years to him, and he was sitting on the bed wearing a pair of tight red velvet britches and nothing else. He looked up at me and showed me a seductive smile that I knew he didn't feel.

I put a finger to my lips. 'I'm not a customer,' I whispered. 'Come on, boy, I'm getting you out of here. Do you have any more clothes?'

His eyes went very wide, and for a moment I thought he might panic and start shouting. Just then Billy popped his head around the door and grinned at the other boy. He gave him a wink and an encouraging wave, and quick as that the lad was off the bed and stuffing his feet into a pair of old boots.

He dragged a patched cloak out of a small chest beside the bed and pulled it around his thin, naked shoulders, and he was as ready as he was going to get. I ushered him quickly out of the room to where Bloody Anne was waiting with as reassuring a smile as her scarred face could manage. She gave the boy a brief, brusque hug and passed him back to Borys, who took him down the stairs and out the back door. Borys stayed outside with the lad, and I went to the next door.

We brought out six boys in all, sending them down to Borys one at a time, before I reached the last room and found one who was working.

The poor little bastard couldn't have had more than seven or eight years to him. He was face down on the bed and sobbing, with a naked man grunting away on top of him.

Memories crashed into my head hard enough to make me vomit.

The man's head whipped around at the sound, his face red and sweaty and outraged at the intrusion. He looked just like my da.

I swung Remorse so hard I nearly took his fucking head clean off.

Blood erupted up the wall and across the ceiling, and the force of my blow made his corpse roll off the bed and hit the floor with a heavy thump. That was bad.

I wiped sick from my chin with the back of my left wrist and held out a hand to the whimpering boy.

'Come on, lad, quickly now,' I said.

The boy just wept and stared at me with wide, terrified eyes. He was naked and bleeding, and I realised that he was in no state to run. I ripped my cloak off and wrapped him in it, and bundled him over my shoulder.

'It's all right,' I said. 'You have to keep quiet, though, you understand me?'

The lad nodded against my back, still sniffling. I hurried back into the corridor and pushed past Anne and Billy on my way to the stairs.

'Burn it all,' I snarled at Billy the Boy as I passed him, and I found that I was weeping. 'Burn it to the cunting ground.'

Chapter 40

It seemed Billy the Boy had formed his own opinion about what went on in the Stables. The fire that consumed the building was apocalyptic.

I sent Borys back to the Stink with the boys we had rescued, leading them through the alleys behind him. He had the youngest lad cradled in his arms, still wrapped in my cloak. I took Bloody Anne and Billy around to the street to meet the Gutcutters as they came boiling out of the tavern entrance into the swirling, firelit snow, shouting and cursing with blades in their hands.

Anne dropped the first with the bolt from her crossbow, and then they were too close and there was no time for her to reload. Remorse and Mercy took their toll, and Billy the Boy stood back and concentrated with a fierce look on his face, and here and there a man dropped clutching his throat as Billy stole his breath. There were too many of them, though, and even as Anne took a man's throat out with her dagger two more stepped up to take his place. I gave one Mercy through the ribs and kicked out at another, almost losing my footing on the treacherous, icy cobbles.

'Tomas!'

I heard Jochan's roar and looked up to see him charging, his bloody axe raised high. I had never been so glad to see my brother in my life. He crashed into the rear of the mob of Gutcutters like a man possessed, like a berserker. The flames from the burning Stables reflected in his eyes, and I knew that he understood all too well why I had done what I had. Cutter slipped into the melee and men died around him, falling back from the evil little blades in his hands while Stefan and Erik fought with the stolid, determined competence of veterans.

I was beginning to think we might just take them all, when a man came out of a house across the street. He put a hand to his mouth and whistled. He whistled a long, shrill note that made my ears first hurt and then scream. I stumbled back a step and clapped my hands to my head, the Weeping Women tumbling from numb fingers as I sagged to my knees. I could feel hot blood against my palms.

The magic was indiscriminate, though. Gutcutters and Pious Men alike were on their knees in the snow as the Skanian magician walked slowly into the street with his long hair blowing around his face.

Everyone was on their knees except Billy the Boy.

The magician stopped and stared at Billy, a frown creasing his pale brow. Billy stood with the fire at his back, outlining him in flame like the devil Old Kurt had feared him to be. He took a step toward the magician and raised a hand.

'No,' he said. 'I won't.'

The Skanian stumbled back a step, his own hands moving in a complicated sequence in front of him. Something invisible seemed to rush through the air between them, but Billy made a chopping gesture with his left hand and whatever it was dissipated like mist on a summer morning.

'No,' he said again. 'I'm going to hurt you now.'

He can mend hurts, Old Kurt had told me, *and now he can cause them too.*

The magician screamed.

I don't have the words in me to describe that scream, save to liken it to a lamb being slaughtered the slow way, like they do in some of the temples. He clutched his hands to his stomach and doubled over, and blood gushed out from the bottom of his robe and darkened the snow around his feet. He pitched to his face on the ground, vomiting more blood, and his entrails left his body through his arsehole at great speed.

The spell broke at once, and I snatched up Mercy and stabbed the nearest man within reach before he could react. Bloody Anne threw herself on top of the fellow beside her and her daggers rose and fell, rose and fell.

Jochan and Cutter made short work of the rest of them, and it was done.

The Stables was a blazing ruin behind us, but I could hear running men, coming closer. Lots of them.

'We need to go,' I said. 'Right fucking now.'

We fled back to the Stink through the alleys, taking wild turns and doubling back on ourselves until I was sure we had shaken off the pursuit. Billy collapsed on the way, ghost pale and shaking like he had contracted the falling sickness. I scooped him up and threw him over my shoulder, and we ran again.

By the time we made it back to the Tanner's Arms I was exhausted, gasping for breath from the boy's weight and frozen to the bone under the sweat that covered me. Mail is not a good thing to wear in winter without a cloak to cover it, and mine was still wrapped around the young lad I had rescued. At least, I very much hoped it was. If Borys had lost those lads I vowed I would kill him myself.

Black Billy let us into the Tanner's with a grin of visible relief as he saw we were all there. Ailsa came bustling over, a worried frown on her face.

'Is young Billy hurt?' she asked, when she saw me carrying him.

'The lad's exhausted, that's all,' I said, and I hoped it was true. 'He fought hard tonight.'

He had done that all right, and no mistake. I remembered the day after he had healed Hari, and how he had looked near death and slept for a whole day afterward. I wondered what this night's work had cost him.

'I'll put him to bed,' Ailsa said, and took the lad from me as though he weighed no more than a newborn.

She disappeared into the back with the unconscious boy, and I sank into a chair and pulled off my frozen mail and leather. Anne brought a coat and wrapped it around my shoulders, and I huddled into it and nodded my thanks.

'Where are the boys?' I asked.

'Borys brought them in about twenty minutes ago,' Luka said. 'They're in the kitchen with Hari, eating us out of house and home.'

He smiled when he said it, though, and I nodded. That was good.

Mika came around with brandies for everyone, leaving a couple of bottles on the tables for us. I drank and shivered, and I saw the others doing the same. That night had been harsh work indeed, the sort of work we had done at Messia, and I knew it would have brought back memories for everyone.

'Get Doc Cordin up here tomorrow to have a look at the lads,' I said, and Mika nodded. 'Some of them aren't in great shape.'

I would worry about what to do with them in the morning. Since the Chains had opened up again I had proper money coming in, and that allowed me to move some of my hidden gold through the business without anyone raising hard questions about where it had come from. Now that I could spend money, I could do things. If I needed to pay some families to adopt the young lads, to raise them and teach them a trade, then I could do that.

And I would.

I sat back in my chair and swallowed brandy, and poured myself another. There was a tap on the door a while later, and Black Billy slid the hatch aside and peered out. He turned and beckoned to Fat Luka.

'One of yours,' he said.

Luka went to the door and opened it, just a little. I could see him talking to someone outside, but their voices were too low to overhear. A moment later Luka nodded and coin changed hands, and then the door was closed and locked again.

'All the Wheels is in uproar,' he said, a satisfied smile on his plump face. 'The traders of Dock Road are asking why they should pay protection to the Gutcutters if they aren't protected, and Ma Aditi is in a fury over losing the Stables and her little boys. There's other talk too, of a powerful man who was supposed to help them and didn't, or did and failed, or died trying. It's confused, is that, but word is the Gutcutters have been let down bad by someone.'

I nodded, and thought of their Skanian magician shitting out his own intestines into the gutter as Billy the Boy pulled him inside out with his mind. I thought that might give Bloodhands something to think on, and no mistake.

'Good,' I said. 'It's been a good night's work for the Pious Men.'

There was a cheer for that, and glasses were raised and brandy downed.

'Fuck a nun, Tomas,' Jochan said, and he started to laugh. 'You burned down the fucking Stables! That's wanted doing for a long time.'

'Aye, it has,' I said. 'Too long. I left it too long.'

I met his eyes, and he blinked back a tear and nodded.

'Aye well, it's done now and done well,' he said.

I felt like a weight had lifted from my heart, to hear him say that.

Chapter 41

A week passed, and I found homes for the Stables boys. Gold opens many doors, after all, and I had gold to spare. The poppy trade was bringing in a fortune, as Ailsa had said it would. Taxes were coming in again too, from all the businesses under my protection, and Will the Wencher had turned the house on Chandler's Narrow into the best and most profitable stew in Ellinburg. It was doing so well, in fact, that I had Sir Eland return there, and put Erik in charge of security at the Golden Chains in his place.

It was a fine morning, cold and crisp, and the sun was shining. Anne and I walked the streets of the Stink together, partly to see how the land lay but mostly so that we could be seen. We looked like lords of the manor in our fine coats and doublets, and we had Stefan and three of the new lads with us as bodyguards. The Gutcutters were still licking their wounds from our attack on Dock Road and the Stables, so that wasn't strictly necessary, but I had to be seen to be guarded and guarded well. Perhaps I should have brought Jochan along, but Jochan was still stinking drunk from the night before and snoring in his blankets.

Billy the Boy had wanted to come too, and I indulged him. He was recovered now, but it had taken him three days to regain his strength after his battle with the Skanian magician. He looked quite the young lordling himself, since I had lavished him with new clothes by way of thanks for his efforts.

'What's that place, Uncle Tomas?' he asked, indicating a baker's shop.

The sign above the door said clearly what it was, but I remembered Old Kurt telling me that Billy seemed unable to read any hand but his own. All the same, the good smells wafting from the open door of the shop were enough to tell anyone what the owner's trade was. He grinned at me to say he was making mischief, and I returned his smile.

'Are you hungry again?' Anne asked in mock surprise.

The lad had done nothing but eat since he regained consciousness, but still he remained painfully thin.

'I could fancy a pastry,' he admitted.

'Then you shall have one,' I said, and ducked through the low doorway of the shop with Anne behind me.

'Mr Piety!' the baker exclaimed when he saw me, his plump, floury hands fluttering nervously at the front of his apron. 'I'm not late, am I, sir? I swear I paid my taxes not three days ago.'

'That you did, Georg,' I assured him. 'Our lad is hungry, that's all. You know how growing boys are, I'm sure. You've two of your own, as I recall.'

'I have, sir, and it's good of you to remember,' he said.

Georg flustered and fussed about behind his counter, and a moment later he presented me with two dried fruit pies and a spiced pastry, wrapped up in waxed paper. Those were his best wares, I knew, but he waved away my coin.

'No charge for you, Mr Piety,' he said. 'There's no charge for the Pious Men, not in here there isn't.'

I nodded and accepted the wrapped package. 'My thanks, Georg,' I said.

We left the shop and I let Billy bury his face in the pastries. It was good to have my streets back again, and I wouldn't forget the respect that Georg had shown me.

It may sound strange, that I taxed these people and they still gave me their wares for free, but that was how respect worked in Ellinburg. They knew that I taxed them fairly, and that my protection actually *would* protect them. Also, I wouldn't see a family starve in the Stink, and that was known too. I had found work for many of their sons and brothers in my businesses, and their daughters too, as guards and messengers and card dealers, as doormen and draymen and cooks and porters. Those who were sick and couldn't afford even Doc Cordin's services had been treated at my expense. Those who were hungry had been fed. That was how I protected my streets, and that was how I earned the respect of the folk who lived there. It was a closed system, to be sure, and participation wasn't optional, but it worked well enough once everyone accepted that.

Anne cadged a mouthful of pastry from Billy and stood on the street corner, munching thoughtfully.

'We should check on your aunt,' she said, brushing crumbs from her chin as she spoke.

'Aye,' I said. 'I suppose we should, at that.'

I had arranged a new house for Aunt Enaid, to replace the one we blew up, and she and Brak had recently moved in. Brak was most of the way to healed by then, although whether his left arm would ever work properly again was still in some doubt.

I saw that he was well paid for his troubles, of course, and everyone else too. The Pious Men were rich again, richer now than we had been before the war. All my crew were dressed like lords, although they were still a long way from learning to act like them.

The new house was down at the end of Cobbler's Row and it was twice the size of her old place. I had hired a maid for her too, one of Doc Cordin's granddaughters, and put a couple of the new boys on duty there to make sure there was no repeat of what had happened last time.

An Alarian lad called Desh had the front door when we came strolling down the row, and he stood up smart when he saw me coming. I think he would have saluted if he had known how, but he had been just slightly too young to be conscripted and had missed the war by a matter of months. He was almost a grown man now, though, and he had a shortsword at his hip and a crossbow hidden behind the garden wall where he could reach it easily.

'Morning, boss,' he said.

He was a good lad, from a poor family down on Hull Patcher's Row. When I had been recruiting new men he had been among the first to take my coin. I thought perhaps Desh might well have grown up wanting to be a Pious Man.

I nodded to him. 'Is my aunt in?'

'Yes, sir,' he said, and opened the front door for us.

Anne and I went inside, but Billy was still eating and spraying crumbs everywhere so I left him outside with Stefan and the guards. It wouldn't do to have him making a mess all over Aunt Enaid's freshly swept floors, I knew that much.

She met us in the hall and ushered us into her parlour, where Brak was taking his ease in front of the fire with his left arm still bound up in a sling.

'Morning, Auntie,' I said.

She squinted at me with her one bright eye. 'That it is,' she said. 'What brings you here, Tomas Piety?'

'Can't I pay a social call on my favourite aunt?'

She snorted and waved us to seats. I spoke briefly with Brak, and then Aunt Enaid picked up her stick and hauled her bulk back out of her chair again.

'Anne and Brak will have a lot to discuss, I'm sure,' she said, although I couldn't think what. 'Come through to the kitchen with your fat old aunt.'

There was something on her mind she wanted to say in private, that was clear enough, so I got up and followed her. Once in the kitchen she chased Cordin's girl out and closed the door behind her.

'What is it, Auntie?' I asked her.

She sat at the kitchen table and I joined her there, letting her take her time.

She didn't take her time at all.

'What the names of the gods are you playing at?' she demanded, as soon as I had sat down.

That made me blink.

'In what way?'

'You attacked the Wheels last week. You burned down the fucking Stables, the way I heard it.'

'Aye, I did,' I said.

'You've got the business *back*, Tomas,' she said. 'It's done. Why go making more blood with Aditi? Everything worked well enough before the war, didn't it?'

'Did it? Was anything well enough, while that filthy place was open?'

'That was never your affair,' she said. 'You run the Stink your way, Ma Aditi runs the Wheels *her* way, that's just how it is.'

'Maybe that's not enough,' I said. 'Maybe I want the Wheels too. Maybe, my dear aunt, I just couldn't stand the thought of that fucking place staying open another week.'

She turned and spat on the floor, and never mind that we were in her own kitchen. Enaid would always be a soldier at heart.

'They'll make fucking war over it!' she hissed at me. 'I should have found a way to keep myself out of that bloody convent. I should have kept a hand on the tiller while you were away, like I said I would. Then maybe we wouldn't be in this mess.'

'You should have married,' I said. 'A long time ago. Made some poor man a terrifying wife, and left me alone.'

'And done what, raised brats?' She snorted. 'This country has twice the mouths it can feed already; that's why we're always at bloody war. No, no brats for me, Tomas. My brother raised two and that's more than enough Piety boys in the world, to my mind.'

Her brother was my da, of course, and I didn't want the conversation going that way.

'This is a good thing for the Pious Men,' I said instead. 'I've got money coming in now, lots of it, and I'm spending it wisely. There's new weapons on their way from Dannsburg, and the men to use them. I mean to clean Ma Aditi out of the Wheels and take them for myself.'

'That's blood for blood's sake,' she said. 'You don't need the Wheels.'

I shook my head. 'It's for the sake of the Pious Men,' I said. 'It's to secure everything we've always worked for.'

It was because Ailsa and the Queen's Men said so, of course. It was to save us all from the horrors of another Abingon, from siege and starvation and slavery, but that was nothing my aunt needed to hear.

'There's a devil in you, Tomas Piety,' Enaid said. 'There always has been, and there's no blaming the war for it. I remember how you were, even as a lad. You were twelve years old when you came to my house in the dead of night with your little brother at your side and you said "Da's dead", and there was no sorrow on your face.'

No, there wouldn't have been.

It seemed there was no keeping the talk away from that subject now. I wondered if Aunt Enaid even remotely suspected what had really happened to Da. I didn't think that she did.

I didn't want to think about it, but her words had opened that strongbox in the back of my mind now and the horrors were crawling out whether I wanted it or not. I felt sweat on the palms of my hands, felt my throat wanting to close up. I could see my da's face all over again.

He'd hit me often enough, hit me and worse beside. Ma died two years after birthing Jochan, and times had been hard. Da was violent and he drank, but that was often the way of men in the Stink. He was still my da, and most fathers had heavy hands. That was nothing in itself but Da did more than hit me. Da put his rough bricklayer's hands where they weren't wanted too. No one wants their own da stuffing his hand down their britches, but I was young when that started. I had only had six or seven years to me, and I thought that perhaps most fathers did that too. I was wrong about that, of course, but I hadn't known any better. By the time I learned different, I was too shamed to tell anyone.

When I turned nine, he came into my bedroom one night and he forced himself on me and used me like boys were used at the Stables.

That went on for three fucking years, and I suffered it.

I suffered it because I had to, because I was a little boy and he was my da and I still loved him, despite everything. He told me that if I loved him then I'd let him do it. He told me that I deserved it, and that I owed it to him, and he made me believe that those things were true. I was only young and he was my da and I loved him and I trusted him, so of course I believed him. But eventually he grew bored with me, or I got too old for him, and he left me be and started on little Jochan, who had just turned eight.

I heard his wails, night after night, and I suffered that too. That was the debt I owed Jochan, the debt I could never repay. I should have done a thing and I didn't, not until it was too late. I remembered lying in my bed one night listening to Jochan cry out in pain in the next room and I *knew* it was wrong and still I didn't fucking do anything. I didn't do anything because he was my da and if I told anyone then they'd know it had happened to me as well, and I couldn't face that. I couldn't face the fucking thought of how they would have looked at me, and the pity and the shame. So I hid my face in my pillow and I wept, and next door my little baby brother sobbed and suffered because I was a coward.

Eventually, though, a thing happened that broke something inside me, something that has never healed. It had been well after midnight, and Da was passed out drunk in the parlour downstairs. Jochan crawled into my blankets with me, crying for what Da had done to him. I tried to comfort him, and Jochan . . . Jochan offered to let me use him, how Da did.

He wanted to please me, I think, his big brother, and that was the only way he knew how. That made me sick to my stomach, and I said it was enough. Fuck the shame, and the pity, and what people might think. People didn't have to know, I realised. I had twelve years to me by then, almost a man grown, and to my mind a man solved his own problems. Something cold woke in my head that night. This was going to stop, that cold thing said to me, and it was going to stop right fucking now.

I got out of bed and I went into the parlour where Da was snoring. He was asleep in his chair, red-faced with drink and sweaty, his mouth half open and dribble on his chin. The hammer had been right there, in his work bag, the hammer he used to tamp down his bricks.

I picked it up and I stood there with it in my hand, and I looked at my da for a long time. I looked at him and I felt the shame in me, the shame of what he had done to me, and more than that the shame of what I had let him do to Jochan while I looked the other way. No one was ever going to know about that, the cold thing said to me. No one ever needs to know.

I lifted the hammer and I broke Da's head with it.

I hit him again, and again, and again, until his head was wet mush and I couldn't see for the tears in my eyes.

If it had been the first time he had done it, perhaps I could have forgiven myself. But it hadn't been, not by a long way. I would always owe Jochan for all the nights of his suffering when I had lain in my bed and done nothing because I was a coward. I knew I could never forgive myself for that.

When I came back to myself I roused Jochan from my bed and told him what I had done, and that it was a secret and that he had to take that secret to the grave with him. I made him promise on Ma's memory, and together we had dragged Da's body to the top of the stairs and pushed him out of his window onto the cobbled street below.

Da drank, everyone in the street knew that, and a drunk man could fall from his bedroom window taking a piss in the night without raising too many hard questions. So that was how it was, and that was how it had stayed. Jochan and I never spoke of that night.

That's where the devil in me came from, the cold thing that killed my da, and it has never left me since.

I looked up at Aunt Enaid, and I clenched my fists and forced the past back into the broken strongbox in my head where it belonged. I loved my aunt, but all the same my voice dropped into the flat tone that meant I was close to violence.

'Don't ever talk about my da,' I said.

Enaid stared at me, and she swallowed. No, she had no idea, but she recognised that voice when she heard it and she must have realised there was *something*. Something she didn't understand, and Our Lady willing never would.

She nodded. 'Aye, Tomas,' she said, and that was wise of her.

Chapter 42

Two days later word reached Ailsa that the wagons from Dannsburg were finally on their way with the men and weapons I had asked for. I started to plan my next move.

I was holding a council of war in the kitchen of the Tanner's with Anne and Luka at the table, and Ailsa unobtrusively listening as she swept the floor.

'Are we going to hit them with the explosives straight away, boss?' Luka asked.

I shook my head. 'No, we're not. I don't know these men. They come from someone I trust, but I don't know a one of them. They're not just bringing flashstones and powder, though. They're coming with swords and crossbows, and we'll try them with those first. I don't want the Gutcutters realising I have blasting weapons until we're ready to go to war, and we're not doing that until I'm sure of every man in my crew.'

Ailsa paused in her sweeping for a moment, a thoughtful look on her face.

'That sounds wise,' Bloody Anne said, and Luka nodded.

'Aye,' he said. 'What, then?'

I pursed my lips in thought for a moment. 'At the top of the riverside path there's a factory,' I said. 'Just beyond the alley that leads up to Dock Road. You know where I mean?'

'Aye,' Luka said again. 'They make . . . broadcloth, I think. I'm not sure. Something with looms, anyway, running off the big wheel at the end of the path. They're weavers, under the mercer's guild.'

'That's right,' I said. 'Ma Aditi takes a lot of protection money from that factory, and I know the mercers think ill of that. If we can take it, kill her guards and smash the machines, the mercers will turn against the Gutcutters. Losing the faith of a major guild will hurt her, and hurt the . . . hurt her backers.'

I coughed to cover my slip. It was getting taxing, remembering who knew what and who didn't, and I had nearly said 'Skanians' in front of two people who shouldn't have ever heard that name.

Luka just nodded, and if he had noticed my mistake he made nothing of it.

'We can do that,' Anne said. 'If we have the men take some planks and rope with them, they can get across from the pilings at the end of the path and go in under the waterwheel. They'll need hammers, too, for the looms. It won't be pleasant work, not at this time of year, but it can be done.'

'Good,' I said. 'Anne, I'll leave it to you to pick who goes with the new lads.'

'Cutter,' she said at once, without hesitation. 'This is sneak-and-kill work, and that's what he's best at. I'd have another couple of lads go with them, but we want to keep the crew fairly small for a job like this.'

Bloody Anne knew what she was doing, so I just nodded. That sounded right to me. Cutter was the obvious choice, as she had said.

'Are any of us going?' Luka asked.

I thought on that for a moment, then shook my head. 'No, we're not,' I said. 'Not this time. Cutter's good at this sort of thing, as Anne says. Put him in charge. I can't keep risking my top table on simple raids.'

Anne nodded. 'Aye, Cutter then, in the corporal's role.'

That sounded good, to me. The right man for the right job.

The wagons finally arrived on Queensday afternoon. There were two of them, with canvas covers over their cargos and ten men in all between them. Rosie was there to meet them, and although she was making a show of having come to see Anne on her afternoon off, somehow we all ended up in the stable yard of the Tanner's. We stood there watching these strange, hard-faced men unload crates and barrels and carry them into the storeroom.

'Well, this is a to-do, Tomas,' Ailsa said. 'I'm sure I don't know where we'll sleep all these fine lads, but then I doubt they'll be staying long.'

I didn't get to keep them, then. That was what she was telling me. I supposed that shouldn't have surprised me. These men were trained soldiers, professional career army by the look of the way they carried themselves, not just conscript veterans like us. This was a loan from the Queen's Men, nothing more.

'No,' I said. 'They probably won't.'

Once the weapons were stowed, Ailsa distracted Anne with some chatter or other while the leader of the new men spoke to Rosie, and I saw a purse move from her hand to his. Then it was done, and she was back at Anne's side.

'Don't you go making eyes at her,' Rosie teased Ailsa, and she and Anne set off arm in arm together for an afternoon stroll while the weather was still fine.

I followed the leader of the soldiers into the storeroom, and a moment later Ailsa joined us.

'My name is Tomas Piety,' I said, holding out a hand to him.

He looked at it for a long moment, and he didn't move. 'So what?' he said.

'So he's the man you're here to serve.'

Ailsa's voice cracked like a whip in the dim room. She took a step toward the soldier and opened her belt pouch. Her fingers dipped inside and came out holding a thick piece of folded leather. She unfolded it and showed the man what was inside, and he visibly paled.

He saluted and clicked his heels, the great fool, right there in my storeroom.

'Captain Larn, ma'am. Queen's Own Third Regiment, sapper company,' he said.

'You're just Larn, here,' she said. 'No ranks, and no saluting. And *definitely* no heel clicking. Take the broomstick out of your arse, Captain. You're supposed to be a criminal.'

'Yes, ma'am,' he said.

'Ailsa,' she corrected him, and her voice changed all at once. 'Just Ailsa, sir, a simple barmaid and Mr Piety here's fancy woman, begging your pardon.'

Larn narrowed his eyes at me, and I showed him an emotionless smile. I was going to have to watch this one, I could tell.

'Let's try again,' I said. 'My name is Tomas Piety.'

I held out my hand once more, and I knew that if he didn't take it this time I was going to stab him.

Larn took my hand and gave it a brusque shake. 'Larn, sir,' he said.

I nodded. That was good. One step at a time.

'Get your men settled in, Larn,' I said. 'It's cramped, but we'll manage. It's no worse accommodation than we had at Abingon, I promise you.'

He looked at me then, and I saw something in his eyes that said I had made a start toward common ground between us. That was how it was done.

'That's good to know,' he said.

I nodded. 'Aye,' I said. 'You'll have had a long journey, I know. There's beer and brandy in the tavern, food in the kitchen, and no charge for my friends. Let your men rest. Tomorrow night there'll be work for you.'

Larn gave me a short nod and stalked out of the room. He wasn't quite marching, but it wasn't far off it.

I gave Ailsa a look. 'Are they all going to be like him? Because if they are, it'll be a fucking miracle if there isn't a fight before sunset.'

'No, I doubt it,' she said. 'His men are sappers, tunnellers and demolition experts. They are most likely as, ah, earthy, shall we say, as your own men are. Captain Larn is a professional commissioned officer and the second son of a minor noble in the capital, with nothing to inherit, everything to prove and no one to prove it to. He is what I believe you would call a pain in the arse.'

I snorted laughter. Hearing Ailsa speak like a barmaid in her aristocrat's voice struck me as funny, but I could see from the expression on her face that she wasn't joining me in amusement.

'Are you listening to me?' she went on. 'These are demolition experts, not rangers. You want to send them on a knife job, to infiltrate this factory of yours? That's *not* the right man for the right job, Tomas.'

'It's a job any soldier should be able to turn his hand to,' I argued. 'These are just Gutcutter scum, not army sentries. If they can't do this, then I won't trust them with the explosives. Anyway, I'm putting Cutter in charge – he'll see them right.'

'Captain Larn will take that extremely ill,' she cautioned me.

'Let him,' I said.

I already disliked Larn, but if he was any sort of soldier at all, then to my mind he would respect the chain of command and do what he was fucking told.

Chapter 43

I sent them out the next night. It seemed strange to send a raid off and not be with it, but then this wasn't Abingon any more. This was Ellinburg, and in Ellinburg I was a prince. Princes don't lead raiding parties, and they don't crawl under waterwheels in freezing temperatures to smash weaving looms with hammers.

The Stables had been different. I had been lacking men, then, and that had been personal. This was just business, and I had good men to take care of business for me. Cutter had briefed his crew in short, hard sentences that left even Captain Larn in no doubt as to who was in charge. Larn might be a career officer but Cutter was a professional murderer, and this sort of work was his bread and beer.

They headed out in a silent column, wearing leather but without their mail, wrapped in old cloaks that they could throw away before they went into the water. I saw Anne watching them leave from across the tavern, and once the door was closed behind them she came and sat with me.

'Rather them than us, I have to say,' she admitted. 'It's fucking freezing out there.'

It was, but sappers are hardy men and once they had done the job there would be no shortage of good cloth in the factory to dry themselves on and wrap around them until they got their warmth back. This late there would be no one there but Gutcutter guards, so their instructions were simple.

Kill everyone, break everything.

That would cripple the factory, enrage the guild of mercers, and turn the workers against the Gutcutters. That last was important, to my mind. From what Ailsa had told me, a large part of the Skanians' plan involved gathering the street-level support of the workers of Ellinburg. Put them out of work, and where would that leave their loyalties? Not with the Gutcutters, that was for certain.

I knew it would mean hardship for some, in the Wheels, but if everything went to plan that would only be for a short while. Anything can be endured for a little while, every soldier knows that, and they weren't my people. Not yet, anyway.

'Aye,' I agreed. 'It's harsh work, but it wants doing.'

'Does it?' Anne asked me. 'I thought we'd be done, once you had the Stink back.'

I didn't need Anne starting on me the way that Enaid had, but just then Fat Luka joined us at the table and showed Anne a wide smile.

'That's a lovely coat, Anne,' he said, nodding to her latest purchase, which hung draped around her shoulders.

It was, at that.

'What of it?'

He shrugged. 'Nothing, nothing. I'm just observing that you've bought yourself a very nice coat. You'll have bought that with money you earned in the Pious Men, I don't doubt. I saw that Rosie had a new necklace around her throat too, a fine piece of goldwork. I'd be surprised if she bought that for herself, or accepted it as a gift from anyone but you.'

Anne scowled and said nothing.

'That money you're spending comes from the business, and the more businesses we have, the more money we all make, isn't that right, Tomas?'

'It is,' I allowed.

Luka was right, of course, but I was surprised all the same.

If anyone starts disagreeing with me or questioning my orders, I want you to explain to them why they're wrong.

I had told Fat Luka that, back in the spring, but I'd never thought to see him argue the point with Bloody Anne. Luka was a good man, and he took his job very seriously. He could be persuasive, too, I knew that. Very persuasive indeed.

'I know,' Anne said, and swallowed her brandy. 'It's just . . . it's more violence, Tomas. More killing. I thought once we had your old streets back we'd be more like a ruling garrison than a fighting force, that's all.'

The Pious Men are businessmen, but you've turned them into soldiers.

'We will be,' I promised her. 'We will be, once Aditi is done. I can't share the city with her, Anne, not any more. You've seen what sort of businesses she runs, and the sort of men her backers have brought against us. The foreign witches.'

That was cheap of me, I knew. I hated having to manipulate Anne, of all people, but the crown's will had to be served and if that meant doing things that I didn't like, then so be it. That was the lighter of the two evils balanced in my hands. It was cheap of me, but it worked. Anne's jaw tightened at the very word, and she gave me a sharp nod.

When you lead, you have to know the levers that move a person.

Cutter and his men came back an hour before sunrise. I was waiting up, with Ailsa and Black Billy for company, and we had kept the fire burning high. I had thought it would be welcome, later. The others had long since gone to their beds, save for Stefan, who had the watch out back.

There was a soft rap on the door and Billy looked through the sliding hatch, then opened the lock and let them in. Cutter and his crew filed into the room, and I counted them all back safe. They were bedraggled and damp and frozen, and they smelled bad from the river water, but they were all back and that was the important thing. Captain Larn had a look on his face that told me he had done things that night that he had never done before.

A professional officer he might have been, and a sapper too, but I'd have bet good silver that he had never met a man quite like Cutter before. I knew that I hadn't. Sappers were brave men and they had done some of the harshest work, in Abingon. Undermining the walls to set charges, fighting in the stifling confines of narrow, crumbling tunnels, that was the stuff of nightmares.

But so was Cutter, to my mind.

The man seemed to have no emotions, no desires, no *soul*. I still had no idea what levers moved Cutter, but if you wanted someone killed quietly and without anyone seeing, then he was the right man for the job.

Black Billy locked the door behind them and they started stripping off sodden leather and ruined wool in front of the fire. They huddled around the warmth in fresh, dry blankets, shivering.

'It's done,' Cutter said, and he spat on the floor to show me what he thought of that.

'How many were they?' I asked.

Cutter frowned. 'Ten, twelve. Dunno. All dead. Smashed the looms like you said, broke the gears and spindles and threw the hammers in the river afterward. Place is fucked.'

That was all he had to say, and he made that plain by walking away to warm himself in front of the fire with the other men. The sappers made room for him there, and I noticed they left a respectful distance around him that spoke of a quiet, underlying fear. When *sappers* fear a man, that man is to be feared indeed.

I wondered again exactly where Cutter had come from, and how he had ended up in Jochan's crew.

Ailsa took my arm and ushered me through to the kitchen.

'You did well not to go with them,' she told me, using her own voice now that we were alone. 'You need to distance yourself now, Tomas, and you need to do it at once.'

I frowned at her. 'Distance myself? How do you mean that?'

'This is a war fought on two fronts,' she said. 'On the streets, yes, but also in the arena of politics. You have men enough to fight in the streets; you don't need to join them any more. What you *don't* have is anyone you can put in front of the governor and the nobility. You'll need to do that yourself.'

'How am I supposed to do that?' I asked. 'I don't move in their circles.'

'Then start,' she said. 'You're a rich man now, Tomas. You need to enter society.'

'Has Ellinburg *got* society?'

'Not particularly, but it's a place to begin. Governor Hauer is a bloated warthog of a creature who thinks he is thrice the man he is, but obviously his position has connections to Dannsburg. Attend a reception here, a ball there, at which I shall dazzle and you shall intrigue, and before you know it we will be in the capital and you will find the ears of more important men.'

'I see,' I said. 'And how would I go about that?'

'The important thing is that you remove yourself from the immediate business of the Pious Men before things start exploding all over the Wheels,' she said. 'There will be no coming back from that, if you or your family are implicated in the resulting carnage. We need to move fast. We will need a house, of course. Something grand, off Trader's Row. And obviously we shall have to marry.'

I stared at her in astonishment. *'Marry?'*

'Yes, of course,' she said. 'I am a lady of court, or at least I am when I choose to be. I can hardly be seen to entertain a provincial bachelor out of wedlock. If I were to produce a husband, though, with mysterious wealth and connections to industry, then yes. That would be entirely acceptable.'

'I see,' I said again. Marry Ailsa? The idea wasn't without its obvious charms, I had to admit, but I hadn't expected this. 'I need to think about this.'

'No, you don't,' she said. 'You just need to do it. We're *already* doing it, in fact. One of my representatives completed the lease of a suitable house yesterday. Servants are being hired, and furnishings purchased. The date of the wedding has been set.'

'Now wait a minute,' I started to say, but she cut me off with a look.

'I don't *have* a minute,' she said. 'I have the Queen's Warrant, Tomas, and you will *do what I tell you*. I can't keep those sappers forever, and we have to hit the Skanians soon. You *cannot* be implicated in that if you are to become a respectable member of society. Which you will.'

There was a first time for everything, I supposed.

Ailsa started to explain exactly what she meant about us getting married, about timing and about how people needed to be able to prove they had been in a certain place at a certain time, and I felt a grim smile form on my face.

Oh, yes, she was a Queen's Man all right. If I had ever met anyone more dangerous than Cutter, I realised, it was Ailsa.

Chapter 44

Three nights later all Hell broke loose.

We had no warning. The first I knew of anything wrong was when a man charged into the Tanner's Arms with his face bloodied and the coat on his back in scorched tatters.

'Gutcutters!' he shouted, and never mind that the tavern was full of customers. 'They're attacking the Chains!'

'Fuck!' I shouted, and rounded on Fat Luka. 'Where was our intelligence?'

Luka had gone pale in the face, and he had no answer to give me.

Bloody Anne was already on her feet and shouting orders. Black Billy and Simple Sam were throwing customers out as fast as they could while men ran around getting into their leather and mail and fetching their weapons. Captain Larn and his men I tasked with holding the Tanner's, and guarding the precious weapons they had brought with them. I had Luka stay there too, and Black Billy. Everyone else was armed and ready in record time.

'Jochan, you'll lead the counterattack,' I said.

He nodded, and I saw the savage gleam in his eye. He was the right man for the right job, I knew that. It was time to unleash the mad dog whether I liked it or not. Jochan picked eight men, Cutter included, and they charged out of the tavern and were on their way to the Chains no more than ten minutes after the alarm had been raised. I looked at Bloody Anne.

'You're with me, with young Billy and the rest,' I said. 'Larn, hold here at all costs.'

Ailsa grabbed my arm as I buckled the Weeping Women around my waist.

'What do you think you're doing?' she hissed at me. 'Distance yourself, I said.'

I gave her a hard look. 'Fuck. That.'

I wrenched my arm free and led my crew out into the biting cold.

'Chandler's Narrow?' Anne said, and the look on her face was almost pleading.

I nodded. 'Aye.'

It was their obvious second target, and of course Anne knew that. Her Rosie was there, and all the other women, with only Will the Wencher and Sir Eland to protect them.

We ran.

As we came up the steps of the narrow I could see we were too late. The front door of the stew was hanging open on one hinge and there was a body sprawled in the courtyard outside the closed chandler's shop, lying half in the light of the single lantern. He was no one we knew, so I simply stepped over him and went inside with Remorse and Mercy in my hands.

There was a stranger in the entrance, leaning on the counter with his hands clutching a wound in his side. I gave him Mercy without breaking stride. The sounds of fighting were coming from down the corridor. Bloody Anne kicked the door open with her daggers drawn.

Sir Eland had retreated to the parlour door, and there he was making his stand.

He hadn't had time to get into his armour when they attacked, of course, and he was standing there in his shirt and britches and bleeding from a dozen cuts, his long sword running scarlet in his hands. Four more men lay dead on the boards, but there must have been another six facing him. One man can hold a narrow space against many, until his strength deserts him or he is overcome by his wounds. It looked like Sir Eland was close to both of those things.

Just as Anne stormed into the corridor a crossbow bolt burst through the neck of one of the Gutcutters, and I heard a ratchet being cranked from behind Sir Eland as someone frantically reloaded. Anne and Mika and me waded into the rear of the Gutcutters while the rest of our crew spread out through the building, searching the bedrooms and killing every stranger they found.

Eland's face split into a savage grin when he saw us, and he attacked.

The hammer and the anvil, that was how we cleared the corridor in Chandler's Narrow. That's a terrible thing in such a confined space, and we butchered them until all of us were red to the elbows and it was done. The floor was littered with corpses, just like it had been at Messia.

'Rosie!' Anne shouted.

She shoved past Sir Eland and into the parlour, and now I could see the women he had been protecting. Rosie was at the front of them, with the crossbow in her hands. Three of the bodies on the floor had bolts in them, I noticed. Rosie had given a good account of herself while Eland held the door.

I clapped Sir Eland on the shoulder. 'You fought well,' I told him.

'I really did,' he said, and collapsed at my feet.

'Boss!' someone shouted from behind me.

'See to Eland,' I snapped at Anne, and turned back down the corridor.

Stefan led me up the stairs and into one of the bedrooms. There were more dead Gutcutters there, who I supposed had been looting the building, and two customers whom the Gutcutters had obviously killed themselves. I saw two of the women dead too, and that pained me. Will the Wencher was sprawled on the floor out cold with an ugly purple bruise on his temple. It looked like he had been trying to protect the girls who had been working when the Gutcutters attacked, but he had been unarmed at the time and had never stood a chance. I respected him for trying, all the same.

Billy the Boy was waiting in that room, and he had something for me.

I recognised the man at once. He wasn't wearing his purple shirt that night, but I recognised him anyway. This was Gregor, Luka's man in the Gutcutters. *My* man, bought and paid for. My man, who should have given us ample warning of this attack, and who had said nothing.

He was backed against the wall, and Billy was staring at him. I didn't know what Billy was doing, but it was plain to see that Gregor was pinned there as helpless as he would have been if four strong men had been holding him in place.

'You'll want this one alive,' Billy said, and as always he was right.

I walked slowly toward the helpless man, Remorse and Mercy dripping red in my sticky hands.

'Hello, Gregor,' I said, my voice taking on the tone that meant harsh justice was coming, and soon.

'Mr Piety, I can explain,' he said.

I nodded slowly, and turned and used Remorse to point at the half-naked woman lying dead on the floor with her guts hanging out of a ragged wound in her stomach. She couldn't have had more than twenty years to her.

'Explain that,' I said. 'Explain to me why two of my girls are lying dead because I didn't know there was going to be an attack on my stew. Explain to me why no *cunt* told me that.'

'I can't—' Gregor started, and I dropped and rammed Mercy through his calf hard enough to smash his shin bone.

He howled.

'Try again,' I said.

'He's got my son!' he gasped around the agony. 'I couldn't . . . he found out I was informing . . . I *couldn't!*'

Some people aren't your friends, however much you pay them. They're just scared to be your enemy. If someone finds a way to scare them more than you do, someone like Bloodhands, then you'll lose them. I knew that well enough.

'I grieve for those two women,' I said. 'I grieve for them, but I didn't know them. You're very lucky, very lucky indeed, that it wasn't a different woman who died here tonight. If Bloody Anne's woman had been killed, Gregor, I would have given you to her. I want you to understand what that would have meant. Bloody Anne would have started at your feet and filleted you like a fish, if you had got her Rosie killed. Do you understand me?'

He nodded, his teeth clenched against the fire in his ruined leg and the pain making flecks of spit bubble between his teeth.

'I don't think you do,' I said, and I smashed Remorse down hilt-first into his kneecap.

He shrieked that time, and a moment later Bloody Anne came through the door behind me.

'Tomas?' she asked me. 'What in Our Lady's name are you doing?'

'This is the man who almost got your Rosie killed tonight,' I said. 'This is the man who Luka pays to tell us what the Gutcutters are doing. This is the man who didn't. Fucking. Tell us.'

I swear to Our Lady that I heard Bloody Anne growl, low in her throat like an animal. I held up a hand to stay her.

'Is Sir Eland still alive?' I asked her.

'Aye,' she said. 'He's weak, but he'll live.'

'Good,' I said. 'I want you to do something for me, Bloody Anne. I want you to go downstairs and borrow Sir Eland's sword from him, and bring it up here to me. Will you do that for me?'

'Aye,' she said again, and left the room.

I looked Gregor in the eye, and I held his fearful stare. Remorse and Mercy are beautifully crafted weapons but they are shortswords, and they're not designed for taking a man's head off.

Sir Eland's heavy war sword, though, that was.

Chapter 45

It was a long night, and it didn't end with the dawn.

Will the Wencher came round in the end, and although he was groggy and having trouble standing I didn't think his skull was broken, so that was good. We put him to bed and left him weeping over his dead girls.

Anne didn't want to let Rosie out of her sight after what had happened, but there was too much to do for me to allow that. Besides, I knew Rosie could take better care of herself than Anne credited her for. Mika and me and a couple of other lads set to repairing the door, and I told Anne to patch up Sir Eland. She was no barber-surgeon like Doc Cordin, but in Abingon everyone had turned their hand as best they could. Anne could clean and stitch a wound well enough, when she had to. There was little enough love between the two of them, I knew, but he had fought well that night. Very well.

It seemed, to my mind, that when Sir Eland had found himself the only thing between those women and death, he might finally have become the hero he had always pretended to be. He had found his place in the world at last.

Billy the Boy was in charge of the big leather bag, and he seemed to take a pleasure in that. It was leaking, of course, but he guarded it well all the same. We held the house on Chandler's Narrow all through the long, tense night, waiting for another attack that didn't come. I wanted to go to the Golden Chains, but that was almost on Trader's Row and I couldn't get Ailsa's words out of my head.

You need to distance yourself, she had told me. *Remove yourself from the immediate business of the Pious Men before things start exploding.*

No blasting weapons had been used, so far as I knew, but a night that bloody was as good as the same thing. If my face were seen at the Chains I wouldn't be able to undo that. I had to put my faith in my brother, for all that the thought made me uneasy.

The sky was just beginning to get light when Borys came to the house and banged on the newly shored-up door. Mika brought him to me, and I looked at the weary expression on his face.

'What happened?' I asked him.

Borys had been with the crew Jochan had taken to the Chains, and he looked like he had seen hard fighting that night. His mail was rent in two places, and he had dried blood splattered over his face and a seeping cut on the back of his forearm.

'It's done, boss,' he said. 'We drove them off and secured the Chains. A lot of them got away, though. Too many.'

'Fuck,' I muttered. 'Where's my brother?'

'The City Guard are all over the Chains like flies on shit,' he said. 'Jochan slipped away back to the Tanner's, to see the lay of things.'

To find a bottle more likely, I suspected.

'Who's got the Chains, then?'

'Cutter, with enough men to hold it and enough coin in the strongbox to keep the Guard from looking at us too hard.'

I nodded, but I didn't like it. My brother put too much trust in Cutter, to my mind.

'Well and good,' I said. 'I'll meet him at the Tanner's, then. Come with me. You too, Anne. Billy.'

They nodded, and the four of us slipped out into the narrow and away down the steps. I left Mika in charge at the bawdy house for the time being, and we returned to the Tanner's Arms as the sun was rising over the riverside streets.

I found Jochan pacing the common room with a brandy bottle in his hand, as I had expected, but when he saw us he put it down and embraced me. That surprised me, I had to admit, but I didn't think it was a good sign. Ailsa was up already, or more likely she had been up all night again. She gave me a smile too, and a hug for appearance's sake. All the same I could tell she was furious with me for going off to fight with the crew.

Luka came over and clapped me on the shoulder. I shot him a hard look.

'Billy,' I said, 'give Luka the bag.'

Billy passed the wet sack over to Fat Luka, and I held his stare.

'Get one of your little spies over here,' I said, 'and have him take that up to the Wheels and dump it in Ma Aditi's breakfast porridge.'

'What's in it?' Luka asked, but I think he knew.

'Gregor's head,' I said.

Luka cleared his throat. 'Aye,' he said.

I could see he felt that he had failed me. That was harsh, I knew. This wasn't Luka's fault, for all that intelligence was his responsibility. I reached out and put a hand on his arm as he turned away.

'It's all right,' I said. 'They had his son. No amount of gold could have prevented this.'

Luka nodded, understanding, and went to send Cookpot out to rouse one of his spies from their bed. I wondered what Aditi would make of my little gift. Truth be told, I hoped she choked on it.

'How bad was it?' I asked Jochan.

He gave me a bleak look and took up his bottle again. 'Bad,' he said. 'We had to storm the place. Erik's dead, and six of the new lads with him.'

Erik had been a good man.

'In Our Lady's name,' I said.

'What the *fuck* has Our Lady got to do with it?' Jochan roared. He turned and hurled his bottle across the room to smash against the wall. 'You're no fucking priest of Our Lady, Tomas, not no more you ain't! All you want is more blood, and more fucking death, and it's never enough for you, is it? You've become a fucking priest of *bones*!'

He rounded on me with fury on his face, fists clenched and the battle shock shining bright in his mad, tear-filled eyes.

I hit him.

I hit my own little brother, who had once crawled weeping into my blankets and offered me the only thing he had to give. I've never been as good with my fists as Jochan was, but I caught him just right. My knuckles slammed into the tip of his prominent chin and sent him reeling backward into a table. He lost his balance and fell on his arse on the floor.

He started to cry.

I was suddenly aware of Captain Larn standing in the doorway to the storeroom, watching us. If he had said a single word right then I would have murdered him with my bare hands, but he was wise and he held his peace, and he turned away.

He had a brother too, I remembered.

An hour later they came at us again.

A runner reached me to say that Georg the baker's shop was on fire, and there were Gutcutters on the streets of the Stink.

I doubted that my little gift had reached Aditi's table by then, so I figured this must have been part of their original plan. It seemed the Gutcutters were throwing everything they had at us. We were all tired, and a lot of us were carrying wounds of some sort by then. I pressed Larn and his men into service.

'It's your watch,' I told him. 'My lads have been fighting all fucking night.'

Larn shook his head. 'We'll carry out planned missions but we're not brawling in the streets,' he said. 'It's too dangerous. If the City Guard were to capture even one of my men and find out who we really are, the implications could reach Dannsburg itself. That is out of the question. I have my orders.'

I wanted to hurt him, right then. I hadn't slept in far too long, and I couldn't get the image of the dead women at Chandler's Narrow out of my mind. Captain Larn was a donkey's shrivelled prick, to my mind, but I knew that I needed him, and more to the point I needed his men and their weapons and their expertise.

I took a deep breath and made myself nod. 'As you say,' I said. 'Hold here, then, and see that you hold fucking hard. Don't forget you're sitting on enough explosives to send half the Stink across the river. It wouldn't do for you to let anyone set fucking fire to the place.'

Larn's jaw tightened at that. All sappers have a healthy respect for the tools of their trade, I knew. He would see that no Gutcutter got inside the Tanner's with fire in their hands, if nothing else.

I went to Jochan and put an arm around his narrow shoulders. 'We have to do it again, brother,' I told him. 'I know you don't want to, but there it is.'

Jochan looked up at me, and the tears were gone from his eyes. There was a hatred there now, not for me but for the whole world, a burning bloodlust that I hadn't seen in a man's face since the walls of Abingon finally fell.

He nodded. 'Get my fucking axe.'

Chapter 46

We stormed onto the streets of the Stink, exhausted and wounded but fuelled by brandy and anger, and our memories. The Gutcutters were attacking the businesses I had sworn to protect, and I couldn't let that pass. Georg the baker was a good man. He had given me three treats for young Billy when I had only asked for one, and taken no coin for them. I have written that I wouldn't forget that, and I hadn't.

By the time we got there the shop was blazing, but Georg and his family were out in the street and safe and that was all that truly mattered. He gave me a stricken look as we marched past, and I stopped to speak to him.

'I will make this right,' I promised him, and I meant it. 'I'll bring harsh justice to those who did this, Pious Men justice, and I won't see you out of pocket for what has happened. There'll be a new shop for you, Georg, and all the coin you need to replace what you've lost.'

'Bless you, Mr Piety,' he said, bobbing his head in something that was almost a bow.

I was a prince, in Ellinburg, and, to my mind, a prince looks after his people. That was how I ruled my streets.

We turned a corner and now we had caught up with them. There were perhaps fifteen Gutcutters on Net Mender's Row, breaking windows and setting fires. This was the poorest part of the Stink, here and Fisher's Gate below it. The folk here had nothing worth taking from them, and I knew very well that the Gutcutters were making a deliberate effort to hurt those who had the least to spare. They wanted to make me look weak, I knew that, like the sort of man who would protect his gambling house and his stew and let his streets burn while he did it. They wanted to turn the very poorest of my people away from me, and in that I saw the hand of the Skanians. This plan had come from Bloodhands, not Aditi – I knew that much and I hated him for it. These people had done *nothing*!

I drew Remorse and raised her above my head to catch the dawn light.

'Company!' Bloody Anne bellowed at my side, in her sergeant's voice. 'Charge!'

We fell upon them like the wrath of Our Lady.

A glorious charge, in the light of the rising sun.

It sounds so grand.

It sounds like the stuff of legends, the act of heroes. Well, we were no heroes, and we were outnumbered and exhausted and hurt, and it was a fucking disaster.

These were fresh men we were facing, and there were just too many of them. Five minutes of battle was enough to tell me that we were going to lose. Two of the new lads were down already, and Jochan was spitting blood from where someone had caught him in the mouth with the pommel of their shortsword.

'This ain't good,' he hissed at me when we found ourselves fighting back to back in the middle of the street.

He was right, I had to allow. It wasn't.

'Anne!' I shouted over the clash of weapons. 'Break and scatter!'

'Break!' Anne roared at the top of her leather-lunged voice, a voice that carried better than mine ever would. Our Lady, but she was loud. 'Company, break and scatter!'

The men did as they were ordered, every man who could, disengaging from his fight and fleeing into the alleyways around us. I found myself in a dank, narrow space with Jochan and Anne and young Billy beside me, watching the rest of my crew split in five different directions as the Gutcutters looked about themselves in bewilderment. These were *my* streets, and I knew them blindfolded. I had been born here, after all, and although most of my crew hadn't been, they had had half a year and more to learn the lay of the area.

The Gutcutters might know the Wheels but they didn't know the

Stink, not like we did, and some of them were young. They weren't all veterans, that was for sure, while most of my crew were.

I was back in Messia, right then. I remembered the close fighting in narrow alleys where numbers counted for nothing, with daggers and the volleys of crossbows that left no one standing.

We had no crossbowmen that day, but we had Billy the Boy.

We caught some Gutcutters ahead of us in an alley between two crumbling warehouses. I pointed, and Billy raised his hands and sent a wash of flame down the alley that turned half of them into screaming, burning travesties of life. I had seen men burned like that before, in Abingon, and I knew there was no coming back from it.

We led them on a wild chase through the alleys of our own neighbourhood, splitting them into small groups to break up their strength. Jochan, Anne, Billy and me stayed together, harrying a group of Gutcutters down toward Fisher's Gate.

'Take them down the narrow to the river!' I shouted to Jochan as we headed into the warren of alleyways behind Hull Patcher's Row. 'Cut them off!'

We needn't have hurried, as it turned out. When we rounded the corner it was to see the remaining Gutcutters surrounded by thin, sick, angry people with barrel staves and kitchen knives in their hands. They looked at Jochan and me, these people of the Pious Men streets, and they fell on the intruders like a pack of wild animals.

When they were done, there was nothing left alive.

Was that shocking?

I supposed that it wasn't, in Our Lady's eyes. When people have run out of food, and hope and places to hide, do not be surprised if they have also run out of mercy.

When it was done I walked among them, and they bowed their heads and competed with one another to kiss my hand.

'Mr Piety,' someone said, and there was a sort of reverence in his voice. 'We don't want their sort down here, not on Pious Men streets we don't.'

Pious Men streets.

That was where we stood, and there could be no more argument about that.

Chapter 47

'It's enough, now,' Ailsa told me, after I had finally managed to get some sleep, and her tone brooked no more argument about *that*, either. 'No more, Tomas. No more violence, not with you involved. I had to spend a lot of money this morning to turn the Guard away from you and your streets.'

'Aye,' I said. 'I thank you for that, Ailsa, and I hear you about the violence. I remember the other things you said too. Did you mean them?'

We were in my room above the Tanner's Arms, where no one could overhear us, and this was Ailsa the Queen's Man I was speaking to now.

'Oh, I meant them,' she said. 'We will marry, and soon. This Godsday afternoon, in fact.'

I stared at her. 'That's only five days away.'

'Yes,' she said. 'Captain Larn and his men have to return to Dannsburg next week, and the timing must be right if you're not to be implicated in what they do.'

'I see,' I said. 'I'll need . . . everything.'

'Everything has been arranged,' she said. 'Your tailor has our clothes ready, and suitable outfits for Jochan and Anne and Enaid as well. Your family *have* to be there, and I assumed you would want Anne to be present as well.'

I nodded. She was right about my family having to be there, and Anne as well. This wasn't just a matter of propriety or respect, I knew. This was deadly serious now. It felt like I was back in the army again, with orders to follow and all the planning done for me. The decisions had already been made and the supplies arranged, and there were no choices left.

'She'll not wear a dress,' I cautioned Ailsa.

'I know,' she said, 'but Rosie will and I need her to be there as well. They will make a handsome couple, to bear witness to our union.'

Our union. I barely knew the woman, even now, and I had no way of telling if what little I did know of her was true. Ailsa was a master of the false face, after all.

'What about the Gutcutters?' I asked. 'If they attack again before Godsday . . .'

'Billy says they won't,' she said, 'and my spies and Luka's agree with him. You hurt them badly last night. Very badly indeed. Now let them wait on our wedding day, and *my* justice.'

Ailsa's justice was the queen's justice, and I knew that was even harsher than mine.

That was good. Once justice was done, all of the Wheels would be mine for the taking and the Skanians would be without their foot soldiers. Whether marrying Ailsa was good remained to be seen. She was certainly pleasing to the eye, but what use is that in a stranger?

'You said something about a house,' I reminded her.

'Would you like to see it? It wouldn't be proper for us to move in until we are married, but it's ready now.'

I paced over to the window and looked out into the street below. This was the Stink; this was my home. I'd lived all my life in Ellinburg save for the war years, and all of it in these streets. Even when I'd had money before, I had never felt a need to move up to the area around Trader's Row. That wasn't for people like me.

I tapped my fingers against the windowsill, and realised I was nervous. Not about the marriage, as I knew that didn't truly mean anything. I was nervous about moving, and about society, and how I wouldn't fit into it. I listened to Ailsa talk about this house she had arranged for us, but I wasn't paying attention to her words. I was listening to the sound of her voice, the way she spoke and how she turned her phrases. I didn't talk like that, and I couldn't see that I ever would. Oh, I could dress like a lord, and spend money like one too, but I would never sound like one. I had seen nobles in the army. Most of the senior officers had been nobility, after all. They didn't even walk like normal people.

And then of course there was my brother. I wondered if Ailsa had given any thought to how we were going to explain Jochan. Truth be told, I didn't care. If this let me do what needed to be done without being dragged off to see the widow afterward, then that was good.

I would worry about everything else later.

The house was splendid, I had to admit. We went to look at it the next day, Ailsa and me, with Jochan and Luka in tow. It was set on the far side of Trader's Row from the Stink, in the shade of the hills below the convent, and with a view of the magnificent Great Temple of All Gods where we were to be married. The house must have had thirty rooms, and all the ones we saw were elegantly furnished and decorated in what Ailsa told me were the latest fashions.

I wouldn't know.

'Fuck a nun, Tomas,' Jochan said, turning around and around in the hall and staring up at the gallery and the high ceiling above him. 'This is a fucking palace!'

'Aye,' I said. 'That it is.'

The servants were lined up in the hall to greet us, and if any of them thought anything of Jochan's language or of my accent they had the grace not to show it. That was wise of them, to my mind.

Ailsa had them introduce themselves to me, the steward and the housekeeper and the cook and the undercook and the valet, the lady's maid and the scullery maid and the three footmen and four household maids and two housemen. What I was supposed to do with them all I had no idea, but I assumed Ailsa would. I was paying more mind to how many guards I would need to put on the house, and where best to station them.

'I'll have a few of the lads come up,' Luka said, as though reading my mind.

I nodded. 'Have them bring crossbows, and plenty of bolts,' I said. 'The high windows have a good position over the approaches.'

Ailsa cleared her throat and gave me a look. 'Tomas,' she said.

'No,' I said. 'No, it's not that simple. Business doesn't stop just because I buy a fucking big house, Ailsa. We're still Pious Men.'

'We're getting *married*,' she said pointedly. 'You know what that means.'

'We are,' I agreed, 'and I hear you, Ailsa, but that won't change everything. Not in one day it won't, not in Ellinburg.'

Jochan frowned at me in obvious confusion, but I ignored him. He would see what she meant, in due course.

Everyone would see what she meant, on Godsday afternoon.

Chapter 48

Godsday came at last. My wedding day.

Pawl the tailor had come by in his cart the day before and delivered all the fine new clothes Ailsa had commissioned from him, and that Godsday morning I didn't hear confessions. We were all too busy getting ready. The place was packed, and almost everyone was there apart from Larn and his men, and Cutter. They had all gone off together the night before, and they hadn't come back.

Ailsa had been gradually changing her voice over the last week, slowly becoming less common, but she did it so smoothly that I didn't think a soul had noticed. The barmaid act was almost a distant memory now, and I suspected it would stay that way. I wanted to see her, to make sure everything was in hand, but that would have been ill luck on the morning of our wedding. I wouldn't see Ailsa again until we stood before the priest together, so all I could do was trust to Our Lady that everything was going to plan.

I was eating an early lunch with Jochan and Anne and Luka, all of us dressed up for the occasion in our magnificent new coats and doublets and britches. Even Billy the Boy looked like a young lord. He would be coming too, of course, as my adopted nephew. Everyone had to be there and, more importantly, to be *seen* to be there.

Aunt Enaid would be joining us later at the Great Temple of All Gods, and Brak with her. She had pitched a fit when I told her I was marrying Ailsa, and all but thrown me out of her house, but I had insisted that she come whether she liked it or not. I had insisted very hard indeed. I couldn't tell her exactly why she had to be there, of course, but my aunt was no fool and eventually she got the general idea about what I meant. All my family and my top table *had* to be seen to be there around me. That was very, very important. Even Sir Eland was coming, to escort Rosie from Chandler's Narrow and give my retinue a bit of class.

Fat Luka was to play the ceremonial part of Ailsa's father, as he sadly couldn't be with us in person. Truth be told, I had no idea if her father was even still alive. She had said that he was and I accepted that, but I knew that it might well not be true. Still, Luka had learned the ceremony, as had I, and that was all that mattered.

It was hot in the common room with the fire burning and all of us wearing too many heavy clothes, and after I had eaten I took my glass of brandy and walked out the back to the stable yard to take a breath of air. Anne joined me a moment later.

'Congratulations on your wedding,' she said.

I looked sideways at her, unable to gauge whether she was making fun of me.

'I wanted you beside me, as my Closest Man,' I said. 'I hope you understand that I had to ask my brother. Appearances.'

'I know.'

'I'm sorry,' I said. 'I wanted it to be you.'

'I know,' she said again. 'Appreciate the thought.'

I nodded and put my hand on her shoulder for a moment. Anne grunted and swallowed her brandy.

'Do you know what you're doing?' she asked me.

'Yes,' I said. 'No.'

Bloody Anne put her empty glass down on the wall beside the back door and silently examined her fingernails, giving me the moment I needed.

'I know what I'm doing *today*,' I said. 'Today is vitally important, Anne. You'll see why, this afternoon. A thing will happen, this afternoon, and then you'll understand. After that, though? No. I don't think that I do.'

She sucked her teeth for a moment, then turned and spat over the wall into the stable yard. 'Didn't think so,' she said.

*

The air in the Great Temple of All Gods was thick with incense and overly hot from the sheer number of candles that burned in there. I knelt briefly to pay my respects before the shrine of Our Lady, one of many shrines in the temple to the great number of gods and goddesses that were held to in Ellinburg. That done, I made the long, echoing walk to join my brother in front of the altar. The worst of the incense was burning there, on that huge stone slab under the tall windows with their thousands of leaded, diamond-shaped panes. I looked briefly over Jochan's shoulder and out those windows. My eye was drawn to the shapes of the great waterwheels turning in the haze from the factories where the river ran along the eastern side of the city. From its vantage point on the hill at the end of Trader's Row, the Great Temple of All Gods commanded an impressive view of the Wheels.

That was going to be interesting.

A moment later the priest joined us there, a Father Goodman who, if the words of the Chandler's Narrow girls were to be believed, was nothing of the sort. There were several of the women among the wedding guests, in fact, sitting in the row of pews behind Anne and Rosie. Each had the bawd's knot proudly displayed on her shoulder, and I could see them looking at the priest and giggling to each other as they waited. Father Goodman was holding his face very still as he made a point of not looking at any of them.

'Is it time?' I asked him.

'Almost,' he said.

There was no clock in the temple, of course, and good clocks were a rare enough thing anyway. I fidgeted, wondering what was keeping Ailsa. This *had* to happen at the right time. Everything did, or we were done.

'Getting nervous?' Jochan asked me.

He winked and passed me his pocket flask. The priest wasn't looking so I took it and had a swift gulp of brandy. Truth be told, I *was* nervous, if not for the reasons Jochan thought. Ailsa would have understood, I knew, but no one else did yet. I wished I could have confided in my brother, and in Bloody Anne even more so, but it was out of the question. The fewer people who know a secret the more secret it stays, to my mind, and there was too much at stake today to risk a wrong word or an overheard conversation anywhere.

I pressed the flask back into Jochan's hand and he pocketed it, and a moment later the doors at the far end of the huge temple opened and the drummers took up their beat.

Ailsa looked breathtaking as she stepped into the Great Temple in a magnificent dress of cream silk that set off her dusky brown complexion perfectly. At that moment I wished with all my heart that I were marrying her for real, in a way that would mean something between us as man and wife.

Her gown shimmered in the light of a thousand candles as she walked slowly down the nave with Fat Luka at her side. She stopped the requisite five paces away and dropped me a low curtsey. Jochan and I bowed respectfully to her in return, and again to Fat Luka, in his place as her father.

The forms obeyed, Luka brought her to my side in front of the priest who was waiting with his back to the altar. Luka and Jochan, my Closest Man, both took two steps backward, leaving us there together. We turned to face the priest, so that we were looking directly out the great windows behind the altar. The drums stopped all at once, leaving an echoing silence that seemed to portend what I and Ailsa alone knew was to come.

'Faithful of the gods,' the priest proclaimed, 'you have come together in this temple so that the most holy ones may seal and strengthen your love in the presence of the temple's ministry and this community. The gods most abundantly bless this love. Let them now bear witness so that you may assume the duties of marriage in mutual and lasting fidelity. And so, in the presence of the gods, I ask you to state your intentions unto one another.'

There was a flash of light somewhere over in the Wheels, and then an almighty bang shook the glass panes in the windows behind the altar. It sounded like a siege cannon firing, but I knew it wasn't. I knew *exactly* what it was.

It had begun, and right on time.

Father Goodman almost jumped out of his robes, and I could hear startled whispering among the congregation behind us.

'Thunder,' I muttered. 'Carry on.'

'Ailsa and Tomas, have you come here freely and without reservation to give yourselves to each other in marriage?' he asked.

'I have,' Ailsa said.

Another roar rattled the glass, and this time I could see flames rearing up in the distance as the first row of factories caught fire. A column of thick, choking smoke rose into the air and spread over the Wheels like the shadow of Our Lady.

This is what happens, I thought, *when you cross me.*

'I have,' I said.

'Will you love and honour each other as man and wife for the rest of your lives?'

'I will.'

Smoke boiled up from a dozen places in the Wheels as merciless fires tore through the timber-and-daub buildings. Another almighty explosion shook the lead in the stone mullions and a warehouse collapsed, sending clouds of dust over the water.

'I will,' I said.

'Will you accept children lovingly from the gods and bring them up according to the laws of the temple and the land?'

'I will.'

A factory exploded like the wrath of the gods. I could see beams and burning laths raining down onto the surrounding streets, spreading the fire and the carnage. Our Lady Herself walked those streets that Godsday afternoon, and Our Lady has no love in Her heart.

'I will.'

Again the priest tried to turn toward the windows.

'Thunder,' I hissed at him. 'Continue.'

The whispering in the congregation behind us was getting louder, more urgent. I shot Jochan a look over my shoulder, and I could see the grim smile form on his face as he worked out what was happening. His eyes gleamed in the light of the candles, mad with battle shock but seeming to welcome the thunder of the explosions, to embrace it as I did.

Another roar, and now the flames had reached the great waterwheels themselves. The wheels might have been wet but the gantries that held them weren't, and they burned. Oh, how they burned! I watched in fascination as the first wheel pitched forward and fell into the river in a great cloud of steam.

'Since . . . since it is your intention to enter into marriage,' Father Goodman stammered, 'join your hands, and declare your consent before the gods and this temple.'

I reached out and took Ailsa's hand in mine. 'I, Tomas,' I said, 'take you, Ailsa, to be my wife. I promise to be true to you in good times and in bad. I will love you and honour you for all the days of my life, for I am an honourable man, as no one here gathered will deny.'

A sixth explosion rocked the Wheels, sending another great cloud of fire and smoke up into the sky. A rippling line of smaller explosions followed, racing down the length of a street and tearing houses apart as they went. The warehouse at the end of the row went up with a roar, and I thought perhaps the fires had found the Gutcutters' hidden cache of blasting weapons. The flames spread in the wind like the wings of devils.

All was death and destruction, and Ailsa squeezed my hand.

'I, Ailsa, take you, Tomas, to be my husband. I promise to be true to you in good times and in bad. I will love you and honour you for all the days of my life, for I am an honourable woman, as no one here gathered will deny.'

The sounds of shouting could be heard through the thick stone walls of the temple now, of screams and running feet and ringing bells even up here on Trader's Row. A fire like that was to be feared indeed, and there would be panic spreading on the streets.

The smoke reached up to touch the heavens, and below it the Wheels had become Hell.

Father Goodman was white as a fresh linen shirt above his black robes now, but my brother held him pinned with a stare that brooked no argument.

'You have declared your consent before the temple,' the priest said, his voice trembling in fear of what was happening outside his walls. 'May the gods in their goodness strengthen your consent and fill you both with their blessings. What the gods have joined, no man may divide. May you both walk in righteousness until the end of your days.'

With that we were married, and all the Wheels burned bright as though in celebration of our union. It was done.

All of it.

Chapter 49

It was the custom in Ellinburg to hold a party after a wedding, and we held ours in the Tanner's Arms. The grand house could wait until tomorrow.

The common room was packed with all the Pious Men and everyone who could be spared from the businesses. So many people from the streets of the Stink came to pay their respects that Sam and Black Billy were serving beer out in the street. Ailsa wasn't working behind the bar, of course, not on her wedding day. Not ever again, in fact, now that she was to be a lady of society once more.

I was standing there laughing, with a full glass of brandy in my hand and my arm around my new wife's waist, surrounded by my family and my closest friends. My brother was making a fool of himself, drunkenly trying to give a speech while standing on a table and waving a bottle around in his hand.

That was when the City Guard arrived.

Captain Rogan himself shouldered his way into the Tanner's with ten armed and armoured men behind him and a look like murder on his face.

'Tomas Piety,' he growled.

I turned to face him, and so did the better part of two hundred other folk. I think that was when Rogan began to wonder if perhaps he had miscalculated.

'Captain Rogan, what a pleasure,' I said. 'Have you come to wish me well on my wedding day?'

'I've come to take you in,' he said. 'I mean it this time.'

'You want to take me to see the widow, Captain?' I asked, my voice quiet and flat but sounding loud in the sudden hush. 'On what charge?'

'What charge?' Rogan spat. 'Half the fucking Wheels is on fire! Blasting weapons were used; flashstones and the gods only know how many barrels of powder. There are whole streets gone! I can't let that pass, not in my city.'

'I'll allow that I'm sure you can't, Captain,' I said. 'However, I have spent the afternoon getting married, in the Great Temple of All Gods. The most reverend Father Goodman officiated, with all my family and friends around me as everyone will tell you. *All* of them. The Pious Men had no hand in this terrible thing, Captain, I can assure you of that. They were all at my wedding.'

Captain Rogan had ten men with him and I had half the Stink with me, and he couldn't prove a fucking thing. Everyone was quite drunk and in a celebratory mood, but a crowd that size with drink inside them can turn ugly very quickly, and an ugly crowd can fast become a riot. I knew no one there would see their prince dragged off in chains. Not on his wedding day they wouldn't.

No one.

I could see that Captain Rogan knew it too.

'One day, Piety,' he said. 'One day I'll fucking have you for this.'

'For something perhaps, Captain, but not for this,' I assured him.

That got a laugh from the crowd, and that laugh turned into some ugly looks pointed at the Guard. Rogan finally decided that he could count after all, and he ordered his men to withdraw. They turned and trooped back out of the Tanner's with jeers following them down the street, and Ailsa gave me an approving look. I raised my glass and bade Jochan continue with his speech.

I never did see Captain Larn and his men again, but the company of army sappers had served me well.

Ailsa and me moved into our splendid new house the next day, as man and wife.

Luka was directing the unpacking, not that either of us had brought much with us from the Tanner's Arms. We hadn't needed to. Ailsa must have been keeping Pawl the tailor and his 'prentice boy in full-time work all by herself, what with the amount of new clothes that were waiting for us in the chests and wardrobes in our bedrooms.

Two bedrooms, I had to accept that. Adjoining to be sure, for the sake of appearances, but we wouldn't be sharing a bed. That didn't surprise me, and truth be told, it didn't sadden me either. Ailsa was clever and fine to look at and she could be good company, when she chose to be, but I didn't know her. I still felt . . . something, I supposed, for her, but I couldn't rightly have said what.

Respect, I supposed. Fascination too, I won't lie about that, but it was the sort of fascination you might feel toward a lioness seen in a travelling menagerie. You admire the power and the grace of the lioness, yes, but no sane man would choose to lie down with her. I remembered thinking how she had the ruthlessness of a businessman and how much I admired that, but this had been something more than business.

Much more.

The attack on the Wheels had been Ailsa's idea, and timing it to coincide with our wedding had been Ailsa's plan. Captain Larn and his men had been utterly ruthless in their efficiency. They were professionals indeed. I had been able to see that even while I said my wedding vows.

The Wheels was a burned and blackened wasteland of devastation.

I had no idea how many had died in the explosions and the fires that resulted from them, but I had no doubt that it was a lot. Too many, to my mind. The blasts had been targeted at the factories and the businesses, and it had been Godsday when those places should have been empty. All the same, fires spread quickly in a timber-and-daub city like most of Ellinburg was, even in late winter. No businessman would have done that.

The butcher's bill for our wedding day was horrific.

I had finally got Ailsa alone late the previous night, after the party had died down and we retired upstairs to keep up the appearance of consummating our marriage. Once the bedroom door was closed she just smiled at me.

'The Skanians will have been hurt by that,' she said.

I would allow that they probably had been, but not so much as the people of the Wheels had. The Gutcutters were all but wiped out, from what Luka's spies told me, and that was good, but the slaughter had been on a scale larger than I had ever imagined.

The Pious Men are businessmen, but you've turned them into soldiers.

I remembered my aunt telling me that, and she had been right. And when specialists had been needed, and weapons that only the army should have, then real soldiers had been found, and they had been used.

This wasn't business, I knew that. I was still fighting a war, for all that it was now a hidden one.

I watched Ailsa, wearing her fine new kirtle as she bustled around our fine new house directing her new servants as though she had no cares in the world, and truth be told, I wasn't sorry that we wouldn't be sharing a bed that night.

There had been a time when I had thought I was falling in love with Ailsa, but I realised now that I had been wrong about that.

If we cannot stop this infiltration, there will be another war and we will lose. *There will be another Abingon, right here in our own country.*

Ailsa had told me that, and she had swayed me to her cause with those words, but when I thought of how the Wheels had looked that morning I wondered if perhaps Abingon hadn't followed me home after all.

I have written that those were my streets and my people, and that I wouldn't see them reduced to the smoking rubble and rotting corpses that we had left behind us in the south. Perhaps I had spared the Stink from that fate, but it seemed to me now that I had done so only at the cost of the Wheels.

I had brought the horrors of Abingon to the Wheels myself, in the service of the crown.

No, on balance I didn't think that I wanted to lie down with the lioness any more.

Not at all.

Late that evening, after we had dined and most of the servants had retired to wherever they went, Ailsa and me were sitting in our parlour. She called it the drawing room, for no reason that I understood, and apparently I was to call it that as well. I couldn't draw to save my life, and I only hoped that I wouldn't be expected to try.

A hearty fire crackled in the grate, and we were making light conversation about nothing in particular while I drank brandy and she worked at some embroidery. The big house was quiet around us, and I found that I was already missing the noise and rude camaraderie of the Tanner's Arms. I heard a thump on the front door and made to rise, but Ailsa lifted a hand.

'Footman,' she hissed at me. 'The steward will come to us if it is important.'

I nodded and sat back in my chair once more, feeling something of a fool. I had no idea how to live in a big house, with servants.

I heard one of the footmen open the door, then some muffled conversation coming from the hall. A minute or so later the parlour door opened and our steward coughed politely.

'Mr Piety, there is a gentleman here to see you. He gives his name as *Cutter*.'

The steward's tone in itself was enough to tell me what he thought of that. I hadn't seen Cutter since the day before the wedding, but I had a fair idea of where he had been. I nodded and waved a hand in what I thought was a suitably noble gesture.

'Show him in,' I said.

The steward coughed again, this time in a way that said I shouldn't be receiving the likes of Cutter in the parlour or drawing room or whatever the fuck it was called, not in front of my lady wife, but he had the grace to do as he was told.

Cutter strolled in with a big wooden box in his hands. 'Evening, boss,' he said.

I nodded to him. 'Cutter,' I said.

'Brought you a wedding gift, ain't I?' he said.

He dumped the box down on the finely inlaid table in front of us that held our drinks, and stood back with an expressionless look on his bearded face. I reached out and flicked back the hinged lid of the box.

'Well done,' I said. 'You'll forgive me if I don't mount it over the fireplace.'

Cutter snorted. 'I'll get rid of it,' he said. 'Just thought you'd want to see.'

'Aye,' I said. 'My thanks, Cutter. You've done well.'

'Right,' he said, and nodded. 'I'll feed it to the pigs then, now that you've seen it.'

He picked up his box again and left with it under his arm.

The box that contained Ma Aditi's head.

Chapter 50

With the Gutcutters crushed and Ma Aditi dead, all of eastern Ellinburg was mine. I would have been happier if someone had brought me Bloodhands' head, truth be told, but I settled for what I had.

No one could tell me what had happened to the Skanian leader who had pretended to be Aditi's second. Captain Larn and his men had done their evil work and vanished like wraiths the way sappers do, never to be seen again. Cutter had been the only one of my crew to go with them, the night before the wedding. I think he was the only one they respected, and after the raid on the factory that didn't surprise me. There was something about Cutter that could give nightmares to the hardest of men.

When I questioned him about it in the Tanner's Arms a few nights later, he just shrugged.

'We killed all that was there,' he said. 'Set the charges and hid. Lit them at the appointed time and legged it. If he ain't dead, then he weren't there.'

'Be happy, Tomas.' Jochan grinned at me. 'That fat boy-fucking whoremonger has finally been kicked across the river where she belongs.'

I nodded. 'Aye, she has at that,' I had to agree.

Ma Aditi wouldn't be mourned by anyone I knew, that was for sure. Least of all not by the boys I had rescued from the Stables.

They were doing well, so I heard, going to school and starting to learn the trades of their adopted parents. That was costing me a pretty penny but it was coin well spent, to my mind. In a way I felt like I was finally paying back an old debt, one I owed to my own little brother.

All the same there was great hardship in the Wheels, now. The Gutcutters were gone, or close as made no difference, but so were a lot of people's jobs and even their homes. Many more than I had bargained for.

I broke open my treasury in the back of the Tanner's to make that right. It was a simple thing now, with the Gutcutters gone, to ride into the Wheels like a conquering prince. I came with open hands and I offered protection, and jobs, and the coin to rebuild what had been taken away from them.

They received me like a saviour.

All but Old Kurt, anyway. I saw him, once, standing at the end of the alley between Dock Road and the river path. I had ridden past on my black mare with ten men around me, and I caught sight of the cunning man out of the corner of my eye. He lifted a dead rat by its tail and held it up toward me, and the look on his face was unreadable.

I didn't think Old Kurt regarded me as any kind of saviour at all, but to my mind that was a conversation we didn't need to have.

A month after the wedding, the Pious Men streets stretched from the bottom of the Stink up through the Wheels and across the docks beyond, all the way to the northern wall of the city. All of that was mine, now, and the people of those streets were *my* people.

I reckoned that might give Bloodhands and the Skanians something to think about.

Two months after my wedding, there was to be a spring ball held at the governor's hall. All the great and the good of Ellinburg were invited, which meant all of us who had lots of money. That was the definition of what passed for society in Ellinburg, after all. There was no way that Governor Hauer could overlook Ailsa and me when he was sending out his invitations, much as I was sure he would have liked to.

We arrived outside his hall in a grand carriage, wearing our most fashionable finery, where we were met by his footmen. The fact that our own 'footmen' that night were scarred and uncouth and heavily armed drew no comment, as though the governor's staff had been prepared in advance for what sort of guest I was. I dare say that they had been, at that.

We were ushered into the hall and this time I *was* allowed to climb the great staircase, with Ailsa on my arm in a beautiful dark-green gown with diamonds at her throat. There was no servant's stair now, not for Tomas Piety there wasn't.

Not any more.

I was a man of consequence, a wealthy businessman wed to a noble lady. Even though Ailsa was obviously of Alarian descent and no one seemed to have actually heard of her, she was unmistakably from an aristocratic Dannsburg family. That carried a lot of weight out here in the provinces.

That alone was enough to secure our place in what passed for Ellinburg society. The open secret that I was the owner of the Golden Chains didn't hurt, either. That had enough of my wealthy patrons looking sideways at me in fear that I might mention poppy resin in polite company to ensure that we were treated with nothing but cordiality and respect.

There was a ballroom on the main floor of the governor's hall. It was grand enough, to my eye, but obviously not to Ailsa's. She looked around herself with barely concealed disdain and wafted a feathered ivory fan in front of her face. That fan had cost more than a carpenter in the Stink made in a month.

'I see little here to entertain me, Tomas,' she said, her tone sounding bored and yet deliberately loud enough to be overheard. 'The Earl Lan Klasskoff throws such wonderful balls that I fear I am completely spoiled for the provinces.'

That may or may not have been the case, but her mention of upper-level Dannsburg aristocracy had the effect she had no doubt intended. Heads turned in our direction, eyebrows rising at the thought that this Alarian woman had attended social functions that they quite obviously hadn't been invited to.

'Perhaps we should retire to the Golden Chains,' I said.

I spoke the words she had given me in the carriage on the way from our house, which was all of ten minutes' walk away, but I felt a fool doing so. My voice was like a clod of wet earth dumped among the fine crystal of those others there. I would never learn to sound like a noble, I knew that much.

'Tomas, where are your manners? I'm sure our lord governor has a most splendid evening's entertainment planned for us,' Ailsa said, in a tone carefully crafted to mean the exact opposite.

I looked across the expanse of the ballroom and saw Governor Hauer glaring back at me with a murderous look on his face. He had a man standing at his right hand, a big scarred brute in a fine coat. I looked at that man, and I felt cold to my bones.

I caught the attention of a footman.

'The man standing with the governor,' I said. 'Do you have his name?'

'The gentleman's name is Klaus Vhent, sir,' the footman said.

The footman's tone said he thought I should have known that, but I ignored him.

I knew that man by another name.

I knew him as Bloodhands.

Tomas Piety will return in

PRIEST OF LIES

Acknowledgments

This book was a real departure for me, and I had a lot of help for which I am eternally grateful.

I'd like to thank my wonderful agent, Jennie Goloboy of Red Sofa Literary, and my equally wonderful editor Rebecca Brewer at Ace. I couldn't have done it without you.

As always thanks are due to my long-suffering beta readers, Nila and Chris, who have helped birth every one of my books so far.

I'd also like to thank Lisa L Spangenberg for her invaluable assistance with historical research and for putting up with my endless weird questions.

Thanks are also long overdue to Mark Williamson, who taught me everything I know about leadership – thank you, sir!

And always, of course, the biggest thanks are for Diane for putting up with me when I'm writing, and for everything else. Love you, hon.

Peter McLean lives in the UK, where he grew up studying martial arts and magic before beginning a twenty-five-year career in corporate IT systems. He is also the author of the Burned Man urban fantasy series.

Find him on Twitter (@PeteMC66), on Facebook (@PeterMcLeanAuthor) and at his website https://talonwraith.com.